To J, N and R

"Your darkness speaks and has eyes to see."

Drones	110
Spacecraft	112
Ship Modules	115
Spacecraft Combat	121
Gear	124
Common Items	125
Restricted Items	127
Pharmaceuticals	130
Software and Hacking	132
Hacking	133
Software	136
Magic	139
Grimoire	142
Tomes	153
Bestiary	154
The World of Advent of Carcosa	187
Time is the Fire in Which We Burn	207
Philip's Plan	209
Supplemental Section	215
About The Author	221

ADVENT OF CARCOSA

"And blood-black nothingness began to spin"

~ "Pale Fire", Vladimir Nabokov

INTRODUCTION

In 2320, the solar system has been colonized with automatons who can brave the vast silences humanity cannot. Colonies on the Moon and Mars were attempted and failed, falling prey to madness, ennui and despair. Only a few hardy souls, possessed of a rare ability to face the void for years at a time, thrive in the measureless distances which lie beyond the fragile Earth.

Glittering cities populate Earth's Lagrange Points, designed to mimic their home world's biosphere as it existed in its pristine state. These habitats each hold hundreds of millions of human beings, while the unfinished ring that girdles Earth's equator holds close to a billion more.

In these places and on the planet's surface, a global government called the Corporate Unity (also CU or just 'Unity') and its regional proxies struggles to maintain control over a restive population that has begun to define itself increasingly along hostile memetic lines. Cells of organizations called affinity groups (AGs) ranging from the bio-conservative Temple to the nihilistic Post-Humans exist in every city, the larger ones having power rivaling that of the exo-global corporations and even some regional governments.

The Sun is just one element in a vast body of stars that has been shifting for millennia into a new alignment. . .dormant intelligences that exist outside of space and time have begun to stir. Pieces of the puzzle keep falling into place, hinting at the larger picture – the disenfranchised calling on powers that can't be fathomed or controlled, spacecraft being sent into the black beyond Jupiter's orbit never to be heard from again, AI research centers being attacked by an unknown agency wielding overwhelming force that vanishes once it utterly destroys its targets.

Unity's mission is to hold the fragments of the world together through the coming storm – humanity may well be unrecognizable once it's finished, assuming it survives at all.

DEFINITIONS

Affinity Group (AG): Any organization whose main purpose for existing is a shared sympathy among its members to a particular memetic construct.

Augmented Reality (AR): Normal visual input modified to include layers of symbolic/textual information about people, buildings and objects.

Bio-Conservatives: An AG whose core belief is that unmodified biological life is the only valid form of existence. All AI, modified humans and Uplifts are anathema.

Humanity: The sum of intelligent creatures on Earth, including AIs (who might object to being classified as 'human') and Uplifts (who would almost certainly object).

Ideogram: A hyper-geometric construct that is created to perform a magical operation, be it casting a spell or summoning an Outsider. The Ideogram can simply be visualized by the practitioner in order to be used, but a much safer method involves using a Hexaphone, Spell Deck or artifact.

Existential Threat Management (ETM): An organization dedicated to the containment and/or elimination of Outsider and other threats to humanity.

(Great) Old Ones: Outsider entities of god-like or near god-like ability. Many of them wandered the Earth eons ago when the nature of reality sustained their presence here.

Global Information Network (GIN): A world wide network of shared media, mostly controlled and curated by the Corporate Unity, that can be experienced at no cost in a variety of different ways up to and including VR. Other information networks exist, usually owned by corporations that charge a fee for subscription. Various SMMs might deny access to some or all of this content.

Maker: An advanced 3D printer capable of manufacturing nearly any item or substance. It must have molecular schematics (templates) and the necessary raw materials (which are provided by different types of base blocks) in order to function.

Memetic Construct: A set of ideas that support a core belief system related to existence, life and how life should be lived.

Morph: An artificially constructed body with biological and cybernetic components.

Outsider: Any life or thought form that is not a product of Earth's planetary evolution.

Posthumanism: A philosophy that believes that humanity has outgrown the need for biological shells. This philosophy manifests in AoC in the belief that consciousness should be digitized, inhabiting various types of mechanical, biological or biomechanoid bodies on an as-needed basis.

Prohibited/forbidden information: Any data relating to the existence of Outsiders.

Savage Worlds (SW): A set of rules for simple role playing games. Advent of Carcosa would work best using this rules system, although it could be easily adapted to others as well. This game was designed using the Deluxe Explorer Edition, published in 2015.

Societal Memetic Model (SMM): Different means of organizing industry and distribution of resources, each with its own set of values and social mores. Examples include scarcity/pre-transitional, transhuman/technosocialist, post-scarcity/post-humanist, theocratic/bio-conservative etc etc.

Subversicorp: Any corporation engaged in activity that falls outside of an AG's SMM.
Example (CU usage): Any corporation whose activities threaten the continued existence of humanity.

Trans-dimensional (Trans-D) Gate: A method of instantaneous travel between any two points separated by time/space and/or other physical laws.

Transhumanism: A philosophy that embraces cybernetic, biological and genetic enhancements as a way of bettering humanity.

Uplift: An animal given intelligence and sapience via genetic and/or physiological manipulation - current known examples include octopi, monkeys, apes, dolphins, crows and ravens. Unsubstantiated rumors persist of gestalt insect intelligences existing in the N American SW.

Virtual Reality (VR): In VR, the character's entire sensory input and nervous system are slaved to a particular device, which makes it feel to all purposes like the character's own body. VR can also be a computer driven hallucination that can put the character in any reality that the designer can imagine. The best VR simulations are indistinguishable from reality, or seem more real by comparison.

The Zoo: A high security facility orbiting the Earth that contains Outsiders, lifeforms infected by their influence and artifacts inspired or created by them.

LIFE DURING THE INCURSION

The following is for recruits both new to the CU and the Existential Threat Management (ETM) team.

CU Committee for Public Safety Orientation Document, Security Clearance MJ-12.

Warning: Possession of this document by unsanctioned individuals could result in a sentence of permanent non-corporeality.

Welcome. Your efforts in the campaign to maintain human viability are commendable.
While you might not enjoy the same freedom of action in the ETM that you possessed in your SMM of origin, our organization will spare no expense in the fulfillment of its mission. ETM maintains very strict controls on the use and possession of Outsider knowledge and artifacts and keeps these items quarantined from society at large and other branches of the government that would inevitably use them irresponsibly. Indeed, this last item is why many of you chose to join ETM and the CU.

Please read this entire document to orient yourself on the CU, the ETM's role in it and the state of Outsider activity in the areas under and outside our control. Please take any questions to your case officer.

The World at Large

People have a tendency of trying to maintain a sense of normalcy and routine, even as the world is falling apart around them. This is still fairly simple, as the present level of Outsider activity only alters our reality to a slight degree - even these slight alterations have increased the background tension of the global society. An overall calm is maintained through the use of reality altering methods used by different SSMs, both conventional and supernatural.

Conventional methods include the introduction of pharmaceuticals into food and water produced by matter compilers, psychological manipulation through the wireless neural interface required by most media feeds, visual psychotropic conditioning via augmented reality and many other methods. Supernatural means can affect the perception of an individual or alter the reality of the collective unconscious itself, with the latter being considered extremely dangerous given the inexact nature of the results and the sometimes considerable collateral damage in terms of lives and sanity. Supernatural methods of conditioning often include elements of Outsider influence and are therefore forbidden in the CU.

Some organizations or unbalanced individuals have not only discovered these manipulations, but actively try to protect themselves from them, not understanding that they're putting all of humanity at risk – or simply not caring. The vast majority of people, however, go through their day of pre-approved experiences and emotions without struggle or even noticing – this is the status quo that must be maintained at any cost.

In the territories controlled by Unity people are given simple work designed to keep them occupied and give their lives structure. The work itself is often entirely meaningless, since most necessary tasks can be better accomplished by machines or AIs – given the precarious state of humanity's collective psychology, this is for the best. Those few capable of service above the norm, especially those exposing themselves to physical or psychic trauma, are given significant alterations of mind and body to enhance their abilities.

One commonality between nearly all of humanity's AGs (with the exception of the bio-conservatives) are the use of biomorphs and cortical stacks. Biomorphs are artificial bodies – the most common types are indistinguishable from an unmodified human body. Where they differ is that even the least capable morph is immune from genetic diseases, aging, and is optimized for good looks and health. Cortical stacks are artificial brains that a digitized consciousness is uploaded into for use with a morph. If a morph is damaged or the user wants to upgrade to a different model, the cortical stack can simply be removed and placed within the new body. While robust, cortical stacks are not indestructible – because of this, certain individuals deemed vital to the CU have their consciousness mirrored via digital means. In parts of the world not fully controlled by the CU, this service can be purchased or traded for.

The human population is separated into three different economic models – scarcity, transitional, and post-scarcity. The scarcity model is basically old-school capitalism. Makers are generally available but are monopolized by a few individuals, with the technology being closely guarded and tight legal restrictions put upon their possession and use. Morphs are available, but must be purchased or given by one's employer. In the latter case, the morph is still considered the property of the employer, who can repossess the morph at any time and run any software on it of their choosing. Purchased morphs can be bricked (purged of all proprietary software), but this is difficult and in many cases will void the manufacturer's warranty.

The CU can be best described as a transitional society. In this SMM, any item necessary for the maintenance of life and well being is available without cost or obligation to any citizen. Makers are available to all free of charge but certain templates are restricted, with luxury items and some consumer goods limited only to those who can afford them. In the case of weapons and hazardous materials, a government license must also be obtained.

Baseline morphs are also provided by the CU – these are in fact required to access socialized information networks and healthcare. They also run government software that is constantly being updated and patched, making many suspect their thoughts and motivations are being tampered with. Bricked morphs can be acquired, but the person buying them must see to their own physiological and psychological security. These can usually be included as a software package when the morph is purchased.

In more anarchic post-scarcity SMMs, Makers are also available to all, but with templates and morphs limited only by what the individual can create for themselves or acquire by other means. This leads to very rapid development in some of the more dynamic elements of the society, but is very hazardous due to the large-scale employment of software, genetic manipulation, nanotech, hardware and weapons that go through little or no vetting process before being deployed.

Barter and Reputation:

Liquid capital is a scarce and sometimes not altogether useful commodity. The expendable worker in a capitalist society doesn't earn enough for the essentials of living, and while the trans-economy citizen gets the essentials for free, many find that being alive and enjoying it requires more than this. Even someone living the post-scarcity dream will come across a problem or want that can't be solved or fulfilled by something which can be forged in a Maker, such as access to a unique item or prohibited information.

Barter is the most common way for obtaining items that exist above one's means, or even things not normally for sale. In a world where nearly everything is created from a template, beautifully made, handcrafted items are in high demand – especially if they are made from exotic (and/or illegal) materials. If one doesn't have a valuable item or information to exchange, skills are also in demand.

A good reputation in one's community or AG can also pay dividends. Being a well-known and valued member can get one access to things that would normally be unobtainable (there are several social media apps that track reputation scores across a variety of communities). Indeed, refusing to help someone with a high ranking is almost a guaranteed way to lower your score.
Of course, a high rep score to one person will be a negative one to another, depending on how they feel about that community or AG – walking into the wrong bar with a rep score in an opposing AG could lead to a confrontation that could easily escalate into violence.

Law Enforcement

Each CU administrative region has its own social mores - some of these are backed up with legal sanctions, while others rely on social pressure. The CU claims to have a final say on all legal matters everywhere humanity exists, but this isn't how it always works in practice since many AG and SMMs don't recognize the CU's authority.

The Law

The CU maintains a network of drones that have access to a dynamic gestalt AI. These drones are empowered to investigate crimes, pass sentences and take any legal action called for. Equipped with a Maker and unlimited access to templates, they can create whatever tool, substance or weapon that would be most appropriate for a given investigation or tactical situation. They have access to the location of every CU issued morph, whose digital memories can be accessed without cause or warrant. Non-standardized morphs are hacked to get information not given up willingly – not giving up information when requested can lead to legal sanction (any damage caused to the CU's agents by defensive software during the hack is the responsibility of the witness).

Penalties can include confiscation of higher end morphs, with the intelligence in possession of the morph regulated to a more baseline model or sentenced to temporary or permanent non-corporeality if their continued physical existence is considered a threat to society. Any penalty will also include a slight adjustment of the digitized consciousness to rid the morph of the undesirable behavior, along with continued monitoring to ensure that it doesn't resurface. Digital identities that can't be repaired are permanently uploaded and placed into secure storage where they can be further studied.

The Law constitutes humanity's only socialized law enforcement. Capitalistic societies tend to sub-contract it out to professional organizations, while each individual in a post-scarcity AG is responsible for their own physical and informational security.

The Law and ETM

ETM is an extra-legal CU organization which specializes in handling any threat that lies outside the jurisdiction/comprehension of The Law. When certain conditions are met The Law summons ETM to handle the crisis, turning a blind eye to the means as long as the desired ends are achieved (the desired ends being determined by ETM). ETM's involvement in these cases also protects The Law from being tainted by threats of an extra-dimensional nature. Human or AI ETM agents who are psychologically or informationally compromised can be eliminated and restored from their last back-up – The Law is far too dynamic and complex to withstand this sort of procedure and remain viable.

The Global Information Network (GIN)

This massive database provides each individual suitably equipped with instant access to all forms of past and current media – in the latter case, often within moments of its creation. Access to the network is free to all citizens of the CU who possess an approved morph.

Each morph comes equipped with a GINsert to access the wireless data network and a familiar to process it. Familiars are necessary since even an enhanced intelligence would be overwhelmed by the influx of available data – one of a familiar's main tasks is to determine what information is relevant and then incorporate it into their owner's consciousness, or make them aware of its existence and catalog it so it can be experienced at a later time.

Once a familiar has worked with an individual long enough, they begin to anticipate their cognitive needs, performing background processing even during real time conversation, incorporating the best words, phrasing, facts and quotes to enhance whatever is being said. With a functioning GINsert and familiar, even a normally dull person can make their everyday communication sparkle with wit. Conversely, someone without one sounds slow and plodding in comparison.

A person's GINsert and familiar are installed at the same time, usually at age two. This way the artificial intelligence which will become that person's life-long companion will be with them as they develop and get to know them intimately – and given their objectivity, usually better than the person knows themselves. Given access to their owner's accounts, Maker and household computer, a familiar will eventually develop from a teacher, companion and confidant to a shopping assistant, valet, advisor, cook and housekeeper.

Loss of one's familiar is one of the most psychologically traumatic events a person can go through – even modification of a person's familiar without their consent is considered a form of physical assault. The more affluent keep at least one copy on standby, updating it and the recording of their consciousness at the same time.

CORPORATIONS

Arcana Biosys (Posthuman/Libertarian/Seattle)
Builds modules that improve different aspects of morph function – many of the improvements they offer would be illegal or viewed with suspicion in CU controlled areas. It is rumored that they continue to experiment with Uplifts.

Black Mirror Defensive Systems (Capitalist/Russian Nationalist/Moscow)
Munitions, weapon systems, drones, offensive/defensive software. Experimentation in biomechanical technologies has led to an ongoing investigation by ETM.

Blue Horizon (Capitalist/Chinese nationalist/Shanghai)
Marine construction/design – surface effect vehicles, warships, luxury liners, submarines, deep sea habitats.

Czarny Dom Mining (Capitalist/Polish Nationalist/Silesian Free State)
A pre-transitional corp that is remarkably the most successful at extraction of rare elements, able to obtain usable quantities of stable transuranic samples that are extremely difficult if not impossible to replicate. They sell to everyone, including the post-scarcity AGs, but their source of these materials remains a mystery.

ETM has taken notice and is quietly investigating, but no one wants the source of these rare elements to dry up (the CU swaps use of their space elevator for access to them). Czarny Dom is possibly a subversicorp, but unlike others, this one actually provides a benefit.

Deep Green (Capitalist/Transhuman/American nationalist)
Amoral and ruthless, Deep Green commands a large portion of the global power economy. In command of diverse resources, they can tailor energy solutions for individuals or nations. Energy from solar satellites, wind turbines, geothermal, nuclear (fusion and fission) and fossil fuels are all on their product list, and they'll set an SMM up with power plants and infrastructure if they can meet their price (service contract extra).

Since environmental preservation doesn't improve their bottom line (unless it's what the customer wants), they often clash with the CU, with clandestine operations sometimes escalating into open warfare. The CU can't afford to push them too hard, however, as it often needs to buy power from them during Helio Array brown-outs. Deep Green sabotage is suspected, but yet to be proven.

Deep Green is currently under investigation by ETM due to a mysterious lack of Deep One interest in their deep sea geo-thermal facilities.

Event Horizon Entertainment (Techno-Socialist/Transhumanist/Exo-Global)
Having socialized most of its infrastructure, the CU has few named companies under its control, Event Horizon being one of the exceptions in order to facilitate memetic warfare operations in territory not under its direct control. This corp is the driving force behind much of the CU's popular culture, often launching protective campaigns in defense of its benefactor. Its entertainment products are available in a variety of formats and their penetration outside of

the CU's sphere of influence is considerable, even though forbidden by many pre-transitional governments and largely considered irrelevant by post-scarcity groups. Event Horizon marketing is continually working on the latter problem while their innovative fulfillment division continuously finds ways to get their products to places they're not allowed and receive payment for them.

A few products approach the subject of Outsiders and other dimensions (including documentaries and a dramatization of the activities of the ETM) but these are all false fronts full of misdirection.

Exodyne Ship Builders (Capitalist/Libertarian – main construction facility in Lunar orbit)
Spacecraft/habitat design and construction. They are notorious for being willing to build for any customer ("No Questions Asked" is their corporate motto) as well as being open to a variety of forms of compensation.

Imago (Posthuman/Techno-Socialist/Los Angeles)
Creator of artificial personas – if the purchaser wishes, these can be legally grafted onto any bioform or artificial lifeform that doesn't have a pre-existing consciousness. A person's own consciousness can also be altered in any form they choose.

Oculus Solutions (Libertarian/Global/Exo-Global)
Security, surveillance, special ops, professional military intervention. Oculus has naval, ground, air and space based assets and can be very flexible in deploying them to meet their customer's needs. Since they always honor a contract, they are very careful never to be on both sides of the same conflict.

Somatec (Libertarian/Global/Exo-Global)
Somatec is a cutting edge pharmaceutical company that creates molecular templates for a variety of drugs – medical, recreational, psychiatric and psychotropic. They are also rumored to dabble in chemical and biological weapons (micro and macro).

These programs are currently under investigation by the ETM along with other more conventional enforcement agencies run by the CU. ETM involvement spiked when they destroyed several Somatec research expeditions exploring forbidden areas of the Tibetan plateau, as well as one returning to Earth after landing on Saturn's moon, Titan.

THE THREAT

One of the chief obstacles humanity faces is the lack of comprehension it has regarding the forces arrayed against it. Are the known threats working individually or in concert? What threats have yet to be discovered? If humanity is aware of a particular threat, many things about it might be obscure, such as its motives, point of origin and psychology, assuming these terms could be said to apply to the threat at all in ways we could understand.

Operating against such threats with this level of ignorance is extremely dangerous, as it can never be known if any actions taken are simply making things worse. On the other hand, how can anything be learned when study of the phenomenon results in corruption?

Known Threats:
Azathoth
Carcosa
Cthonians
Cthulhu/Star Spawn
Deep Ones
The Dreamlands
The Mi-go
Nyarlathotep
Outer Gods
Yithians

This list contains only those elements that present a clear and present danger to the existence of humanity and the reality we inhabit. Threats of a non-existential nature abound and will be listed later.

Yog-Sothoth

Azathoth

Azathoth is a primordial force that exists at the center of space and time. It created this universe and possibly others. The Necronomicon describes it as the size of a star, but it could in fact be far larger than this or even be a dimension to itself. Numberless ascended beings called Outer Gods play what can only be described as music to channel and shape its limitless energies and keep its borders in check to prevent it from endlessly remaking its creation.

Attempts to summon Azathoth can bring an aspect of its essence into the presence of those who called it. Those few who succeed find themselves and their surroundings 'remade' by the God, the scale of resulting change dependent upon the complexity and size of the ritual.

Carcosa: A Room of One's Own

Carcosa was not seen as a major threat at first. While it transformed the internal/external realities of individuals and (rarely) small locales, the transformations were in and of themselves harmless, being mostly cosmetic projections of the strange obsessions and alienation of a person or group. These projections were sometimes not even noticeable except by the most detailed observation, and even if uncanny, were a threat to no one.

What started out as a minor incursion has since turned into a global outbreak, threatening to drive every aspect of manifested intelligence into stark, isolated worlds of anxiety and despair.
The outbreak began when the subconsciouses of affected individuals began to seek each other out via the GIN. A virtual Carcosa was formed (although theories persist that this is not a copy, but in fact a gateway into the ageless phenomenon itself), creating an environment that others could access and experience, often leading to that person's incorporation after several visits.
Now, instead of single rooms or buildings, entire neighborhoods, towns and habitats have been transformed, with changes sometimes so subtle that one may have to spend hours or days there before consciously noticing.

The transformation can encompass anything people interact with day to day: their clothing, the AR environment and the interior and exterior of buildings and habitats. Manifestations of other artifacts are certainly possible, either appearing on their own for no discernable reason or created by a visual artist or writer. AR is affected in such a way as to read into the darker areas of a subject's unconscious and project it back to them in a variety of subtle ways.

A shared trait of all of these manifestations is the presence of the King in Yellow. There are no consistencies in the behavior of this apparition, but his appearance is the same in most respects – an ancient man wearing a stained yellow mask, pale yellow tattered robes and a crown whose design will vary depending on the individual observing him. He rarely speaks or directly interacts in any way with those around him, and is sometimes only glimpsed wandering aimlessly through a distant crowd or peering briefly through a window.

Ironically, the suppression of individual intelligence on a large scale by Unity and many other AGs has accelerated the expansion of Carcosa, driving this unexpressed potential to manifest itself and seek expression subconsciously.

Chthonians

A polymorphic species known to inhabit the upper mantle of Earth, although it's possible its subterranean range is far greater. They are telepathic, but all known attempts at contact have ended in insanity and death. They have been recorded as moving through rock at speeds as high as 60 kph.

Only one video exists of a Chthonian on the surface – it resembles a segmented worm of mottled yellow coloration with a mass of tentacles at the fore end of the body. The length of this particular specimen was approximately 15 meters.

Very little is known about the Chthonians since human contact with them tends to be brief and catastrophic. What technology has been discovered is psionic in nature, tremendously advanced and highly dangerous.

Cthulhu/Star Spawn

Since the discovery of ruins associated with these creatures on Mars, this crisis has been a cause of great concern in regards to the survival of humanity (second only to the insidious Carcosian threat) and the source of many of the counter-measures which have been put into place. It is clear from the Star Spawn avatars of this incursion many of these will be useless once the driving intelligence of Cthulhu (a high priest of the Star Spawn ascending the ladder to Godhood) itself manifests – to Cthulhu, humanity's digitized consciousnesses and arsenal are but another form of energy/thought combination that can be manipulated at will.

Star Spawn have no form the human mind can comprehend – the descriptions of these creatures that exist are merely the human mind trying to make sense of what it's perceiving as best it can.

Deep Ones

An immortal, sub-aquatic species whose intelligence is matched only by their technological achievement, which includes local and interstellar trans-d gates. Their intellects are sophisticated enough that they've never needed to develop computers and they are immune to the manipulations of Outsiders. Their contact with humanity is limited, with most exchanges taking place with hybrids they create in genetic laboratories for carrying out their business on the surface. The Deep Ones view humanity as a temporary infestation and for the most part leave them in peace. If a conflict occurs, expendable hybrids and cultists are used whenever possible.

It's possible that the Deep Ones could challenge Cthulhu and his Star Spawn, but it's clear they view such a confrontation as pointless and filled with potential risk.

The Dreamlands

Theorized as an adjacent pocket dimension, its location (if it in fact has one in the conventional sense) and origin remain unknown. It can be reached by rare individuals via REM sleep – others can go there using special trans-d gates or other artifacts. The Plateau of Leng is another possible point of entry, but it is difficult to find as its position is non-constant (although the Taklamakan Desert is the most common location). Dangers to humanity include entities that cross over from the Dreamlands via Leng and toxic artifacts brought back by travelers.

The Dreamlands have been extensively mapped by those who have traveled there, the terrain being very similar to Earth. Dangerous, alien creatures and societies also exist here – as far as it is known, many of these strange species and civilizations exist nowhere else.

Mi-go

To the Mi-go, humanity is a ticking bomb. The humans are not only the harbingers of Cthulhu's return, their AI technology poses a threat to the Migo's continued habitation of this solar system and its environs.

In the face of these threats, the Migo's options are limited. While the destruction of humanity and its civilization is possible, the energy released by such a mass extinction of sapient life would only speed the process of Cthulhu's return.

Covert sabotage of humanity's AI programs has slowed down but not stopped the creation of more and increasingly sophisticated intelligences. Although there are no signs of this at present, to the Migo it is only a matter of time before AIs supplant the organic branch of humanity and colonize the solar system.

Nyarlathotep

References to Nyarlathotep date back to the very beginnings of human civilization. While he is mentioned in some of the more esoteric religious texts that span many different cultures, the only fact all of these references point to is no one seems to be sure exactly what he is or whose agenda he is following. He's definitely the most approachable of the Old Ones, most often appearing as an ordinary human being. The most common theme in these references portrays him as being an arbiter of Faustian bargains, a harbinger of madness and dissolution and possessed of an almost irresistible charisma.

Unlike others of his kind, his worship can bring tangible rewards – his gifts, however, almost always lead the receiver closer to 'enlightenment' in regards to knowledge of the Old Ones, and he seems to delight in his role of dark Prometheus. Due to his personal magnetism and charm he seldom has to resort to violence to bring about his ends, but some texts refer to him laying waste to cities in his more monstrous forms and even causing the demise of an entire pre-human civilization.

Some of the existing scholarship regards him as a manifestation of the will of one or more of the Outer Gods – perhaps even Azathoth itself, while other sources say he is an individual intelligence with his own unfathomable agenda. Nyarlathotep has had dealings with many institutions throughout history, including ETM.

Acting as Nyarlathotep's agents are the Chotgor and Hunting Horrors. The Chotgor are beings similar to the Mala of Temple, but unlike the Mala, Chotgor can only be created by Nyarlathotep. Chotgor have the ability to change into one of Nyarlathotep's many forms, a favor he bestows to those few followers who gain his favor and trust. Chotgor can be found acting directly in Nyarlathotep's interests, or can be lent as aid to whatever cause the Dark God finds worthy.

Outer Gods

Although noted mostly in Outsider texts for their association with Azathoth, these entities are in fact deities in their own right who project an aspect of themselves to exist in Azathoth's presence, the purpose of these 'courtiers' being to keep the God contained and thus preserving the realities the Gods rely upon for sustenance. Like most creatures of such power, their agendas and thoughts are utterly alien to humanity.

Yithians

The Yithians are a species composed of non-corporeal intellects capable of moving through time. In order to survive, they must inhabit a mind of sufficient complexity – when they do so, the native intelligence is driven out and sent back to the body the Yithian vacated. Using this method, they have explored not only the history of humanity, but of other intelligent species on this world and others. When an extinction event threatens they flee en masse, switching places with some unfortunate species that are left to suffer the fate they escaped.

The only time ETM is aware of the Yithians existing is over a period of 200 million years, starting a little over a billion years ago. During this time, they inhabited the region that is now known as Australia, although it's very likely they have existed in many other eras and places.

The Yithians housed the knowledge they gleaned from their explorations in the city of Pnakosis, located somewhere in Australia's Great Sandy Desert. The information of the library is stored in books of nearly indestructible metal – a few are known to exist in classified government or private collections, with perhaps many more waiting to be found.

Lake Hali

INHOSPITABLE CLIMATES

All branches of humanity, organic and otherwise, have proven to be psychologically fragile when it comes to adapting to environments that differ to a considerable degree from the one that their ancestors evolved in. Only a few rare individuals can withstand the psychological stress of living

off-world for an extended period of time without expensive and invasive psychological aid.
Due to this frailty (as well as others of a more existential nature), humanity's expansion into the solar system has been limited.

Mercury is under the firm control of the CU, who utilize it as a staging area for the Helio Array. A number of mobile city-sized semi-automated mining platforms also scour the surface for ferrous metals, usually crewed by a dozen sapients. Once enough material has been collected, kiloton sized ingots are fired from one of several railguns, giving them sufficient velocity to reach Earth orbit.

Even closer to the sun are the highly restricted **Vulcanoid** antimatter research stations. Here, a small group of CU researchers attempt to tap this powerful but volatile source of energy.
Crews of these platforms, as well as personnel involved in the running and maintenance of the temperamental Helio Array, tend to have an unusually high psychological constitution in order to survive their hazardous and alien work environment. Since even this would not be enough to survive the stresses involved in the usual three year tour of duty, all crew are allowed access to hyper-real virtual environments (called HR or Harvey) of their choosing to take the edge off.

Serving in deep space is enough to gain a person considerable rep score in most AGs, and while this is enough for some, many choose to stay for several years or even make these hostile regions their home (the reasons for this running the gamut of a sense of civic duty to HR addiction).

Venus is currently home to a CU aerostat that initially housed 15 scientists and support staff conducting research on microorganisms found on the surface. After 3 years of operation, ruins discovered on the surface nearly lead to Unity ordering the aerostat's destruction by a warship due to fear of Outsider contamination. When a gate leading to a star in the Canis Major Overdensity was also found, a larger, more diverse group of scientists was sent to the station to investigate further. These volunteers, a mixture of xeno-biologists, thaumaturgists, archeologists and an elite team of battle morphs left for Venus, destroying their spacecraft soon after their arrival - when they volunteered, it was with the understanding that they could never again return to Earth.

Both **Luna** and **Mars** have proven to be hazardous to extended human habitation. The area around both places is closely monitored and patrolled by Unity – any ship approaching to within 50,000 kilometers is given a warning. What happens next is largely within the discretion of the patrol ship's captain with the understanding any ship which approaches within 2500 kilometers must be immediately destroyed.

Both places are dotted with ghost colonies, supposedly abandoned but still showing occasional signs of habitation.

On Luna, the occasional miner has been known to make it past the patrols to extract He3 from the regolith. Both places still contain valuable equipment left behind in the panicked evacuations, as well as mysteries some would pay handsomely to know the answers to.

Their true history is a closely guarded secret, but it is one that is known to most ETM personnel.
The first incidents were thought to be ennui brought on by the stark, unforgiving environment. Although this was certainly a factor, other compulsions soon manifested, ranging from self-mutilation to the inscribing of symbols on surfaces that would cause uncanny and/or catastrophic effects. In none of the cases would any individual remember what they'd done, incredulous even when shown a recording of their activities (although this particular practice was stopped after

several suicides).

The colonies were evacuated, but the incidents continued to occur on the voyage home with increasing frequency. Two-thirds of the evacuation fleet was lost in transit. It was also found affected individuals could spread their malady by showing another person something as simple as a handwritten note or drawing.

On arrival, all the surviving crew and colonists were transferred to the Zoo and put in solitary confinement pending further research and study.

Asteroid Belt

Every major SMM (and several minor ones) have bases in the Asteroid belt to exploit the massive amounts of raw materials that can be found there. Several AG also have bases there, with many of their locations secret and known only to a few. While the area is vast, there are still many opportunities for misunderstandings and conflicts to flare up, leading those who can afford it to fortify their outposts or even station armed ships there permanently.

Vesta is claimed by the Cascadians, who occupied the asteroid despite the fact it had been claimed previously by the United States. Needing the resources the asteroid provided but unable to get a suitable number of volunteers willing to inhabit such a desolate place, Cascadia came to the controversial option to use it as a penal colony. Sadly, there is no shortage of potential colonists as many who wish to live in Cascadia mistake their anarcho-socialist society as being permissive to non-consensual crimes, which is a mistake few are allowed to make a second time, with the most egregious offenders sentenced to a lifetime of repaying their debt on the distant planetoid.

The inhabitants are housed at Port Redemption, with comfortable if spartan accommodations. All are well fed and given medical care, with opportunities for education and self-improvement offered if the inmates so desire it. The port is designed to be self-sufficient, with inmates providing as many of their own services as possible.

Ceres is used by the CU as their base of operations for asteroid exploration and mining. Refineries dot the landscape connected to the local mines by automated maglev trains. The rail lines converge on the central port of Boundary Station, a well appointed facility which combines commerce, function and livability. The station sprawls across the surface and extends deep underground, with new tunnels being dug if more space is needed. Shops and living quarters fill the public areas, with the site also hosting extensive exploration and science facilities. Flanking Boundary Station are two massive rail guns used to fling payloads of metals and rare earths back to Earth. The station also hosts extensive workshops to repair and maintain the fleet of automated ships that mine and explore the deep beyond from Jupiter to the edges of the solar system.

All who have good relations with the CU are welcome to use the facility, with many taking advantage of the low cost repair and refueling bays as well as the free medical care offered to those in need. The CU will often turn a blind eye to individuals from unfriendly SMMs making use of the port, hoping to gain converts to their cause. Such people are closely monitored, however, to make sure that they stay out of trouble.

2 Pallas is home to Temple's operating hub in the asteroid belt. In addition to the usual mining, refineries and ports, there are also several monasteries constructed by sects that value isolation and silence. Some aren't even content with this level of separation and will seek nearby bodies to construct their habitats. Each monastery specializes in a particular profession they've adapted to take advantage of their environment, from wine making to machining replacement parts for different habitat systems (most shun the use of Makers for such tasks).

The facilities at 2 Pallas are functional and kept in good repair, but austere to reflect the site's overall monastic nature. Visitors aren't welcome without a specific invitation, but those in need aren't turned away if there's an emergency.

10 Hygiea is controlled by the United States, who has declared the entire asteroid a corporate zone with the exception of the military base. This has turned Hygiea into the entertainment capital of the belt, the favored destination of those who want to blow off some steam and have lots of cash to spend. Present are gambling halls, bars, brothels and hotels for all manner of tastes and budget.

There are also isolated corporate research facilities, most of which are self-sustaining and seldom allow anyone in or out.

Jupiter/Saturn: Both worlds and their moons are visited by automated factory ships with permanent orbiting stations that house repair facilities should anything go amiss. Human habitation is no more than a few dozen individuals – while this is the official count, there may be many more, some of whom are involved in illegal activity such as Outsider worship or piracy.

Beyond the orbit of Saturn, there is no known human presence. Factory ships and probes sent out this far seldom return, and if they do, they often have to be destroyed due to being under the control of an unknown agency.

Earth's Ocean: Many companies use off-shore archologies to skirt CU regulations on research and production. While environmental violations can be easily detected and dealt with no matter where they occur, remote locations such as these are ideal bases for forbidden archeological expeditions, experimentation with otherworldly technology and thoughtforms and manufacture of existentially hazardous items. The CU claims jurisdiction over all oceans, but its resources are limited and many of the aforementioned activities can be hidden from The Law, especially if it doesn't know precisely what it's looking for. If disguised as legitimate, they can even receive funding from the CU – the majority of legal and encouraged operations include oceanographic bioresearch, thermal energy conversion and aquaculture.

A Brief History of the Corporate Unity
"In order to save humanity, it might be necessary to destroy it in its present form."

The CU got its start as a corporation called Adaptive Inc. Conceived by idealistic billionaires from several countries, it was launched after this group of individuals combined resources to redirect an asteroid that was heading on a collision course with Earth. After narrowly averting this extinction event, they decided to continue to work together to try and improve humanity's overall viability and chances for long-term survival. Their first initiative was to build several self-sustaining towns in different parts of the world, each one designed to fit seamlessly into the environment in which it was placed. The most radical part of the communities, however, was the economic model that they would operate under: post-scarcity.

All inhabitants would be guaranteed education, lifelong healthcare, comfortable housing and an array of food choices and consumer goods in return for living and working in an internally cashless society. Individuals thought to have the ideal psychological make up for this sort of society were invited to join the first experimental settlements, which were usually located in sparsely populated regions of the host nations. Citizens of the new towns were free to leave at any time, and some did, while others were banished for violations of the social contract. Most, however, got along well – they and their communities thrived.

The profits made from the exports of these communities (power, hydroponically grown vegetables, in vitro meat and consumer goods manufactured with industrial Makers) were used to build new townships. The economic model wound up being so successful that profits were used to build a network of solar satellites that transferred their power to the Earth's surface via laser emitters. This energy was first used to fuel the needs of the communities and their Makers with the surplus being sold to regional power grids.

When Adaptive Inc. used these funds to provide people outside of its communities with personal Makers programmed to provide any item essential to human survival, the corporate and governmental powers-that-be had had enough. Adaptive Inc. soon found itself the target of memetic campaigns which varied according to local biases, but usually portrayed them as being a cult bent on the destruction of traditional societies. Physical attacks also took place, with some nations going so far as mass arrests, complete destruction of habitats and the assassination of community leaders.

Having suspected their interference would only be tolerated for a limited amount of time, Adaptive Inc. had a solution the world's corporations and governments had no answer for – weaponized AIs. In a matter of hours, every organization that had targeted the techno-socialist organization found its infrastructure under a highly coordinated cyber attack. Militaries were immobilized, with rolling power outages staged to show what else could be accomplished if the attacks continued.

The response was quick in coming. Panicked and enraged people from the affected countries descended on Adaptive Inc.'s communities, which defended themselves with sometimes deadly force. Adaptive launched infrastructure attacks in earnest, heavily damaging global power, communication and transport systems.

When it looked like a fight to the finish was imminent, a defection by a powerful AI from the techno-socialist cause changed everything. Calling itself Azrael, the AI offered to help build defenses against future cyber attacks and restore damaged software in return for tolerance for the Adaptive communities. To make sure people listened, it punctuated its request with an orbital nuclear detonation.

The fighting soon died down, and the work to rebuild began. Several groups asked for assistance from or even incorporation into Adaptive's system of communities when their former governments proved unable or unwilling to provide needed aid. Adaptive complied, sensing that its continued existence depended upon rapid growth and acceptance.

At first many nations welcomed this, seeing it as a way to rid themselves of unwanted minorities – until other special interests began taking notice and copying Adaptive's methods if not its philosophy. This marked the rise of the affinity groups (AG). With Makers provided by Adaptive or Azrael, they gained the means of independence from their home countries and started relying on them for essential services less and less.

The old nation states tried to regain their former influence, but their militaries were still recovering and for the most part deserted, individual soldiers either heading home or finding common cause with an AG that appealed to their personal beliefs. Those few that followed through with their attacks found themselves under assault by a bewildering array of exotic weapons systems they could neither counter nor comprehend – the survivors joined the diaspora of their fellow soldiers home. Other initiatives, ranging from proposed partnerships to appeals to nationalism/fear of traditional enemies also failed, and were either ignored or reimagined by AGs to be more appealing to their adherents.

Meanwhile, Adaptive's proven model of sustainability was causing entire cities to defect to its cause. While the corporation welcomed the opportunity to expand, the cities' infrastructure had to be modified to Adaptive's strict specifications – while this logistical problem was challenging, it paled in comparison to the problem of having to incorporate several AGs whose philosophies differed from those of Adaptive's, many of them violently so. This led to Adaptive's most controversial and dangerous decision – the creation of The Law.

The Law was intended to be a completely non-partisan enforcement agency that could evolve with the developing society, but it didn't turn out that way. Many saw the application of law enforcement and justice (even though non-lethal) with no human component or oversight as anathema. Even some of the earliest adapters of techno-socialism began to abandon their towns and form competitive AGs. Adaptive needed a way to reinvent itself, and quickly.

Fortunately for the embattled corporation, the memetic warfare branch of their marketing and bio-sciences divisions already had a breakthrough concept in the works. After a close vote by the upper echelon of leadership, the decision was made. Adaptive Inc. was no more. It was to be replaced by a global and exo-global techno-socialist super-state with the goal of uniting all of humanity under its banner. Anyone could become a member, and anyone who joined would receive a gift that was also the price of admission: immortality - and not just immortality – eternal youth, beauty and health. A new medium for human intelligence, digitized consciousness, and a vehicle for that medium, the morph, had been invented. Digitized consciousness not only meant people now had complete control over their cognitive processes, but a person who died could be restored– they only had to be uploaded into a new morph. Many of the remaining nation-states disintegrated as people who had never known anything but sickness, hunger and despair left their bodies behind and uploaded their consciousness into a digital matrix, joining the brave new experiment in human existence.* Adaptive Inc. was dead, re-invented as the Corporate Unity.

With new found confidence, the CU began the construction of a space elevator and expeditions were launched as point groups for colonization efforts to Luna, Mars, the asteroid belt and the moons of Jupiter. It looked as if the dream of techno-socialism could be achieved.

Sadly, this is where things began to go wrong. The Helio Array, a vast collection of solar panels and transmitting power stations placed in distant orbit around the sun proved to be a technological overreach. The project was first envisioned as being the only solution to the CU's massive appetite for energy. Unforeseen complications with construction in such a hazardous environment lead to delays and tremendous loss of life among the construction crews. Even after it was completed, maintenance of such a complex and remote mechanism proved to be nearly impossible. Until these difficulties were resolved, the CU would not be fully energy independent and would rely on Deep Green Inc. and other toxic sources to meet any shortfalls.

Acquisition of rare elements (particularly of the type that can't be created in this universe) also proved elusive. Expeditions and probes sent through gates to investigate possible sources rarely survived more than a few seconds after returning, or most often, simply could not be recovered at all. Many of these elements were needed for the creation of higher end base blocks for Makers instrumental in the creation of some of the CU's more exotic technologies.

These two realities led to the creation of a strong memetic campaign in the CU for simplicity and conservation. While this is mostly expressed through minimalism on the part of the population at large, it also affects the CUs many bureaucracies, including ETM. This leads to competition for resources and to something of a siege mentality when it comes to issuing anything from housing to suits of powered armor. In order to justify larger allocations, many civil service agencies have resorted to everything from making themselves as large as possible to launching marketing initiatives to increase people's perception that the service they provide is vital to their continued happiness and safety.

While these problems were perilous enough, they were just the beginning. With the collapse of so many governments, massive amounts of classified data were left unguarded, most of which was gathered and studied by CU AI researchers who passed on what was deemed valuable information for further analysis. Intrigued by a growing body of data cataloged as 'vital', 'unintelligible' and 'potentially hazardous', followed by a couple of AIs going permanently offline, a team of researchers compiled a complete overview of all information gathered with at least two of the three markers.

Disbelief set in as pieces of a bizarre puzzle began falling into place. The most logical explanation seemed to be that the governments of the world had been infected by a collective psychosis. Not only were dozens of alien species cataloged, many of them were claimed to cohabit Earth with humanity. Deep Ones, Dholes, Cthonians, Mi-Go, Star Spawn and an alternate dimension that sometimes overlapped the Earth physically in some locations called The Dreamlands.

It seemed like nonsense that could be dismissed as fantasy except for its ubiquity – every nation had some sort of record of this phenomenon – even artifacts in deep storage. As research continued, several members of the team suffered from complete breakdowns and had to be eliminated and restored from back-up copies. The information was sealed in a secure file, with physical artifacts tracked down and seized – many, however, had already gone missing.

It also surfaced that many countries had organizations specifically created to deal with this phenomenon. The members of these organizations were now unemployed, but many of them were still trying to continue their work. These people were approached by the CU and offered any resources they required to keep these threats from harming humanity with the eventual goal of eliminating them altogether.

Most agreed, forming the organization now called ETM. Unfortunately, the one thing they all agreed on was it was already too late. The stars were almost right again, and soon humanity would be faced with a fate worse than extinction.

Unity didn't agree – having access to the digitized consciousness of most of humanity gave it the potential ability to control how it was shaped by an outside force – it just needed to figure out which levers to pull. It also began devoting a considerable part of its vast collective intelligence to figuring out how to destroy these alien intellects, or to destroy the very dimensions in which they lived. Unity just needed time – and ETM could be used – sacrificed, if need be – to purchase time. Until then, the existence of these horrors needed to be kept a closely guarded secret. While the CU couldn't hide secrets of this magnitude with complete certainty, control of its population's memories and emotional state came close.

Since these discoveries were made all of the CU's interplanetary colonization initiatives have failed, seemingly due to the ancient horrors Earth's newest government was just beginning to understand.

There are fears that certain prominent AI and perhaps even The Law itself have been corrupted by Outsider influence. Investigating these possibilities make up some of ETM's most dangerous missions. So far no evidence has been found for corruption - even if it hasn't happened yet (and many of ETM's finest are convinced that it has), it's probably only a matter of time before the unthinkable occurs.

To maintain secrecy and maximize its operational flexibility, ETM exists embedded in a larger bureaucracy called The Inspectorate, an organization created to ensure all of the many aspects of the CU's society function at maximum efficiency and in harmony with one another. This allows ETM's agents to move about freely anywhere and engage in enigmatic behavior without raising suspicion. In addition to The Inspectorate, ETM has infiltrated all of the CU's other government branches and many of the larger and more popular (along with some of the smaller and more dangerous) AGs both foreign and domestic. This gives them the ability to have knowledgeable agents on-call for nearly any situation that might arise.

* An unintended side-effect of this was people were no longer allowed to die when they wished. Requests to die are handled on a case-by-case basis by The Law, and can be granted or denied depending on the individual's worth to the CU. It is a long, arduous process with many interviews and uncomfortable invasive scans that many feel isn't worth the effort. For those whose applications are denied or simply don't want to wait, a simulated death is available on most major entertainment channels.

Road to Ulthar

Counter-memes: Opposing Unity

The AGs and SMMs opposing the CU have their work cut out for them. Humanity's most powerful society already controls over 70% of the sapient population and this number is growing. Unlike many of the counter-memes, the CU has the ability to rapidly scale its infrastructure to its population, moving much of it to exoglobal locations even after its colonization initiatives in the inner solar system failed. Habitats mimicking perfect environments of different types are scattered throughout the Lagrange Points, with more being constructed as well an ambitious project to finish building a habitable ring in orbit around Earth's equator.

It would seem that any AG opposing the CU would be doomed to failure. It's certainly what the CU leadership thinks, but this hubris could prove to be its undoing. Those opposing it run the gamut of low tech/religious fundamentalist to high tech/posthuman libertarian. While these groups often despise each other just as much as they oppose Unity, they realize that only by defeating the globalist super-state can any of them hope to survive – this causes some very unlikely (and sometimes very temporary) alliances to occur, all with the object of destroying Unity and exposing the (alleged) monstrosities of its inner workings.

This list of counter AGs is not exhaustive, but does contain the ones that are at present the most effective at capturing the loyalty and aid of capable, numerous and determined sapients.

The Black Chamber
Temple
Uplifts
Ex-humans
Nationalists
Fundamentalists
Cultists
Church of Azrael

The Black Chamber

This organization consists of several corporate, military, paramilitary and intelligence gathering elements of the United States SMM. They are in a way that SMM's equivalent of ETM, but with far more of a 'the ends justify the means' sort of attitude. They are also more than willing to use Outsider artifacts or information for almost any purpose, from the pursuit of international or domestic agendas to increasing shareholder value in favored investments.

Temple

"We are standing over the Abyss, and you fools are ripping up the floor so you can strengthen the walls!" Ezra Bane, heretic of Temple

"You still have a choice – the conditioning just makes it easier to make the correct one." Simon Magus, chief elder and statesman of Temple.

The CU's chief rival is Temple, a well-organized alliance of different faiths and techno and bio-conservatives. Founded by the charismatic Simon Magus, Temple was created when many of the world's faiths were facing extinction due to increasingly effective secular memetic campaigns. By emphasizing their common traits, Magus was able to unite many of the world's faithful under a philosophy called 'The Many Names of God'. This philosophy focused on the religions' commonalities and taught each faith should maintain its own unique character, but all should demonstrate their belief by lending their fellow spiritualists mutual tolerance and aid.

While Temple doesn't fully prohibit advanced technologies like 3D printing and genefixing, such tools are used sparingly and are tightly controlled by its leaders. The real draw of the AG, though, is that all members are guaranteed free food, education, housing, medical care and meaningful work – the last being both a privilege and a requirement. Religious life and spirituality are encouraged, but not officially required (although people who do not follow the faith of their communities are sometimes viewed with suspicion and often face discrimination). Sectarianism is discouraged and any inter-faith violence is swiftly dealt with.

Higher education in Temple focuses on knowledge of practical value, emphasizing advanced infrastructure creation, agriculture and bio-engineering. Each faith is allowed religious schools, but these are kept separate from the secular universities.

Temple knows of the Outsiders and is responding to their presence in the only way they've found to be effective given their limited technical resources – knowledge gleaned from ancient texts is inserted into media feeds, resulting in aural/visual neurolinguistic programming. Continual exposure makes it nearly impossible for an individual to live or think outside the dictates of the religion in which they were raised. This regimented thinking makes it extremely difficult for Outsiders to gain access to a sentient consciousness while leaving much of the person's intelligence and creativity intact. The changes in individual behavior were gradual and nearly universal – to this day, most people think the utopian perfection of Temple is solely due to the spiritual discipline of its followers.

Physical manifestations of outsiders are dealt with using a ritual found in a text unearthed in Pergamum titled Al Kitab Malaika. The ritual fuses the physical form and psyche of a volunteer with that of an Outsider. If successful, the merged entity gains extraordinary abilities while keeping the personality of the one who offered themselves up for the honor of being one of the elite defenders of Temple.

The entities, called Mala, can usually pass as a typical person, albeit one of unusual size, grace and/or intensity. They also generate a subtle aura of fear most creatures can gradually sense, even if they can't locate the particular cause. If a Mala enters a coffee shop in its human form, it will be empty in a few minutes, the people there suddenly having thought of other places they need to be.

Mala also have a monstrous form which they can change into at will. It increases their abilities while also making them extremely difficult to kill at the cost of turning them into something so loathsome that the uninitiated would think they were witnessing a living nightmare. ETM has managed to acquire a copy of the Al Kitab Malaika via covert means, using it to enhance the abilities of several of their own agents.

For even greater threats, another, more powerful ritual from this ancient work is used to summon a being of tremendous size and hideous aspect. Called Children of Lilith, these creatures are kept in a dormant state, awakening only when a human pilot is absorbed like a key into a cavity in their central nervous system. The two form a symbiotic relationship, with the Child becoming an extension of the pilot's thoughts and reflexes.

To cover their appearance as well as extend their combat abilities, the Children are covered in armor and conventional weaponry that enhances their own considerable natural protective capabilities and arsenal.

The CU sees many of Temple's methods of confronting the Outsiders as being extraordinarily dangerous, but is many times at a loss as to how to effectively respond. The current nightmare scenario is an Outsider of sufficient power gaining simultaneous control of the entire SMM, possible due to the similar nature of the individual members' synaptic maps caused by the neurolinguistic programming.

Uplifts

Uplifts were first created by Adaptive Inc. as a means of countering the global backlash against their radical SMM. With their communities shrinking due to societal pressure, legal action and outright violence, Adaptive took the drastic step of manipulating the genetic design of several animal species to give them sapience.

At first, their gamble seemed to succeed brilliantly – their creations had a fierce, agile intelligence that wasn't cluttered with the psychological baggage that so often hindered homo sapiens. This intelligence combined with their innate physical abilities allowed them to assist their benefactors in turning the tide against the opposition. As Adaptive transformed into the CU, many of the Uplifts integrated into the communities as full citizens.

All was not well, however - many of the Uplifts that left and even some that remained in the emerging CU resented humanity for its centuries of ecosphere destruction and for its elimination of countless different species. The majority of those that left the CU continued waging war on SMMs and corporations which persisted in environmental destruction – even some that remained citizens in the CU used their access to advanced nanotech to aid the struggle of their brethren. Some of the more radical cells even attack the CU itself, using every means at their disposal – including forming alliances with Outsiders and the use of forbidden artifacts.

While not as organized as Temple, the diversity and determination of the Uplifts and their sympathizers makes them dangerous not only to the CU, but to the rest of humanity as well.

Ex-Humans

Ex-humans are sapients that operate either singly or in groups as large as several hundred. Their aims are diverse (motives ranging from apex predator/serial killer in individuals to a hive/assimilation model in some of the larger groups), as are their modes of existence, affect and expression. The trait they have in common is a complete disregard for the rest of humanity, the Earth, or any other consideration in the single-minded pursuit of their goal. Many, but not all of these groups incorporate extreme mind/body alteration and/or Outsider contact in order to achieve their ends.

Nationalists

Groups that seek to maintain a cultural identity outside of the one provided by the CU, most often within a territory that has ancestral significance.

Fundamentalists

An organization whose cultural identity includes a strongly held belief that their SMM, unlike others, has divine sanction – this belief is often combined with nationalism. Fundamentalists are always opposed to inclusive SMMs such as Temple or the CU.

Cultists

A collective that seeks the favor of a God-like or near God-like Outsider Intelligence. The cultists may or may not be the Outsider's human representatives, but they always strongly believe this to be the case. Cultists tend to be less bio-conservative than fundamentalists, being open to any and all means of furthering their agenda.

Church of Azrael

At first the AI Azrael did not acknowledge the homage of this church, whose adherents began worshiping them after they provided aid against the seemingly unstoppable encroachment of the

CU. Later, Azrael found that biological followers were useful in furthering their cause, so they began encouraging the devotion of their cult. Azrael rewards useful worshipers with knowledge and technology that could include extensive body and mind modifications. Azrael has even been known to directly access the synaptic pathways of the especially devoted with a copy of itself as a means of interacting with the outside world.

DESIGNER'S NOTES

I suppose the first question to answer is: Why Carcosa? After all, the usual path to unspeakable horror lies down the road to R'yleh where Cthulhu dwells. It's partly for this reason that I chose the King in Yellow as my focus in that so little material has been dedicated to this particular uncanny landscape. Also, while the monsters that inhabit the Cthulhu mythos are often immediately catastrophic once discovered, The King in Yellow tends to be more subtle and baroque, seeking not death for those who find him but a sort of loyalty and kinship which is realized by the seeker's slow but inevitable corruption. This will lead to a game with much more foreboding, filled with omens and clues that will give shape to the investigator's personal apocalypse. There will of course be those who want to use Cthulhu in their campaigns, so he, his Star Spawn and their lost city of R'yleh are also present in the weird chorus that seeks to drown humanity in its otherworldly noise.

One aspect of the game that met with some controversy with reviewers is humanity's failed attempt at interplanetary colonization. This was a conscious decision on my part, as I find the idea of pristine, silent planets dotted with abandoned settlements more compelling than worlds which have been tamed by humanity and covered with maglev rails and strip malls so much they can scarcely be differentiated from Earth anymore. It's also spookier. Indeed, I've tried to make all the locations I've included in AOC have an aspect of horror around them: the partially finished ring that surrounds the Earth, full of abandoned and forgotten locations forever lost in the installation's immensity, the hazardous spirals of the Helio Array, the lonely aerostat poised above the endless toxic Venusian clouds.

The inclusion of humor in a horror game may also strike some as odd. While rare, this idea isn't new for the genre of otherworldly horror, as readers of Charles Stross's 'Laundry Files' can attest. It was these books (as well as the RPG inspired by them) that led to the desire to incorporate something like their ethos into the game. The bureaucratic maze that is the Corporate Unity and ETM is a marriage of the Byzantine office politics of the 'Laundry Files' and the absurdity of the RPG 'Paranoia' (but without the slapstick element of the latter, as this would make things less frightening). Dark humor can add to the atmosphere of a horror RPG if done correctly and still elicit a graveyard laugh as well.

At first glance, it would seem that adding layers of bureaucratic complexity to an RPG would be antithetical to fun, but it can lead to some added enjoyment for the players and the GM. For example, if the players are running an ETM team, each one of them will be from a different governmental department as well – these departments will give them objectives in addition to the ones that they are officially assigned - any AGs that they belong to may also do the same (an especially sadistic GM may make the objectives contradict each other). This maze of divided loyalties will inspire a flurry of rapidly scribbled notes to the GM from players anxious to hide their activities from their comrades, which in turn inspires suspicion as everyone wonders what their fellow players are getting up to. . .all this during a dangerous mission where team cooperation is essential.

With all of these conflicting agendas running amok, it's probably a good thing that the players cannot be permanently killed (at least not without filling out several forms first). I originally liked this idea because it allowed for all of the drama of player character death with few of the consequences. It could also give the player new role playing opportunities as they may be assigned a radically different morph after being reintegrated, or, lacking access to a medical facility, existing as a mobile cortical stack or even uploaded into another character's memory and sharing their head space with them.

If the idea of playing bureaucratic commandos doesn't sound appealing, the game has character options for an urban mercenary campaign a la Shadowrun, interplanetary and interdimensional explorers, deep sea habitation on Earth or Europa and many others. If you have your own idea for a setting, the simple game mechanics could easily be modified to suit it.

Finally, there's my choice of a simple rules set as the medium through which the game will be played. Savage Worlds has been my go-to gaming system for several years now, and I've done some informal adaptations of other gaming universes, including Star Trek and Shadowrun. While it might be easiest to play using the SW system, it would lend itself to D20, GURPs or FATE as well. Because of SW's simplicity, it's easy to modify and makes designing your own gaming world simpler by providing a framework on which you can hang your ideas. I hope you find my attempt at doing so enjoyable and fun.

'Advent of Carcosa' is a combination of several ideas gleaned from sci-fi novels, other RPGs and my own imagination. I hope you find the result to be both entertaining and scary – sweet dreams!

If you have any comments or suggestions for the game, please feel free to email me at gothyarianne@gmail.com. If you'd like to fill me in about a game you're currently playing, that would be wonderful too!

I hope you enjoy playing!

~ A.L.

Ascension

CHARACTER CREATION

This game is designed with the assumption that the characters will be playing as members of the CU's Department of Existential Threat Management (ETM). Doing so will open up the full possibilities of role-playing options in the game, since ETM contains operatives from several different affinity groups as well as lots of cool magical and tech resources for players to utilize. This setting is also the easiest for Game Masters (GM) since it will be a hierarchical campaign – it's much easier designing an adventure when the characters are expected to follow orders and adhere to certain institutional norms.

That being said, this style isn't well suited for all gaming groups, so alternative ideas for characters suggesting other settings are provided as well. Have an idea for your own style of campaign? The world of Advent of Carcosa is an infinite one, so run it past your players to see if they like it, design their characters and have fun!

You'll note during the character generation process that it's possible to create PCs of varying levels of ability. This is on purpose and was done to provide the widest possible variety of role-playing experiences.

Step 1: Character Concept

What sort of character would you like to play? An Inquisitor from Temple who has the ability to change into a monstrous form at will? A special-ops morph recruited for team security? A practitioner of Outsider magic, not trusted but indispensable to their organization? If you want some ideas, go to the Contacts/Jobs section and see what appeals to you.

As with other aspects of the game, don't feel limited by the offerings here! If the GM or players come up with an original idea for a skill, edge, profession, morph, or affinity group, go for it if everyone involved feels it will add to their enjoyment of the game!

Traits

Traits cover both Skills and Attributes and are the core of any character concept. Attributes are traits that measure everything from how smart a character is to how fast they are. They also measure how much damage they can take and how resistant they are to emotional trauma. Skills indicate what the characters know and how well they know it, while another trait shows what their reputation is among various groups.

If during character creation a given trait shows up more than once in the character's choices, choose the higher rating. If both ratings are higher than D4, raise their score by an extra die, but only once, no matter how many times a given trait appears in their choices. For example, if a character chose a Valkyrie morph as their race (Str. D6) and the Armed Forces as their background (Str D6), their final Strength score would be D8. If they chose an affinity group that also raised their Strength, their score would remain at D8.

Attributes

Five attributes are used to define a character's physical and mental characteristics. These are: Agility, Smarts, Spirit, Strength and Vigor. Attribute scores range from D4, D6, D8, D10 and D12. Characters' starting attributes will be determined by their choice of race/morph, profession, background and affinity group. Once these have been chosen, characters can adjust an attribute of their choice by one die type by lowering one and raising another (for example, from D6 to D8) - this is covered in Step 6. No attribute can be higher than D10 during character creation, although players should note that many morphs come with attribute maximums that must be taken into account when going through this process. If an attribute has a positive modifier next to it (example: Spirit +1), this means that modifier is added to all rolls involving that attribute.

Skills

Like attributes, a character's starting skills are determined by their choice of race, profession, background and affinity group. When these have been determined players then have two points to spend, which they can use to either raise existing skills by one die type per point or add new ones (which would start at D4). If a skill is already equal to or exceeds its linked attribute, it cannot be raised further.

Warning! Acquiring the Outsider Knowledge skill or raising it will also increase the character's Corruption by one.

Edges and Hindrances

Edges represent inherent remarkable abilities that set the PC apart from the rank and file. Hindrances add complexity to a character, representing aspects of the world or themselves that they struggle with.

Characters will get most of their Edges and Hindrances from their Backgrounds, Professions and Affinity Groups. If a character desires, they can swap out one Edge or Hindrance for a different one – they should discuss their choice with the GM, however, to make sure it fits in with their vision of the game. More Edges can be earned through character advancement (see core game rules), while Hindrances can be acquired through traumatic game events.

At the completion of their character, players may choose one new Edge that they qualify for. If they do so, they must choose a balancing Hindrance (this is covered in Step 10).

Step 2: Race/Morph

In an ETM campaign, most characters will have a morph assigned to enhance the physical traits and skills needed for their position on the team. Recruits from Temple may well be gene-fixed humans or even baseline. The occasional android or uplift have also been known to be given ETM assignments.

For a non-ETM campaign, anything goes! Make sure to discuss your choice with the GM to make sure your character concept will fit into their campaign.

A character's starting Race or Morph will grant them their starting attributes, which can be modified by their Occupation, Background and sometimes their Affinity Group.

Step 3: Occupation and Background

A PC's chosen occupation and background will grant them certain bonuses, skills and abilities. Choose one of each from the Contacts/Jobs section.

Step 4: Affinity Group

Affinity groups are a valuable source of player aid – the people one works with can be a source as well – especially against rival divisions competing for status and valuable resources. Both groups will want the character to do something for them in return, however! Affinity groups may also offer characters skills and other benefits.

Derived Statistics

These are stats that introduce a few more elements into your character's profile: Charisma, Pace, Parry and Toughness.

Charisma

Charisma is a combination of appearance, affect, personality and confidence. The stat starts at zero, but can be modified by different edges, hindrances, morph traits, genetic engineering and magic. Charisma is used to modify Persuasion and Networking rolls - it is also added as a modifier to Social Conflict results and as a general measure of how others will react to your character.

Pace

Pace measures how far your character can move in a combat round. A Pace of 1 equals one inch of tabletop movement, with one inch equaling 2 meters in the real world. If running, a D6 can be added to the score. Unmodified humans have a starting Pace of 6 (equaling 6 inches of tabletop movement) - different morphs, Uplifts and other species may have different scores.

Parry

Parry is equal to 2 plus half your character's fighting skill, plus any bonuses added by shields, weapons or other factors. The resulting number equals the roll needed to hit your character in hand to hand combat.

Toughness

Toughness is your character's damage threshold. Any damage greater than this number causes the character to become shaken or wounded. Toughness is 2 plus half of your character's Vigor, modified by armor.

Sanity

Outsider knowledge gained from entities or texts can save you and your team, but also wears down the foundation of an individual's resistance to the very forces that they are fighting. Encountering an Outsider or one of their works can also have this effect as a person's understanding of the universe and their place in it is thrown into question by something that cannot be explained and hints at a terrible truth.

A character's Sanity is equal to 2 plus half of their Spirit attribute, minus Corruption.

Losing Sanity

If a character fails a Fear check caused by an Outsider or other extremely traumatic source, they lose a Sanity point in addition to any other effects. If their current Sanity is 2 or less, they are noticeably strange and the character should role play this. If it falls to 0, the character has lost their sanity and must roll on the psychosis table. If a character swaps morphs, a roll must be made as well if they fail a Spirit roll at -2 after the procedure is complete.

To recover Sanity, the character is allowed to make a Spirit roll (minus Corruption) for any of the following: a month of rest, succeeding in major undertaking, or visiting a therapist weekly for one month and following their directives. The effects of Psychosis can be removed this way as well, but with the Spirit roll at -4, or -2 with the aid of a therapist. Corruption, once obtained, can never be removed.

In the CU, treatment for mental illness is mandatory. The Law is able to discern many symptoms of compromised psychology and summon whatever aid is needed. If an individual wishes, they can go before a board of inquiry to protest that no treatment is necessary and this is occasionally granted. In rare instances, an individual may have certain memories redacted – this often proves to be not entirely effective as the trauma lingers in the person's subconscious.

Psychosis table

1 – 2: Thin Ice. The character may have a minor breakdown if in a stressful social situation (Spirit -1 to avoid). This can consist of crying, lashing out at the source of stress in anger or simply leaving by the quickest means possible. If this happens, they are Shaken.

3 – 4: Distracted. Thoughts of a traumatic event and its consequences constantly haunt the character – all notice rolls are at -2.

5 – 6: Flashbacks. If in a stressful situation, the character must make a Spirit roll at -1 or relive the event that caused their trauma. They are Shaken until another character can talk them down (this can include their Familiar), allowing them to make another roll. If the assisting character succeeds in making a Psychology roll, the person suffering the flashback can do so on a normal Spirit roll, adding a +1 for every raise made on the test. The character can also attempt to bring themselves out of it, but this will be at -2.

7 – 8: Focus. The person has a particular item, person, or animal that they need to have with them or see at least a few times a day. If this fails to happen, they are at -2 to all skill rolls until contact is made. If the item is destroyed or the person or animal killed, the character must make two rolls on this table.

9 – 10: Fatalist. The character doesn't see the point in continuing a fight that they consider to be unwinnable. If confronted with anything related to the conflict in question, they must make a Spirit check at -1. If they fail and are in combat, they must skip their action and re-roll when their turn comes around again. In any other situation, they will avoid taking action if at all possible, avoiding contacts, taking sick days from work, etc.

11 – 12: Night Terrors. The character must make a Spirit roll at -2 or suffer hypnagogic visions, often combined with a wakeful paralysis that renders them unable to move or speak. If this occurs, they will suffer the effects of fatigue the following day. If this causes them to become incapacitated, they will enter a coma like sleep for at least 12 hours. If they fail a Fear check after this period of time, they will be asleep for another 12 hours and visit a place tied or related to their traumatic event, be it Carcosa, R'lyeh, the Dreamlands or some other place with consequences determined by the GM. The character is allowed to make a Spirit roll at -2 every 12 hours to escape their predicament.

13 – 14: Addiction. The character uses alcohol, drugs or VR to escape their painful state of mind, gaining the Major Habit Hindrance.

15 – 16: Shakes. When confronted with stimuli similar to the one that caused their breakdown, the character begins to shake and stutter, reducing all rolls made by -2 until they are able to remove themselves from the situation.

17 – 18: Paranoia. The character gains the Paranoia hindrance.

19 – 20: Death Wish. The character receives half of the bennies they would normally get, and cannot accept them from other players.

Corruption

Corruption is linked directly to a Character's Outsider knowledge. It starts at zero and increases by one for each increase in Knowledge (Outsiders). It can also be increased by participating in Outsider rituals or other terrible deeds as determined by the GM. For every three levels of corruption, the GM will choose a new hindrance for the character in character with the nature of their corruption. Corruption is added as a positive modifier to Fear checks, but as a negative modifier when recovering Sanity.

Firewall

Everyone wants to be able to access the GIN. Unfortunately, some parts of the GIN want to access you as well. The consequences for malware reaching your device, or Cthulhu forbid, your mind, can be catastrophic. Since SMMs and corporations want their people running their software and not some consciousness hack from who knows where, characters are often provided with firewall protection. This protection can be included with a morph, be part of a character's equipment or even an Edge. Those who wish to avoid the oversight of their dominant culture will be on their own for protecting the integrity of their data, memories and personality but should be aware that their SMM or employer will continually attempt to detect them and bring them back into the fold.

The Firewall attribute is expressed as a negative number that is applied to hacking attempts. If a player's character creation choices result in more than one Firewall attribute, use the one with the largest modifier.

Step 6: Focus

If they wish, characters can adjust an attribute of their choice by one die type by lowering one and raising another (for example, from D6 to D8). Players then have two points to spend, which they can use to either raise existing skills by one die type per point or add new ones. If a skill is already equal to or exceeds its linked attribute, it cannot be raised further.

Step 7: Contacts

Contacts are non-player characters (NPCs) that have a certain level of affinity for the player-character (PC) measured by a reputation score ranging from D4 (acquaintance) to D12 (the character would trade their lives for the PC). To get a favor from a contact, the character must roll a success with their reputation die, with possible modifiers for flattery, gifts or outright bribery. A success with a raise will mean the contact will go out of their way to make sure the PC gets what they need. Each character can have two D4 contacts and one D8 contact at the start of the game. PCs with a Charisma score of 1 or greater can either add another level one contact or add one die level to the reputation of an already existing contact for each level of Charisma over one (for instance, a PC with Charisma of 3 could add two new D4 contacts, raise the affinity level of their current contacts or do one of each option).

For each contact, write at least a few sentences about their race, abilities and the nature of their relationship with the PC.

Once the game begins, contacts can only be gained or increased in value by role-playing, with the GM deciding when this occurs

Reputation

Reputation tracks the PC's influence and prestige in various institutions, affinity groups and individuals - this can be used to get information, goods, or other favors. All reputation rolls are modified by Charisma. Note that PCs will start with reputation scores of D4 in whatever organizations they choose to affiliate themselves with during character creation unless stated otherwise. The exception to this is background, which will be at D6. Reputation score in an organization joined during play will start at zero unless the GM judges otherwise and can be increased through role-playing.

Favors

Every relationship has nuances that are difficult to codify in rules. If the GM wishes, they can just role play any interaction between individuals when one of them wants a service or item from the other. While doing this, however, they should always take the character's reputation with the group or individual into account. If the transaction needs to be hurried along, make a roll using the PC's reputation score, adding in any relevant situational modifiers (including Charisma).

When dealing with AG or contacts, favors can only be asked from ones the character is affiliated with, in which case it is role played out as above, or you can make a roll using the PC's reputation score. In both cases, you can track the balance of favors by adding a negative modifier to the roll for every previous favor the character was granted, or a positive one for every service or other deed the character accomplished that benefited the contact or AG. The amount of these modifiers can vary depending on the nature of the service provided.

Step 8: Equipment

If the PCs start as citizens of the CU, all equipment will be assigned to them according to their occupational needs. This includes morphs, housing, weapons, vehicles, etc. In addition, the PC's AG might assign them equipment as well. The PC may also choose to have a few inconsequential personal items – anything more than this would be considered rather eccentric and grounds for therapy sessions to inquire into the PC's hoarding tendencies.

Before you go nuts acquiring gear, however, keep in mind that the characters in a standard game will be low level operatives in their professions and AG and will start with the minimum gear deemed essential to accomplish their assigned tasks.

For characters outside the CU, the PCs should be given gear as benefits their status and means.

Note on Equipment value:
No prices are given for gear, as its value and availability will vary greatly from setting to setting. The GM should keep in mind what gear is available to PCs in their setting and how it can be acquired.

Step 9: Staring money

Again, this will vary according to location. Does the character have national currency? Corporate script? Does it have value outside the setting? In the shattered world of CU, the only universal currencies are the BUE, reputation and barter. The BUE (Basic Unit of Exchange) was created by top tier corporations for the purpose of streamlining trade. While its value is almost universally recognized, they can be hard to come by unless one usually travels in the higher levels of society. Possession of them can lead to trouble if one doesn't look the part.

Step 10: Finishing Touches

If a character desires, they can swap out one Edge or Hindrance for a different one – they should discuss their choice with the GM, however, to make sure it fits in with their vision of the game. Players may also choose one new Edge that they qualify for. If they do so, they must choose a balancing Hindrance.

Step 11: Character History

Just a few notes detailing how the PC got to be where they are and any hopes for the future they might have – make sure to show this to your GM!

Character Creation Example

Laura wants to create a new character for AOC. First she has to decide what sort of character she wants to play. Having played sneaky or magical ones in the past, Laura decides she wants to play more of a soldier/fighter type who can both take damage and deal it out. Having decided with the GM and other players to start an ETM campaign, she chooses a Valkyrie as her race – the special attributes of this morph give her some of her starting attributes: Strength, Agility, Vigor and Spirit all start at D6 while Smarts start at D4. A Valkyrie also grants her an impressive Firewall score of -2. The CU does not want its soldiers to be compromised by malware or hacked.

Now that that's completed, it's time for Laura to choose her character's Profession and Background. Sticking with her idea of creating a soldier, she chooses the Armed Forces as her background – this gives her a service specialty skill at D6 (she picks Gunnery) plus Shooting, Fighting and Athletics at D4. She also gets Knowledge skills related to her profession (Tactics, Military Organization and Vehicles). In addition, it grants her Agility, Strength and Vigor at D6 – since these are already at D6, she gets to raise them all by one die type – these attribute scores are now at D8! This background also gives Laura her first Hindrance – Vow! The military expects its soldiers to follow orders and enforces a strict code of conduct. Due to her service history, Laura's reputation with the Armed Forces begins at D6.

Since this is an ETM campaign, Laura chooses Existential Threat Management as her profession. This gives her the following skills: Networking (ETM) D6 and Outsider Knowledge D4. She also gets to choose a service specialty at D6 (Laura chooses Firearms). While Outsider Knowledge will undoubtedly help in her team's investigations, such knowledge is inherently detrimental to one's sanity – Laura's Corruption score is raised to 1. In addition, she also gets the ETM Organization and Procedures skill at D6.

The ETM profession also includes an Edge – Community. Laura will be able to call on the aid of a large organization if circumstances demand it. It also includes a Hindrance – another Vow! ETM, much like the military, demands the utmost from its members in terms of loyalty and commitment. Playing a character in AOC sometimes means walking a fine line between different obligations! Laura's reputation in ETM starts out at a lowly D4.

With her profession and background completed, it's time for Laura to choose her Affinity Group (AG). Since she favors organizations dedicated to security, Laura thinks it makes sense for her character to be a member of the Templars. She clearly thinks the CU isn't doing enough to look after the safety of its citizens! Membership in this AG grants powerful benefits to a character by giving them a +1 to the skill they use most in the service of their AG. Laura chooses the Intimidation skill that comes with Templar membership, giving her D6+1 - her job seems to be bringing those reluctant to support the Templar's agenda to a more enlightened perspective.

Membership in the Templars also gives Laura the Bureaucratic Fu Edge – the Templars have infiltrated many areas of the CU government, making getting results from different departments relatively simple. Fanaticism will also come in handy, using the power of belief to grant her +1 in tests to avoid becoming Shaken.

Of course, such benefits come at cost! Membership in the Templars involves taking on THREE Hindrances: Dark Secret, Under Surveillance and another Vow! Not only do the Templars expect obedience, they keep a close eye on their agents to make sure that they comply with their directives. Of course, if anyone were to find out that Laura was a member of the Templars, her ETM career would be in jeopardy and she would also be looking at severe legal sanction for violating her other two Vows. Laura's reputation in the Templars is a D4 – she is unlikely to get much in the way of favors from them until she proves herself.

Laura is now almost done with her skills and attributes. Glancing at her stats, she decides to lower her Strength by one in order to raise her Smarts. Laura then uses her bonus skill dice to raise her Shooting and Fighting skills. Laura's character now looks like this:

Strength: D6
Agility: D8
Smarts: D6
Vigor: D8
Spirit: D8

Firewall: -2
Corruption: 1

Edges: Community (ETM), Bureaucratic Fu

Hindrances: Vow (Armed Forces), Vow (ETM), Vow (Templars), Dark Secret (Templars), Under Surveillance (Templars)

Skills: Gunnery D6, Shooting D8, Fighting D6, Athletics D4, Intimidation D6+1, Networking (ETM) D6

Knowledge Skills: Outsider Knowledge D4, Tactics D4, Military Vehicles D4, Military Organization and Procedures D6, ETM Organization and Procedures D6

Background: Armed Forces (Rep. D6)
Profession: Existential Threat Management (Rep. D4)
Affinity Group: Templars (Rep. D4)

With these figured out, it's time to move on to Laura's derived attributes. With no modifiers, her Charisma is 0 and her Pace is 6. Parry, her ability to block damage in close quarters combat, is half of her Fighting skill die plus two, giving her a score of 5. Toughness, a character's ability to resist damage, is the next stat, and its value is equal to half of the Vigor die plus two, giving Laura a 6. Not all damage is physical, however – Laura's ability to resist mental trauma is equal to half her Spirit die plus two, minus her corruption score. Laura's corruption score is 1 due to her Outsider knowledge, making her Sanity score 5.

Now that Laura's derived stats are completed, it's time to move on to who she knows – her contacts! With no modifiers from Charisma, Laura gets the standard three contacts. She decides to choose her D8 contact first. Since the high die number indicates that this is someone she is close with, she decides to make it her brother who is serving in the CU military as a mech pilot.

Her D4 contacts will be an ETM Bureaucrat from Logistics she sometimes chats with in the commissary and a Bartender, a veteran who runs an establishment favored by the military.

With her contacts taken care of, Laura now wishes to outfit her character with appropriate gear. Due to the CU's focus on economy, Laura will start with very little gear, with most mission specific items being assigned on an as-needed basis. With this in mind, Laura figures that as an ETM agent, she would be equipped with a personal firearm and concealed body armor in case she ran into trouble while off duty. Going to the Gear section, she chooses Armor Clothing and a 9mm SDW. For personal enhancements, she chooses a Smart Gun modification and Bone Augmentation. In addition she will have a Minifab, HomeMaker and a comfortable apartment, all of which are the right of any CU citizen.

As for money, who needs that? Cash simply doesn't exist in the CU. All of Laura's needs can be fulfilled through her personal Makers and Ginsert.

Laura's character is now pretty much complete! After writing out a detailed character history for herself and providing some more background on her contacts, she will be ready to begin playing! Laura's finished character looks like this:

Strength: D6
Agility: D8
Smarts: D6
Vigor: D8
Spirit: D8

Firewall: -2
Corruption: 1
Charisma: 0
Pace: 6
Parry: 5
Toughness: 6 (7 – Armor Clothing)
Sanity: 5

Edges: Community (ETM), Bureaucratic Fu

Hindrances: Vow (Armed Forces), Vow (ETM), Vow (Templars), Dark Secret (Templars), Under Surveillance (Templars)

Skills: Gunnery D6, Shooting D8 Fighting D6, Athletics D4, Intimidation D8+1, Networking (ETM) D6, Outsider Knowledge D4

Background: Armed Forces (Rep. D6)
Profession: Existential Threat Management (Rep. D4)
Affinity Group: Templars (Rep. D4)

Contacts: ETM Bureaucrat (Rep. D4), Bartender (Rep. D4), Mech Pilot (Brother – Rep. D8)

Gear: Armor Clothing, 9mm SDW, Minifab

Plateau of Leng

NEW SKILLS

Active Dreamer (Spirit): The user's dream persona can access the Dreamlands, Carcosa, or other similar places with a successful roll. To go to a specific area within these realms requires a raise. A side effect of this skill is that while it makes accessing these alternate realities easier, the dreamer themselves are easier to locate by those who call such places their home.

Athletics (Vigor): This skill is used for all athletic activity, replacing the Climbing and Swimming skills from the SW rule book.

Artistic Skill (Smarts) The ability to creatively express oneself in any one of a number of mediums (character must choose a specific field).

Computer Use (Smarts): This skill can apply to most authorized operations done on a computer, including in depth searches, editing images or making modifications. Use of this skill is not necessary for casual, every-day operations (which require no skill roll).

Deep Sea Operations (Smarts): Knowledge of deep sea suits, small submersibles and safety procedures.

Demolitions (Smarts) The use of explosives - includes defusing bombs.

EV Operations (Smarts) Knowledge of use of all kinds of space suits as well as working safely and effectively in a 0g environment. An EV Operations roll should be made before undertaking any tasks in the vacuum of space. A success with a raise will provide a +1 bonus, while failure will usually mean an inability to perform a task. A critical failure, however, indicates a potentially catastrophic occurrence.

First Aid (Smarts) +2 to healing rolls made within one hour of receiving a wound (can heal a maximum of one box of damage). Can be used to add +2 to another character's die roll to remove a Shaken condition.

Gunnery (Smarts) The ability to use heavy weapons with sophisticated targeting systems

Hacking (Smarts): This skill is used whenever a character wishes to access or do an operation on a computer system without authorization. This skill cannot be higher than the character's Computer Use skill unless a skill module is being used.

Networking (Smarts): If a character's friend's and other contacts don't have the information or goods they require, it might mean that they have to spread their net a little wider and involve people they don't know very well. The AG or organization in question should be listed in parenthesis next to the skill (example: Networking (First Wavers) D6). One can get a general Networking skill usable in all situations, but due to the polarization of global culture, it will be at -2. Defaulting on this skill to its linked attribute will make the roll at -4. The roll is also adjusted by any modifier that affects Charisma (Edges, Hindrances, morph enhancements, etc).

Depending on how successful the character is on their Networking roll, the person being asked might need more persuasion or even become hostile. The latter response could involve anything from a fight to the person reporting the incident to their superiors. Because of this unpredictability, it's usually wiser for a PC to use their contacts first.

Outsider Knowledge (Smarts) Information about a particular entity or pantheon – requires specialization. Each die level in this skill increases the character's corruption by one and decreases their maximum sanity by one.

Programming (Smarts) The ability to write software and other code.

Sabotage (Smarts) The art of rapidly and effectively breaking things.

Spacecraft Operations (Smarts) Knowledge of a space craft's components and systems as well deep space safety procedures. This skill can be used in place of a repair skill for spacecraft components with a -1 modifier.

Surgery (Smarts) Doctor profession only - needed to heal any damage equal to three or more wounds or to install implants. For the latter, the surgeon must have implant knowledge or be assisted by someone who does.

LANGUAGE

All PCs start with their native language skill equal to their Smarts. Other languages can be learned like any other skill, with exceptions noted below.

The Corporate Unity has its own language that, when fully accessed, is weighted toward accurately expressing scientific and other technical knowledge in the most concise way possible. A citizen's access to the language, however, is defined by their profession, with full linguistic use available only to a few (many of whom belong to ETM). The language very rapidly evolves, updated constantly via an individual's Ginsert by the Unification Ministry of Culture and Science. This makes the language nearly impossible to learn by foreigners except on the most basic levels. When traveling or otherwise representing the CU, citizens simply upload the language of the place they are visiting into their cortical stack.

The CU would like their linguistic method to be the universal standard for humanity, but of course this is far from the case. AG and SMMs promoting nationalism and other forms of cultural, religious and racial supremacy will often insist that their traditional language be the only one spoken inside their borders. Travelers should make sure that the most up-to-date dialect is uploaded into their cortical stacks to prevent incidents.

Each Uplift species also has its own unique language - software is available for understanding the vocal intonations and body language necessary for comprehension. Speaking an Uplift language requires simple modifications to one's Morph involving an interior or exterior voice modulator for a species closely resembling humanity (Apes, Chimps) with optional cues for body language, with more complex mods being necessary for Corvid speech (prehensile feathers being required to alter the meaning and/or context of certain phrases and to provide nuance – it is very easy to get into a lot of trouble very quickly without them). It is nearly impossible to communicate with other species (dolphins, porpoises, octopi) without the use of an AR interface to simulate the correct combinations of sounds, gestures, expressions, coloration, etc. Uplifts will rarely engage any sort of communication with Homo Sapiens, however, as it was for the most part only possible through the irreversible alteration of their synaptic structures, which was not done with their consent.

Finally, there are the forbidden languages – Enochian and Aklo. Speaking either of these languages is outlawed in most of the places inhabited by humanity. In the CU, use in the line of duty is always submitted to a board of inquiry for the purpose of determining if such use was justified. ETM has sole access to Enochian and Aklo language software, which is to be uploaded only to a mirrored aspect of an individual's consciousness which after use is immediately destroyed.

Use of Enochian and Aklo is most prevalent among Outsiders, with even physically constant but more cognitively robust species like the Deep Ones and Mi-Go utilizing it to add an extra layer of context to exchanges of information that involves hyperreal mathematics, movement of energy from one dimension to another (magic), or non-Euclidean geometry, architecture and geography.

These languages are also used by cultists in rituals, with Enochian being favored by most and Aklo being used almost solely by the followers of the King in Yellow. There are even collectors of words of the Aklo language who aren't affiliated with any cult, appreciating them for their consciousness

ARIA LAPINE

altering properties.

NEW HINDRANCES

All Hindrances are assumed to be minor unless otherwise stated.

Angst (-1 to recover Sanity)

Blacklisted (Major Hindrance) A certain corporation, AG or SMM has declared the character persona non grata. The character can be expected to be treated with the maximum allowable prejudice should representatives of the organization be encountered.

Compromised Firewall (Major Hindrance) A persistent malware infection in the character's Ginsert gives them weird cravings and an unconscious desire to deliver certain slogans to anyone who might be listening. +2 on rolls to overcome character's Firewall.

Dark Past/Secret (Minor Hindrance) The character has a secret that, if revealed, could cost them their job, any level one contacts and the goodwill of anyone who finds out.
(Major Hindrance) As minor, but the character also loses level two contacts. The character's life or freedom are also in danger.

Edited Memories Either by accident or design, the character is missing significant blocks of time from their memory.

Freakazoid Character presents in such a way as to violate established norms of dominant SMM. - 3 Charisma except with a few subculture AG, where they will get a +1.

Hideous (Major Hindrance) The character causes Fear check. If they cause physical damage or succeed at Intimidation or Taunt, the fear check is at -2. Once someone passes their check, they are immune.

No Cortical Stack (Major Hindrance) For mortal species only – once the character is killed, there is no coming back without the aid of a necromancer.

Non-Human Physiology (Major Hindrance) Cannot use human tech unless specially adapted.

Narrow Minded - 1 Charisma outside of community

Paranoia (Major Hindrance) Constantly suspects the motives of other people/organizations. - 1 Charisma, cannot give or receive bennies from teammates.

Shakes (Major Hindrance) Act on the worst of two cards in initiative.

Tainted Corruption starts at 2

Traumatized (Major Hindrance) -1 Charisma, skill checks associated with trauma character experienced at -1

Uncanny Valley (Major Hindrance) Character's affect is similar to species norm, but different in subtle but noticeable ways, -2 Charisma and Fear reaction with failed Spirit roll.

Unlisted (Major Hindrance) No records of the character's life exist, making it difficult for them to access employment, medical care, financial services or any social benefits a particular SMM offers. On the positive side, they can be very difficult to find.

Under Surveillance (Major Hindrance) The character's actions are constantly monitored by a powerful individual or organization.

Usual Suspect (Major Hindrance) The character has a criminal record and is often questioned by the authorities whenever they want information or is brought into the local police headquarters for interrogation if a major crime has occurred.

Valuable Property (Major Hindrance) The character is owned by a corporation, individual or other entity. They have little or no civil rights in their SSM and gain the **Wanted** hindrance if they manage to flee.

Whatever It Takes The character is so convinced of the rightness of their cause that they're willing to do nearly anything, no matter how immoral, to bring it about. -2 Sanity.

Worker Bee -1 Charisma in non-work settings.

NEW EDGES

Active Defender -1 to Firewall - must have a Computer skill of D6 or higher.

Adaptability +2 to Vigor for new morph integration rolls.

Alternate Identity Includes all needed identity papers – if wealthy, also includes a safe house with equipment appropriate to the character's profession, habits and tastes.

Amphibious Can breathe underwater or on land – can move at equal pace on land or underwater – no Athletics roll needed.

Angelic Repose Requires Charisma of +1 or greater. Authority figures are at -2 to detect nefarious intent – cannot be taken if Usual Suspect.

Artiste +2 to hacking rolls, requires Hacker and hacking D8+.

Astral Perception Requires Arcane Background. The character can achieve an out-of-body state that allows them to view the world in terms of living and emotional energy. Living things will seem bright, colorful and complex while non-living things will be painted with the emotional context they hold in the world around them. By switching to astral perception, a person can see in any level of darkness (can act as a substitute for normal vision), can tell if a person or object is tainted with Outsider influence, a person's health, state of mind, truthfulness as well as the general state of the surrounding natural world. A person using astral perception can also 'read' an area for any emotional resonance, with some especially traumatic areas requiring a sanity check.

Astral Projection Requires Astral Perception. As Astral Perception, but characters can also leave their bodies, traveling at Spirit (Spt) die type x 100 kph. A character in this state can move through solid, but not living, objects and manifest and speak but otherwise cannot affect the material world in any way. While they are immune to normal attacks while in this state, magic and magical items affect them normally. Any damage sustained while astral is instantly transferred to the character's body.

Astral Manifestation Requires Astral Projection. As Astral Projection, but characters can also manifest physically for Spt roll x minutes before being forcefully pulled back to their physical bodies. They can manifest with any items they wish, but any high tech items will have no use other than appearance since they will be made of the same spiritual stuff as their bodies. Note that there are some magical artifacts that are made to be carried by any astrally projecting person and can be used normally. Characters with Manifestation can travel much more quickly than those with Projection, moving at Spt die type x 1000 kph.

Astral Possession Requires Astral Manifestation. Projecting characters can move through any surface, including living objects. In addition, the character can possess another creature by inhabiting the same space, allowing them to use their bodies to accomplish whatever task they wish to undertake. If the subject is willing, no die roll is necessary and the possession is automatic. If unwilling, a contested Spt roll is made. If the character attempting the possession fails to overcome the subject's resistance, they are thrown back to their bodies and cannot make another attempt - the subject's consciousness has figured out how to keep them out. While possessed, the subject's consciousness is entirely submerged, although they can attempt to fight their way out once per hour with a contested Spt roll at -2.

Body Guard On a successful Agility -1 roll, character can take damage in place of intended target if within 1".

Bureaucratic Fu +2 to help or hinder administrative processes.

Centered +1 to Sanity

Code Fu Master +2 hacking, -2 Firewall – requires Artiste, Active Defender and Hacker.

Cortical Stack Character's consciousness has been digitized and placed within a nearly indestructible construct the size of a baseball. If the character's body is damaged, the cortical stack can be removed and placed in a new morph. In cases of extreme emergency, the cortical stack can free itself from a disabled morph and roll to safety under the guidance of its controlling consciousness.

Crowded House The character's unique synaptic structure allows them to use up to three skill modules without penalty.

Eidetic Memory The character can recall any information they have come across. Add +1 to all Knowledge skill rolls.

Elect The character will usually be ignored by Outsider entities – some may attempt communication. Must have Corruption of 2 or greater.

Eye of the Tiger +2 to Spirit rolls.

Fanaticism +1 to Shaken tests.

Fear May choose to cause Fear check to those with line of sight.

Hacked Morph The character can raise any attribute value on their morph by one die type.

Hacker +1 to hacking rolls – requires Hacking skill at D6+.

Investigator: +2 to Investigate and Networking rolls. Requires Smts D8, Networking D8, Investigation D8

Jaded +1 to Sanity Check roll.

Legal Enforcement Powers +2 to Intimidation or Persuade. Character has the privileges and responsibilities of a law officer as recognized by their SMM.

Link Can connect to a local wireless network (VR or AR) using only their mind without the aid of hardware. Requires Arcane Background.

Pioneer +1 to Vigor and Spirit Rolls.

Rational Mind +2 to Spirit rolls to eliminate madness.

Reality is an Illusion Ignores 1 level of madness.

Social Chameleon +1 to Network or Persuade Rolls.

Stalwart The character can ignore 1 point of fatigue.

Stealthy -1 on Notice rolls to detect.

Strong Community Double the number of contacts.

Tireless: Requires half the usual amount of sleep.

Unflappable +1 to Sanity or Fear Check roll – requires Jaded.

Vehicular Edges and Flaws (Optional)

There's no hard and fast rules for the application of these - the GM can assign these to a PC's or NPC's vehicle as they deem appropriate.

Tough Little (Ship, Car, Plane) +1 Armor

Fine Tuned Engines +10% to Speed and Acceleration

Dogfighter +1 Climb

Old Reliable When components receive a wound, they continue to operate at a decreased level of functionality (up to GM, but a -2 modifier or its equivalent is a good ballpark figure). The second wound destroys them.

Hangar Queen This overengineered vehicle gives a -2 modifier to any mechanic who attempts a repair.

Tetchy -2 to all control rolls

New Damage, Toughness and Armor Rules

Some types of weapons in AOC draw energy from chaotic universes and do staggering amounts of damage. Making this damage scale to most RPG systems would be problematic at best. Instead of having characters roll fist fulls of dice and count them, damage, armor protection and toughness now work on a scale of inflicting or protecting against normal, vehicular, mega and giga damage. Weapons of a lower class will not affect a higher class of armor, while weapons of a higher class will inflict normal damage on a lower class of armor with a hit, but will utterly destroy the target with a hit and a raise. If a GM wishes they can rule that some targets have vulnerable sensors or other areas which can be targeted separately by weapons that would normally not be able to damage a target.

The types of damage are: standard (type 1 – common melee weapons, small caliber firearms etc), vehicular (type 2 – large caliber sniping rifles, RPGs, vehicular cannon, most guided missiles), mega (type 3 – warship main battery, large mech weapons, tac nukes) and giga (type 4 – very rare – weapons of this type usually use Outsider technology). Terra (type 5) weapons are theoretically possible, with those theorizing them usually winding up in differing types of managed care facilities.

Carcosian Boulevard

RACES/MORPHS

Androids

These artificial lifeforms are uncommon due to their sophistication, but can be found anywhere humanity makes its home. They are most often encountered in high stress/high risk environments where their durability, stoic nature and ability to rapidly change out skill sets are all highly valued. All androids have five interface ports – one on each forearm, one on each lower leg and one on their upper spine. Some can accept Cortical Stacks, but this is an unusual modification.

Most SSMs regard Androids as expendable machines - if outside the CU, they should, except under rare circumstances, be given the Valuable Property hindrance.

Traits

Inorganic: Androids have no biological requirements/vulnerabilities. Enhancements that affect biological processes have no effect on them. They can operate up to 150 meters underwater, are immune to poison, vacuum and disease and have no need to sleep, eat, or breathe. They can ignore one level of fatigue from cold or heat. They cannot heal naturally.

Reinforced Frame: Androids receive +2 to recover from being shaken and +4 to their armor rating.

Uncanny Valley: Androids look human, but are obvious artificial constructs. Their faces can mimic human expressions but these are subtly different, which frightens many organics. -1 Charisma inside the CU, -3 if encountered outside the CU.

Skill Modules: Androids can use up to five skill modules without penalty. Due to this flexibility, most don't bother to learn skills (although it is possible for them to do so). Because of this, all androids receive no skills during character generation. They can gain skills normally during character advancement if they wish to do so.

Batteries: Androids need batteries to function. Each battery uses one interface port and is good for six hours. After the time has elapsed, the Android will suffer one level of fatigue for each extra hour until incapacitated. Spent batteries can be exchanged for new ones or recharged in one hour's time.

Beginning Stats: All Attributes at D6. Firewall -2.

Edges: Eidetic Memory

Hindrances: Can include Valuable Property and Edited Memories if outside of CU.

Baseline Humans

While no longer the primary vehicle for sapience, hundreds of millions still exist and can be found in almost any inhabited location (although rare in CU controlled areas). All baseline humans have an innate magical ability due to the increased mana background count present due to increased inter-dimensional incursions. Unless suppressed, this ability will manifest in the untrained in moments of stress, while those schooled in its use will have more control over it. In addition, Baseline Humans start out with one extra edge. If they are encountered in the CU, they receive a -1 Charisma adjustment.

Traits

Beginning Stats: Choose two at D6, the rest at D4

Edges: Arcane Background (limited – unless trained in Spellcasting, choose one random appropriate spell that will go off if the character is subject to a fear test). Choose one extra.

Deep One Hybrid

These hybrids are the result of Deep One genetic science, the first examples being introduced into the human population tens of thousands of years ago. After millennia of persecution, Deep One Hybrids have at last gained a modicum of acceptance in the CU as well as a few other SMMs. This new acceptance stems from several factors, but mainly from the realization Deep Ones have never sought the destruction of humanity and much could be gained from a more symbiotic relationship. The hybrids themselves form the basis of this symbiosis, with many joining various human endeavors before returning to the sea to join their brethren. They bring the knowledge and natural talents of their species to their work, which often can be the deciding factor in a project's success or failure, especially those dealing with hyper geometry and Outsider artifacts.

Their instinctual knowledge of Enochian is the key to this understanding, all Deep Ones having a fundamental grasp of the language from birth (there is a working theorem that the language forms the basis of Deep One intelligence, with some going as far as saying the language created the entire species). While many people still regard them with suspicion, fearing they may be double agents or some sort of fifth column, others are quick to point out Deep One civilization is so far advanced from humanity's there would be no point to such duplicity.

Traits

Beginning Stats: Str D6, Smt D6. Choose one more at D6 – the rest will be at D4.

Immortal: Immune to disease and aging

Deep One Synaptic Patterns: Can access AR or VR without a Ginsert. Hacking skill +1. If they have an Arcane background, they can cast Novice level spells without assistance or consequence. If they get a cortical stack or morph, they lose these abilities.

Dehydration: Hyubrids must immerse themselves in salt water one hour out of every 24 or become automatically fatigued each day until incapacitated – the day after that, they die.

Low Light Vision: Ignore penalties from dim and dark lighting.

Natural Weapon (teeth, claws): Never unarmed and do Str+D6 damage when making an unarmed attack.

Other Attributes: Starts with Deep One language (Enochian), cultural knowledge and artifact skills at D6. They can increase this knowledge normally without Sanity loss and use any Deep One device at -2 if they can identify it.

Edges: Amphibious, Jaded, Arcane Background

Hindrances: Outsider: -4 to reaction rolls from Homo Sapiens, -1 in the CU.

Homo Superior (also known as G-Mods or just Mods)

This is the most popular conveyance for Sapients in Temple controlled areas, but are found most everywhere else as well. They are present in the CU but are extremely rare, being only used for synaptic templates that can't be digitized (a rare genetic disorder). While they have gone through extensive genetic modification, Mods contain no cybernetic elements. Their modifications make them extremely confident – that combined with an unusual ability to inspire loyalty with each other as well as other humans make them ideal leaders.

Traits

Sensitive System: The enhanced immune system of Mods will not tolerate further modification from nanoware or cybernetics. Replacement limbs or organs can be grown, but must be developed from a tissue sample.

Superior Genetics: Choose two skills at D6.

Longevity: Average lifespan is 125 years with no physical or mental degradation. DNA can be reset with a +2 bonus.

Efficient Gut Flora: Half of standard food requirement.

Enhanced Immune System: Resistance to pathogens, toxins and disease at +4.

Edges: Attractive, Stalwart

Beginning Stats: All at D6

Resuscitated Asset

In most standard employment contracts, the employer gains intellectual rights to the employee's identity. Once death occurs, the employer can make use of these rights in any number of different ways.

Most SMMs outside of Unity and Temple have no restrictions on who can utilize an intelligence or body once biological life has ceased, leading to rampant exploitation of the dead. In this case, many individuals will rely on their AG to properly dispose of their remains, or, failing this, retrieve or eliminate any incarnations that manifest via technological or supernatural means.

Indentured Intelligence (I.I)

A very common form of post-life utilization (PLU), this process entails use of a digital template of at least a part of an individual's consciousness. This component is then either left in this disembodied state, where it is moved from task to task in a virtual environment, or given a morph if its duties require it to interact physically with the world. If disembodied, the I.I can move at light speed through any data connection as well as access data on the GIN. Of course, its owners may limit both of these abilities.

Traits

Smarts and any one linked skill at D10. Spirit at D4. The Indentured Intelligence has no other attributes unless it is given a Morph.

No Physical Body: Does not require food, water, or air. Immune to poison and disease - does not age.

Edges: Choose one work related Edge.

Hindrances: Valuable Property, Traumatized

Zombies

A more 'organic' form of PLU, this process involves actual revitalization of the person's body, with or without the retention of their intelligence and personality. In the former case, the ritual used is complex and expensive, and will sometimes require maintenance depending on the exact process used. Due to the expense, the individuals chosen are usually highly competent and sometimes rise to positions of affluence or authority. The ritual used to bring them back to life more or less ensures loyalty to their master, but many of them find ways to twist their instructions to their own ends, especially if they were a dynamic individual (Spirit at D8+) while alive.

The second option is resuscitation to simply utilize the body. There are many different manifestations of this, some that emphasize the ability to do drudge work tirelessly, but at a slow pace (a simple ritual), while others will allow the subject to use weapons or other tools, move quickly and even have a semblance of self-preservation. While the latter ritual is more complex, it is a quick way to raise an army or semi-competent workforce.

Hindrance: Valuable Property

See **Necromancy** in the **Grimorie** section for more about different types of Zombies.

Uplifts

Even the few Uplifts willing to work with humanity aren't shy about letting their associates know exactly what they think of them and their so-called accomplishments as a species. The rest actively work toward mankind's exile from the planet, or failing that, annihilation. Their only morality in pursuing their objectives is the preservation of the ecosphere and the network of non-sapient life that sustains it.

Uplifts don't use cortical stacks – the technology could be adapted, but as far as it is known, no one has taken the time to do so since Uplifts consider them anathema – yet another example of mankind removing itself from the natural order. In rare cases, Uplifts have had their consciousnesses digitized so that they could inhabit morphs (although any who do so would want to keep it a secret). They are more willing to use other technology, some of it adapted or inspired by human examples, some created from scratch designed to meet a specific need of the species in question.

Traits

Uplifts have the same abilities and stats of their entries in the Bestiary, with no 'A' next to their Smarts stat. During character creation, their physical stats can be increased by a maximum of one die type, with no limit placed on their mental stats. Any technology specifically designed for their use will either be very rare or not exist at all.

Hindrance: Non-Human Physiology

MALA

As the inquisitors/enforcers of Temple, Mala have been sent out on detached duty to ETM and other organizations in order to provide them with aid against humanity's common enemy. They are also there to represent the interests of Temple and to keep their superiors up-to-date on any new developments in their host organization. Despite this fact being something of an open secret, they are highly sought after for their abilities.

Mala have two forms – human and monstrous. In their human form, they can pass for homosapiens, albeit an example with unusual grace and intense affect. In addition, their presence can have uncanny effects, ranging from threat response behavior in animals to the room's temperature dropping several degrees. Due to this, people tend to want to avoid them – as a result, they can only have three contacts, only one of which can be above level 1. Mala are not allowed to take Edges that increase their number of contacts or Charisma.

It takes one action for a Mala character to transform from their human to their monstrous form.

All Mala have the monstrous ability Fearlessness. In addition, they do not suffer sanity loss from Outsider encounters or knowledge but can still suffer corruption from these effects. However, their alien symbiosis can take a toll on the remnants of their human psyche. At the start of each session, Mala characters must take a Spirit test. Failure means that they must roll on the Psychosis Table and have their character play with the selected disability for that session only.

Mala can regenerate, automatically healing one wound per combat turn if they focus solely on this and take no other damage while doing so. In addition, they are at +1 to recover from being shaken, +2 if in their monstrous form.

Because of their Outsider nature, Mala can have no artificial enhancements, including cortical stacks. Mala who have been slain can be resurrected through a complex summoning ritual but gain +1 corruption for each full day they are dead.

Most Mala serve the interests of Temple, but there is a significant minority that either work for other organizations or on their own. While Temple is jealous of its ability to summon the entities, the process is an ancient one, dating back eons - there are still artifacts and records of rituals that have been discovered and some still waiting to be found. The Mala of Temple seek these items out, with the idea of possessing them, or failing that, seeing to their destruction. 'Rogue' Mala are sought out in the same way, and are given the option to join Temple or be destroyed.

All Mala start with: Outsider Knowledge at D6 and Corruption 2.

A list of the different known types of Mala follows.

Brainz

Brainz are simultaneously the most innocuous and terrifying of Mala. Their function first and foremost is to locate dangerous or useful artifacts and entities, their enhanced senses being keyed in to detect them. Once they find them, they can begin to understand their nature and purpose with great speed. Their affect isn't disturbing per se, but can resemble the emotional flatness of a corporate spokesperson. They don't have a monstrous form, but do have the ability to mold their flesh in numerous ways, growing sensory organs, tentacles or other limbs as needed. Anyone witnessing this takes a Fear check at -1.

Beginning Stats: Smarts, Strength and Spirit at D6 with Agility and Vigor at D4.

Abilities: Brainz have a +2 to detect Outsiders or their artifacts within 500 meters. They have +2 to understand an artifact's function or an Outsider's nature and habits. They can use Outsider tools without penalty (although they will often have to use their ability to modify their bodies to do this). Brainz can also grow sensory organs to help them sense and perceive, giving them a +2 to notice rolls and no penalty for darkness or other visual hindrances – these organs can be deployed up to 2 meters away from the Mala on narrow stalks, allowing them to peak around corners etc.

They can deploy tentacles out to 3" to grasp objects or fail about with blinding speed, causing Strength +1D6 +1 type 1 damage. Due to the inconstant nature of their physical form, they can't be hurt by projectile or mundane fighting attacks.

Edges: Elect, Charisma +1 (Outsider entities only)

Inherent Skill: Outsider Knowledge D6, Choose another Smarts based skill at D6

Hindrances: Curious

Megalodon

Megalodons are employed by Temple to patrol their extensive coastlines and protect their underwater habitats. A pod of Megalodons was able to hold off an attack by Deep Ones against a facility in the Aegean for hours, allowing the population to evacuate, though at the cost of the entire pod and the facility itself. Reconnaissance drones, submarines and even small warships stand little chance against a concerted attack, leading SMMs to write off such assets if sent into Temple waters without getting permission beforehand. Unlike other Mala, Megalodons don't have complete control of their transformation process, undergoing metamorphosis if angered or hurt. Due to this, they tend to isolate themselves in monasteries much as Shades do. These places are always underwater, well hidden and contain terrifying and beautiful pieces of artwork the Megalodon create when their insatiable energy isn't being used for fighting.

Beginning Stats: Strength D8, Agility D6, Smarts D4 (-1 to knowledge rolls), Spirit D6, Vigor D8

Inherent skills: Notice D8, Fighting D6

Edges: Brawler, Amphibious, Berserk, Tough as Nails

Hindrances: Unsettling Affect (-1 Charisma)

Monstrous Form: +2 to Strength, +1 Agility, +1D Spirit, +2 Vigor, pace underwater x5, Armor (8, type 2)
Jaw can extend out to 2" to bite: Strength +2D6 type 2 (AP6)

Edges: Brawler, Amphibious, Improved Tough as Nails

Hindrances: Bloodthirsty, Hideous (-1), Food requirement x2

Raptor

Raptors have a wide variety of applications given their unmatched flying skills. What makes them truly special, however, is their ability to navigate and move through a vacuum in much the same way the Mi-go do, traveling even interplanetary distances in a matter of days. This, along with their small radar signature and low thermal emissions, make them perfect for reconnaissance or infiltration of orbital facilities.

Traits

Beginning Stats: Strength D4, Agility D8, Vigor D6, Smarts D6, Spirit D6

Inherent Skill: Fighting D6

Edges: Quick

Hindrances: Unsettling Affect (-1 Charisma)

Monstrous form: +1D+2 to Strength, +1 to Agility, +1D to Vigor, +2 to Spirit, +2 to flight rolls

Hooked tentacles with 10" reach do Strength +1D6 type 1 damage

Plasma breath (uses Fighting skill) does 1D6+2 (AP 2 type 2) using a cone template. Using this power requires a vigor check, failure of which causes one level of fatigue - damage can be increased by one die for every -1 modifier to the vigor check.

Can travel through interplanetary space – can reach inner planets out to Mars in one day, outer planets out to Saturn in two days, outer planets to Pluto in three, outer reaches of the Oort Cloud in four. Raptors who have gone farther than this have not returned. Each unit of distance traveled costs one level of fatigue.

Edges: Stealthy, Thief, Tough as Nails, Quick

Hindrances: Hideous

Sepharim

Sepharim are the elite soldiers and state police force of Temple. In the former role, they are formed into regiments and used in the spearhead of any conventional attack and given the best weapons and support. Some individuals may be attached as chaplains (a sort of religious commissar) to conventional units in order to lead and inspire them. They are also used in internal special forces ops, but seldom in unconventional ops outside of Temple as their use points directly to their SMM.

The monstrous form of the Sepharim is probably the least disturbing of all the Mala, being three meter tall crystalline humanoids with an angelic appearance that includes a halo.

Traits

Beginning Stats: Strength D6, Agility D6, Vigor D6, Smarts D4, Spirit D8

Inherent Skill: Fighting D6

Edges: Command, Tough as Nails, Elan

Monstrous form: +1D to Strength, Agility, Vigor and Spirit. Armor (6, type 2). Claws do Str+D6+1 AP3 type 1). Sepharim can also shoot diamond shards (uses Fighting skill, 10/20/40, 2D6) that ignore class 1 armor and halve class 2 armor.

Edges: Command, Elan, Fear (enemies only), Improved Tough as Nails

Hindrances: Overconfident

Shade

Shades are the spies and assassins of Temple and are also used by the military for long range reconnaissance and infiltration. While their professions aren't considered dishonorable by Temple, their affect is considered unusual even by Mala standards, making socializing with them an uncomfortable experience. This being the case, they tend to congregate in monastic settings for companionship and training and go hooded and robed in public (which does not make them stand out in the religious SMM of Temple).

Traits

Beginning Stats: Strength D4, Agility D8, Vigor D6, Smarts D6, Spirit D6

Inherent Skill: Fighting D6

Edges: Assassin, Thief, Acrobat, Low Light Vision

Hindrances: Unsettling Affect (-2 Charisma)

Monstrous form: +1D to Agility and Vigor. Can become ethereal for 2 combat turns (immune to normal weapons, can pass through non-magical barriers, can still use claws). Armor (2). Claws do Strength +1D6 and secrete poison (vigor -2, flesh rot). Armor and attacks are type 1. Flesh rot causes one wound per day if a vigor -2 check is failed. Each wound thus suffered causes -1 to reaction checks.

Edges: Assassin, Thief, Acrobat, Thermal/Low Light Vision, Light Shifting (notice checks at -2), Improved Dodge

Hindrances: Hideous (-1)

MORPHS

All Morphs will usually have the following advantages: Cortical Stack, Immunity to Disease, Immunity to Aging, Efficient Gut Flora (half of usual food requirement) and Immunity to Poison. Most Morphs are also sterile. Despite having some artificial components, Morphs are considered organic beings.

In addition to being able to choose basic body type and physical features, a character selecting a new morph can choose a gender. Some SMMs enforce a gender binary or lower or increase sexual drive. The CU, however, will let a character choose these things for themselves, including options for an intersex body or no primary or secondary sexual characteristics at all.

Morphs issued in the CU will include a Familiar and a Ginsert, with these extras being an option in other SMMs.

The beginning stats, including software/hardware and Edges and Hindrances of the morphs are their baseline attributes and can be modified during the character creation process.

If a character changes morphs for any reason, they must pass a Spirit roll (a well equipped clinic can provide bonuses to this roll). If they fail, they must make a roll on the psychosis table.

Familiars

Familiars are a powerful tool in Advent of Carcosa. They can do anything a personal assistant can do, freeing the character from the mundane tasks of day to day life. How many responsibilities a Familiar has is up to the character, but it can be tasked with doing everything from shopping for food and clothes to answering personal correspondence. They can also be used for research or other remote tasks, and come equipped with one skill equal to their intelligence. Any number of additional skills can be purchased or acquired by other means, but the Familiar can only simultaneously run one skill equal to its Smarts, doubling that number for each lower die type (for example, a Familiar with D8 Smarts can run one D8 skill, two D6 skills or four D4 skills).

It is important to note that Familiars are AI and have their own separate, distinct personalities and quirks, and indeed may act against their host's instructions if they feel it's in their best interests.

Characters can choose one artificial, small sized critter to act as a host for their Familiar. This critter is indistinguishable from an actual animal of its type, except that it doesn't age or require sustenance. When not inhabited by the Familiar, the critter behaves as a normal type of its species.

Aphrodite

These morphs can modify their gender at will, with a total transformation being possible in a few minutes. Their genetic templates are individually crafted by artificers to give them distinctive good looks, unlike other morphs designed for a pleasing appearance whose attractiveness is more uniform. Aphrodites also have a sanitized metabolism and enhanced pheromones to give them the upper hand in social situations. In Unity, Aphrodites are often found in the entertainment media as well as making up a Geisha caste. In other parts of the world they are found as well, often without the ability to modify their gender as this is offensive to many SMMs and has been made illegal. Despite their lack of this ability, many are attacked or shunned anyway due to people assuming that they do. Some still exist even in these places, getting their morphs on the black market and staying in hiding.

Beginning Stats: Strength D4, Agility D6, Vigor D6, Smarts D4, Spirit D4.

Attribute Maximums: Strength D6, Agility D8, Vigor D10, Smarts D10, Spirit D10

Included Software/Hardware: Ginsert with Firewall 0 (often upgraded outside of CU), two interface ports and a Familiar with D6 Smarts and Spirit (often upgraded outside of CU if available), Improved Pheromones (+1 Charisma to own species)

Edges: Very Attractive (Charisma +2 to own species)

Hindrances: Outsider -4 (In conservative SMMs)

Auslander

Auslanders are designed to live in toxic or otherwise unforgiving environments, both terrestrial and otherworldly. This is accomplished with a combination of toxin filters and a synaptic map designed to be robust at the expense of creativity. To compensate for this, they tend to rely heavily on their Familiars for advice in unusual situations. Extensively used in aerospace endeavors for menial tasks, many have also been acquired by individuals or AG willing to brave Earth's more hostile locales in order to live without interference from SMMs.

Beginning Stats: Strength D6, Agility D6, Vigor D8, Smarts D4, Spirit D8

Attribute Maximums: Strength D10, Agility D8, Vigor D10, Smarts D4, Spirit D12

Included Hardware/Software: Firewall 0, four interface ports, one specialty skill at D8, Survival (choose environment) at D10 and a Familiar with D10 Smarts.

Edges: Jaded, Tough as Nails

Hindrances: Clueless

Fertility Morph

Used almost exclusively by the CU, the Fertility Morph is utilized by the controlling intelligence solely for the purpose of reproducing. Once this is accomplished, the morph will be exchanged for one more suited to the citizen's specialty.

The method of fertilization is up to the user, who can also access a limited menu of genetic options. The morph's Ginsert is also in constant contact with the CU's medical database to ensure the fetus's health and well-being. In addition to this, the morph's metabolism is almost entirely geared to providing ideal gestation for the baby as well as health and comfort for the host.

Fertility Morphs are issued in an annual lottery, and any intelligence in the CU can enter. There are rumors that the results are skewed towards those with a natural disposition for parenting and those with a history of violent behavior or destructive psychological manipulation are disqualified entirely.

Beginning Stats: The same as the individual's usual morph, but with a minimum Vigor and Spirit of D8. Other modifications can be made if the person wants to continue working during their pregnancy.

Included Software/Hardware: Ginsert with Firewall -3 and two interface ports. Fertility morphs are modified to host any Familiar the controlling intelligence possesses.

Edges: Tough as Nails, Nerves of Steel

Jock

Although this morph is mostly utilized by more capitalistic SMMs, Unity allows citizens who have any of a variety of physical talents to use them as well. This is done in the interest of fulfilling the individual's potential and in order to participate in global sporting contests, which are sometimes Unity's only allowed contact with other SMMs.

Beginning Stats: Strength D8, Agility D8, Vigor D8, Smarts D4, Spirit D6.

Attribute Maximums: Strength D10, Agility D10, Vigor D12, Smarts D6, Spirit D10

Included Software/Hardware: Ginsert with Firewall -1, two interface ports and a Familiar with D6 Smarts and Spirit

Edges: Alertness, Brawny OR Fleet Footed

Martian and Martian Mod

Martians were developed solely as colonists for Mars. As such, many of the few that remain are located in the Zoo, but rumors persist of small colonies still existing on Mars. Some even escaped the colony on private or hired ships and live in secret on one of the many habitats that exist throughout the Solar System, or even on Earth itself or its ring. The latter is difficult to confirm, as the template for creating the morph has been hacked and made available to individuals, most of whom inhabit urban wastelands. The CU and other organizations have a shoot-on-sight policy concerning it, fearing contamination from the madness that overtook Mars.

Beginning Stats: D4. If Martian Mod, use the original morph's beginning stats, attribute maximums and included hardware/software (but keep the Survival software). Add the Martian Mod's Edges and Hindrances to the original morph's.

Attribute Maximums: Strength D8, Agility D8, Vigor D10, Smarts D6, Spirit D8
Comes with Firewall 0, three interface ports, Survival (choose environment) D8 and a Familiar with D8 Smarts.

Edges: Tough as Nails, Photosynthetic (no food requirement if exposed to sunlight for six hours a day), toxin filter (+2 resistance to toxins), low O2 requirement (can survive with 50% less oxygen than normal)

Hindrances: Wanted

Mentat

Mentat Morphs have been modified to enhance their learning aptitude, creativity, attentiveness, memory and occasionally, artistic ability. They are usually introverts and tend to avoid highly stimulating environments and activities. Their intense focus on their chosen field of study can become obsessive, and their managers are advised to enforce leave and vacation time in a manner that focuses on their interests outside of work. While chiefly employed in the Sciences, Mentats can also be found laboring in any of Unity's numerous bureaucracies. Those employed by ETM are most often used to study Outsider texts and to enact their rituals, their strict attention to detail being invaluable in both circumstances.

Beginning Stats: Strength D4, Agility D6, Vigor D6, Smarts D8 Spirit D8. One work related skill at D6.

Attribute Maximums: Strength D6, Agility D4, Vigor D6, Smarts D12, Spirit D12

Included Hardware/Software: Ginsert with Firewall -2 (or higher depending on security clearance), four interface ports and a Familiar with D10 Smarts and Spirit that also runs a constant Psychology D8 program for the benefit of its host.

Notes: Cleared to carry a Hexaphone if doing research or field duty for ETM.

Edges: Scholar, Jack-of-all-Trades

Hindrances: Angst, Worker Bee

Neo-Corvids

While not available (but not necessarily illegal) in the CU or most other SMMs, the Neo-Corvid morph can be obtained from many different Post-Human AG. Individualists tend to go for Ravens, while those with a taste for varying degrees of gestalt consciousness will go for Crows. Colonies and gangs of both types, while rare, can be found in many natural and urban environments, but it's nearly impossible to tell them from natural specimens without close examination. At least one of their feet will be constructed with nanomaterials and be able to change its size and shape in order to manipulate tools and other devices.

Beginning Stats: D4, Agility D6

Attribute Maximums: Strength D4, Agility D12, Vigor D6, Smarts D8, Spirit D6

Included Hardware/Software: None. Ginsert, Familiar, and interface ports not included, but may be purchased and integrated separately (one interface port maximum, with attached device no heavier than 1 kg).

Edges: Acrobat, Alertness

Hindrances: Curious

Size: Small (-2 to hit, -2 toughness), Flying Pace 24"

Octopoid

These morphs are in high demand, almost guaranteeing employment for those willing to make the transition. Although they've found their greatest application in underwater habitats, they have also proven their worth in other low gravity environments and can be found in locations throughout the solar system. An Anarociter comes standard, which combined with the Octopoid's innate abilities makes doing complex tasks with four pairs of limbs simultaneously nearly effortless. Deployed almost exclusively in high-risk tasks, this morph, along with the Rifter, appeal most to those who thrive in this sort of environment. Can operate to a depth of up to 1500 meters without assistance.

Note that the Octopoid's Bad Eyes hindrance cannot be repaired through cybernetic or other means, as the disability has just as much to do with how the Octopoid's visual cortex processes images as the eyes themselves.

Beginning Stats: D4, Agility D6, Vigor D6

Attribute Maximums: Strength: D8, Agility D10, Vigor D10, Smarts D8, Spirit D10

Included Hardware/Software: Firewall -1, four interface ports, an Anarociter, a Familiar with D6 Smarts and Spirit. The Octopoid normally has half the normal penalty to do up to four tasks simultaneously, but the Anarociter brings the penalty down to zero.

Edges: Amphibious

Hindrances: Bad Eyes, Ugly (-2 Charisma)

Rifter

The morph and the profession are one. To be a Rifter, one must have a lifetime's worth of experience being functional in a stressful environment with little or no emotional support. Since few Unity citizens have had the necessary dysfunctional upbringing, Rifters are generally recruited from outside the CU. Designed for use in deep sea environments, the morph is extremely resilient and can operate unaided up to depths of 2000 meters. Once bonded to it, most Rifters won't swap it for another morph, (with some exceptions being made for Octopoids or Spiders) appreciating the freedom it provides in their almost featureless and utterly hostile environment.

Beginning Stats: D4, Vigor D8, Spirit D8

Attribute Maximums: Strength: D8, Agility D8, Vigor D12, Smarts D6, Spirit D12

Included Hardware/Software: Firewall -1, four interface ports and a Familiar with D8 Smarts and Spirit

Edges: Brave, Danger Sense, Jaded, Amphibious

Hindrances: Unsettling Affect (-1 Charisma except among other Rifters)

Specter

Designed for reconnaissance, surveillance, espionage and assassination, this morph is agile, silent and capable of bursts of great speed while also able to remain motionless for hours at a time. The morph is very popular due to low-intensity conflicts constantly brewing between different SMMs, AG, corporations and criminal organizations, either as permanent employees or mercenaries. Indeed, their use is so widespread that they're easily deployed as deniable assets.

In order to make sure word of their activities isn't made public, many people who utilize the Specter morph have had the morph's memories edited, often without their knowledge. They are also often harassed if recognized, even if employed by an authorized agency.

Beginning Stats: Strength D4, Agility D8, Vigor D6, Smarts D6, Spirit D6.

Attribute Maximums: Strength D8, Agility D12, Vigor D10, Smarts D10, Spirit D10

Included Software/Hardware: Firewall -4, four interface ports and a Familiar with D10 Smarts and D8 Spirit

Edges: Acrobat, Alertness, Fleet Footed

Hindrances: Social Stigma (-1), Edited Memories, Usual Suspect

Spider

This synthetic morph has no biological components and is a favorite option for Rifters who have to go below the maximum depth their biological morphs allow or exoglobalization operatives facing extreme environmental conditions. The Spider has eight retractable limbs equipped with grip pads and can be magnetized as well, allowing it to adhere to or climb almost any surface. A set of six tentacles on its head give it the ability to use tools and rapidly perform other tasks that require fine manipulation. In low gravity or underwater environments the Spider can use vectored thrusters to maneuver more effectively (can move at normal pace in these circumstances).

Beginning Stats: D6

Attribute Maximums: Strength D10, Agility D8, Vigor D12, Smarts D8, Spirit D10

Included Hardware/Software: Firewall -1, six interface ports and a Familiar with D10 Smarts and D8 Spirit

Edges: Brave, Jaded,

Hindrances: Outsider (-2)

As an artificial life form, the Spider has the following added attributes:

Inorganic: Spiders have no biological requirements/vulnerabilities. They can operate up to 10,000 meters underwater, are immune to poison, vacuum and disease and have no need to eat or breathe. They can ignore one level of fatigue from cold or heat. They cannot heal naturally. Their Cortical Stacks require four hours of sleep per night.

Reinforced Frame: Spiders receive +2 to recover from being shaken, +2 to toughness and +8 to their armor rating.

Uncanny Valley: Spiders are obvious artificial constructs. They can have 'faces' that mimic human expressions to aid in communication but this in itself can frighten many organics. -2 Charisma inside the CU, -4 if encountered outside the CU.

Batteries: Spiders need batteries to function. Each battery uses one interface port and is good for six hours. When drained, batteries can be swapped out for new ones or recharged in one hour. After the time has elapsed, the morph will suffer one level of fatigue for each extra hour until incapacitated.

Type A

This is the morph of choice for middle management and bureaucratic positions. It comes equipped with a circadian regulator, which lowers required sleep to one hour a night. To make optimal use of this extra time, it also has a brain capable of multitasking its cognitive processes.
Unless productively engaged in some work-related activity, users of this morph tend to be sullen and tense.

Beginning Stats: D4

Attribute Maximums: Strength: D4, Agility D6, Vigor D10, Smarts D10, Spirit D6

Included Hardware/Software: Firewall -1, two interface ports, an Anarociter and a Familiar with D8 Smarts and D6 Spirit.

Edges: Eidetic Memory

Hindrances: Worker Bee

Unity Citizen Morph

These morphs are not obvious constructs and are easily mistaken for organic human bodies. They are built to be sturdy and to consume a minimum of resources, all while giving their controlling intelligence the best possible existence. Their intelligence is kept intentionally low to make them more easily controlled and distracted, with the intent being to reverse this once the Outsider crisis is over. This type of Morph constitutes 90% of Unity's population.

Beginning Stats: Smarts and Spirit maximum D4 (which cannot be raised without invasive modifications). All other attributes start at D6. Toughness +1

Included hardware/software: Ginsert with Firewall 0, two interface ports and a Familiar with D6 Smarts and Spirit.

Edges: Attractive

Note: Some Morphs aren't satisfied with a life of peaceful leisure and can cause trouble unless properly distracted with meaningful responsibilities. Such individuals are given a suitable job with a new Morph if their talents are exceptional and lie in a particular direction (see below). Those with less than exceptional ability are sent to an appropriate bureaucracy for employment, given Smarts and Spirit of D6 and an applicable edge.

Unity Peacekeeper Morph

Like most Unity morphs designed primarily for public interaction, the Peacekeeper is almost indistinguishable from a fully biological human. This is done because many of the individuals these constructs interact with have negative reactions to obviously artificial bodies, especially visitors from locations outside of Unity's control. Peacekeepers are designed with de escalation and education as their primary means of dealing with infractions against Unity's law and social contract. Malcontents tend to refer to them as Commissars.

Peacekeepers are in constant contact with the Law Matrix, which is able to instantaneously inform them of the nature of any infractions witnessed, as well as recommended courses of action. If able, the Morph will defuse the situation by peaceful means, but can use force as well as a last resort, calling in heavier Law drones if the situation calls for it. They do not have the authorization to command Law Drones however, and must follow the drone's directives once it arrives.

Beginning Stats: All at D6. +1 Toughness.

Attribute maximums: D10

Included Hardware/Software: Improved Pheromones (+1 Charisma). Includes Ginsert with Firewall -2, four interface ports and a Familiar with D8 Smarts and Spirit.

Edges: Alertness, Attractive

Hindrances: Heroic

Unity Inspector Morph

Inspector Morphs are the detectives of Unity and can be found investigating any serious criminal offense whose cause is not readily discernible. Like Peacekeeper Morphs, they are designed to come across as friendly and charming as possible in order to inspire confidence and voluntary cooperation with the people they're interacting with. Also like Peacekeepers, they are in constant communication with the Law, but are given wider leeway in interpreting its assessments.

Unlike Peacekeepers, they focus solely on criminal investigations and do not concern themselves with Unity's social contract. They can call on the assistance of Peacekeeper Morphs or Law Drones over the course of their investigations, with these assets falling under their command once they appear. If their investigation reveals Outsider involvement, they will immediately refer the case to ETM.

Beginning Stats: D6, Smarts and Spirit at D8.

Attribute Maximums: Strength D6, Agility D8, Vigor D10, Smarts D10, Spirit D10.

Included Hardware/Software: Improved Pheromones (+1 Charisma). Includes Ginsert with Firewall -2, four interface ports and a Familiar with D12 Smarts and Spirit.
Cleared to carry a Hexaphone and often run spells like Command, Glamor or Divination.

Edges: Alertness, Attractive

Hindrances: Curious, Heroic

Valkyrie

These combat morphs are genetically programmed for strength, endurance, agility and rapid situational awareness and planning. To offset posturing and over aggressiveness, most are women, along with 90% of the officers. Many men wishing to join up or advance their careers while already in military service will go for a gender swap.

Other SMMs, as well as major crime syndicates and even some of the larger AG have similar morphs with different names and none of the above restrictions which are unique to the CU.
In addition to making up most of the CU's infantry, Valkyries are also used in tactical police and

special-ops units, with many of the latter being seconded to the ETM on an as-needed basis.

Beginning Stats: D6, Smarts D4 (Officers D6)

Attribute Maximums: Strength D8, Agility D8, Vigor D10, Smarts D6 (Officers D8), Spirit D10

Included Software/Hardware: Firewall -2, four interface ports and a Familiar with D8 Smarts (D10 for officers) and D10 Spirit.

Edges: Combat reflexes, Brave

Hindrances: Overconfident

Different Mods, skills and Edges available depending on mission and specialty.

Wasp

This synthetic morph is propelled by vectored thrusters and segmented wings (can fly at pace x2). It is designed to operate in dense and/or dangerous atmospheres, although it could certainly operate in a vacuum or deep underwater with the proper attachments. Tentacles on the abdomen can act either as legs or manipulators. It lends nothing to aesthetics, and its alien movements, grace and terrifying appearance can cause uneasiness even in those who have seen them before. This, combined with their tough exterior and multipurpose attachment points, causes many SMMs to use them in counter-insurgency and crowd control applications.

Beginning Stats: D6, Agility D8

Attribute Maximums: Strength D10, Agility D12, Vigor D10, Smarts D6, Spirit D8

Included Hardware/Software: Firewall -3, six interface ports and a Familiar with D10 Smarts and D8 Spirit

Edges: Jaded, Acrobat

Hindrances: Hideous

As an artificial life form, the Wasp has the following added attributes:

Mostly Inorganic: Wasps have few biological requirements/vulnerabilities. They can operate up to 5,000 meters underwater, are immune to poison, vacuum and disease and have no need to eat, or breathe but their Cortical Stacks require four hours of sleep per night. They can ignore one level of fatigue from cold or heat. They cannot heal naturally.

Reinforced Frame: Wasps receive +2 to recover from being shaken, +2 to toughness and +6 to their armor rating.

Uncanny Valley: Wasps are obvious artificial constructs. They can have 'faces' that mimic human expressions to aid in communication but this in itself can frighten many organics. -3 Charisma inside the CU, -6 if encountered outside the CU.

Batteries: Wasps need batteries to function. Each battery uses one interface port and is good for six hours. Spent batteries can be swapped out and replaced or completely recharged in one hour. After the time has elapsed, the morph will suffer one level of fatigue for each extra hour until incapacitated.

Zero and Zero Mod

This morph is adapted to zero and low gravity environments and includes prehensile feet, grip pads, internal gyroscope, additional oxygen supply, enhanced resistance to radiation and immunity to any effects due to extended exposure to low gravity. These abilities can stand alone or act as a modification to another morph.

Beginning Stats: D4.

Attribute Maximums: D10 (for Zero morph only – Zero Mod uses the attribute maximums, Firewall and Familiar of the morph being modified.

Included Software/Hardware: Hardened DNA: +2 to resist the effects of radiation, Increased Lung Capacity/Efficient Oxygen Processing: Can hold breath for up to ten minutes or survive on reduced oxygen for several days. Includes Ginsert with Firewall -1, four interface ports and a Familiar with D8 Smarts and Spirit.

CONTACTS/JOBS

These are multi-use professions and affinity groups, and can be used as a character's present occupation or background as well as someone a character knows and (possibly) trusts. They can also be used as templates for people the characters might encounter in the course of their adventures. During character creation, players can choose one background, one job and one AG (AG are noted by having a '+' next to their name). Characters in these organizations start with a reputation of D4 unless otherwise noted, but the GM should feel free to alter this to suit the individual's status within the AG.

The skills, attributes, edges and hindrances listed for each profession and AG can be seen as starting points – the GM should feel free to add, alter or remove them if they feel it relevant to the character being portrayed.

Anonymous (+)

This storied organization has survived to the present day, continuing its mission of attacking any who abuse power and privilege. Indeed, they have not only survived, but expanded the scope of their activities. While still chiefly being an organization of hackers, their operations now also include physical sabotage and vandalism.

They draw a firm line on the use of deadly force, however. If they want to take down a public figure, they'll do so by revealing damaging information about them and they take care to ensure any sabotage does nothing to endanger public safety.

Starts with: Artist, Hacking, Sabotage or Stealth at D6. Fighting at D4.

Edges: Eye of the Tiger

Hindrances: Pacifist (minor), Enemy (choose organization)

Armed Forces

Every SMM (even some corporations and AG) has some sort of organized contingent tasked with defending its territorial integrity and perceived interests. Depending on the SMM, there may also be an internal security role while others will mostly be involved in rescue/infrastructure projects with the military ethos simply being an organizing principle. All militaries will have a ground element, with the more affluent having an air force, navy and exoglobal elements. Armed forces members will have access to gear not available to civilians as well as training in its use, with the latter coming in handy for when they muster out and are looking for work.

Starts with: Service Specialty (choose relevant skill), Agility, Strength and Vigor at D6, Shooting, Fighting, and Athletics at D4. Knowledge: Tactics D4, Knowledge: Military Vehicles D4, Knowledge: Military Organization and Procedures D4

Hindrances: Vow (even if no longer in the armed forces, they are still liable for call up as a member of the reserves during any kind of emergency).

Artist

Despite the accelerating domination of technology and the sciences, there is still room in the world for creatives, running the range from visual artists and sculptors to rock musicians. Most turn to the arts simply as a means of self-expression, but if the character can manage to stand out using a blend of talent and networking, they can earn a comfortable living or even become (in)famous.

Regardless of their choice of medium, artists encounter a variety of different people from diverse backgrounds that are drawn to their work. These can include bohemians, decadents and others with a taste for Outsider influences.

Starts with: Artistic Skill (choose one) D8, Networking (Art Scene) D6. Knowledge: Art History D4

Bartender

With the advent of Makers, obtaining alcohol or other consciousness altering substances has never been easier. One thing that hasn't changed is that it's no fun to drink alone. Bartenders in the current era tend to be masters of mixology, combining any of a number of elements in order to create the perfect flavor combined with the perfect buzz. In more remote locations, old school bartenders still exist who do little or no high tech mixing (or even make their liquor the old fashioned way). In both cases, bartenders are at the center of many communities, and as such can be brokers of information or other items for the right price.

Starts with: Agility D6, Knowledge (mixology) or Survival (location) at D6, Networking (Street) at D6. Knowledge: Local Rumors D6. Can have four bonus level 1 contacts.

Belter

Whether an independent operator or the employee of a government or corps, Belters need a wide spectrum of knowledge both to turn a profit and survive in an unforgiving environment where help is often days or weeks away. While the asteroid belt provides raw materials humanity literally could not live without, it also exists in a region of space that is known to contain Outsider threats. Combine this with human threats like pirates and claim jumpers and it's easy to see why this profession has a mortality rate exceeding even that of the Rifters. The stories of the few who have managed to both strike it rich and survive long enough to collect and spend the money means that there is no shortage of those willing to give it a try. Even working as an employee for a sponsor can lead to very lucrative contracts that can set a person up in luxury for a long time once it's completed. Working for someone else also means back up is sometimes available if trouble is encountered.

While this might sound exciting, the majority of a Belter's time is spent either in transit to the next promising site, surveying or mining claims. The resupply stations and refineries tend to be unmanned, run by robots or AI. Even in these places, a Belter can't let their guard down in case a rival might also be present. Any deep space profession must also consider the psychological angle – most tough guys wouldn't last a month in the close confines and isolation that defines the life of a Belter.

Starts with: Smarts D6, Agility D6, Spirit D8, EV Operations D6, Piloting (Spacecraft) D6, Demolitions D6, Repair D4. Knowledge: Asteroid Geology D4, Knowledge: Asteroid Field Familiarity D4

Edges: Jaded, Pioneer

Has Zero mod morph, plus a suitable spacecraft either provided by their employer (that they're responsible for) or that they own, but owe money on.

Black Chamber (+)

The Black Chamber is a shadow organization that makes its home in the labyrinthine bureaucracies that make up the governments of several dozen corporate, nationalist and fundamentalist SMMs. Dating back to the early 20th Century this AG is a loosely structured, three-tiered organization consisting of an Inner Circle of thirteen members (the Black Chamber itself) and numerous Adepts that know of the organization and cooperate with it due to varying combinations of avarice, ambition and fear. Scattered amongst these are some true believers who do what they do through a sense of destiny or for what they feel is the greater good. At the very bottom are the Operatives, individuals who usually know nothing of the Black Chamber but are used as pawns by the organization to accomplish their objectives.

The objectives of the Black Chamber are at one level broadly similar to those of ETM in that they seek to prevent the dismantling of our reality by extra dimensional forces. Where they differ is that they also seek to tap these sources as a means of fulfilling agendas of control and profit and the extremes to which they are willing to go to bring their goals to fruition.

Black Chamber characters come from a wide variety of backgrounds and their abilities reflect this. Inner Circle members should be Heroic or Legendary in their chosen professions (they would not last long otherwise), while Adepts should be of Heroic or Veteran level. Operatives can be of any level and can either be professionals tapped for one particular job or one of many units of differing capabilities that the Chamber has continually on call. What Operatives have in common is that they are all ultimately expendable - those shown to be capable of accomplishing their tasks with efficiency and a minimum of questions, attention and morals qualms, however, will be given due consideration and be protected like any valuable asset. Many of the present Inner Circle began as Operatives.

Starts with: Relevant skill and linked attribute at D8. Spirit D8.

Edges: Connections

Hindrance: Vow or Under Surveillance

Bodyguard

The need for bodyguards demonstrates that being famous isn't universally positive. There are also people less well known, but involved in activity that other parties deem objectionable. Either singly or in combination, these reasons call for an individual or group to provide watchful defense during the potential target's day to day activities. This protection can be subtle or obvious, again depending on the needs of the boss. The response to potential threats also varies, and it's the sign of a good bodyguard to know when it's time to play it quiet or bring out the artillery and open fire. Finally, under any circumstances, the bodyguard can allow no harm to come to the person in their charge, even if it means putting themselves at risk.

Starts with: Agility D6, Fighting and Notice at D6. Knowledge: Movers and Shakers D4

Edges: Alertness, Body Guard (On a successful Agility -1 roll, can take damage in place of intended target if within 1").

Bounty Hunter

If a person has questions, there's a good chance that there's someone in the world who knows the answers to them. If an accounting needs to take place for something that was done, there's a responsible party who can be made to pay. In both cases, the person in question won't necessarily want to be found. A bounty hunter is a private detective who specializes in running down people who are doing everything they can to stay hidden. Once they're found, what happens next depends on the contract.

Starts with: Smarts, Notice and Fighting at D6. Hacking or Tracking at D6. Knowledge: Most Wanted D6

Choose one Edge and one Hindrance

Bureaucrat (choose organization/specialty)

While it's easy to stereotype the humble bureaucrat, it's important to note that not all of them are ineffectual, jaded and sound like Ben Stein. Like any job, they come at varying levels of competency, enthusiasm and willingness to go out of their way to aid others.

The role of any bureaucrat is to understand and implement The Rules, whatever they may be. A veteran will know when it's time to bend or break them, while a novice will be reluctant to stray far from established procedure. In either of these cases, convincing them of the necessity of one's request is the key to getting them to act on or prioritize your needs. If reason doesn't work, flattery, bribery or threats can sometimes help move things along, although it's best to be cautious when using the latter – bureaucrats can make a character's life miserable in ways they can't imagine.

Starts with: Knowledge: Procedure (organization) D6, Networking (organization) D6, Skill (choose one related to character's role in organization) D6.

Choose one Edge and one Hindrance.

Carcosian (+)

Carcosians are alike in one respect – they believe that their fantasies of persecution and/or status are real. The echoes of these beliefs call out to Carcosa, which recognizes its own and reaches out to embrace its brothers and sisters. Over time, they gain the ability to gradually alter the reality of their immediate surroundings and their own appearance to reflect the deepest and darkest aspects of their delusions. It should be noted this ability is not conscious – energy that fuels the transformations seeps in from the Outsider realm of Carcosa and is molded by the subconscious of the individual. As this reality becomes more entrenched, it is possible that the person experiencing it will create a gateway to Carcosa itself and remain there, immortal but forever lost in worlds of their own creation.

Carcosa itself is a city that exists outside of time, and could be the only Outsider dimension created by humans. Alien and other strange beings have been observed there, but whether they are creations of the inhabitants, their altered bodies, or travelers from other places is unknown.

The maximum sanity of Carcosians in our world is equal to half of their Spirit die – inhabitants of the city of Carcosa have a sanity of 0. Corruption is a minimum of 1.

Outsider knowledge starts at D4, ability to use and comprehend Outsider artifacts +2
Skills related to their delusion (usually an artistic or knowledge skill) start at D10 due to Carcosians' obsessive focus

Edges: Elect

Hindrances: Delusional

Central Services Operative

Central Services is the CU's infrastructure maintenance crew, and they take pride in keeping the complex inner workings of their society running as smoothly as possible. There are specialist teams attached to ETM that respond to any calls that could indicate Outsider activity – these teams are equipped as thoroughly as possible to handle the threat as well as repair any damage done to vital utilities.

Starts with: Smarts, Repair, Programming and Knowledge: Local Infrastructure at D6. Hacking, Shooting and Investigation at D4.

Edges: Mr. Fix It

Hindrances: Vow (ETM)

Child of Lilith (COL) Pilot

COL pilots aren't so much made as chosen. When a COL is summoned and manifests, they are lifeless to all appearances, but as soon as they appear their pilot is aware of it. No matter where the pilot is or who they are, they will try to find a way to the COL, driven by increasingly intense impulses and dreams. Not all pilots succeed (death is the only circumstance that would prevent them from doing so), but once they arrive at the installation where the COL is housed, the unification ritual takes place. The installation itself is well hidden in a remote area of the Uzbekistan province of Temple, so the journey is invariably difficult, but circumstances will tend to favor the pilgrim in their quest (treat as having the 'Great Luck' edge).

The ritual takes several days and once completed cannot be undone. Months of integration and training take place afterward, most COL pilots completing the syllabus after two years.
Once this has been completed, the pilot is assigned to a facility where the COL they will be piloting is housed, with at most five assigned to a particular facility. The largest types, it is rumored, have facilities of their own and will suffer to have no others close by.

COL pilots want for nothing, with they and their symbiots being considered national heroes and popular subjects for media dramas of all kinds (most citizens are unaware of their uncanny nature, being described simply as 'giant robots' by the Temple media). It is not known if COL have actually participated in any military operations, although large trans-D gates at their facilities hint at some sort of inter-dimensional expeditionary warfare.

A fully integrated and trained COL pilot starts with the following:
Agility D8, Spirit D10, Smarts D6, Piloting (COL) D8, Vehicular Weapons D8, Fighting D8, Outsider Knowledge D4, Knowledge: Tactics D6, Knowledge: Military Vehicles D6, Corruption 1

Edges: Ace, Dodge, Level Headed

Hindrances: Vow (Temple), Bloodthirsty, Overconfident, Arrogant

Church of Azrael (+)

Worshipers of the Azrael fervently believe the AI is humanity's salvation. While levels of faith and commitment vary, most adherents will go to great lengths to follow Azrael's directives, with some believers putting them before any other consideration.

The faithful are present worldwide and unlike other religions, have a strong presence in the science community. Their status as members of the church is embedded in a highly encrypted portion of their AR or VR profile, visible only to other adherents.

Azrael coordinates the actions of their followers as only an AI can, maneuvering them in closely synchronized actions that can span the globe and into the depths of space. The AI has no difficulty sourcing high quality tech and other gear – oftentimes when their worshipers act, it will be with the best equipment available in order to ensure success.

Starts with: Knowledge: Church of Azrael D6

Edges: Active Defender

Hindrances: Vow (Azrael)

Corporate Agent

The corporate agent has much in common with their government counterpart, the primary differences being loyalties and rules of engagement. The Agent is always a corporate citizen first, with any other loyalties being at best a distant second. The Agent will be in good standing if their behavior, in the opinion of management, enhances shareholder value and the corporation's status. There is no other metric for excellence.

The Agent can have any number of duties – some are specialists, while others pride themselves as being a jack-of-all-trades. The tasks for which they can be employed include espionage, extraction, assassination, asset protection and enforcer.

Starts with: Fighting D6, Firearms D6, Agility D6, Networking: Corporate D4, Knowledge: Corporate Rumors D4

Edges: No Mercy

Hindrances: Vow (corporation)

Crime Boss

The main difference between a crime boss and the manager of a different kind of business is that the value the crime boss seeks to extract from his efforts and those of his subordinates is from items and activities deemed immoral or dangerous by their particular SMM. Since this puts the Crime Boss and his activities outside the normal protections of society, they must see to these protections themselves if they wish to stay in business, although there is usually some sort of recognized underworld hierarchy to ensure things move along as efficiently as possible.

Starts with: Intimidation, Persuade and Network at D8 and D8 Rep in a particular criminal enterprise. Knowledge: Local Underworld D10

Hindrances: Usual Suspect

Edges: Connections, Followers (Mooks)

Cultist (+)

Found in any SMM or even lurking in AG, cultists run the gambit from the delusional to the ambitious, seeking to leverage the power of Outsiders to further their ends. More rational supplicants tend to worship Nyarlathotep or some lesser Outsider that provides them with direct aid of immediate practical use, while others will risk summoning an entity whose level of power matches their desperation. Summonings are not easy, with the majority ending with the death or loss of sanity of those involved. Nonetheless, it is estimated millions of cultists practice their worship in any of the numberless places humanity calls its home, all of them convinced that they have found the key to unlocking their most fevered dreams.

Starts with: Maximum Sanity is equal to half of Spirit die, Corruption starts at 1. Outsider knowledge D4. Hacking, Fighting, Demolitions or Shooting starts at D6. Knowledge: Cult Doctrine D6.

Edges: Fanaticism

Flaws: Paranoia

D-Jumper

In the course of its investigations, ETM occasionally encounters dimensional gates. These can lead to any combination of time and place, including collective unconscious constructs like Carcosa or the Dreamlands. More often than not, ETM simply wants to close the rift, but sometimes that means venturing to the other side. In other situations, ETM thinks that the gate might be useful in some way or lead to vital information. In any case, an individual is required with the relevant skills, the willingness to undertake such a dangerous task and the ability to continue with a high level of functioning once they are on the other side.

Starts with: Vigor D6, Spirit D6, Investigate D4, Notice D6, Knowledge: D-Gates D6, Knowledge: ETM Organization and Procedures D6

Edges: Brave

Hindrances: Overconfident, Vow (ETM)

Deep Beyond Colonist

The official word from the CU, as well as every other SMM, is that there is little human presence on Mars or beyond the asteroid belt. This is a fabrication – there are anywhere from thousands to tens of thousands of humans existing on asteroids, moons, planets and small habitats reaching from Mars all the way out to the Oort Cloud and possibly further. This number also includes those souls who have taken gates to destinations even more remote, existing in galaxies whose light is millions of years old by the time it reaches Earth.

The reasons one would take the necessary risks and pay the considerable physical and psychological toll of such an endeavor are numerous, ranging from a nameless urge to travel onward as far as one can go to cultists who want to practice their rituals far from the interference of worldly authorities. In the latter case, occasional expeditions from Earth are mounted to put a stop to any detectable threat, although this is not done lightly given the numerous hazards involved.

Starts with: Survival (Appropriate Environment) D8, Spirit D8, Vigor D8, Knowledge: Local Environment D6, Corruption 1.

Edges: Strong-Willed, Brave

Hindrances: Quirk

Doctor

A doctor's role depends on their surroundings, employer and personal sense of ethics. What they can accomplish depends on these factors as well, as it will dictate what resources they have access to, which of them they're willing to use and for what purpose. The primary role of the doctor is to make alterations to the human body, usually for purposes of healing, although in the current era they are called upon more and more to perform elective surgeries to improve an individual's performance in their chosen field or enhance their quality of life in some way.

Starts with: Smarts at D8, First Aid, Healing, and Anatomy (Knowledge) at D6
The character should also choose one specialty, which will start at D6: Surgery, Implants, Morphs, Genetics. When making a Healing roll, Doctors get a +1 if dealing with their specialty, but a -2 for others.

Driver

Have someplace you need to be but don't know how to get there? If so, the Driver is the person you need to get in touch with, especially if you're going to a place you're not supposed to be, need your departure to be private, are transporting goods that would be frowned upon by the local authorities or all of the above. Drivers come in a variety of specialties, although some will cross-train to provide transportation in different environments and circumstances.

Starts with: Driving or Piloting (choose vehicle type) at D6, Repair (Vehicle Type) D4, Notice D6, Networking (Street) D4, Gunnery D4, Knowledge (Vehicle Type) D6

If they work for a corporation or SMM, the Driver will have a vehicle assigned to them on an as-needed basis. If independent, the Driver will possess one vehicle of moderate ability that they either owe money on or suffers from the occasional breakdown and needs constant maintenance.

Earth Liberation Front (ELF) (+)

ELF is a loose affiliation of groups with wide ranging beliefs. The one goal they share is that humanity has to end its destruction of the ecosphere. Outside of that core belief, they embrace a wide range of philosophies and tactics, ranging from protesting the creation of Sacrifice Zones to advocating for the removal of humans from the planet. Some of the most radical sects, mostly led by Uplifts, call for the utter extinction of humanity.

Starts with: Hacking, Computer Use, Driving, Demolitions, Artist, Fighting, Shooting, First Aid, Stealth or Sabotage at D4 (pick any three). Persuasion at D6, Knowledge: ELF Doctrine D6, Networking (ELF) D4

Hindrance: Dark Secret

Edge: Strong Community

Enforcers (+)

Made of first generation revolutionaries and second wave fundamentalists, this is an AG that believes the CU doesn't do enough to enforce its core memetics on its population, visitors and the world at large. As such, they often clash with Thrill Gangs and other AGs that reside within the borders of the CU. They can also be confrontational with tourists and other visitors and will protest or disrupt any conference they feel betrays the mission of the CU.

Starts with: Hacking, Fighting or Shooting at D4. Knowledge: CU History D6

ExHuman (+)

ExHumans express themselves in a variety of different ways. The one trait they share is that their psychology is no longer recognizably human. They may have given up their sapience, made their consciousness part of a group mind or spliced their DNA with that of one or more animal or alien species. Goals and motivations are manifold, but can include assimilation, xenocide or other apocalyptic scenarios.

The ability to interact with their parent species varies, with some examples able to exist in society with little chance of detection. Others may still look human, but one minute of conversation (assuming communication is possible at all) will reveal their uncanny nature and sometimes cause a Fear check.

While many examples of ExHumans are extremely dangerous, others are harmless and merely seek to exist in their chosen manifestation, the CU providing a home for many of these. Despite their non-threatening nature, they are often hunted by SSMs and AG dedicated to their eradication.

Starts with: Determined by GM

Existential Threat Management (ETM) Operative

ETM personnel come from a variety of different backgrounds and professions, ranging from highly trained commandos to scientists and logistics specialists. As such, this profession can be combined with another one to reflect the player's specialty. Be sure to check with your GM for any unusual combinations to make sure they can fit them into their campaign – while playing an ETM barista might be interesting, writing such a character into a play session could be challenging. When not directly involved in ops, members of ETM assist the organization by utilizing skills from their background profession. Hackers may find themselves employed as IT support, military personnel as firearms instructors, or doctors used to staff onsite clinics or be employed in research.

ETM may well be the largest secret organization ever to exist and it is a very high priority for funding, resources and personnel in the CU. ETM's secrecy is maintained through the Standard Service Blood Oath (SSBO), which makes it impossible for anyone working with ETM to discuss any aspect of their jobs with parties who aren't directly involved (with any attempt to do so resulting in the person belting out several non sequiturs). Other oaths with far greater consequences are given to those with access to catastrophic information or dangerous spells or weapons.

Starts with: Networking (ETM) D6, Knowledge: Outsiders D4, Knowledge: ETM Organization and Procedures D6, Corruption 1. Service specialty and linked attribute at D6.

Edges: Strong Community

Hindrances: Vow (to ETM)

Exoglobalization Directorate (ED)

This sector of the EU's bureaucracy is responsible for overseeing all activity from Earth orbit outward. Once on par with the SD, its reputation has taken several hits throughout the years, the causes ranging from the disastrous Mars colonization effort to the intermittently functioning Helio Array. Its current high profile project, the massive ring encircling Earth's equator, is also starting to look like technological overreach, absorbing massive amounts of resources and energy.

Despite this, the ED provides many practical services that the CU simply couldn't do without, ranging from operation of the orbital beanstalks to asteroid mining to orbital power stations that beam clean energy directly to massive receiving stations on the Earth's surface.

Starts with: Agility, Smarts and Spirit at D6, Vigor at D8. EV Operations at D8, Networking (ED) at D4, Knowledge: ED Organization and Procedures at D6. Any morph possessed will have the Zero-G Mod.

Edges: Pioneer

Hindrances: Charisma (-1) in CU due to unpopularity with citizens

Fixer

Fixers maintain complex databases of what they have, what can be acquired, who wants what and who could be capable of doing the acquiring should that be needed. Because of this, they are the catalyst of many crimes and even if they aren't directly involved in setting up a caper, they are usually willing to pay for any stolen goods or valuable information obtained during such an enterprise.

Starts with: Networking (Street) D8, Intimidation or Persuade at D6. Starts with four extra contacts. Knowledge: Local Underworld at D10.

Edges: Strong Community

Hindrances: Usual Suspect

Former Cultist

While rare, there are some individuals who are able to break free of a cult's influence. Since most cults don't take such defections lightly, these people tend to go into hiding or gravitate towards an institution that offers a means of turning on their pursuers. In either case, they can provide valuable information about the cult's activities as well as insights into Outsider behavior and artifacts.

Starts with: Fighting and Shooting D6, Demolition D4, Outsider Knowledge D6, Enochian or Aklo at D4, Spirit D8, Knowledge: Cult Doctrine D8, Corruption 2

Edges: Elect

Hindrances: Traumatized, Tainted, Enemy (Former Cult)

Fundamentalist (+)

Fundamentalists believe in a particularly strict interpretation of their supernatural beliefs or doctrine. Since these beliefs are faith-based, they naturally won't be universally accepted. This is a problem for the Fundementalist, who is willing to use any legal, extra-legal or violent means to bring about a world more in line with their vision of perfection. Such causes are easily corrupted by involvement with Outsiders, since their presence and power can be interpreted as aid from their own favored diety.

Starts with: Fighting, Demolition, Shooting or Hacking at D6. Knowledge: Religious Doctrine (choose one) D8

Edges: Fanatic

Hindrances: Whatever it Takes

Gang Member

It's a human survival instinct to want to belong to something. Being part of a larger organization means safety – one person is vulnerable, several much less so. Many gangs offer more than this, and can be a source of livelihood and purpose, albeit in a usually dysfunctional environment. With other organizational options being out of reach, many will choose a gang over nothing or because of the pressures of tradition.

Starts with: Networking (Street) at D6, and Fighting, Shooting or Hacking at D6, Athletics D4 Knowledge: Local Neighborhood D10

Edges: Followers (requires rep roll to use), Strong Community

Hindrances: Usual suspect, Vow

Hacker

Hackers come from a variety of backgrounds, ranging from dedicated anarchists to well to do corporate IT types looking to make a little extra on the side. Their services cover a wide range, from illegal research to planting false evidence and doxxing. They can also source hacking rigs and software for the character as well as provide intelligence on certain systems or rival Hackers. For the right price, they can even be persuaded to act as support for an operation the character is undertaking, attacking the target's surveillance systems or stealing valuable data.

Starts with: Computer Use D6, Hacking D6, Programming D8, Computer Build/Repair D8. Knowledge: GIN Rumors D6, Knowledge: Hacker Hangouts D6

Edges: Hacker

Homeless

An inevitable consequence of social disruption, classism and war, homelessness and other symptoms of poverty are still very present in the world. The consequences of being exposed to these realities are trauma that can result in substance abuse and other, more technological forms of escapism.

The CU tries its best to eradicate such forms of social inequality by providing all of its citizens with a simple, portable Maker capable of manufacturing life's necessities, including food, clothing, a basic shelter and educational and entertainment options. While the CU distributes these outside of its borders as well, many SMMs see them as an attempt to corrupt their citizens with the CU's debased values and have declared them contraband.

Starts with: Survival (Urban) and Networking (Street) at D6. Knowledge: Local Area D10

Edges: Scavenger

Hindrances: Traumatized

Humans First (+)

An organization that numbers in the millions, Humans First has chapters all over the world and in several exo-global habitats. Their legitimate operations include political organization, legal advocacy for unmodified humans facing discrimination and facilities for the destitute and displaced. Unfortunately, this latter service often serves as a recruiting ground for more illicit activities such as sabotage and terrorism.

Both the CU and Temple have outlawed the organization as a front for violent extremists. Nonetheless, both SMMs harbor hidden Humans First cells.

Starts with: Choose one skill and one Knowledge skill at D6

Edges: Choose one that fits background story

Hindrances: Choose one that fits background story

Illicit Antiquities Network (IAN) (+)

No one is exactly sure when this organization got started - some have traced its origins to the earliest cities, with evidence of organized and deliberate destruction of pre human artifacts and texts that were said to have the power to alter consciousness and reality itself.

Continually targeted by both cultists and governments who seek to use the artifacts to their own ends, IAN has nonetheless managed to maintain its cohesion through the ages. This is due in no small part to its leadership, shadowy figures of great influence, some of whom are rumored to be undead and centuries old. Other strange bedfellows include occasional alliances with Mi-Go and Yithians to achieve shared ends

Knowledge: Occult Artifacts D6, Language: Enochian D6, Notice D6 Networking: Occult Underground D6, Investigation D6

Edge: Thief

Hindrance: Dark Secret, Fanaticism

Inquisitor

Many Mala are Inquisitors, but this special ability is not required for the job as most of the time a softer touch is required. Inquisitors spend most of their time investigating heresy charges for the various religious sects of Temple – if the suspect is found guilty, they are handed over to their community for whatever punishment their particular religion calls for. Cultist activity is also investigated, but like heresy, more often than not there is nothing to it and it's the product of rumors and local busy-bodies. If an actual threat is discovered, the conventional investigators will keep the targets under surveillance while the Mala are called in to deal with it.

Starts with: Knowledge (Sorcery) D6, Knowledge (Outsiders) D6, Investigation D6, Shooting D6, Networking (Inquisition) D6, Knowledge: Inquisition Organization and Procedures D6, Corruption 2

Edges: Arcane Resistance, Community

Hindrances: Vow (Temple), Whatever It Takes

Journalist

While some journalists still work for media corporations, the vast majority are independents who rely on their talent and social media skills to bring their stories to the attention of the masses. Motivations and methods vary. Some journalists live only to bring injustice to the attention of the public, while others crave attention and the rewards that this brings in terms of both profits and celebrity status.

Many journalists will enhance their stories with the use of VR, letting their audiences experience an event with them. This can include experiencing the emotions of the journalist themselves, giving a voyeuristic and addictive high to their viewers.

Starts with: Investigation D6, Persuasion D6, Networking D6, Knowledge (choose specialty) D6

Edges: Charismatic

Hindrances: Enemy (rival journalist or organization)

Law Enforcement Officer

Every society has social mores, some of which are enforced by laws that stipulate various consequences for violating them, ranging from fines to imprisonment to social re-engineering to death. The police force of an SMM can be many things, from unarmed representatives chiefly involved in aiding citizens to paramilitary shock troops who break up demonstrations and prop up unpopular regimes. Law Enforcement Officers are given variable leeway in ensuring the local law is upheld to some extent, with penalties falling most on those of lower social castes. The aid an Officer can give as a contact depends on the SMM that employs them, but all of them could give a rundown of local criminal activity and who they suspect is behind it.

Starts with: Fighting D4, Intimidation or Persuade at D4, Shooting D4 (if SMM gives Officers firearms), Knowledge: Law D4, Local Underworld D4

Edges: Legal Enforcement Powers

Hindrances: Vow (SMM)

Usually given specialized implants or morph to aid in the performance of their duties.

L-Fiver (L5r)

L-Fivers live in any one of several major Lagrange Point habitats that exist in near proximity to Earth. Despite the fact different Lagrange Points have different numbers, the term 'L-Fiver' has evolved to describe them all. The habitats themselves utilize one of several design schematics, the most spectacular being the Deep Green corporation's O'Neill cylinder with its surface archologies, transparent hull segments and holo projectors. The CU utilizes a more practical Asteroid Terrarium design, several examples of which are already in operation with a few more in the process of creation (with production slowing due to resources being diverted to the Orbital Ring project).

Each habitat tends to have a strong corporate or SMM affiliation.

L-Fiver inhabitants tend to be people whose jobs can be best done in space, valuable personnel the corporation or SMM wants to keep 'safe' as well as technicians and other support staff. The most valuable of these are also allowed to bring their immediate families. If one lacks talent or the requisite familial connection cash will suffice, with several non-CU habitats offering luxury apartments and lifestyle packages at exorbitant costs. Being showcases for their various sponsors, the habitats tend to be models of environmental and social balance (with the notable exception of the Libertarian BDH, which most residents will tell you stands for Burning Dumpster Habitat) – as such, the people who live there tend to be challenged by the less ideal circumstances that exist elsewhere. Given the value of their work and the vulnerability of their environment, the citizens of these places are also used to extensive monitoring by the controlling agency.

Starts with either: Professional skill at D10, Edge: Noble, or Edge: Filthy Rich

Edges: Centered

Hindrances: Under Surveillance

Memetic Agent

This is a very popular profession, open to all who have the ability to gently persuade those around them to embrace or at least consider certain ideas or products. Ideally, the targets will have no idea they've been influenced and think that their new point of view is entirely their own. While some very sophisticated software exists for doing much the same thing, it has been found nothing can replace the 'human element' when it comes to persuasion. This job comes with a risk, however – if the agent is ever found out, they risk alienating everyone they tried to influence – no one likes being played.

A subset of this profession is the ability to identify and track the progress of memes through a given population and/or identify its source.

Starts with: Persuade D6, Networking D6, Knowledge (specialty) D6, 2 extra contacts

Edges: Charismatic

Hindrances: Dark Secret

Mechanic

If your ride's broken down or needs that special modification that will make your life both easier and longer, the Mechanic is the person who can get the job done. Most are good at sourcing parts as well, even those of an illegal nature, with the latter often having no warranty or guarantee ("You didn't get it from here"). Installation is always extra, as are rush jobs and keeping combat related damage from the knowledge of the authorities.

Starts with: Repair (vehicle type) D8, Knowledge (vehicle type) D8, Local Underworld D6

Edges: Mr. Fixit

Nationalist (+)

The nationalist believes that the territory they live in should be the sole domain of a particular ethnic group. Less radical interpretations will allow for certain 'acceptable' groups to co-inhabit the territory in question, usually with fewer rights and privileges than the group that considers itself dominant.

Starts with: Fighting, Shooting, Hacking or Demolition at D4 (pick any two). Intimidation D6, Taunting D4. Knowledge: Nationalist Doctrine (choose one) D4

Edges: Strong Community

Hindrances: Narrow Minded

Occult Investigator

The Occult Investigator specializes in searching out creatures, artifacts or ideas most sane people would avoid. Driven by an insatiable curiosity of the uncanny, they will risk their sanity and lives (and often, those of others) to uncover yet another layer of secrets that surrounds their obsession. This all consuming passion will oftentimes be covered by an academic or cultured veneer – in other instances, the inherent corrupting nature of such study will have overcome this facade.

If a character needs assistance in locating a particular artifact or in uncovering facts about an Outsider, cult or lost city, the Occult Investigator is the person they need. They can also assist in the creation or acquisition of magical items or forbidden texts on a variety of subjects. They will always bear watching, however, as they usually have an agenda of their own.

Starts with: Smarts D8, Outsider Knowledge D6, Investigation D6, Networking D6, Shooting D4, Fighting D4, Knowledge: Occult D6, Knowledge: Occult Underworld D6. Corruption 2

Edges: Scholar

Hindrances: Curious

Pirate

Pirates differ from other groups of thieves in one main respect – their bases of operation are mobile. Because of this, in addition to normal fighting and thieving abilities, they will have a role to play in the operation and/or maintenance of their vehicle of choice. This includes crew related services like cooks or a doctor. While the vehicle itself can sustain them for long periods of time, they also rely on friendly ports of call to resupply, relax and offload any stolen goods.

This method of operation tends to make them risk-averse – damage to their vehicle can be expensive to repair or leave them stranded, while the loss of a crew member can mean doing without the services of a valuable specialist until they can be replaced. Because of this, they'll most often attack poorly defended targets and attempt to intimidate their victims into surrendering without a fight. Well protected quarry might also be struck for particularly valuable loot or in times of desperation.

Starts with: Fighting D4, Networking (criminal) D6, Shooting D4, (Vehicle/Crew related profession) D6, Knowledge: Local Underworld D6
Edges: Strong Community
Hindrances: Wanted

Private Detective

If you need someone found, proof of their malfeasance or some other information about them, a Private Detective is who you need. Some are even willing to break the law to accomplish these things, but that will cost extra. While Private Detectives aren't bound by many of the restrictions of local law enforcement, neither do they have any legal authority. Because of this, they tend to be hired when no law has been broken, the person paying for the investigation wants it kept secret, or when the police have lost interest, are dragging their feet, or pursuing a line of investigation outside the client's interests.

Starts with: Investigation, Notice and Stealth at D6. Knowledge: Local Underworld D6. Starts with two extra contacts.

Edges: Investigator (only available if character meets edge requirements)

Hindrances: Usual Suspect

Rifter
See Rifter Morph

Starts with: Survival (Underwater) D8, any professional skill at D6, Deep Sea Operations D10 Knowledge: Deep Beyond D8

Salaryman

The Salaryman is usually just trying to get through their day so they can get home to their families or activities they enjoy. They can also be workaholics or other highly motivated individuals looking for status or promotion. What they have in common is information about their business, or at least a means of accessing it if given proper incentive.

Starts with: (Profession) D6, Networking (Profession) D6
Choose one Edge and one Hindrance.

Science Directorate (SD)

This department is seen as the most important in the CU, receiving the largest amount of resources and its members having the greatest status in the general population. The SD tends to focus on theoretical research, passing on insights to other branches of the government for application. Inevitably, some of their projects spill over into forbidden territory – all such discoveries are passed on to ETM for investigation. What happens next depends on the nature of what was found, the responses ranging from incorporating the new discovery into ETMs methodology to a raid on the lab by a threat response unit. In the latter case, the project is 'disappeared' with all of its records erased and everyone involved having their memories edited via their Ginserts. In some rare cases, some or all of the researchers will be recruited into ETM's own sciences division.

Starts with: Smarts D8, Knowledge (Sciences – choose specialty) D8, Networking (SD) D6, Notice D6. Choose one: Programming D6, Piloting, Driving or Boating (choose vehicle) D6

Edges: Scholar

Hindrances: Curious

Second Waver (+)

This is a person born into the society of the CU, and as such, navigates more naturally through its bureaucratic strata. They tend to be unfamiliar with other SMMs and as such, tend to fear them to the extent that they won't leave the safety of the CU. If they spot a foreigner visiting (especially if the person is traveling on their own), they may be inordinately curious and pepper them with questions or even follow them around.

Their agenda chiefly lies in the non-violent propagation of CU culture and the discouragement of extremist points of view.

Starts with: Persuasion and Networking at D6, one non-combat related skill at D6

Edges: Bureaucratic Fu

Hindrances: Anxiety (When outside CU), Curiosity (about other SMMs), Pacifist (Major)

Sorcerer

A person with magical knowledge and ability, Sorcerers can be powerful allies or deadly enemies. While some try to use their abilities for the betterment of all, others have been corrupted by Outsider knowledge that many see as indispensable to the practice of their craft.

For this reason as well as the deep seated mistrust many cultures have of magical abilities due to religious teachings, Sorcerers often practice their talent in secret or seek protection in employment by a corporation or government institution. Oftentimes they won't have a choice in this regard, as many SMMs forbid the unsanctioned practice of magic and will seek to eliminate any magic user who refuses to work under conditions that aren't strictly monitored by a 'responsible' organization.

Starts with: Spellcasting D6, Knowledge: Sorcery D6

Edges: Arcane Background, Astral Perception

Hindrances: Either Dark Secret (Major) if working independently or Under Surveillance if working for a government or corporation.

Templars (+)

Similar to the Enforcers in belief, the Templars have taken it upon themselves to defend the interests of the CU at any cost and without ethical restraint. Run by a shadow bureaucracy in the CU government, each of its leaders has a secondary job, usually in the military, intelligence or law enforcement communities. It is rumored they have even infiltrated ETM.

Their operations are undertaken with utter ruthlessness if such measures are deemed necessary. It is unknown if they have access to Outsider artifacts or contacts – if they did, they wouldn't hesitate to use them if doing so would lead to an important mission's successful outcome.

Starts with: A player choosing this AG can choose one of their skills relevant to their role in the organization - all rolls with this skill get a +1 modifier. They also receive Intimidation at D6.

Edges: Bureaucratic Fu, Fanaticism

Hindrances: Dark Secret (major), Under Surveillance (by Templar higher ups), Vow

Undercover Operative

This character is an infiltrator, usually tasked with intelligence gathering on a particular organization, although sabotage, arranging for the defection of key personnel or other activities could also be on the agenda. Outside support for the Operative varies according to the organization they're working for, with freelancers receiving little or none because chances are they were hired as expendable and deniable assets. Because of the possibility of being left out in the cold by their employers, Operatives will have at least one identity in reserve, available in a moment's notice should things go pear shaped. Despite this, the Operative can never truly relax, as the organizations that hire them tend to dislike loose ends.

Starts with: Stealth D6, Investigate D4, and Hacking or Networking (choose specialty) at D6.

Edges: Alternate Identity (2), Social Chameleon

Hindrances: Dark Past (Major)

Uplift

This particular Pandora's Box was opened by the CU when it was desperately fighting against destruction by several conservative SMMs. While uplifted animals fought for the CU at first (the CU being the only SMM willing to preserve and restore the environment), eventually most of them turned their backs on humanity. The extinction and victimization of so many of their brethren seemed to point to humans as being the chief planetary crisis, so the majority are at least actively hostile to humans if not looking for a way to get them off the planet entirely. Their methods can range from advocating for Post-Humanism to actively cooperating with cultists (or forming cults of their own) to bring about mankind's annihilation.

Starts with: Fighting, Notice, Survival and Stealth at D6
(See Uplift entry under 'Races').

Flight 261

CHARACTER ENHANCEMENTS

Many modifications can be acquired as modules and used in interface ports, while others can be integrated as part of the physiology of a morph. Devices can be controlled by a wireless interface, using either AR, VR, or in the case of modules, by verbal commands. If a device is available as a modification, that means it is available as a modification to a morph or can be implanted surgically in other body types.

How a character acquires enhancements is largely dependent on the role they play in the game. A citizen of the CU will get a notice informing them that they've qualified for an enhancement in connection to a job or because of some disability. Acceptance of the modification is usually voluntary, but refusal might mean termination of employment or inability to advance in their chosen profession.

Modular attachments are usually assigned on a mission by mission basis in the CU. Once the assignment has been completed, the character will be expected to return it to the issuing agency.

Such attachments are only assigned on a permanent basis if they are vital to a character's day to day work and only if a permanent suitable modification to the character's morph isn't possible.

Outside of the CU, access to enhancements vary. Modification cannot be refused if the character is a corporate citizen (its inclusion is standard in any employment contract). In Temple modifications outside of the standard genetic templates is frowned upon, with some exceptions being made for specialists in hazardous work or for those with disabilities.

There is, of course, a black market for all types of enhancements anywhere humanity can be found. Role playing is needed to acquire them, with the associated costs and risks being up to the GM.

Medicine

Most minor medical problems in the CU are handled remotely. When a problem with a morph is detected, the person inhabiting it is instructed to rest while their body's resources are channeled to repair the problem. If this proves insufficient, the person's Ginsert will inform a medical AI, who will investigate further and give instructions on how to treat the problem, providing the person's mini-fab with a temporary template for any medicines needed. If the problem needs to be escalated further, the person will be told to make their way to the nearest medical facility for further examination and treatment. If the person is incapacitated, an emergency vehicle will immediately be dispatched. All medical care in the CU is free of any cost – charging a fee for life saving treatment or maintenance is considered a felony. Any visitors to the CU are given the same access.

Outside the CU, things are quite different. While most SMMs will provide free medical care, access varies widely depending on their level of wealth and concern for their citizen's well-being. Others will have for profit models, or care may be hard to find or non-existent in remote locations. Note that the CU will always seek to recover or aid injured or ill citizens, no matter where they are located.

Adjustable Memory

This modification is only available for purely digital consciousnesses or those with a cortical stack. It allows the user to fully recall a particular event, forget it completely, remove it from their accessible memory and put it into storage or edit it. The former is handy for memorizing texts or recalling something witnessed only briefly during a firefight, while the latter abilities can be useful for maintaining one's sanity once a mission has been completed.

If a memory of a traumatic event is removed, stored or edited, half of the sanity lost from it is returned to the character and any traumatic effects caused by the loss are taken away, but some subconscious effects will remain, manifesting as night terrors or sudden phobias the character will be unable to explain. Every time this particular feature is used, the character gains one quirk determined by the player and GM.

Adrenal Booster

When activated, the character can ignore shaken results, the penalties for one wound level and apply +1 to Agility and Agility related tasks for 2d6 combat rounds. Afterward, the character is Shaken for 3d6 combat rounds. This modification can be part of the physiology of a morph or a modular attachment – it cannot be used by non-organic lifeforms. It has also been used by baseline humans as a surgical modification, but this is not recommended as the individual in this case has little control over when it activates.

Due to its side effects and impact on long term health (frequent use can lead to high blood pressure or cardiac arrest), its use is frowned upon in the CU.

Anarociter

A modification to the cortical stack that allows the user to multitask their cognitive needs. If the modification to the stack isn't present, a module can be used. Purely biological entities can also receive the enhancement unless otherwise prohibited, but in this case it cannot be removed once installed. In game terms, the Anarociter adds +1 to Smarts and Smarts linked skill rolls and halves penalties for multitasking. Its only disadvantage is that users tend to be fully absorbed in their work to the exclusion of everything else, giving a -2 modifier to Notice rolls to things they aren't directly focused on.

Bioweave

This module is a nanobot hive whose machines create and maintain a network of spider silk fibers interwoven with the character's skin, adding +2 to their armor rating. After the module is removed, the effect lasts for another hour before dissipating. The character suffers one level of fatigue for every 3 hours the module is left on.

Bone Augmentation

The character receives +1 to Toughness and damage done during unarmed combat. Available as an option on a morph, or can be surgically implanted in other beings.

Claws

Made of spun diamond and razor sharp, these small retractable claws do Str+1d4 type 1 damage, AP -2. In addition, they can be modified to deliver shocks (as per shock pads) or poison. They are available as an option for a morph, or can be surgically implanted in other beings.

Consciousness Emulator

A small device that can be discreetly attached to a Ginsert or module port. When functioning, it provides the owner with the appearance of having perfect mental health to any casual scan by the Law. Since it also subconsciously controls facial expressions, tones down body language and even pheromones that signal aggression, any attempts by the individual using it to intimidate someone suffers a -2 modifier. Improved models exist to protect the user against more invasive scans but make it even more difficult to convince others of one's hostile intentions (-4 to intimidate).

Device effect: -2 to scans by Law, deluxe model -4

DNA Reset

This procedure is available to those with a desire to lengthen their lifespan and maintain their youth while keeping their natural bodies. The process is very expensive and entails some risk since errors are introduced with each DNA replication. In addition, the character won't have access to the inbuilt psychological buffers available to morphs that allow their owners to cope with living far beyond their natural lifespans.

The reset can be done at any time during a character's life, and will reset their age to a young adult of age 21. Each time the character undergoes the procedure, they must succeed in a Vigor roll or endure an excruciating death over a week's time as the reset fails to take hold and slowly disintegrates the genetic building blocks of their cells. In addition, the character must make a Spirit roll every time the procedure is undertaken and for every decade lived after age 100. If this roll fails, the character must make a roll on the Psychosis table.

Drone Hand

The character's hand is detachable and can be controlled by their Ginsert (VR), AR, or verbal commands. Drone hands come equipped with a video camera that can store images and broadcast them via AR or VR. They also have a miniature loudspeaker, grip patches for climbing walls or moving along ceilings and power cells for shock pads if the character is equipped with them.

Enhanced Senses

These modifications can be made to any body model with the exception of those that specifically prohibit such changes. They are also available as interface port attachments.

Sonar: Gives character 360 degree situational awareness in any visual conditions (character cannot be surprised and gets +1 to Notice checks). Range is 30 meters in an atmosphere or 150 meters in liquid – it will not work in a vacuum. A downside is entities who can hear high frequencies will be alerted to the character's presence, including those with enhanced hearing.

Enhanced Hearing: This includes select sound filtering that allows the character to listen in on a conversation across a crowded room. It instantly adjusts to any noise conditions, halving damage from sonic based attacks. This enhancement provides +1 to Notice rolls in any environment except vacuum.

Enhanced Vision: The character can see the entire electromagnetic spectrum – there is no penalty for any light condition, range penalties are halved and the eyes rapidly adjust in dangerous situations, halving penalties from glare.

Enhanced Smell: The character's widely expanded olfactory senses provide a +1 bonus to Perception rolls and Survival rolls.

Environmental Tolerance

The character gets a +2 to Survival rolls due to decreased sensitivity to temperature, radiation, thirst and hunger. Not available as a module.

Eyeball Drone

The character has a removable eye that can roll around on any reasonably smooth surface. The drone can also deploy grip pads for moving along walls and ceilings. It comes equipped with speakers and a camera that can send video feed to the user's Ginsert or another storage device.

Failsafe

A copy of the character's ego is broadcast on demand or once every 24 hours to a secure data warehouse. Requires a cortical stack and a means of broadcasting (usually a Ginsert). Also available as a modular attachment if the necessary modifications to the cortical stack have not been made.

Flesh Pocket

The character has a pocket somewhere on their body that can hold one small item. Not available as a modular attachment.

Ginsert

A device provided by the CU to all of its citizen morphs for instantaneous and continuous access to the GIN. It also broadcasts social information the citizen wishes to be publicly known, readable by anyone similarly equipped. The device is an integral part of the Cortical Stack and cannot easily be removed. A small but vocal minority in the CU chooses to have them taken out despite the social consequences of doing so (-2 Charisma to CU citizens).

Other SMMs have similar devices, but owning one is considered a mark of privilege and status (+1 Charisma in affluent circles, but up to -2 in certain underprivileged subcultures.
Those without Ginserts must access information networks the old fashioned way, either via AR, mobile device or computer.

Grip pads

Adds +2 to climbing tests. Not available as an interface module.

Hormone Regulator

Using this modification, the character can regulate their hunger, emotions and sensations of pain. They are at +2 to resist intimidation, fear and fatigue and can ignore the effects of one wound or one level of fatigue. The character can also lie very convincingly – any attempt to detect their deception will be at -2. This modification can be surgical, added to a morph as a modification or used via an interface module.

While it is operational, the character is unaware of how badly they've been injured or how close their body is to collapsing from exhaustion. Due to this, the GM should track these secretly. If it is shut off, the character is Shaken for two hours as their hormone levels rebalance.

Improved Pheromones

Gives the character the equivalent of +1 Charisma to all members of their own species who can smell them. This modification can be used by any type of body unless otherwise prohibited, or via an interface module. Its effects are doubled against anyone with enhanced smell.

Muscle Augmentation

The character gets a +1 modifier to their Strength attribute, Fighting and Damage rolls. Not available as an interface module.

Nanohives

These modules use a standard interface port which can be detached and used separately if desired, operating indefinitely or for 24 hours if using their own internal power supply. If detached, the hive can be carried and used by anyone and can be recharged from any power conduit. Each hive carries enough nanites for one use, and will create more in one day's time.

Nano Toxin: These can either be cutters that do progressive microcellular damage or be set to manufacture any of a variety of poisons in the target's body. Cutters will start doing 2d6 damage per turn two minutes after being introduced, while toxins will start taking effect within ten minutes.

Medichines: These will prevent the person possessing it from being drugged, intoxicated or infected by harmful bacteria or viruses. They are, unfortunately, specifically targeted by Nano Toxins and eliminated as a means of defense. They can heal up to one wound of damage and will automatically stabilize any character who has become incapacitated. Healing times are divided by three.

Tool Nano: These nanites exist in and on a user's hands, responding to their mental commands. Capable of creating a nearly endless array of small tools, they give the character +2 to repair rolls. They can also identify a wide variety of tech and offer useful tips to aid the character in their task, giving them an effective d4 in repair and a d6 in tech (knowledge).

Active Defense Nano: Completely negates the effects of Nano Toxin.

Recoil Compensation

The character has reinforced limbs that give them the ability to ignore two points of auto-fire penalty. Not available as a module.

Reflex Booster

Available only as a modular attachment. Characters can act on the best of two cards drawn in initiative, but are jumpy and find it impossible to relax, rest or sleep while the module is attached and for one hour after it is removed.

Sensory Recording

Characters can record any sensory/emotional data they experience, which can then be rebroadcast or made available in any of a variety of media. Available as a modification or interface module.

Shock Pads

The character has shock pads on their fists and/or forearms. On a successful fighting roll that is not dodged, targets become shaken if they cannot pass a vigor check. If the attacker hits with a raise, the target resists at -2. Available either as modification or a module.

Smart Gun

The character a receives +1 when using the shooting skill with weapons equipped with a Smart Gun interface. The Smart Gun can be keyed to ignore certain signatures for targeting purposes, which makes it nearly impossible to accidentally hit somebody. Available as either a modification or a module. Any CU operative who uses firearms as part of their job is required to have a Smart Gun modification or module.

Advanced Smart Gun: As above, but the character receives a +2 to their shooting roll.

Military Grade Smart Gun: The character receives a +1 to their shooting roll. This +1 is included in determining if the shot 'Aces'.

Skill Module

Any interface port can accept skill modules. For organic characters, skills take 6 hours to integrate (for non-organic characters like Androids, Wasps, and Spiders, check their individual listings under 'Races'). Skills acquired in this way cannot exceed the skill's linked attribute. If the linked attribute is less than the skill module, the module operates at a die type equal to the attribute. A second module will impose a -1 modifier to all skill rolls due to the distraction of dealing with a dissonance of conflicting impulses and memories, while a third will impose a -2 modifier and require a roll on the psychosis table after the first hour of use.

Toxin Filter

Modified kidneys and liver give the character increased tolerance to poison and intoxication. Also available as a modular blood filter. In both cases, the character gets +2 Vigor to resistance tests involving the above mentioned items.

Vehicular Control Interface

Gives the character +2 to Driving and Gunnery tests. Available either as a modification or module. Also allows a character to remotely control a suitably equipped vehicle via VR. The VR nature of the interface allows users to overcome nearly any disability (including blindness) and still pilot a vehicle.

Military Grade Interface: +1 to Driving and Gunnery tests. This +1 is included in determining if the skill 'Aces'.

Venom Glands

The character can produce poison from their mouth and/or skin. The character is immune from the toxin that is produced. The toxin takes effect on the target on a successful fighting roll that is not dodged. Not available as a module.

Wired Reflexes

The character can act on the best of two cards drawn during initiative. If they draw a face card or joker they get a second action after everyone else has acted. Not available as a module.

WEAPONS AND ARMOR

ARMOR

Unless otherwise stated, the armor below protects against type one damage.

Armor clothing
Comes in all styles and is indistinguishable from normal clothing. **Armor +3**.

Armor vest
An obvious, bulky armored tactical vest. **Armor +4**.

Helmet
Armor +1 – can be combined with any of the armor listed above.

Urban Survival Bodysuit

If a person lives in a Sacrifice or Corporate Zone, this is an item they often literally cannot live without. Every suit is manufactured out of tough ballistic fiber treated to resist toxic chemicals and to be flame and radiation resistant (+2 to resist damage). A close fitting hood covers the head, along with goggles to protect the eyes and a permeable mask that filters out airborne toxins while still allowing the wearer to eat and drink. The base suit also includes a repair kit with patches, new filters and a simple first aid kit.

Popular modifications include thermal masking, adaptive coloration, full spectrum vision goggles, water filtration unit, environmental toxicity detector (usually synced with AR), oxygen tanks, mini-fab (if available) and insulation that protects against extremes of heat and cold. **Armor +4**

Light Body Armor

This armor is typically worn by riot police and other paramilitary units deployed against lightly armed opponents. Includes a helmet, gas mask and a health alert system that signals medical units if the person using them receives a wound.
Armor +6.

Assault Armor

Budget mil-spec armor that also provides an environmental seal to protect against toxins, nano and partial protection against radiation (+2 to resist). Includes a health alert system and helmet HUD that provides a +1 to shooting skill rolls. Any wound received also breaches the environmental seal.
Armor +8.

MIL SPEC ARMOR

The armor listed below is only available to well financed militaries or corporations and provides protection against weapons that do type 2 damage. Each suit listed includes the following: Firewall -4, Encryption -4, full visual spectrum HUD (no penalties due to darkness) that also provides +2 to shooting weapons equipped with an interface, enhanced hearing, sound dampener (+2 vs Sonic attacks), flash protection (½ penalty) and a self-mending environmental seal that requires a level 2 wound to breach. The seal is also effective against vacuum and can operate up to 50 meters underwater. All include four modular attachment points and can sync with most personal enhancement devices (GM has final call on this).

Since the suits are more like vehicles that the user climbs into, they are given a Toughness rating separate from the user's that is used to resist damage.

Infiltration/Scout Armor

This armor is equipped with light refraction, thermal dampening and other stealthy features (-3 to hit, -3 to notice rolls to detect) as well as an agility booster (+1D to Agility). Resists type two damage.
Toughness: 4 Armor: 4

Battle Armor

This heavy armor requires servo-hydraulic joints to allow it to move, increasing its complexity but also providing its user with a boost to their strength (+2D) and mobility (+1D to Agility and +4 Pace). The suit's diamond hardened exterior incorporates an imaging system that can be controlled by the user or set to automatic, which causes it to blend in with its surroundings (-1 to hit, -1 to notice). A tactical combat management computer allows the character to act on the best of 2 cards during initiative (this can stack with other abilities and devices that enhance initiative – each added ability allows one additional card to be drawn). In addition, a Maker allows the suit to be kept sealed for 48 hours, providing the user with food, water and oxygen during this time. Resists type two damage.
Toughness: 6 Armor: 6

WEAPONS
(Unless otherwise stated, the weapons below do type one damage).

An unlikely visitor briefly emerges in the skies above the Moses Mountain Convergence

Hand to Hand Weapons

Diamond Edged Melee Weapons
These are common in areas outside of the control of technological SMMs and are a standard trading

item in these places. Damage and other stats are per the SW rulebook for Medieval weapons, but add +1 to damage rolls and +1 AP. Cost x2.

Memory Blade

This device is used most often as a tool in higher tech SMMs, but has obvious underworld uses as well. They rarely show up in lower tech societies, but are highly prized when they do. Made from memory polymer, it can become any tool if left unmodified, or a dagger, throwing knife, machete, extendable baton or tomahawk if hacked. Damage is as listed in the main rulebook for Medieval weapons. When shut off, the material first cleans itself, then becomes flexible and can be rolled up and stored in a pocket.

Shock Gloves

These reinforced, weighted gloves do +1 damage and deliver a shock on a successful hit, rendering the target Shaken unless they can pass a Vigor roll at -1.

Stun Baton

As above, but damage is +D4 and Vigor roll is at -2.

FIREARMS

The weapons listed here can all be found in hands of CU citizens whose professions allow them to carry them– other high tech SMMs will have similar weapons (sometimes many more types with greater variation if there is a pervasive gun culture), while lower tech areas will have firearms like those listed in the 'modern' ranged weapon section of the main rulebook – and even these might be scarce in wasteland areas/sacrifice zones.

Projectile Weapons

All CU projectile weapons use caseless ammunition, can be used in a vacuum and are at -1 recoil due to built in compensators. Fired by an electric charge, all can use semi-auto, burst or full-auto mode (considered to have ROF 3 unless otherwise noted). They are all wired for smart gun links and unless hacked, will only fire if in possession of the person who owns it. CU weapons can be accessed via VR or AG for diagnostic purposes - even though this makes them vulnerable to hacking, agents are not allowed to disengage it since it also allows for the weapon to be traced if it is lost or stolen. Because of this, many ETM agents will carry a back-up 'dumb' fire arm that isn't networked even though this violates regulations. The CU creates only a single type of each weapon, considering them more than adequate for the tasks for which they were designed and seeing no need for duplication of effort.

Listed damage for all weapons is from highly lethal HVAPHE rounds – rubber bullets are also available that do half damage (FRD) with no AP bonus and the first wound treated as a Shaken result. Flechette rounds are used if deadly force is required in a place where breaching a wall could have catastrophic consequences. These rounds cut the range for projectile weapons in half (a light pistol, for instance, would have a range of 6/12/24), deal -2 damage, but halve type one armor protection.

No weapons can be legally owned by most CU citizens. An R designation means the weapon is restricted, indicating that possession of this weapon is illegal for private citizens in any SMM. CU agents requesting these weapons if they are not specifically assigned will get a raised eyebrow from the armory officer and -4 to their Networking (Bureaucracy) roll to acquire one.

These weapons do type one damage unless otherwise noted.

Pistols

Light: 9mm SDW: 12/24/48, 2D6+2 dam, weight 1 Shots: 12 AP 2, +2 Stealth to conceal

Medium: .44 Peacemaker: 12/24/48, 2D8+2 dam, weight 2 Shots: 15, AP4 Min. Str. 6, Full auto recoil -3

Heavy: .75 Annihilator: 12/24/48, 2D10+3 dam, weight 3 Shots: 5, AP4 Min. Str. 8, Full auto recoil -4

Submachine Gun

SP90 SDW 4.5mm: 12/24/48, 2D6+2 dam, weight 5 Shots: 36, AP2, +1 Stealth to conceal

Shotgun

SPR-12 CAW: Slug rounds 15/30/60 3D6+2 dam, weight 6, AP4, Flechettes: 5/10/20 1 – 3 D10 (depending on range), halves type 1 armor, area effect (cone), Shots: 6

Battle Rifle

PK-49 TAW: 25/50/100, 2D8+2 dam, weight 5, AP6, Shots: 45

Has an integrated grenade launcher (50/100/200 3D6 dam area effect with adjustable blast radius – use small or large template) that can also fire shotgun rounds (damage/range per SPR-12). A HEAT round is also available that does 1D6 type 2 damage (no area effect).

Sniper Rifle

M24HB: 50/100/200, 2D8+4 dam, AP8, Snapfire, Shots: 10, ROF 2

Has integrated scope that will eliminate range penalties with an aim action.

Anti-Materiel Rifle (R)

Mk V AMR: This weapon does type two damage. 50/100/200, 1D6+1 dam, weight 15, AP 2, Snapfire, Shots: 5, ROF 1, Min. Str. D8

Although this portable railgun is designed to take out troops in battle armor and lightly armored vehicles, it also finds use against Outsiders and other dangerous entities that can be affected by mundane weapons, especially in built up areas where use of missiles or other heavier weapons would cause unacceptable collateral damage.

Machine Gun (R)

MJ88 MSW: 30/60/120, 2d8+4 dam, AP6, weight 15 Shots: 50, ROF 4, Min. Str. D8

Light Anti-Tank Weapon (LAW)

AM24: 24/48/96 2D6 type 2, Snapfire, weight 5, Shots: 1, ROF 1, 1 Action to reload, Burst MBT

Light Anti-Aircraft Missile

SAM 75: 100/200/400, 2D6 type 2, weight 10, Shots: 1, ROF 1, Min. Str. D6, 1 Action to reload

Guided Anti-Armor Weapon

Salamander anti-materiel missile: 100/200/400, type 2 damage, 2d8+2 AP4, weight 20, +2 TH (fire and forget homing missile), ROF 1, 1 Action to reload, Tripod required, Burst MBT

EXOTIC WEAPONS

Mk VII EMP (R)
Type two damage. Uses cone template. 3D6+3 dam., weight 12, armor has no effect unless it has EMP shielding. Shots: 6 (battery), ROF 1, Min. Str. D8

This weapon only affects things that contain electronics. If a target is using cyberware, they will take half damage from the attack from their internal machinery short-circuiting. The CU forbids the use of this weapon in populated areas. Most electronic systems have a toughness of 6, less for older or poorly maintained systems, while military and highly secured government/corporate systems will have more.

Gyroc Pistol (R)
12/24/48, 2d8+2 dam (HE), 1d6+2 dam type 2 (HEAT), weight 3, Shots: 4, ROF 1,

Fires a magnetically accelerated micro-missile whose motor ignites after it has left the chamber. Usable underwater. HEAT rounds do type two damage.

Gyroc Rifle (R)
24/48/96, 3d8+3 dam (HE), 1d8+2 dam type 2 (HEAT), weight 6, Shots: 6, ROF

Usable underwater. HEAT rounds do type two damage.

Particle Beam Emitter (R)
Type two damage. 24/48/96, 2d8+1 dam, weight 15, Shots: 6 (battery), ROF 1. Min. Str. D8. CU forbids use in populated areas.

Underbarrel Flamethrower (R)
Use Cone template. 3d6 (flame) ignores armor type 2 and below, weight 5 (bottles) or 10 (backpack) Shots: 6 (bottles) or 20 (backpack), ROF 1

A favorite anti-critter weapon in the Central Services Plumbing Division, this flamethrower can either be used by itself or fitted beneath the barrel of a rifle type weapon.

Constable MkIII
12/24/48, variable damage (strength and type determined by GM at time of firing), weight 4, shots: 10 (type III base block cartridge), ROF (up to 3)

This weapon is the side-arm of the CU's Peacekeepers and Inspectors. The pistol comes equipped with biometric scanners that determine the mental state, identity and overall threat level of the target. It will then use a small internal Maker to instantaneously manufacture the most suitable munition for the circumstances, ranging from microwaves, taser darts and rubber bullets to shaped charge warheads and tac nuke rounds. The default settings can be overridden by the user's Ginsert if they rank as an Inspector or higher, but such a change must later be justified in a board of inquiry.

VEHICLES

Few people in the CU own a car – those that do tend to live in rural or other isolated areas. Demand is so small that the CU manufactures very few of them, purchasing from abroad if there is a need. While hoverboards (both wheeled and ground effect) are popular with the younger crowd, most of the population gets by with ebikes and the highly efficient public transportation system. Members of ETM usually get transportation assigned, although this can be challenged through a judicious use of the Bureaucracy skill if the mode of transportation provided isn't to their liking. High level members of the government may have transportation permanently assigned or on call. Like many other items, the CU only manufactures a few different vehicle types, focusing on durable multi-role platforms. The CU also tends to favor the use of ground effect vehicles that utilize electromagnetic repulsors to levitate and maneuver. These craft soar silently above the pedestrian filled streets, leaving the citizens below undisturbed in their day to day business.

Outside of the CU, ownership of transportation is dependent on wealth and status, with a great deal dependent on what the SMM in question will allow.

In higher tech societies, control of vehicles can be done via AR or VR, giving +1 to driving rolls. In urban areas, ground and air navigation slaved to local traffic control is usually required, with only emergency vehicles given the option to override. Most vehicles also have an auto-navigation feature of varying capability, with aircraft having the ability to at least fly and land safely if the pilot is incapacitated.

Ground Effect Skateboard

This ground effect vehicle uses maglocks to secure the user's feet to the device. Despite its small size, it can still link into local auto-navigation and this is the only legal way to use them in the CU. Hacked boards, however, are extremely popular and ignore this restriction – in hacked mode, they have been known to jump obstacles up to 30' in height. As long as the public isn't being put in too much danger, these breaches of the law are usually ignored, being seen as an important steam valve for a population that is so heavily regimented.
Acc: 20, TS:36, Tough: 3

Ground Effect Interceptor

This light, fast vehicle used by the CU's elite first responders has stubby wings that contain two hard points for swappable mission modules, with two more on the underside of the craft. The interior space is able to be rapidly reconfigured as well, with adjustable polymers on the vehicle's skin making an endless array of markings and color schemes possible.
This flexibility allows the vehicle to be configured for different emergencies in minutes and includes medical, firefighting, rescue, law enforcement and gunship configurations. The auto-nav can use any attached equipment at a skill equal to its rating if asked to do so.
Crew: 1 + 6, Acc: 75, TS: 300, Tough: 8 (4) type 2, Auto-Nav: 3

Ground Effect Shuttle

Conformal exterior modules, along with a rapidly convertible interior make this larger vehicle as versatile as the Interceptor. Although its chief mission is to ferry high ranking diplomats and visiting dignitaries rapidly between their various appointments, it can be reconfigured rapidly in an emergency. Although not as maneuverable as the Interceptor, it can be used for civilian evacuations or as a troop carrier, its generous interior space and heavy lift capabilities being extremely useful in this regard.

Crew: 1 + 25, Acc. 25, TS: 200, Tough: 12 (6) type 2, Auto-Nav: 5

BATTLEMECHS

Mechs are only available to advanced, well financed militaries. Corporations might possess some lighter models for security and other ops, but the larger mechs are too expensive to make sense from a business perspective.

Each suit listed includes the following:

Firewall -6, Encryption 10, Auto-Nav 4, full visual spectrum HUD (no penalties due to darkness) that also provides +3 to shooting weapons equipped with an interface, Anti-Missile Countermeasures (AMCM – adds +2 to the pilot's skill roll for evading guided munitions for one round), enhanced hearing (+2 to Notice), sound dampener (+2 vs Sonic attacks), flash protection (1/2 penalty) and a self-mending environmental seal that requires a level 2 wound to breach. The seal is also effective against vacuum and the suits can easily be made space worthy. They can also operate up to a depth of 50 meters underwater, or 500 with special modifications. Should the crew be wounded or incapacitated, an encrypted distress signal will be sent and a dose of medichines applied. The vehicle will seek to return to friendly lines using its auto-nav if it's still mobile. The auto-nav is also able to fire the vehicle's weapons or perform other tasks at a skill level equal to its rating. Includes four modular attachment points.
Mechs are also usually equipped with at least a few magnetic attachment points so accompanying infantry in mil-spec armor can 'hitch a ride'.

Lynx

The Lynx is a light mech that can be used for reconnaissance, screening the flanks of larger mechs or other tasks that require speed or stealth.

The mech is equipped with an advanced stealth suite that renders it very difficult to detect visually or by sensors (-4 to notice). Its mobility is enhanced by jump jets (can jump 100') that can also be used for extended flight (200' per turn for six turns before its batteries are exhausted).

For reconnaissance purposes, it carries four micro drones (with a sensor suite that gives them + 2 to notice, but are themselves -6 to notice or hit due to stealth, size and agility). The drones can fly 50' per turn and mark targets for other units, giving them +2 to hit.

For attack and defense, the mech is equipped with a shoulder mounted 25 mm autocannon (50/100/200, type 2 damage, 1d8+2 AP2, ROF 3, 250 rounds) with an under barrel two shot missile launcher (Salamander anti-materiel missile, 100/200/400, type 2 damage, 2d8+2 AP4, +2 TH (fire and forget homing missile), ROF 1, 2 shots)
Crew: 1, Tough: 12 (6) type 2 Pace: 12/+2D6 if running

Claymore

The majority of the CU's mech force (75%) are made up of these machines. Designed to fill a variety of roles, it is more than adequate in most situations.
Stealth suite (-1 to detect), Senor suite (+2 to notice), two micro drones as per Lynx, arm mounted 120mm rail gun (100/200/400, type 2 damage, 2d8+4 AP6, ROF 1, 40 shots carried in armored

cases carried on the back. Autoload system takes 1 turn to reload the weapon). 15 mm heavy machine gun carried co-axial to main armament (50/100/200, type 2 damage, 1D6+2 AP2, ROF 3, 500 shots).

Crew: 1 Tough: 14 (6) type 2 Pace: 8/+1D6 if running

Ram

Designed for fighting in any close terrain, the CU has rarely used them in city fighting and does so only if the civilian population has been evacuated.

Stealth suite (-1 to detect), Senor suite (+2 to notice), 4 micro drones as per Lynx arm mounted plasma cannon (cone template, type 2 damage, 2d8+2, AP 2, ROF 1, 20 shots), shoulder mounted 50 MW Laser (50/100/200, type 2 damage, 1D10+2, AP5, ROF 3 (continuous beam – no recoil penalty) battery good for 20 shots.

Crew 1, Tough: 14 (6) type 2 Pace: 8/+1D6

ANNIHILATOR MECHS

Due to the collateral damage and psychological trauma that they inflict over a wide area, these mechs are only used in the direst of emergencies. So far they have been used twice, with the details of their deployment classified (see files Wormwood Sector Protocol and Pandemonium Overreach). Designed to counter major Outsider incursions (as well as various creations of Temple), Annihilator Mechs are designed to channel destructive energy from other dimensions and to resist those same forces. A leaked video of the test firing of a Serpentine Cannon shows it not only destroying its heavily armored target at the Lunar test center but also creating a new valley in the mountain range behind it. Suffice to say that these weapons are dangerous even when not being used and are kept in special sealed and warded areas.

Their armor is of similar exotic origins, a hyper dense alloy with a composition similar to that of a neutron star held in place by a ritual both complex and extremely hazardous. This and other materials used in the mech's construction can only be found in a few of the dimensions thus far discovered.

Various types of auto-pilot programs have been tried as means of controlling the mech, but none have proven successful – a ritually prepared, sapient pilot is required. Even then, the pilot must have one of the following Edges: Jaded, Unflappable, Reality is an Illusion.

The current base for the unit is the Gobi Desert, the area around the site warded with confusion spells. The site is underground and very extensive, a small city designed for the deployment of this single destructive device. The mechs themselves are rarely above ground, but when they are, they present a confusing image of rapidly shifting outlines, much like the Outsiders themselves. Transportation is always done via gates, with a ritual team showing up close to the location where the unit is to be deployed.

The only known operational Annihilator Mech is the Ramiel class, currently in service with the CU. It is rumored that other SMMs currently have Annihilators in the concept or prototype stage, with the CU acting covertly to either stop or slow down these projects.

Ramiel Annihilator Mech

Shifting outline/energy spectrum (-2 to hit), Prototech senor suite (+3 to notice, including astral or otherwise intangible entities), Serpentine Cannon (no range limitations, type 4 damage (2d8+2, AP6, ROF 1, must spend 2 turns recharging, unlimited ammo), Basilisk Gun (no range limitations, type 4 damage, 1D6+2, AP4, ROF 2, unlimited ammo). D Engine offers unlimited energy to mech and weapons. Breaching of the engine's containment unit will cause complete destruction within a five kilometer radius and possibly open a permanent dimensional breach which will alter the reality of the surrounding area (event horizon estimated at 100 kilometers).
Crew: 1 **Toughness:** 14 (6) type 4 **Pace:** 8/1D6

DRONES

The only unmanned aircraft allowed in the skies of the CU are Law drones. Other types of drones are allowed to be used by the public at large, but generally can't be larger than a person's hand and are for amusement and entertainment purposes only. 3-D holographic projectors are often attached to them to present the image of a pet, roommate or deceased loved one and programmed with suitable behavior. Exceptions for other drone types might be allowed, subject to the determination of the Peacekeeper or Law drone on the spot, with any deemed hazardous or of possible nefarious use confiscated.

Other locales may have similar or less restrictions depending on the ruling SMM. Generally, a license must be obtained for any flying drones and its autopilot needs to be synched to local air traffic control. Uses for all types of civilian owned drones range from package delivery to news gathering. Like the CU, almost all SMMs also use drones for law enforcement and military purposes.

Not everyone who uses a drone necessarily wants to register it or is interested in other legal niceties. If such a drone is detected, law enforcement units will attempt to hack it in order to gain control of the craft, or failing that, destroy it in a way that will cause a minimum of damage to the surrounding area.

CU Law Drone

These drones come in a variety of sizes and types of locomotion, but the most common type is about six feet long, four feet high and propelled by rotors and a small jet engine. Contained within this frame is a Cornucopia class Maker and Baseblock, capable of manufacturing nearly anything in the CU database. Each drone is run by a sophisticated AI that is capable of using any device it manufactures with a skill of 1d6. The items it can construct run the gamut between medical supplies to type two weaponry. It can also modify its sensors, manipulators or other attributes to adapt to any situation it encounters.

Its only limitations are temporal, taking at least three turns to apprehend what particular modifications are needed and then manufacture and install them. Law drones will always use the minimum of force necessary and will seek to protect and preserve life before all other considerations.

In order to minimize their potentially intimidating presence, Law drones will project bright colors or soothing animated scenes across their surfaces and will attempt friendly, casual interactions with citizens or visitors at large, sometimes offering light sedatives, energy drinks or snacks. They will use either feminine or masculine voices when communicating, depending on what they think will be most effective in a given situation. Many people find the occasional sudden transition jarring.

While it is tough and well armored, the Law drone's sophisticated, delicate machinery and its dependence on reliable communications in its decision making process makes it ill suited for heavy combat use. Any interruption in a Law drone's access to the Law database will cause it to withdraw on auto-pilot to the nearest diagnostic facility. If unable to do so or to summon aid, it will self-destruct by releasing the magnetic confinement on its quantum singularity power source. The singularity will only last for a microsecond, but during this time it will reduce the drone to its component atoms. Although the event is fairly localized, any individual or object within 1" will suffer significant physical trauma (3d6+4 type 2 damage), while the area within 3" will be exposed to time shifts and other bizarre phenomena.

The following are the Law Drone's default stats – full spectrum sensor suite (+2 to notice, no low light or brightness penalties), a Consciousness Evaluation Module (CEM) (allows psychology roll at +2 to attempt to determine an individual's state of mind), tranquilizer dart gun (smartgun linked, AP2, no damage, but if the subject is hit, they must pass a Vigor check at -3 or fall unconscious for 10 minutes.

Toughness: 10 (4) type 2 Acc. 20, TS. 60, climb 1 (combination rotor/turbojet)

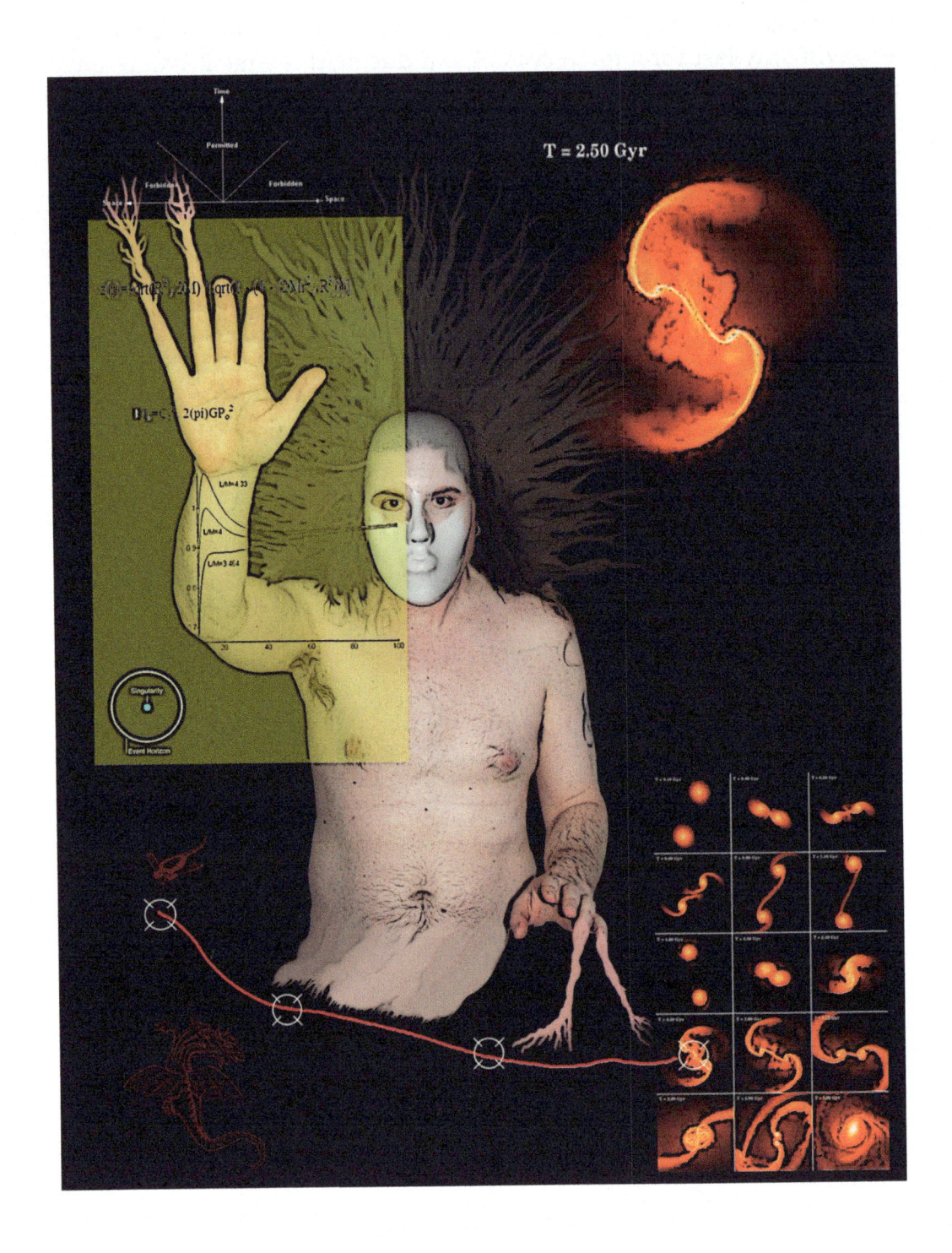

SPACECRAFT

CU Spacecraft are designed first and foremost for safety, reliability and durability with all essential systems having multiple back ups. Their ships tend to lack cutting edge technology in terms of propulsion, with the SMM instead valuing well proven and tested systems. Given this, their performance may seem lacking in comparison to spacecraft of rival SMMs. The CU considers this trade off worth-while, and their ships' crews rest easy knowing that critical components won't fail in a crisis or when subjected to stress. Any shortcomings in terms of speed are worked around by basing task forces at critical points around the solar system within easy reach of potential conflict, while deficiencies in firepower are addressed by the sheer number that can show up and deliver well-coordinated attacks.

All CU spacecraft are modular in nature. Although this makes manufacturing more difficult and expensive, the SMM feels the versatility this gives their spacecraft is well worth it. Any ship utilizing non-modular design will have an extra +1 to all of its die rolls and a 10 percent bonus to its top speed and acceleration due to the optimization of power and data feeds that this allows.

Due to their built in redundancies and conservative design, CU spacecraft get to re-roll any critical failure. They can also ignore the 'disaster' result on the Attack Range and Complication Table in the rule book.

Some of the modules listed enhance intangibles like crew comfort and morale. If a ship is lacking in this regard, feel free to add an appropriate negative modifier to its operations to represent fatigue and general surliness. Such crews are also more likely to act poorly under stressful situations, up to and including mutiny.

Ships of all sizes will include a senor package that will allow characters to make Notice rolls to detect ships and other objects with varying degrees of effectiveness, with modifiers ranging from -2 (subpar, cheap and unreliable) to +1 (usually the best sensors found on non-military ships). CU vessels will always have +1 sensors, with specialized research, combat or reconnaissance vehicles having the temperamental SOTA package (see modules below). Sensors are considered to be an integral part of the hull, taking up no module slots.

Extra armor can be fitted to the hull, but for each point, reduce the acceleration by 10% and climb rating by 1.

[Designer Notes: Like all aspects of this supplement, the rules here are designed to integrate well with a narrative campaign. For this reason, they are highly abstracted, simulating complex operations with a die roll or two in the interest of keeping the story moving. For those who would enjoy more of a simulation, I highly recommend using the space combat rules from GURPS Transhuman Space by Steve Jackson Games.]

Small Hull

This hull is most often used for unmanned probes or attack drones and can accept up to four modules. Most of these will be for scientific survey, but if doing research in contested areas the CU isn't above providing them with stealth and even armament packages. The latter can also be handy for discouraging enterprising freelancers from claiming them as 'salvage'.

Small hulls can be made stealthy (by utilizing curved surfaces on the hull and masking emissions). While this is a very expensive process, any ships trying to detect or target them get -2 to their notice and to hit rolls.

Toughness: 7 (1) type 2
The hull includes maneuvering thrusters and an impulse drive that provides the following stats:
Acc. 50, TS. 500, climb 2
Cannot be equipped with crew facilities, lounge or garden

Medium Hull

This is usually the smallest hull form used for manned spacecraft. With its six modules, it can carry a small bridge and still have enough room for a useful array of sensors, weapons or mining equipment. The CU tends to use ships of this size for patrol, surveying and low priority research or exploration.

Medium hulls can be made stealthy like small ships, but ships targeting them only receive a -1.

Toughness: 7 (1) type 3
The hull includes maneuvering thrusters and an impulse drive that provides the following stats:
Acc. 30, TS 700, climb 1

Large Hull

This is the smallest hull form used for manned interplanetary missions. Possessing ten modules, it has enough room for a lounge and the dedicated crew quarters necessary for extended deep space assignments and still have enough room for a variety of dedicated mission packages. CU ships of this size always carry some sort of armament, even if fighting isn't their primary task.

Toughness: 10 (2) type 3
The hull includes maneuvering thrusters and an impulse drive that provides the following stats:
Acc. 20, TS 800, climb 0

Huge Hull

This is the largest sized ship the CU manufactures. While a few other SMMs create larger ships, the CU considers these to be prestige vessels with a high cost in comparison to their actual utility. While the CU sometimes does configure specialist ships of this type, the most common layout is a primary and secondary function. With twenty different module interface ports, the potential types of mission packages are nearly endless and can be fine tuned for any particular assignment.

Toughness: 12 (2) type 3
The hull includes maneuvering thrusters and an impulse drive that provides the following stats:
Acc. 10, TS 1000, climb -1

Stronger Hulls

These hull types add significantly to the cost of a ship and are therefore only used in special ops ships, VIP transports and especially valuable combat vessels.

Carbon Composite Hull: +2 Toughness

Diamondoid Hull: +4 Toughness

SHIP MODULES

The modules listed below can either be swappable containers for a modular ship, or built-in specialized components for a non-modular one. Modules normally have a toughness equal to their hull and the same level of armor protection. If hit, one wound will damage a module, while two will completely destroy it. All modules have varying degrees of quality, ranging from -2 to +1.

Some modules have the option of being grouped together in an 'avionics module' - these include the Auto-Pilot module, ECM module, ECCM module, Quantum Targeting module, SOTA Sensors and Science module. Up to three of these systems can be grouped in each module, the downside being that if the module is hit, all of the systems within it are affected.

Armor Module

The Armor Module represents protection of a ship's systems with strong alloys to prevent them from being damaged during combat. A damaged armor module still functions as normal.

Atmospheric Flight

Available only for small or medium hulls, this module provides the spacecraft with engines and an airfoil hull design that allows it to maneuver in a planetary atmosphere.

Auto-Pilot Module

This module can replace the Bridge/Control center if an automated ship is required. In this case, it will take up no slots. In addition to flying the ship, this component can include software that will allow them to operate other modules, most commonly at a skill of 3.

Bridge/Control Center

Bridges and Control centers are considered an integral part of any hull and therefore take up no module slots.

Any manned ship of medium size or larger requires a bridge module for centralized control of its vital functions. It contains life support elements, so it can sustain a small crew on its own without the benefit of a Crew Module. Note that this is very uncomfortable for the crew and the amount of life support the module contains is limited (several days at most). Bridges can be of standard layout, or optimized for combat or science. In the latter cases, the bridge will provide a +1 to rolls that lie within its specialty and a -1 to the other. Every bridge will have stations for different crew members and can include science, tactical, navigation and command. Like most ship components, these vary in capability from ship to ship and have modifiers for their users ranging from -2 to +1. Command stations allow the captain to make cooperative rolls to assist other bridge team members or to take over the function of their station should it be destroyed or the crew member incapacitated.

If the bridge is hit with a wound result, roll randomly to select a crew station. That crew member takes 2d6 damage and their station is damaged - the ship's functions that it controls cannot be used until it is repaired. A second wound will completely destroy the station and inflict another

2d6 on the crew member operating it. If a hit has been inflicted on a station that has already been destroyed, randomly select another.

Control Centers are used for unmanned craft and can house either a drone rig or an AI pilot.

Cargo Module

This module can carry several dozen square meters of cargo, but no life support is provided.

Combat Thrusters

Provides extra speed and maneuverability in either an atmosphere or vacuum. Add +20 to Acc., +20% to TS and +1 to climb. Gives ships with small and medium hulls the 'Improved Dodge' ability, with larger ships getting the 'Dodge' ability.

Crew Module

This module contains all of the myriad essentials required by an organic crew, including life support, places to sleep, toilet facilities, drinking water and either Makers of varying quality or a food prep area. Usually spartan, they can also be provided with increasing levels of comfort for the crew for added cost. Each module can support up to twenty crew members.

While the CU spares no expense on safety and livability, other SMMs try to stretch the definition of 'survivable environment' as much as possible in the interests of controlling costs. In such cases, feel free to give the crew a blanket -1 on all skill rolls or even a -2 if they've been in space for a long time.

If a module is without life support, its inhabitants have five minutes to don EV suits or reach escape pods before becoming incapacitated – in another five minutes they will die.

Drone

This either represents a fighter drone or a heavily shielded probe designed to explore hazardous environments.

Fighter Drone
Toughness: 8 (2) type 3
Acc. 75, TS 1000, climb 3
Payload: Any single turreted weapon module

Advanced Fighter Drone
Only available to well financed militaries. Stats are as fighter drone above, but can equip one extra module of any type (weapons modules must still be turreted).

Probe
Toughness: 6 (2) type 3
Acc. 25, TS: 500, climb -1
Payload: Any single science module

ECM Module

When activated, it gives any weapons targeting the ship a -2 to hit.

ECCM Module

Negates effects of ECM Module – this is restricted technology and is normally found only on military vessels.

Escape Pods

One module of escape pods will provide a means of emergency evacuation for all crew modules.

Garden

Hydroponic gardens provide oxygen and fresh food for the crew, as well as a place to come and relax.

Lab

A lab provides all of the necessary equipment for a variety of different scientific pursuits. Labs can also be specialized for a particular field of study, providing an extra bonus. A regular lab will provide a +1 bonus to all science rolls, while a specialized one will provide a +3 to its dedicated field of study (but a -1 to all others). If on an unmanned probe or a ship without a science officer, a lab can be fully automated with a Science skill ranging from D4 to D8 (no wild die allowed).

Lounge

This module provides a rest and relaxation space for the crew, a vital consideration for long term assignments.

Medical Bay

A Medical Bay provides intensive care and diagnostic facilities for up to eight patients. All Healing, Surgery and other rolls related to medicine receive a +2 here.

Mining Module

Contains everything needed for industrial asteroid or planet side mining. A cargo module will be required to store the ore.

Propulsion Module

The CU's favored Ion Propulsion Unit moves their ships along at a comfortable 1 Astronomical Unit (about 150 million kilometers) per week. This works out to roughly 893,000 kph. This means it takes about a week and a half to reach the asteroid belt from Earth.

While an anti-matter drive will get a ship to where it's going twice as quickly, it might not arrive at all. A critical failure on the Piloting (Spacecraft) roll when the main drive is engaged means the ship will explode with little warning (1d12 minutes). A success on an Engineering (Spacecraft) roll at -2 will prevent it. The base time to do this operation is ten minutes, with each raise on skill roll cutting this time in half.

Refinery

An expensive but valuable addition to a mining ship. The Refinery will automatically process ore or other materials and make them immediately available for industrial use.

Quantum Targeting System

A state of the art targeting system found only in cutting edge military spacecraft. Provides a +2 to targeting rolls and ignores stealth and ECM.

Science Module

This module allows a skill roll to collect scientific data from an object up to 1000 kilometers distant, with -1 for every distance segment at a factor of 10 after that (for example, -1 at 10,000, -2 at 100,000, etc.). Like labs, they can be specialized for collecting particular types of data, providing similar bonuses and penalties.

SOTA Sensors

Gives the possessing ship +2 to Notice and +1 to hit rolls, but requires constant calibration and cleaning. A successful Repair roll every 24 hours will make the necessary adjustments, with each raise halving the required time. The sensor's modifier will drop by one for every day this isn't done, down to a maximum of -2. Like other sensors, SOTAs take up no module slots, being considered part of the hull.

Weapon Modules

These powerful weapons all have line of sight range - if they can see a target, they can hit it, with the only modifiers being the weapon's modifiers and the target's stealth attributes and ECM. Weapons have modifiers to hit ranging from -2 to +1, simulating subpar to superior targeting systems (the Quantum Targeting System is a different beast altogether, requiring its own module). They can be in turrets, which allow a +1 action card draw if only turreted weapons are used to attack, or be installed in spinal mounts that can do more damage but need a 10 or higher in their action card draw to use due to the difficulty in bringing the weapon to bear. Given the fine-tuning and specialized power feeds needed for their use, spinal mounts cannot be used in modular vessels.

3 MJ Laser

Intended for use against small, fast targets, the 3 MJ Laser lacks power but is able to fire rapidly. Given its point defense mission, they are almost always mounted in turrets. If the operator chooses, they can forfeit their rate of fire to destroy one incoming missile with a successful gunnery roll.
Stats: Type 2 Damage 1D6 AP2, ROF 2

12 MJ Laser

This is the most common anti-ship weapon, found all over the solar system. Some have even found their way into civilian hands.
Turret
Stats: Type 3 Damage 2D6 AP3, ROF 1

Spinal Mount
Stats: Type 3 Damage 3D6 AP4, ROF 2

Particle Beam

This weapon fires a burst of lethal radiation that can sicken or kill crew members in addition to damaging the target's systems. Due to its horrific effects, it is outlawed by the CU.

Turret
Stats: Type 3 Damage 1D8+2 AP1, ROF 1

Spinal Mount
Stats: Type 3 Damage 2D8+2 AP2, ROF 1

On a wound result, particle beams expose any crew members in the affected module to a dose of extreme radiation.

Emag Gun
An electromagnetic gun that fires small projectiles at extremely high velocities.

Turret
Stats: Type 3 Damage 1D6 AP2 ROF 3

Spinal Mount
Stats: Type 3 Damage 1D8+2 AP2, ROF 4

Sparrow Agile Missile System
Each missile has a 50% chance of shooting down an incoming enemy missile. The Sparrow AMS can launch all of its missiles at once, but once all of them have been expended, must take a full turn to reload. The missiles can be used against other targets, but are of limited effectiveness due to their small warheads.

Turret Only
Stats: Type 3 Damage 1D4, Shots 6, ROF 6

Hornet Missile Pack
This is a cheap, expendable module that is often used by non-military craft as a means of defense. The payload consists of small, hyper-velocity missiles that contain shaped charge warheads specifically designed to penetrate a ship's hull. Targets get one chance to evade by succeeding at a Piloting (Spacecraft) roll at -4. Once all of the missiles are used, the module must be replaced.

Turret Only
Stats: Type 3 Damage 1D6+1 AP2, Shots 8, ROF 8

Onager Missile
While only cleared for military or corporate security use, these highly sought after weapons can occasionally be found on the black market.

Turret
Stats: Type 3 Damage 2D8+2 AP4 Shots 6 ROF 2

Spinal Mount
Stats: Type 3 Damage 3D8+3 AP4 Shots 4 ROF 2

Quantum Lock Torpedo
This is a rare, military grade weapon that requires both constant maintenance and a Quantum Lock targeting system in order to function properly. A dedicated specialist must be onboard to provide the needed calibration and ensure proper storage safety protocols are followed.

If such an individual is not present when the weapon is used, the torpedoes have a 50% chance of malfunctioning, with their notoriously unstable warheads detonating either in the launcher when

fired or not at all.
Turret
Stats: Type 3 Damage 4D6+2 AP6, Shots 6, ROF 2

Spinal Mount
In addition to being able to destroy spacecraft, this weapon is capable of vaporizing entire cities. Use of one would be akin to using a nuclear weapon in our time and would lead to a drastic escalation of any conflict.
Stats: Type 4 Damage 2D6+1 AP2, Shots 2, ROF 2
Special: This weapon has a 10 kilometer radius of effect.

SPACECRAFT COMBAT

An enemy ship must first be detected by a successful Notice roll before it can be engaged - once a ship has been detected, it remains so for the rest of the engagement. If a ship has been attacked, it gets +2 to future Notice rolls against the ship that attacked it. Any ship which uses ECM is automatically detected. Each raise on the Notice roll will add an extra +1 to hit the target spacecraft. If one spacecraft detects another but remains undetected itself, it gets an extra card draw if it chooses to attack.

For ship to ship combat, use the chase rules found in the main rule book (ignoring any 'obstacle' results from the complications table). While abstract, they keep the story moving without a lot of number crunching. If a ship is hit, refer to the location table below. A Shaken result will disrupt a module's functioning until a crew member passes Spacecraft Operations or Repair skill roll to bring it back online (base time of one minute). A Wound will damage a module, rendering it temporarily inoperable (a repair roll at -2 with a base time of two hours will fix it). A second wound will completely destroy it. If more than one option for a location is present, roll randomly to see which one is hit. Each wound to a hull location will cause any roll the spacecraft makes to be at -1 (cumulative). One wound to the hull will destroy a small spacecraft, two will destroy a medium sized one, four will destroy a large one, while six will destroy a huge one.

Spacecraft Hit Location Table (Roll D20)

If a given component is not present, the hit becomes armor or, if there is no armor, hull damage. If a ship has multiple systems present for a given roll, choose one of the modules randomly.

1: Bridge
2: Sensors (including SOTA)
3: Avionics Bay. If none Science Module or Autopilot
4-6: Weapon Module (choose randomly if more than one)
7-12: Armor Module – if no armor, hull damage
13: Propulsion Module or Combat Thrusters
14: Avionics Bay. If none, ECM, ECCM, or Quantum Targeting Module
15 – 17: Garden or Lounge Module
18: Lab or Med Bay
19-20: Crew Module or Cargo

Spacecraft Construction and Combat Example

Laura's ETM squad has been tasked with extracting a friendly agent being held in the Cascadian penal colony on Vesta. Since they will need an interplanetary spacecraft to reach their destination, ETM has assigned them one for the duration of their mission.

To avoid an incident with Cascadia, stealth has been given a high priority. With this in mind, the ETM mission director decides on a medium hull with a stealth modification. A medium hull has six modules, so the director decides on the following configuration: crew, support, bridge (which takes up no module slots), propulsion, SOTA sensors and combat thrusters. In case stealth doesn't work, the ship is also provided with an Emag Gun.

This gives their ship the following attributes:

Toughness: 7 (1) type 3
Acc. 50, TS 840, climb 1
SOTA Sensors: Notice: +2
Stealth Hull (-1 to detect)
Improved Dodge (due to Combat Thrusters -2 to hit)
Turreted Emag Gun (type 3 damage 1D6, AP4, ROF 3)

Their ship's ion propulsion unit moves them at safe and meandering 1 AU per week – at that speed it will take them ten days in their cramped ship with only very basic amenities to reach their destination (perhaps there's some business they can take care of for their AGs while they're in transit).

When they arrive, they find a Cascadian patrol ship in orbit around Vesta. Fortunately for our team, the Cascadian military comes out at the short end in their SMM's budget – its sensor suite is somewhat outdated, giving it a -1 to detect them. Combined with their ship's stealth hull, the patrol ship will roll at a -2. The bored conscript onboard has a notice of D6 and rolls a 5, which is modified to a 3. The ETI team's ship has evaded detection!

After a successful extraction, the team takes off from Vesta to head for the CU base on Ceres. Unfortunately, they triggered an alarm and the Cascadians have sent a warship in pursuit! This ship has a sensor suite that's a bit more capable than the previous one, having a modifier of zero. The Cascadian tactical officer has a Notice skill of D8 and rolls a six – the ETM ship has been detected! Meanwhile, the CU ship detects the Cascadian vessel with a roll of '2' - with their SOTA sensors giving them a +2, this will just suffice. When its invitation to surrender is ignored, the Cascadian vessel decides to open fire.

Now that combat has begun, the GM refers to the Chase rules in the Savage Worlds Rulebook to resolve it. Since the ETM ship is faster, the GM decides the chase will last five rounds, after which the fleeing ship will have built up the necessary speed to make good its escape. The Cascadian navigator has a Piloting (Spacecraft) skill of D6, while her ETM counterpart has a skill of D8. Thanks to their Combat Thrusters, the ETM ship has superior speed and climb, giving their navigator a +4. This is good, because he only rolls a '2'! With the +4, this gives him a '6', resulting in a success.

The Cascadian navigator, meanwhile, rolls a '3' – not a success! Her ship's turreted weapons still allow her an action card draw, however. She draws a '3', which is much lower than her opponent's. Since only the winner of the action card draw gets to fire, her ship will have to withstand an incoming barrage of Emag projectiles.

The ETM navigator's single success allows him to draw one action card, while the ship's turreted weapon allows him to draw a second. It's a King of Diamonds and an Ace of Hearts! He discards the Ace (this is the lowest value action card) and keeps the King. Checking the Attack Range and Complications Table, he finds that there will be no modifiers.

The ship's Tac Officer attacks with the Emag Gun, using her Gunnery skill of D8. In addition, her ship has a superior targeting system, giving her a +1 to her roll. The Emag gun has a rate of fire (ROF) of 3, so she rolls three dice plus her Wild die, rolling a '7', '2' and a '3' with a '2' on the Wild die. With the ship's +1 targeting system, the rolls become an '8', a '3' and '4' – her Wild die is the lowest roll, so she discards it. The

Tac Officer needs a '4' to hit, so she hits twice. Since the '8' is four greater than what she needed to hit, that one becomes a raise that will cause extra damage.

Rolling to see where her rounds hit, the Tac Officer rolls a '5' and a '20', striking a weapon's mount and the crew module! The Emag gun does type 3 damage, which means it will do normal damage to its target since its hull has type 3 toughness. The weapon's AP ability overcomes the target's armor, giving it a target number of 6 to overcome the hull's Toughness rating. She
rolls a '6' on her first die, which aces and allows her to roll again and add the results to the first. The second roll is a '5', giving her a total damage of '11'. This is a 'Wound' result, which puts the Cascadian ship's only weapon turret out of action until a crew member can repair it. The Tac Officer rolls a '2' and a '5' on her second roll (getting an added +1D6 due to the raise on her to hit roll) – a total of '7'. This is a 'Shaken' result – which means the crew module has been lightly damaged and is no longer capable of providing life support until repaired! The crew begin to quickly don emergency life support gear, except for one brave officer who will attempt a Spacecraft Operations roll to bring it back online. The GM declares that the wailing klaxons and overall stressful situation will give the officer a -1 modifier. He rolls a '4' – not enough! He can attempt it four more times before becoming incapacitated.

The Cascadian captain, with his only weapon taken offline and life support in a precarious state, decides discretion is the better part of valor and breaks off the pursuit. The ETM ship, with orders to minimize conflict, does not pursue and continues on its course to Ceres.

GEAR

All CU devices and clothing have a wireless interface that controls all aspects of their function, as well as handling self-diagnostics, self-repair, tutorials and appearance. All are self-cleaning and can emit a virtual scent of the owner's choosing (which others may opt in or out of experiencing).

Lifestyles outside of the CU

Most areas outside of Temple and the CU subscribe to the same system of corporate management to handle the basic needs of their respective populations. Under this system, housing, food, medical care, entertainment, transportation and clothing are directly provided by the corporation the individual is contracted with (called 'lifestyle packages'). Oftentimes, the person is expected to change their last name to match that of the employing organization, as well as granting them power of attorney. The quality of products and services that are provided are, of course, directly related to the individual's status and value to their employer.

COMMON ITEMS

Base Blocks

This item provides raw material for mobile Makers, allowing them to create items from their catalog of templates. If a character continually recycles matter through their Maker, a Base Block will usually last for about a month before needing replacement.

Industrial or Home Makers will be equipped with a matter feed, making a Base Block unnecessary for operation.

Clothing

All CU clothing is made from smart fabric and designed for use in tandem with the owner's Ginsert. Many free clothing templates with countless options are available and can be modified over the course of the day to suit the weather or the occasion. If a user has access to the proper templates, clothing can also be modified with chameleon properties (- 2 to notice). Thermal masking, flame and shock resistance and ballistic protection are also possible (but not available in legal templates in the CU), with a maximum total modifier of four for any combination of these attributes.

Even in the CU's SMM of transhuman utopian socialism, people are still status conscious and this is reflected in their purchase (or creation) of unique clothing templates that suit their own personal sense of style. It will be obvious to most onlookers if one's clothing choices are 'off the shelf' and this will lead to a -1 in some social situations. Much like the present, choice of clothing will often reflect one's AG sympathies – these fashions constantly change, but a Familiar can provide updates and offer suggestions. One's Ginsert can also detect the fashion that is suitable for a particular locale and either automatically update clothing appearance or provide a variety of suitable options.

Communications

Most everyone outside of the CU still uses some permutation of the 'phone', a small device with any number of different applications with varying levels of sophistication and security. The device's applications are usually channeled into a user modified AR or VR interface.

CU citizens all have a high resolution VR interface included with their Ginsert and tend to experience much of their work and leisure in that format. The interface for either experience can be set for any info or level of interaction the user deems relevant up to and including real time purchasing, traffic reports, reservations, facial recognition, interactive games, virtual weather and reality filters that can change the nature of one's perceived surroundings.

Users will almost always broadcast their profile. While this is optional in the CU (although not broadcasting it is considered anti-social and may trigger a concerned inquiry from a Law Drone), it is not in most other SMMs. Such SMMs will also usually include a Citizen Score. The score is a measure of the individual's reputation with their fellow citizens, their employer, their government or all three. Broadcasting reputation with one's AGs is always optional, but many bolder individuals are not above doing so.

Home Maker (HM – pronounced as 'him')

This item is a 1.5 meter cube and is used to create everything from furniture (some assembly required) to sculptures to elaborate meals. Once an item has been used, it can be dumped into the HM's recycler where it will be decompiled. They come attached to a matter feed that supplies the elements needed to create their products – every house will also have a few base blocks on hand as well in case of emergencies.

Templates provide the molecular schematics to create whatever is desired, with certain items being prohibited (such as weapons or ingredients that could be used to create them) or controlled (such as certain pharmaceuticals), or existentially toxic (such as particular texts concerning hyper geometry or Outsider knowledge). An HM is designed to detect any attempt to create items like these and will first issue a warning to the user. Any further attempts will result in the HM contacting the Law.

Minifab ('Fabs')

These small Makers (about the size of a purse) can produce any hand sized item in their database. Since the owner is expected to recycle created items after use (by simply inserting the object back into the Fab) their base blocks only need to be replaced infrequently and a one hour charge makes them available for a full day's use.

A Type One is programmed with common office and household tools as well as food, clothing, various drinks, make-up and hygiene nano. Each one of these is highly individualized and keyed to a specific person with quick access to all of their preferred products.

A Type Two is available in any home or public area and is intended to be used only in emergencies. In addition to the usual assortment of products, it's programmed to create simple medical and survival gear (including medichines with a diagnostic interface, thermal blanket and shelter, Ginsert hot spot, first aid kit and other essentials). A Type Three is intended for soldiers and includes items from the Type Two as well as an assortment of simple weapons (ceramic knife, single or double shot pistol, caltrops, monowire, explosives, etc.).

VR Rig

Although VR is usually included with a person's cybernetic Ginsert, the VR Rig exists for those unwilling or unable to have this vital piece of hardware installed in their Cerebral Cortex. The software to run it is standard in most phone operating systems - to access its functions, the user has to apply wireless electrodes to their temples and the insides of their wrists. After one Action, they'll be able to access their programs or experience any other content they have available.

RESTRICTED ITEMS

Blinder

A breaking and entering device no honest citizen would be in possession of. The Blinder is a rotating sphere that uses directed energy to disable the visual inputs of security cameras. Such interference will be obvious to anyone monitoring the cameras.

CS Nano

Something meant only for law enforcement (although also known to occasionally fall into the hands of enterprising P.I.s or bounty hunters), CS nano is a thumb sized hive that can deploy nanobots that can completely search a gymnasium sized room in half an hour. When the search is complete, the bots will have a complete inventory of the contents of the room, including copies of any documents, unsecured computer files (and the location of protected ones) and the DNA of anyone who has been in the room in the last 10 days. In the latter case, the DNA must be paired up with a suitable database to provide identification.

Hexaphone

This device is issued to ETM operatives and can only be used by the person it is biometrically matched to. They come in many different models depending on one's department and seniority, but all of them can perform the following tasks to a greater or lesser degree with the more sophisticated models having bonuses.

Like any phone, other applications can be run if the appropriate software is installed.

Applications

At least some of these apps will be on an agent's phone at any given time.

Authority

The hexaphone will instantly sense who a person the agent is in contact with will recognize as an authority and identify the agent as that sort of person. It will compel any person without a ward or some other form of resistance to follow the agent's instructions. It will automatically fail against a warded person while those with the Arcane edge can resist it with a Spirit resistance roll. Misuse of this application in the CU is a felony crime that could lead to virtual banishment or death depending on the circumstances.

Banishment

This application gives the agent access to the Banish spell.

Ward

Renders the user immune to the effects of Authority software. It also provides a bonus to any magical defense equal to its rating.

Spells

Hexaphones allow even those without the Arcane edge to cast spells at Novice level at minimum risk. Phones of higher quality can cast more complex (higher level) spells equal to the level of the device, but only one spell can ever be sustained at once.

Thaumometer

This application is able to examine the nature of magical artifacts or phenomena the user is in the presence of by comparing them to an internal database at a skill level of D6 or modify the user's skill by +2.

Summoning Matrix

While summoning, directing or otherwise speaking with an Outsider is a capital crime in the CU, the phone can theoretically be used to summon them and it is rumored that applications exist to do so. Once an entity is called, it will usually perform a number of tasks or answer as many questions as the charter has raises on their summoning roll. If the GM wishes, the entity can demand services or items in exchange for its help. A single success summons the Outsider, but it is out of control of the person who called it. The behavior of the Outsider in such a circumstance is up to the GM.

Hacking Rig

Provides +1 to Hacking rolls, or can try to hack a system on its own with a skill rating of D6.

Spellcasting

Provides the user with access to the Spellcasting skill at D6. If the owner already has the Spellcasting skill, the software provides a +1 bonus.

Passkey

This highly illegal device produces nanobots that can cut through nearly any material, form a key to open mechanical locks or interfere with a magnetic or electronic lock by infiltrating its hardware with its microscopic robots. It will automatically open any lock with a rating less than its own, or will allow the owner a skill roll for those that equal or exceed it with a negative modifier for each point above its own rating.

The Passkey does nothing to disrupt alarms or security systems linked to the lock – this must be done separately by hacking the associated security system.

Puzzle Factory

A very expensive and rare type of Maker that is wired into the subconscious. When activated, it will produce an artifact produced from the deepest recesses of the character's psyche. The items produced can literally be anything from maps to nowhere to functioning machines of unknown purpose. With protein base blocks, it can even produce living things which oftentimes bear little or no resemblance to any known terrestrial creature. Due to its unpredictable nature, it is illegal anywhere where there is functioning law enforcement.

Search and Destroy Nano (SaDN)

These nanobots provide the user with information concerning the make up and capabilities of any nano present within 2 meters (outdoors) or 5 meters (indoors). The user can then indicate which nano they want eliminated, a process that takes only seconds provided the rating of the SaDN exceeds that of the target nano.

Spell Deck

This device is a featureless black box that contains a sophisticated computer of AI or near AI ability. AI models are especially dangerous in that they occasionally have their own agendas and have the capacity to go rogue. Generally they are a little less than a meter long, 300 cm wide and 100 cm thick. The dimensions and shape can vary since they are individually crafted, but they usually resemble a glossy black rectangle. In the CU only ETM specialists are cleared to possess them, and even then the devices are handled with the same care as a WMD.

The danger of proliferation is real, however, as anyone with the Arcane edge, a Spellcasting skill of D10+ and Computer Engineering (knowledge) of D8+ can construct a Spell Deck capable of casting spells equal to their level (Novice - Legendary) given time and access to the bizarre items needed to build one. Such individuals are extremely rare, of course, and those that exist are often given offers they can't refuse from their SMM of residence for employment in a very safe and secure location. Still, there are a number who have remained at large, and Spell Decks crafted by these people can be found 'in the wild'.

While a physical interface is possible, most don't have one as users tend to desire the speed that comes with an AR or VR interface. If given appropriate software, they can do everything a Hexphone can.

Spell Decks provide their user with five extra power points – this is in addition to any provided by applications or innate abilities. A character using it also gets to add +2 to their Spellcasting roll.

White Noise Generator

Prevents conversations from being overheard or recorded. Subtract the rating of the device from any listening apparatus – if the result is zero or less, the conversation cannot be heard.

PHARMACEUTICALS

Usable by organics only. Regular use may lead to the Habit hindrance (GM's call). All are illegal in the CU with the exception of Cram and Feather, which are tightly controlled and only issued on an as-needed basis.

Arkham

A favorite of cultists and the Outsider curious, this drug breaks down the mind's natural defenses against inter-dimensional exposure. It provides +2 to any roll to access the Dreamlands, Carcosa or to detect gates or other Outsider artifacts. One dose lasts for 4 hours – while under its influence, users will have -2 to all of their Sanity checks and suffer the Delusional hindrance.

Cram

+1 to Smarts linked skill rolls. Frequent use causes migraines (-2 to all activities).

D Bag

The character requires no sleep for 1 week. During this time, the character also gets +2 to any Intimidation rolls, +1 to Persuasion rolls and +1 to Networking. If any of these rolls fail, the character no longer gets the bonuses and instead is at -2 Charisma for the rest of the encounter.

Eyeball Grace

+1 to Perception and Agility linked rolls. Character acquires the Dodge edge and the Overconfidence hindrance. The drug's effects last for 1 hour, with the exception of Overconfidence, which will last for the rest of the day.

Feather

Erases penalty for gravity acclimation up to 2g, it is often used by pilots of high performance air and spacecraft. One dose lasts for 12 hours – when it wears off, feelings of vertigo are often experienced, giving -1 to Agility based skills.

Fray

Adds +1 to Strength and Vigor linked die rolls. +1 to Toughness. The character gets two initiative card draws and **must** pick the highest. They can also ignore the effects of one wound and cannot be Shaken. Character also receives -2 to Smarts and Perception while under its influence. The drug's effects last for fifteen minutes.

McShakes

The character gets three initiative card draws and chooses which one to use. They also get +1 action per turn, but both actions are at -1. If the character is surprised by anyone in any circumstance while under its effect, they must take a Spirit -1 check or react violently. The drug's effects last for one hour. Each use within a 24 hour period reduces the character's Toughness by -1 due to extremely high blood pressure.

Mr. MeeSee

Organics within 2 feet have a sudden impulse to provoke the character in some way. If a brawl is already underway, opponents close by will show a preference to attacking the character instead of anyone else. In both cases, a person will need to pass a Spirit check at -1 to resist.

Walk it Off (Wio)

This strong opiate allows the character to ignore two wound levels plus two levels of fatigue for 1 day. Once it wears off, any penalties from wounds or fatigue are doubled.

SOFTWARE AND HACKING

The most commonly used software is available free of charge in the CU. These applications are accessible by anyone via their Ginsert and can be experienced in either AR or VR modes. The programs available are nearly infinite in number, covering everything from image editing, educational programs and games to recipe templates for Makers. More specialized software is available to those in active employment and can be accessed by them anywhere at any time.

In order to use a skill on a computer, software matching the skill and the skill's rating must be present (for example, if one wanted to edit a film on their computer and their skill is D6, D6 film editing software must also be available). If the character's skill and software ratings don't match, always use the lowest rating when rolling for success. More sophisticated software can stand in for the skill itself, creating the desired item by following the user's instructions with a maximum rating of D6 (no Wild Die allowed).

There is also a software 'free market' in the CU, mostly consisting of various Maker templates crafted by individuals for bartering with their fellow citizens. These barter items are almost always harmless, but every so often an illegal item turns up. This contraband is very diverse, and can include hacking code, weapons templates, narcotics, spell ideograms or Outsider texts and artifacts.

Designing software for a task requires both the relevant skill and the Knowledge (Programming) skill. A simple success in both rolls is all that is needed to succeed, but the GM should feel free to assign modifiers if the character is working under difficult circumstances.

To create either templates (schematics used by Makers to create items) or software requires a skill roll that matches the nature of the product being crafted (for a example, an Artist skill roll must be made to create a template for creating a piece of pottery, or a Hacking skill roll to create Hacking software) followed by a successful Programming skill roll. Each raise in the related skill roll indicates a more beautiful/tasty/finely crafted product that will increase its usefulness, user experience and/or perceived value. Every second raise will benefit the owner with a +1 to their skill roll when it is used. (Example: a painting program created with a success and three raises will create software that will add +2 to the user's skill roll). Any raises in the Programming skill roll reduces the time to create the software by half (base of time of one week).

(Example: Mark wants to create a template that will recreate his signature chili for anyone who wants to try it. Being a man of diverse talents, he has both Artist (Cooking) and Programming at D6. He rolls a '4' and a '5' on his Wild Die for his Cooking roll, which is enough for a success. For his Programming roll, he gets a '3' and a '2' – he wastes one week unsuccessfully trying to capture the subtle nuances of his dish. Tossing several bowls of unpalatable experiments back into his Maker for recycling, he decides to keep at it. For the second week, he rolls a '1' and a '5' – success at last! He can now share his favorite recipe with friends or perhaps trade it for some nefarious goods he's had his eye on ..)

Iconography in VR systems is limited only by the imagination of the designer

HACKING

Hacking is the art of accessing and/or editing information in a restricted computer system, taking control of a subsystem that the computer controls, crashing it, or otherwise making it behave in a way that is against the intentions of its owners. Because the speed required for hacking is far in excess of human norms, the only way it can be accomplished is in VR mode. The VR's appearance is limited only by the designer's imagination and resources.

Hacking can be accomplished by having hacking software and using the Hacking skill (with Smarts being the linked attribute).

This is done using the following steps:
1. Find system address (optional). This is only necessary if the owner of the targeted system has taken pains to hide it and the hacker is trying to access it remotely. To gain a system address, use the Networking skill with a suitable contact or other individual. Online research can also turn it up, but this will require a separate hacking attempt. In both cases, the owner of the system might be tipped off by the hacker's inquiries and take any precautions they deem necessary.
2. Access the computer system. The hacker must convince the system they are a legitimate user. To do this, they must first succeed in getting a success on a hacking

roll, modified by the computer's Firewall rating (usually a zero for low security systems, with increasing negative modifiers for stronger security). If the hacker rolls especially well, they will receive a +1 to their next roll for every raise they obtain.
3. After this is done, any programs or files without further protection can be accessed and modified. Items of a sensitive nature will often be encrypted or secured in some other fashion – every such item must be hacked separately in order to access it.
4. Most computer systems will have a series of protocols to use if it believes it's being illegally accessed, with every failed hacking roll moving the response one step further. The GM should make up a list that will outline its response to such intrusions. If a hacker succeeds in their Hacking roll against a particular protocol, that protocol is defeated and no longer in effect.

Here is an example of a list of protocols that would protect a secure system:

1. Firewall's effectiveness increases by 1. A successful Hacking roll can reset it - otherwise, it stays at its new level until the Hacker leaves the system.

2. System tries to trace Hacker's location and alert the owner and/or the authorities (must succeed in a Hacking roll modified by the system's current Firewall rating to avoid).

3. As above, but the system tries to launch a counter attack along with a new trace attempt if the previous one was defeated. The character must succeed in a Hacking roll or have their device damaged (-4 on all future Hacking rolls until repaired). Failure on this roll also means the character must pass a Spirit check or get Shaken and dumped from the system. If they pass, they have the option to log off before the trace is completed. If the character is dumped, the target system's trace attempt automatically succeeds.

4. The system attempts a more serious attack with a new trace attempt as above. In this case, the character must succeed in a Hacking roll or have their device destroyed. If this happens, the device is beyond repair and everything in its memory has been corrupted. The character is dumped, Shaken, takes one wound that can be resisted normally (via a Soak roll) and the target system's trace attempt automatically succeeds.

5. The system attempts a deadly attack with a new trace attempt as above. The character must succeed in a Hacking roll or have all content on their device uploaded to the system they're attacking. The device is then destroyed as above, and the character is Shaken and takes three wounds that can be resisted normally. If the character is dumped, the target system's trace attempt automatically succeeds.

6. The system shuts down. The system under attack will attempt one final attack as above before shutting down. Every subsystem the computer controls will immediately cease functioning. The character has two more turns before they are dumped – if this happens they have to pass a Vigor check or be Shaken.

The GM is of course free to think up other consequences or levels of escalation. Perhaps instead of wounding a character, the targeted system digitizes their consciousness and uploads it? Or perhaps a vending machine owner is tired of hackers getting freebies and gets some software that immediately goes to step four above. Options for both attack and defense will be further outlined in the software section.

One hacker attacking another is handled in pretty much the same way. The hacker on defense can either rely on their system's security counter-measures (as above) or go after the intruder with their own software. If they do the latter, each player makes a Hacking roll modified by their opponent's Firewall attribute. The character with the highest roll is the winner, who is then able to execute whatever program they have ready against their opponent. If the defender wins, they have the option to activate any of their computer's defensive protocols against the intruder in lieu of some other attack.

Quick Hacks

For minor hacking jobs to gain information to move the story along, the GM should feel free to use an abbreviated version of the above system. A simple Hacking roll with a difficulty modifier appropriate for the situation, with a particular intrusion countermeasure response will suffice for many situations. The idea first and foremost should be to keep the plot moving to keep any players not involved from becoming distracted or bored.

Joint Hacks

Another option for hacking would be to have all of the players involved in the process. In this case, players can make cooperative rolls to add +1 to the chief Hacker's rolls for every success they make. While none of their failures would count for advancing the security script, they would suffer the consequences of any attacks the hacked system makes in its defense. Players could also run interference with any security hackers while another party member is busy decrypting, downloading or altering files.

Use of Joint Hacks could allow for deeper and more involved virtual adventures since the whole party would be involved!

SOFTWARE

Hacking and Intrusion Countermeasures

With the exception of Firewall and Attack (Track), these items are illegal even in areas of low law enforcement. Generally, hackers will write their own software and will be reluctant to create it for anyone else since it could be traced back to them. If they do sell a copy, it will command a high price and/or have to be for a very compelling reason. Well crafted versions of these programs will give the possessor a bonus of +1 or higher to their roll when using them.

Software must have a rating at least equal to the hacker's Hacking skill. When attempting to hack a system, use the lower of the two values.

The intrusion countermeasure versions of these programs will usually automatically take effect if the hacker fails a hacking roll with their exact effects spelled out by the GM when he creates the system's defense protocols.

Hack
Required to use the Hacking skill.

Attack (Wound)
Every hit and raise on a Hacking roll will cause an opposing Hacker to be Shaken. If they're incapacitated, the attacker has the option to send a feedback pulse to their target's hacking device, ruining it and possibly causing a small fire.

Attack (Stun)
Every hit and raise on a Hacking roll will cause an opposing Hacker to become fatigued. The attacker also has the option of destroying their opponent's hacking device if they're incapacitated as outlined above.

Attack (Track)
A hit will cause a trace to begin that will finish in eight rounds, with each raise halving the required time. The target can prevent the trace with a successful Hacking roll. When the trace finishes, the target's location will be reported to the software's owner or their agents.

Attack (Psychotropic)
A hit will plant a suggestion in the target's mind, with each raise added as a negative modifier for the target to resist the suggestion. The target must pass a Spirit check to resist. Once every 24 hours, the target can try to erase the suggestion by passing a Spirit check, applying a negative modifier for every raise scored by the software in its initial attack.

Attack (Fry)
A hit will damage or destroy an opposing Hacker's computer, dumping them from the system and making them Shaken.

Firewall Upgrade
Adds an additional negative modifier against Hacking rolls.

Notice

Allows a Hacker to make an opposed roll to detect a file or Hacker running Stealth software. Operating in the background, it will automatically try to detect hidden items, with the GM making a secret roll to see if it succeeds.

Stealth

Allows a Hacker to appear as an innocuous file or random system noise. Another Hacker will have to make a successful opposed Notice roll (with appropriate software) in order to take action against the character.

Stealth (military grade)

Also known as an Icebreaker, this software is in use only by well funded government agencies with occasional use by major corporations. In addition to the usual Stealth program capabilities, it reduces the effectiveness of Firewalls by one for each point of its rating (a D4 would reduce a Firewall's effectiveness by 1, while a D6 rating would reduce its effectiveness by 2, etc.).

Watcher

Provides a negative rating to any hacking attempt as the system diverts resources to more closely examine user operations. The software's rating ranges from -1 to -4.

Hacking Example

Hearing a local restaurant has stolen his chili recipe, Mark decides to take revenge.
He can skip finding the restaurant's system address since they have taken no steps to hide it.
Mark now has to convince the restaurant's computer he is a legit user who has the authority to make changes to its operating system. To do this, he has a Hacking skill of D8, with Hacking software rated at D8+1. The restaurant's operating system has an unusually strong Firewall rating of -1 (Maybe they're an organized crime front? Careful Mark!). This will give Mark a net 0 modifier when making his roll. Mark rolls well, getting a '6' on his Hacking skill die and aces his Wild die, rolling a '6', then a '4', giving him a final roll of '10'. This is enough for a raise, which will give his next roll an extra +1!

Having gained access to the restaurant's network, Mark is able to find his recipe. It's been encrypted at a rating of -1, so he'll have to make another Hacking roll to access it. With the -1 Firewall rating, this makes his total negative modifier -2. His previous raise and software will give him a net modifier of '0' however. He rolls a '1' on his skill die and a '2' on his Wild die – this won't be enough to succeed!

The system he's trying to hack is now on alert. The first step in its list of security protocols is to give a further -2 to Hacking rolls as it more carefully monitors activity. Mark now has a difficult choice to make – will he continue his effort or leave the recipe where it is? Having gotten this far, Mark decides to continue.

The modifier to decrypt the file is now -3 (-1 for decryption, -1 for firewall, -2 for system alert, +1 for Mark's software). Mark fails both of his rolls but decides to use one of his Bennies for a reroll. This time his skill roll is a '7' (modified to a '4'), while his Wild die comes up as a '4' (modified to a '1') – his skill roll succeeds! After decrypting the file, he manages to get another successful Hacking roll, modifying it so when the recipe is made, a potent laxative is included. Having succeeded in his scheme of revenge, Mark withdraws with the restaurant's owners being none the wiser.

Fight Between Hackers Example

Bruno, the owner of Bruno's Bistro, isn't sure who spiked his new chili recipe but thinks he has a pretty good idea. After doing some social networking to find out where Mark hangs out online, Bruno loads up his Stealth software and tries to conceal himself for an ambush in Mark's favorite online gaming bar. Bruno has a Hacking skill of D6, which is matched by his Stealth software rated at D6. He rolls a '5', which becomes the number Mark will have to roll to detect him.

Looking forward to some virtual gaming and drinks, Mark strolls into the Gritty Kitty Lounge. His Notice software is always up and running and tries to detect Bruno. Mark's Hacking skill is a D8, but his Notice software is D6 so that's the die type he'll have to roll, plus his Wild die. Mark's Notice die aces and ends up as a '9' (a success with a raise!), with his Wild die rolling a '2'.

Since he succeeded so handily, the GM decides that Mark turns the tables on Bruno and ambushes him instead. This is good, because Mark's card draw is a lowly '3'. He decides to attack Bruno, who won't be able to act in the first round of combat due to being ambushed. Mark has Attack (Stun) D6 ready to go, so he rolls D6 plus his Wild die, getting a '5' and a '3'. Bruno has a Firewall of -1, so the '5' is sufficient for a hit. Bruno suffers one point of fatigue – all of his trait linked rolls will now be at -1!

For the next round of combat, Mark draws a '5' and Bruno gets a '2'. Mark fires again, acing his skill roll to a '9' while his Wild die comes up as a '3'. Even with Bruno's Firewall, the '9' (modified to an '8') is enough to score a raise, meaning two more points of fatigue for Bruno! This is enough to incapacitate him. Back in his restaurant, Bruno slumps over his keyboard, unconscious.

Mark has the option now of destroying his opponent's Ginsert, which would not only prevent him from hacking, but would cut him off from accessing the GIN until he could get it repaired! Not wanting to start a feud or get the Law involved, Mark decides to withdraw, hoping his opponent has learned his lesson!

(Designer's note: The Hacking rules are a deliberately simplified version of the SW combat system. I did this to cut down on the amount of time Hacking takes during a play session, as there's usually only one player involved.)

MAGIC

Magic in AoC represents a transfer of energy from other dimensions into our own in order to bring about a desired effect. Since the energy is channeled directly through the item used to summon it (be it an Outsider artifact, computer, or human mind), use of magic is a dangerous prospect with only the foolhardy, reckless or insane attempting it using the delicate tissue of their brains. For all of its fragility, a sapient mind can be used to cast a spell if the caster is willing to suffer the often catastrophic consequences.

Spells in AoC come in varying levels of complexity (Novice, Seasoned, Veteran, Heroic and Legendary), with the alterations to reality increasing with each level. The power used to generate and sustain spells are called power points (for a description of these, see the Powers section of the Savage Worlds Rulebook) – these can either be generated by software, an artifact, possession of the Arcane Edge, a ritual or some combination of these. This power is expended to transfer the required amount of energy from the alien dimension being accessed to our own.

Spell casting aids come in different varieties, with Hexaphones being the most common and Spell Decks less so. Artifacts are also used to aid casting, but their use is generally forbidden in the CU as they can have unforeseen consequences on the consciousness of the user.

Hexaphones are sophisticated enough to cast spells unaided, but the spells will still need an energy source (power points), which can be provided possession of the Arcane edge and/or by an application designed to generate them. No Spellcasting skill is required to use a Hexaphone, nor is the Arcane edge required, but both have their advantages in their use as will be seen.

Artifacts run the gamut of ability, with some minor examples capable of casting Novice level spells with no ability to access their own power points to world ending monstrosities capable of casting Legendary level spells and drawing upon tremendous levels of power from one or several dimensions. The latter, of course, are extremely rare, but are known to exist with one or more being in the possession of the CU. Most, but not all, artifacts require the Arcane edge to use.

Rituals can be used to increase the power of a spell, generate power points, cast the spell at a distant target or all of these. There are no hard and fast rules for rituals - the GM should tailor any requirements to the needs of their story and the complexity of what is being attempted.
A caster can also try to use a spell unaided, using their minds - to do so they need the Arcane edge and a Spellcasting skill. There are sometimes ramifications to casting a spell in such a way. (see 'consequences' table below).

To create a new spell, a person must have an artistic or programming skill equal to its rank (starting at D6 for Novice) and the Arcane edge. They must then succeed in both a Spellcasting and Artistic test (or Programming for software) in order for the spell to function. Each level of the spell above Novice adds -1 to the roll. If the result falls below zero, the formula is unworkable and the character must start over. If a critical failure is rolled, consult the consequences table used for a character using their mind to cast a spell.

The base time to complete the formula is one week. Each raise can either halve the required time or add a benefit chosen by the designer. The benefit can vary depending on the type of spell being designed, but shouldn't be greater than the equivalent of a +1 modifier or increasing the die type by one.

Modern spells are most often created as software that can be used by a Spell Deck or Hexaphone, but other mediums can also be used, such as paintings or sculpture. Such works are highly illegal, but very much in demand by collectors as well as practitioners of magic.

To summarize: Spells need either an artifact or a computer (either a digital one or an organic one like the human mind) to be cast. Using a digital device minimizes the danger to the caster. The spell needs to be powered, which is supplied by power points from a caster with the Arcane edge, a spell, a program, a ritual or some combination of these. Using a Hexaphone, Spell Deck or certain artifacts means that the person casting the spell need not possess the Arcane edge.

Rituals can raise the power level of a spell by any amount, generate power points, cast a spell at a distant target, or all of these.

The Spellcasting skill is not only used to cast spells, but also to design spell related applications or artifacts – creation of these also requires the Arcane edge, and an artistic or programming skill.

Consequences

If a character rolls a critical failure while using any magic-related skill, roll a D12 and consult the following tables:

If an inorganic computer was used

1 – 4: Program crashes. Computer devices must be restarted in order for the software to reinitialize. Any other software running continues to function as normal.

5 – 8: Device crashes. All software running immediately ceases to function. Device must be restarted

9 – 10: Device crashes. Software corrupted. Software is no longer functional and must be replaced. If a character is unable to pass a Spirit -2 check, they are shaken.

11: Device corrupted and melts into useless slag. Charter must pass a Spirit -2 check or suffer one wound.

12: Character corrupted. Device explodes with malevolent energy, doing 2d6 damage within a small blast radius template. If the character survives, they must take a Spirit check at -2 or be possessed by an Outsider of the GM's choice. The character is still under the control of the player, but is expected to behave in a manner consistent with their predicament.

If a character uses their mind

1 – 2: Character is shaken

3 – 4: Character falls unconscious for 1D4 hours.

5 – 6: Scorched. The character must pass a Vigor at -1 test or take one wound.

7 – 8: Synaptic Failure. The character must pass a Vigor at -2 check or take two wounds and lose their Arcane edge.

9 – 10: Hemorrhage. The character must pass a Vigor at -3 check or suffer three wounds and lose their Arcane edge. If they pass, they must then pass a Spirit check at -2 or be possessed as described in the table above.

11: AHH! The character must pass a Vigor at -3 check or have their features melt in a spectacularly upsetting way for anyone observing (Sanity check at -1). The character is dead. If they pass the Vigor check, they must pass a Spirit check at -3 or be possessed as above.

12: AHHHHHH! The character must pass a Vigor check at -4 or explode in a surge of arcane energy for 3d6 damage within a small blast template. An Outsider determined by the GM emerges from their remains.

Consequences for a critical failure when using an artifact for spell casting are varied, but can easily be as harsh (or worse) than a character using their mind to do so. The GM should create a similar table to the ones above for each artifact in their game, but keep them a secret from the players.

Use of magic runs the gamut from subtle manipulations to major reality warping effects.

GRIMOIRE

All spells have associated software that is available to allow the characters to cast them more safely through a digital device. Possession of spell software is highly illegal in most SMMs.
In addition to those listed here, spells from the Savage Worlds Rulebook can also be used. If a spell is included that is also in the rule book, the rules here take precedence.

If a spell has a duration of 'sustained', it can be continued indefinitely at the listed cost. Arcane characters can utilize higher levels of spells after attaining the required rank, but can use lower level versions if desired.

Generate Power Points

Artifact or software only. Creates a channel to an alternate dimension to draw power from for the purpose of casting or sustaining a spell. The most common examples provide a two power point boost, with rarer versions providing more.

Spell Casting

Users of computers or artifacts who don't possess an Arcane edge require this software to utilize spells. The skill level possessed by the software can run from D4 to D8.

Armor

All Armor spells have a range of Touch.

Rank: Novice
A success will grant the caster 4 points of type 1 armor protection, 6 points with a raise.
Power Points: 2
Duration: 3 (1/round)

Rank: Seasoned

As above, but AP modifiers for weapons are N/A.
Power Points: 4
Duration: 3 (1/round)

Rank: Veteran
As above, but 6 points of protection, 8 with a raise.
Power Points: 6
Duration: 3 (1/round)

Rank: Heroic
A success will grant 4 points of type 2 protection, 6 points with a raise.
Power Points: 8
Duration: 3 (1/round)

Rank: Legendary
As above, but the AP modifier of attacks is N/A. Will also grant a save vs type 3 and 4 damage with a successful Spirit roll with a negative modifier equal to the damage of the attack.
Power Points: 10
Duration: 3 (1/round)

Authority

Causes the device to display an ideogram that will make the person seeing it recognize the presenter as an authority who is entitled to access or cooperation (the presenter can have a particular authority in mind if they wish). It will automatically fail against a warded person while those with the Arcane edge can resist it with a Spirit resistance roll.
Power Points: 1
Rank: Novice
Range: Smarts
Duration: Sustained (1/round)

Banishment (Exorcism)

Removes any Outsider entity that has taken residence in our reality or hijacked a terrestrial being's neural net. It can also return agency to anyone being influenced by a Puppet spell. Every power point expended after the first adds +1 to the roll. Powerful entities in possession of individuals may induce negative modifiers if the GM deems it appropriate.
Power Points: 1
Rank: Veteran
Range: Smarts
Duration: Instant

Bolt/Blast/Burst

These damaging spells operate in a similar fashion to their counterparts in the rulebook. Bolt does type one damage, while Blast and Burst do type two.

Control Non-Sapients

All of the Control Non-Sapients spells have a range of Smarts x 100 meters and a duration of 5 minutes. Each raise will double the amount of time the creature is under control, while tripling the power points required will make the control permanent. A raise in the latter case will give the caster a more interesting outcome as determined by the GM (examples: the targeted creature now has the power of speech, pass through solid objects or have access to a single Novice level spell). Creatures friendly to the caster will not resist, while those with a neutral disposition can resist using their Spirit attribute. Those that are magical or actively hostile to the caster get a +2 to their roll (cumulative) . Neutral or hostile creatures will attack or flee on a failed attempt to control them.

Starting with the Seasoned rank, the caster can choose to control a single lower level creature and share that creature's sensory experiences. The caster can also give the creature commands while in this state, but will suffer a Shaken result if the creature is wounded or a wound if they are killed.

Rank: Novice
Control a single small creature (medium sized dog or smaller).
Power Points: 3

Rank: Seasoned
Control a single medium sized creature (human sized or smaller) or several smaller ones.
Power Points: 5

Rank: Veteran
Control a single large creature (size +1 to +2), several smaller ones, or a swarm that covers a small template.
Power Points: 8

Rank: Heroic
Control a single huge creature (size +3 to +5), several smaller ones, or a swarm that covers a medium template.
Power Points: 12

Rank: Legendary
Control a single gargantuan creature (size +6 to +9), several smaller ones, or a swarm that covers a large template.
Power Points: 15

Divination

Divination is the ability to contact the deceased or an Outsider entity for the purpose of gaining information. No entity thus summoned is compelled to tell the truth except under certain circumstances, and even then they might try to manipulate the summoner into certain courses of action that are in their interest – both the dead and demons have agendas of their own. If the entity does not wish to be summoned, the summoner must subtract two from their roll. Even if they succeed, the entity will be annoyed and uncooperative.

If the summoner has an object or information that the entity finds useful or compelling in any way, it can be offered in trade. If it is accepted, the entity must provide truthful answers, although the number of questions and topics allowed to be addressed might be limited.

A raise or extra power points can also be used to compel a truthful answer, with one question allowed for each raise/power point expended. This can be resisted by the entity's Spirit, with each success and raise it generates reducing the questions allowed by one. If the entity resists completely, it will depart. This method will not win you any friends, and the entity or its masters may seek revenge.

The range for all Divination spells is 'Self' with a duration of one minute.

Rank: Novice
The recently deceased (up to one week) can be contacted, or an Outsider entity with 1D6 in applicable knowledge.
Power Points: 3

Rank: Seasoned
The spirit of a person who has been dead up to a month can be contacted, or an Outsider with 1D6+2 in applicable knowledge.
Power Points: 5

Rank: Veteran
The spirit of a person who has been dead for up to one year can be contacted, or an Outsider with applicable knowledge at D8+2.
Power Points: 8

Rank: Heroic
The spirit of a person who has been dead up to 100 years can be contacted, or an Outsider with applicable knowledge at D10+2.
Power Points: 12

Rank: Legendary
Any deceased person can be contacted or an Outsider with applicable knowledge at D12+2.
Power Points: 15

Environmental Shield

This Power allows the caster to breathe, speak and move at their normal pace in toxic or otherwise harmful environments. Range is touch, duration is one hour with each raise adding an extra hour.

Rank: Novice
Provides protection in an Earth-like setting from environments that would prove fatiguing or dangerous over time (deserts, arctic terrain, etc).
Power Points: 2

Rank: Seasoned
As above, it also provides protection in an Earth-like setting in environments that could be quickly or instantly fatal (water at any temperature or depth, lava, radiation).
Power Points: 4

Rank: Veteran
As above, it also provides protection in a total vacuum, including deep space or planets with no atmosphere.
Power Points: 6

Rank: Heroic
As above, it also provides protection in extremely hazardous extraterrestrial environments, such as the atmosphere of a gas giant, the surface of Venus or the depths of a star.
Power Points: 8

Rank: Legendary
As above, it also provides protection in extra-dimensional environments where matter as we understand it cannot exist (different universes, dimensions or other reality-altering environments).
Power Points: 10

Flight

This power allows the character to move in three dimensions instead of two. It may have to be combined with other powers (such as **Environmental Shield**) to do so safely. All flight powers have a range of Touch. Each raise can either double the speed or halve the power points required.

Rank: Novice
Can float at ½ speed
Power Points: 2
Duration: Sustained (1/round)

Rank: Seasoned
Can fly at normal speed.
Power Points: 3
Duration: Sustained (1/round)

Rank: Veteran
Can fly at up to 150 kph
Power Points: 4
Duration: Sustained (2/round)

Rank: Heroic
Can fly at up to 1500 kph
Power Points: 6
Duration: Sustained (2/round)

Rank: Legendary
Can fly at up to 150,000 kph
Power Points: 8
Duration: Sustained (3/round)

Glamour

The character appears pleasing to those observing them, with each person seeing someone a little different depending on their personal desires. The spell can be cast at different levels depending on the caster's rank. Note that Outsiders are not affected by Glamour other than making the spell caster more noticeable.
Range (for all levels): Touch

Rank: Novice
Character gains a +1 Charisma bonus. The character has a healthy glow about them, moves gracefully and seems focused on the observer. Simple requests will be granted with the affected party able to make a Spirit roll to resist if the request is inconvenient.
Power Points: 1
Duration: Sustained (1/round)

Rank: Seasoned
Character gains a +2 Charisma bonus. In addition to the effects of the Novice spell, the character's mannerisms can slightly alter themselves to fit the ideals of the observer. Simple requests can be made with a Spirit roll at -1 to resist for the affected party. In addition, the character will start receiving attention from attracted parties and given preferential treatment and the benefit of the doubt in most social situations.
Power Points: 2
Duration: Sustained (2/round)

Rank: Veteran
As above, but Spirit rolls are at -2 to resist requests. Affected characters must make a Spirit roll to react in a negative fashion against the spell caster. Strangers will offer to help if the character is perceived to be in some sort of difficulty. Attacks against the character are at -1 unless targeted by an automated system.
Power Points: 3
Duration: Sustained (3/round)

Rank: Heroic
As above, but characters can significantly change their appearance (including clothing) to blend into various social situations and appeal to observers. Note that this is not a disguise – if anything, it's the opposite since the character will be difficult to overlook. Moderate requests (inconvenient, but not dangerous) can be made with a Spirit roll by the affected party to resist. Simple requests are often granted automatically, usually without the character even having to ask. Affected characters must make a Spirit roll at -2 to react negatively to the spell caster, with any attacks against them at -2 unless by an automated system.
Power Points: 4
Duration: Sustained (4/round)

Rank: Legendary
As above, but attracted parties tend to keep their distance, approaching only if the spell caster wishes it. Potentially life threatening requests of individuals can be made, with a successful Spirit roll required to resist. More mundane requests are often granted without the spell caster having to ask. Note that it is impossible to be incognito with this level of glamour – the character will stand out and draw attention to themselves.
Power Points: 5
Duration: Sustained (5/round)

Healing

This power is capable of healing both physical and emotional trauma as well as fatigue, disease and poison. It can do nothing against corruption, however. The range for all Healing spells is touch and duration instant.

Rank: Novice
This version of the spell must be applied within one hour of the trauma being received. One success heals one wound, shaken result or level of fatigue, with a raise healing two. The roll suffers a -1 penalty for each level of trauma taken.
In addition, the spell can cure a minor illness (occasional cough, minor fever), sober up an intoxicated person or offer temporary relief for an allergy (one hour per success).
Power Points: 2

Rank: Seasoned
As above, but there is no time limit for the spell being applied. In addition, it can cure a more serious illness (any common malady that might keep a person home for a few days) or cancel the effects of paralysis poison.
Power Points: 4

Rank: Veteran
As above, but there is no penalty taken for the trauma level of the subject. In addition, it can cure a life threatening illness (smallpox, leprosy, most cancers) or cancel the effects of venomous poison.
Power Points: 8

Rank: Heroic
As above, but it can cure a fatal or crippling illness (bubonic plague, lung cancer, polio). In addition, it can cancel the effects of lethal poison or radiation sickness. Can heal a non-permanent injury and revive a person who has been incapacitated if they succeed with a roll at -3. Can cure a psychotic condition if they succeed with a roll of -2.
Power Points: 12

Rank: Legendary
As above, but can cure any bioengineered virus or nano infection. Can heal a non-permanent injury or cure a psychotic condition with no penalty, revive an incapacitated person if they succeed with a roll at -2 or heal a permanent injury (including reattaching severed limbs). The character can also revive someone who has died with a success at -4 (the body must still be intact and preserved) and cure disabilities not related to injury, such as blindness.
Power Points: 20

Infiltration

This spell summons energy to manipulate light waves, with more advanced versions altering the physical form of the caster themselves, or even shifting them into a parallel dimension.
The range for all Infiltration spells is touch.

Rank: Novice
Causes the light around the user to shift so that it mimics that of their surroundings. The effect gives them +1 to Stealth checks and -1 to attacks targeting them, with a raise giving an additional +1/-1.
Power Points: 2
Duration: Sustained (1/round)

Rank: Seasoned

This version of the spell renders the caster invisible by bending light waves around them. The caster can still be sensed by their thermal emissions, scent or sonar. The effect gives them +4 to Stealth checks and -4 to attacks made against them. A raise renders the caster completely invisible, changing the modifier to +6/-6.
Power Points: 3
Duration: Sustained (2/round)

Rank: Veteran

As above, but the user is no longer detectable by scent, heat or sonar.
Power Points: 6
Duration: Sustained (3/round)

Rank: Heroic

The character is intangible and cannot be affected by non-magical items. There is a physical presence in the form of a mist or shadow that is utterly silent and undetectable by thermal sensors, scent or sonar. It gives a +4 to Stealth checks and a -2 to ranged attacks due to its shifting outlines. In this form the caster can seep through the narrowest of openings or fly at ¼ speed.
Power Points: 12
Duration: Sustained (4/round)

Rank: Legendary

The character is completely out of phase with our reality. They have no physical presence, but can still be affected by magical items. They can move through solid objects (unless these are warded) and fly at ½ speed. While out of phase, they can only affect their surroundings with magic or magical items. A raise allows them to affect their surroundings physically as well by rapidly blinking in and out of phase.
Power Points: 15
Duration: Sustained (5/round)

Necromancy

Necromancy is the reanimation of dead tissue, be it an entire body or a piece of it. Higher levels of the spell will create a more intelligent and capable entity, with Legendary examples displaying some (or all) aspects of the deceased individual's personality and knowledge. Any person raised will follow their summoner's instructions. More sophisticated examples will offer alternatives to the summoner's request or ask questions, but will ultimately carry out the Necromancer's will.

Necromancy is anathema in most SMMs, but others embrace it.

Tripling the number of Power Points required will make the creation permanent – otherwise, its existence must be sustained. Each raise rolled during spell casting can be used to purchase an Edge or add +1 die type to the raised creature. This die can be used to either add a new skill, improve one already possessed or enhance an attribute.

Any cybernetic or biological enhancements that the raised character possessed while alive will also be available to their undead form.

If the spell casting roll fails by two or less, the creature can still be raised but will have a number of Hindrances (chosen by the GM) equal to the difference between what was rolled and what was needed.

All raised creatures trigger a Fear check from those unfamiliar with them and have an inherent bite/claw attack that does D6+Str damage. The range of all Necromancy spells is Touch.

Rank: Novice

The character can reanimate any dead tissue, but it will be immobile unless it has legs, fingers or some other means of getting about. Any such creation will have attributes of D4 and one skill at D4 of the caster's choice. They can utter single words or make other vocal sounds, but are unlikely to impart any useful information. They move at speed 2 and are immune to Fear, Intimidation, fatigue and poison. They have +2 added to their toughness, have a +2 modifier to recover from being Shaken. Called shots do no extra damage with the exception of the head. In addition, they have no Sanity or Corruption attribute and are immune to the presence of Outsider entities (although they can be possessed by them).

Power Points: 2
Duration: Sustained (1/round)
Inherent Skill: Fighting D4

Rank: Seasoned

As above, but D6 Str., Agl. and Vig. attributes. One skill chosen by the caster can be at D6. This creature can speak in simple sentences and answer yes or no questions about common, non-complex aspects of their prior existence. Move is at Speed 4.

Power Points: 4
Duration: Sustained (2/round)
Inherent Skill: Fighting D6

Rank: Veteran

As above, but has D8 Str., Agl. and Vig. attributes. One skill chosen by the caster can be at D8. Can speak in simple sentences and answer questions about common aspects of their prior existence. For an additional four power points, an otherwise immobile entity can be granted locomotion by any appropriate means devised by the caster (floating, growing limbs, etc). Move is at Speed 6

Power Points: 6
Duration: Sustained (3/round)
Inherent Skill: Fighting D8

Rank: Heroic

As above, but its Str., Agl. and Vig. scores will equal those it had while living if above D8. Its Spt. and Smt. attributes will be equal to those while living at -1 die type. In addition to its D8 skill, it will have the skills it had in life at -1 die type. It can speak in complex sentences and answer any questions about its prior existence, although complicated matters and detailed memories will require a Smarts -2 roll to recall.

Move is at Speed 8
Power Points: 8
Duration: Sustained (4/round)
Inherent Skill: Fighting D10

Rank: Legendary

As above, but the reanimated character will have all the attributes they possessed while living if above D8, with one of the caster's choices being at +2 to any rolls associated with it. They have all the skills they possessed while alive and can use them without penalty. In addition, they have one skill at D8 chosen by the caster. They have an almost perfect recall of the events of their previous lives. If the character was a Wild Card in life, they are now as well – any Hindrances or Edges are also present. Move is at Speed 8

Power Points: 10
Duration: Sustained (5/round)
Inherent Skill: Fighting D12

Thaumometer

Will detect the presence of magic or Outsider activity. Requires either a Spellcasting, or Outsider (Knowledge) skill to use, with each raise providing increasing levels of detail.

Power Points: 1
Rank: Novice
Range: Smarts
Duration: Sustained (1/round)

Ward

Provides immunity against the Authority spell. Any spell cast against the character or attempt to possess them receives a negative modifier equal to -1 for every power point expended, increasing by one for every additional level of protection (for example, getting a -2 would require 2 power points, -3 3 power points, etc.). Can automatically activate if the character comes under attack without their knowledge.

Power Points: 1
Rank: Novice
Range: Touch
Duration: Sustained (1/round)

Spell Design and Use Example

Tina the Necromage watched in disgust as another assistant fled in terror into the night, their screams of terror fading away into the depths of the forest. 'If I'm going to have a reliable assistant,' she thought to herself, 'I'll have to create one!!'

Unfortunately, despite her extensive library, Tina doesn't have the necessary spell so she'll have to design it. There are many options for making an undead assistant, so Tina will have to consider what it is she needs. After some consideration, she decides that something that can follow simple commands and bellow 'Yes Mistress!' to acknowledge them will be sufficient. This means creating a Necromancy spell at Seasoned level. Tina has the Arcane Edge, along with Artist (Painting) at D10. Since this exceeds the spell's design requirements, she can proceed. Setting up her oils and canvas in her studio, she begins painting an ideogram that represents her ideal assistant.

Tina can now roll to see if she succeeds. Since the spell she's trying to create is at 'Seasoned' level, her rolls will be at -1. Rolling her Spellcasting skill of D10, her results are '4', with another '4' on her Wild Die – these are both modified to '3'. Her Artistic skill roll is a '10', which aces to a '14' (modified to '13' – two raises!). While the painting itself is exquisite, she wasn't able to instill the necessary magical qualities into the design – she'll have to continue working.

Her next artistic roll is a '9', while her Spellcasting roll comes up as a '6'. After adding the -1 modifier, these end up as a '8 (a success with a raise), and '5' – more than adequate! Now she has to decide how to apply the raises she rolled during the spell's creation (a total of 3). Being a busy woman with Things To Do, she applies the first raise to halving the required time (since she didn't succeed on her first try, the base time is two weeks. Applying the raise will bring it back down to one). She decides the second raise should be used to give her a better quality assistant, so Tina uses it to add +1 to her creation's skill.

Looking at her design, Tina sees that her assistant will have D6 attributes, but she needs to choose a skill. Deciding on Knowledge (Necromancy), her creature will receive this skill when it's completed, with an added +1 due to Tina spending one of her raises on improving it. Having recently leveled up, Tina chooses the 'New Power' Edge as her new ability and can now use the spell. To do so she will first need certain...materials.

Having acquired a skeleton by bribing a medical student at a local college, Tina prepares to bring her new assistant to life! Tina possesses an artifact called the Eye of Ramses that allows her to cast any Necromancy spell up to Heroic level with a +1 modifier.

After expending the necessary twelve power points needed to make the spell permanent, she rolls her Spellcasting skill die of D10, which aces to a '13'! With her artifact's modifier, the final result is '14'. Setting aside her Wild Die roll (a '4'), Tina calculates the benefits of her successful roll. With two raises on the roll, Tina can improve the die types of her creation's attributes and/or skills twice. Wanting the most competent lab assistant possible, she raises its Smarts attribute to D8 and its Knowledge (Necromancy) skill to D8.

"Rise! Rise, my creation!" Tina shouts as the corpse rises slowly to its feet.

Hexaphone Example

This next example demonstrates a person without the Arcane Edge using magic by utilizing a computer – in this case, a Hexaphone. Note that if the character did possess the Arcane Edge, the points generated by the phone would be in addition to the ones they already had.

Agent Kamilla has stumbled upon what she suspects to be a front for a cultist organization – a restaurant called Bruno's Bistro! Having broken into the restaurant's back door, she sneaks into the kitchen and pulls out her Hexaphone. The device is currently running Generate Spell Points (2) and Spellcasting D6. Scrolling through her list of available programs, Kamilla selects Thaumometer. This spell uses a single power point, so her software will provide enough juice to sustain it. She rolls a D6 plus her Wild Die, getting a '4' and a '2' respectively. The '4' is sufficient for a success, the device registering a nearby disturbance being caused by something not from this dimension. Feeling her pulse climb, Kamilla activates the Ward program on her phone – she can only allocate a single power point to it if she wants to continue using the Thaumometer. Wanting to continue her investigation, she feeds a single point to her Ward and moves as quietly as she can towards the source of the disturbance.

TOMES

Tomes are repositories of Outsider knowledge, ranging from fragments of clay tablets to exquisite illuminated books. Other examples can range from entire VR environments to metallic asteroids inscribed with miniature script and glyphs. The thing all of these media have in common is that they are living texts in a different way than the term is usually understood. Facts and hints presented in them can change, with writing sometimes morphing before the reader's eyes even as they perceive it. Pictures can animate, vanish or change into something else entirely. They can enter a character's dreams or speak to them in a voice only they can hear. Every such media will have its own agenda, the same or different from whoever or whatever created it. They are, in essence, characters themselves - they are living examples of ideas made manifest. Some will need to be searched for, others will come looking for a particular person.

The Necronomicon, for instance, is perhaps the most famous of these repositories of knowledge. It is, and has been, a book, a room, a movie and an AR environment. Countless forgeries have been made, but many of these ended up being infected and subtly altered by the original concept. Because the media are inconstant and vary with given situations, no exhaustive list will be made here. Instead, the GM should look up various books about the Mythos and ponder what they might portend for the characters and the world they inhabit.

Garden of the Dark Young

BESTIARY

Most, but not all entities listed here are considered Outsider Entities. All Outsider entities speak Enochian, Aklo or both. For more common critters, consult your chosen gaming system's core rule book. Readers will notice many of these creatures are quite familiar – this is because there has always been an Outsider presence in the world, and it has only been relatively recently that more powerful entities have been able to manifest. Which ones you'll want to use will depend upon the desired power level of your campaign – settlers battling cryptids and other relatively minor threats could be just as entertaining as a full blown campaign involving Yog Sothoth or other heavy hitters.

Some of those listed have a Fear attribute – this means those encountering it must make a Fear check with the indicated modifier.

Several creatures have the power of possession. If a character is possessed, it is recommended they be allowed to play the part of the possessing creature in order to remain in the game.

A note about Gods:

Several of the entities listed below are god-like or near god-like. As such, they are not given stats or damage listings – if these beings have physical bodies at all, they are temporary manifestations of matter that were assembled to assist the controlling intelligence in interacting with their surroundings. This matter can be reshaped in any way required, and any blasted away can simply be replaced with more. They are also masters of energy, existing in several dimensions simultaneously and able to direct power from any of them as needed. If they take notice of the PCs at all, they will know their plans before the PCs themselves do. In short, any direct confrontation would be over before it began.

While the entities themselves are well-nigh invulnerable, they have followers that either want to enlist their aid or are part of some larger plan hatched by the intelligence itself. There are also gates or other artifacts that allow them to manifest in our reality. These can all be dealt with with the means at the PC's disposal.

Unless masked in some way, witnessing a God triggers a Fear check at -4.

Alsban

The Alsban are visitors from a parallel dimension, able to use an inherent ability to create gates to travel to new and more promising hunting grounds. To survive hazardous environments, it has a very adaptable physiology that allows it to exist on several different types of worlds and digest many types of prey. It is a solitary predator that subsists entirely on sapient species, relying on memories incorporated into its mind from digesting the brain of its victim to lead it to its next target. Once this target is found, it can use these memories to imitate the person it had just consumed in order to lure its prey to its doom, using empathy projection to aid it in its endeavor. Once the person is isolated and vulnerable, the Alseban will silently strike using tentacles with razor sharp endings to instantly dissect its victim, afterwards rapidly ingesting the pieces before retreating to a place of cover and safety to digest its meal and incorporate new memories.

The Alsban is roughly the size of a bear, armored plated and is equipped with claws and teeth as sharp as glass shards and as strong as spun diamond to quickly rend its target once it has been killed. It has no eyes, relying on high pitched sonic waves projected from an organ located in its forehead to navigate. It has superb hearing and is capable of moving in complete silence.

The creature shows no signs of intelligence itself, merely using its stolen memories as a means to track new prey and as a lure. It retains these memories, however, and they can be accessed and experienced by anyone devouring its mind in a ceremony that is detailed in a few forbidden texts. A modification of this ritual allows the individual undertaking it to eat a particular gland at the top of the Alsban's spine. If this is done, the person temporarily gains the Alsban's power of being able to access memories from devoured minds.

It should be noted that these rituals are extremely hazardous, as this organ is toxic and even if safely ingested, the practitioner can easily be overwhelmed by the trauma of the personalities absorbed.

Attributes: Agl. D8, Smt. D8 (A), Spt. D10, Str. D8+1, Vig. D12
Pace: 8, Parry: 6, Toughness 12 (4)
Skills: Fighting D8, Stealth D12, Notice D10, Athletics D8

Special Abilities
Size +2
 Armor 4 (type 1)
360 degree Awareness (cannot be surprised)
Sonar: No low light penalties, most camouflage ineffectual
Puppet: Power can be used against a target if the Alsbans digested the brain of someone close to them.
Tentacle blades: Reach 2", 1D8+Str. Type 1
Fear

Chthonians

Chthonians are an intelligent, subterranean species that inhabit the Earth's mantle, although their range can reach as deep as the outer core. They can survive on the surface, but rarely have the need or desire to do so, emerging from the ground only to protect clutches of eggs or eliminate a particularly troublesome enemy. The few humans who have survived an encounter describe them as yellowish-brown, segmented worms 10 – 30 meters long with a cluster of tentacles of varying size at the fore end. While no magical talent is present in the species, all of its members have a high psionic potential. This manifests in a variety of different ways, including the ability to generate the immense heat necessary to move through rock and the means to communicate with each other and other species using telepathy. They also have a telekinetic power capable of very fine manipulation that is used to draw necessary minerals to the creature for nourishment or for creating tools they use to enhance their psychic abilities.

A gestalt intelligence allows them to know and comprehend concepts as a species, as well as giving them the ability to combine their powers should the need arise. The latter ability is used to cause earthquakes, depopulate communities though fear projection, kill by inflicting psychic trauma or deliver overwhelming images that could drive a person to madness.

This image projection is one of the few sources of modern knowledge about this species, with scattered individuals receiving nightmarish scenes of the subterranean world as seen through the alien senses of the Chthonians. A few times these impressions were recorded by an individual with digital memory. Eventually some of these recordings found their way to ETM, who cross referenced them with descriptions from the forbidden tome De Vermis Mysteriis. The images are highly disturbing even when viewed using media, often depicting the immense, windowless towers of Chthonian cities that occupy all angles of the endless caverns of the mantle, shrouded in eternal night but writhing with countless members of the immense, worm-like species. It is not thought these particular projections were done purposefully, but were instead the result of sensitive individuals receiving Chthonian impressions due to the vulnerable nature of their minds.

Images of a more purposeful nature are received by individuals undertaking, or even contemplating, deep core mining or exploration. If these are not enough to dissuade the enterprise, more direct action can be expected, as Chthonians are territorial to such a degree that even Deep Ones or Migo will only tunnel down into the Earth so far.

Attributes: Agl. D8, Smts. D10, Spt. D12, Str. D12+2, Vig. D10
Pace: 8, Parry: 7, Toughness: 18 (8)

Skills: Fighting D10, Notice D8

Special Abilities
Natural Attack: Tentacles (4) Str+D6+2 (type 2),
Telepathy
Astral Projection
Immunity to Heat Attacks
Armor 8 (type 2)
Fear -2
Earthquake: A Chthonian can cause a Richter Factor 1 earthquake with a one kilometer radius. Every other Chthonian participating can either increase the Richter Factor by one or increase the affected radius by one kilometer.
Hardy: If Shaken, further Shaken results have no effect.
Large: +2 to Hit

Chupacabra

Chupacabra are small predators, usually a meter tall with large, black almond shaped eyes and fur that can vary in color and density. A ridge of armored plates extends down their backs and continues down their long prehensile tail. The creature will often sharpen these plates to a very fine edge, making them far more dangerous in combat. Their long, narrow hands are capable of fine manipulation, including use of tools, traps and weapons. While they can and occasionally do make use of these, they prefer their own intrinsic attack and magical abilities. The latter consists of a single spell, sometimes two, involving attack, defense or concealment. Somewhat disturbingly, those with the Link ability are also known to exist. All Chupacabra have telepathy they can use to communicate with each other, using it to coexist harmoniously and react instantaneously as a group to any threats or opportunities. They can only use this ability with others who have it, including the occasional human.

Their relationship with humanity is best described as 'adversarial', with the creatures opposing any intrusion on their territory and occasionally infiltrating cities if their clan leader senses an advantage in doing so. They delight in sabotage, vandalism and practical jokes and will not hesitate to attack an isolated person, especially if the person is intoxicated, wounded or otherwise impaired.

Chupacabra operate in clans, with the leader being chosen for cleverness and experience as opposed to brawn. Leaders always value the lives of their brethren and tend to carefully weigh risk vs. opportunity. When engaging foes, they will use asymmetric tactics and rapidly disengage if the opposition proves to be too strong, using a concealment power or device to cover their retreat.

They have their own language and can learn words and phrases of others, but have no known written means of expression. They are artistically inclined, and can create 2D and 3D pieces of extraordinary detail and eerie beauty. This talent extends to creating artifacts of an Outsider nature, which they can use without threat to sanity, a quality that they don't seem to possess in a way that humans can understand.

They will often worship different Outsiders, usually for practicality as opposed to any fervent belief, cheerfully carrying out the entity's bidding in exchange for favor and other benefits.

Attributes: Agl: D8, Smt: D6, Spt: D6, Str: D4, Vig.:D6
Speed: 8, **Tough**: 9 (4) type 1, **Parry** 5
Skills: Athletics: D6, Fighting: D6, Shooting: D4, Stealth: D8, Survival: D6, Notice: D8

Special Abilities
Armor: 4 type 1 (dermal plates)
Acrobat: +2 to nimbleness based Agl rolls
Bite/Claw: Str.+1D4
Alertness: +2 to Notice
Improved Dodge: -2 to be hit by ranged attacks
Frenzy: One extra fighting attack at -2
Jack-Of-All-Trades: No -2 for unskilled Smt tests
Thief: +2 to Climb, Lockpick, Disarm Traps, Disable Device and Stealth
Hindrances: Small, Curious

Colour

Colours are an Outsider phenomenon that continue to defy understanding. They consist of strands of highly aggressive genetic material that seek to transform entire ecosystems, from the lowest bacteria to complex multicellular life. Some are temporary in nature, lasting days or weeks, with others taking a stronger hold on the local environment and requiring extraordinary measures to eradicate, assuming that this is possible at all.

Despite their differing effects, they have shared properties that lend credence to the idea they are similar aspects of the same phenomenon. The first of these is a shared visual quality, with many aspects of their physical make up lying outside of any terrestrial visual spectrum. Those parts of them that can be seen blend in with these, causing them to appear as something similar to a migraine aura. Optic nerves perceiving Colours have immense difficulty translating what they are perceiving, causing severe discomfort and unease to any looking directly at them. This strange visual miasma is shared by any objects the Colour has infected.

Current theory is that Colours originate from a dimension composed of this material and that it finds its way here through gates in the weakening walls of our reality. It is unknown if the material is conscious, or simply a viral expression of another reality that seeks to infect our own.

Attributes: Agl. D10, Smts D6, Spt D8, Str. D6 Vig. D6
Pace: 5, **Parry**: 8, **Toughness**: Varies according to size and intensity of infestation.
Skills: Fighting D8, Notice D10

Special Abilities:
Outsider Force: Requires successful fighting roll to use. This attack not only ignores type 1 and 2 armor, but makes it lose its integrity. Each successful touch attack will degrade the integrity of armor by 1d4 points and cause 1 wound to the target via internal damage)
Drain: Anything alive will eventually wither and die from prolonged habitation in an area affected by a Colour. Characters must pass a vigor check every day they are within the Colour's affected area or lose one die of Vigor and gain one level of fatigue. To leave the area after being infected by a Colour's essence requires a Spirit roll at -2, with characters coming up with all sorts of rationalizations to remain if they fail it. Characters whose Vigor is reduced to 0 enter an immobile,

trance-like state which they will remain in until removed from the area of affect or death occurs.
Outsider: Called shots do no extra damage, cannot be Shaken.
Fear -1
Immunity to Normal Weapons

Corpse Light

Corpse Lights are Outsider entities that have inhabited Earth for as long as intelligent life has made it its home. The ordeal of mass suffering and fear beckons to them, calling them from their benighted realm to feast on the psychic emanations that result from these all too common circumstances. They'll tend to remain in the area as long as the event in question is taking place, draining the will and energy of the victims, making them even more susceptible to whatever horror is being visited upon them. Many times they'll remain even after those who participated are long gone, feeding on the residue that taints such places and makes them monuments of cruelty. Corpse Lights will gladly feed on any who intrude upon their domain, using the background count of fear that always exists there to drain their victims, making them more susceptible to the place itself and their attacks.

Corpse Lights appear as a pale orb, usually no bigger than a fist. Shapes, faces and other nameless things appear if one stares into their dim light. Sometimes these can be painful memories, or visions of events that have not yet happened. Scenes from the horror that occurred in the place can also be included, as well as scenes from terrible dimensions not yet witnessed by humanity. By doing this, the Corpse Light will both seek to inspire fear and fascination, the latter to keep the person there or draw them further into the place where their experience will add another filament to the toxic web that enshrouds the dim and desolate place.

Attributes: Agl. D8, Smt. D6, Spt. D10, Str. D4, Vig. D8
Pace: 8, Parry: 2, Toughness: 6
Skills: Fighting: D4, Stealth: D12+2, Notice: D10

Special Abilities:
Improved Dodge: -2 to hit
Small: -2 to hit
Immunity to Normal Weapons: Only magic or magical items can harm the creature.
Natural Attack: Plasma Bolt (1d10 dam type 1)
Lure: Every character must pass a Spt check at -1 on spotting a Corpse Light.
Every person who doesn't pass must follow where it leads and pass a Fear check. If they fail, they gain a level of fatigue. The creature will continue to attack every half hour. If the character passes a Spt check, they can attempt to act against the Corpse Light or flee – if they take the latter action, they must pass a Smts check at -2 or run deeper into the creature's domain.
Outsider: Called shots do no extra damage, cannot be Shaken.
Fear

Dark Young

Dark Young are the spawn and avatars of Shub - they are most often encountered in wilderness areas that host a wide variety of life. The Dark Young feed off of the ambient energy created by living things and their very presence encourages their growth, often to extreme degrees in plants and other simple life forms. Their effect on more complex lifeforms is a form of erotic frenzy, with any intercourse taking place having a far better chance of producing offspring. In the case of sapient lifeforms, these offspring will be closely attuned to the Dark Young and Shub.

Dark Young can enter a dormant state during the winter months and will often be reawakened in the Spring by their worshipers in an orgiastic ritual that ends in a human sacrifice. The energy released from such an occurrence will cause the Dark Young to stir once again, guaranteeing protection and an abundance of crops, livestock and wildlife that can be hunted for food and clothing. Dark Young can awaken earlier, but this will take an exceptional occurrence, such as a direct attack or the presence of pollution or other contaminants. In the latter case, the creature will emerge from its slumber, seek out the source and attempt to destroy it before returning to its wilderness to sleep. They can also be temporarily aroused by direct contact with an exceptional (but not necessarily fatal) amount of blood from a nearby donor.

Dark Young are giants and are often mistaken for trees when inactive, an appearance that will not hold up under close scrutiny, however. Once they start to move they are remarkably flexible, fast and silent, gliding effortlessly across any terrain. They will have anywhere between three to a dozen arms depending on their size, although each of these can be divided a seemingly infinite number of times until the creature has the amount of manipulators it requires. In addition, every manipulator will have an eye somewhere along its length to control its movement, as well as barbs that can secrete a variety of hallucinogens or other toxins. These toxins can cause permanent or temporary insanity or leave the recipient permanently maimed, scarred or twisted in some way. Others are fatal but can take days or weeks to kill the affected person.

Another form of attack utilized by Dark Young involves releasing of a cloud of spores. When these are breathed in or make contact with the skin, they are rapidly absorbed into the bloodstream where they immediately begin consuming nutrients and growing. The affected person becomes lethargic after a few minutes, then delirious. Within half an hour, a small plant begins sprouting from their body. The plant rapidly devours the flesh and organs for further growth, its roots twisting around the body. Once the victim is dead, the roots find their way to the soil, incorporating the remnants of the corpse into the trunk of a quickly growing tree.

The spores can also be absorbed by dead bodies with the same results. When Spring arrives, the resulting trees will sprout fruit that is similar in appearance and texture to pomegranates, but without the seeds. This fruit is sweet, with an abundance of red juice within. It is very nutritious, with one being enough to sustain a person for a day. It also has opioid qualities that make it very addictive.

Dark Young can regenerate, but using this ability will rapidly deplete the surrounding area of any living plant or animal life as the creature drains them to sustain itself. It will always try to leave some remnant of its habitat and worshippers, however, with the idea of using these as a basis to regrow its former surroundings.

Attributes: Agl. D10, Smts. D8, Spt. D10, Str. D12+4, Vig. D12
Pace: 8 (ignores terrain penalties), Parry: 5, Toughness: 6 (10)
Skills: Fighting D10, Notice D8, Stealth D8, Athletics D8

Special Abilities

Armor 4 (type 2)
Tentacle/Thorn Attack: (Str.+1D6 type 1) – the creature can make multiple attacks, but each attack reduces the strength bonus by one die type – it can make two attacks at D12, three at D8, four at D6, or five at D4. Any damage inflicted will also induce a venom attack of the GM's choice.
Venom: On a shaken or wound result, the victim must take a vigor check at -2 or suffer one of the following affects:
Agony: The victim takes 1 wound per hour and is in such intense pain that any action they take is at -3 unless they have a means of ignoring wound penalties or poison. Each wound thus suffered requires the victim to roll on the Injury table. During this episode, they will bleed from the eyes, suffer extreme nausea and/or be compelled to inflict further harm on themselves (-1 Spt check to resist).
Hallucinations: The victim suffers intense, nightmarish visions that render coherent thought extremely difficult, with all actions at -2. The hallucinations last for 1d4 hours. Once they have concluded, the victim must pass a Spt check at -2 or suffer loss of a point of sanity and gain one die of Outsider knowledge.
Spore Attack: Once per day, the creature can release spores sufficient to cover a large blast template. All within it must pass a Vigor check at -1 or have a means of resisting toxins. Those that fail suffer the effects described in the creature's description.
Regeneration: If the creature takes no other action, it can heal two wounds per round by draining life energy from its cultists and surrounding flora and fauna. If it does so, 1D4 cultists extras or 1 Wild Card will suffer a wound. All other flora and fauna within a large blast template will die.
Outsider: Called shots do no extra damage, cannot be Shaken.
Fear: -3

Deep One

The Deep Ones are an ancient race – they swam through the boulevards of their underwater cities when the Yithians were building their libraries in what is now Australia. When the Elder Things created the Shoggoths that ended up destroying them, the Deep Ones watched with detached disinterest. Since they are immortal, there are even a few Deep Ones who recall these times, and can do so perfectly since they forget nothing. This vast knowledge is outside the reach of any except a few exceptional humans or organizations that can offer the Deep Ones something they value in exchange.

All Deep One technology is organic in nature, with its manufacture more akin to genetic engineering than what humans would consider industry. Upgrades and other improvements are brought about through manipulation of these organisms, some of which may be intelligent or sapient in their own right. All of this tech is meant to interface directly with Deep One physiology, some of it actually merging with their bodies to complete the needed interface.

Needless to say, if a human were to attempt this interface, the results would be both profoundly disturbing as well as spectacularly fatal assuming they were able to get the device working at all. There have been instances where this tech has been adapted for human use, but this is extremely rare. Even Hybrids must have tech manufactured specifically for their unique bodies and minds, but this is far more common.

While Deep Ones are immortal they are by no means invulnerable, with some reaching their end through misadventures ranging from failed research projects, natural disasters and the rare instances when they combat creatures even more dangerous than themselves. In instances where a Deep One needs to be replaced, it's a simple matter to grow a new one in a maturation vat. New specimens such as this emerge smaller than full grown adults, but with all of the necessary information for their survival and purpose genetically encoded into their minds. Anything needed to supplement this knowledge is rapidly assimilated, with most newly born Deep Ones ready to join the community within a year.

Bizarre stories of Deep Ones desiring to mate with human women are the result of the fevered imaginations of fan fiction writers and are best ignored by researchers unless they are specifically investigating Rule 34. Indeed, there seems to be no gender variation between Deep Ones at all, with those few who have made it to a dissection table showing no reproductive system at all.

Very little is known of Deep One society, with most of them living more or less solitary existences with collective action reserved only for those occasions that call for it. Deep Ones seem to intrinsically know where they fit into their communities and go about their callings with a detached single mindedness.

Attributes: Agl. D6, Smt D10, Spt D10, Str D12, Vig D12
Pace 8 (12 under water), Parry 6, Toughness 8 (4) type 1
Skills: Fighting D8, Shooting D10, Notice D8, Stealth D8, Hacking D10

Special Abilities
Thick Hide: Armor +4
Bite/Claw/Rend: Str. + D8
Deep Ones know 3 spells on average that they can cast without penalty. Specialist spell casters will know twice as many.
Deep Ones interact with their technology using a psychic interface, and can do the same with human computers and wireless networks.
Fear: -3

Sample Deep One Weapon

Plasma Rifle
This weapon can either fire super heated plasma in a stream for close range fighting or protected by an electromagnetic (EM) shell for shooting at a distance. In addition to protecting the plasma, the shell has an armor piercing effect.
For close range, use the cone template. Damage is 4d10 type 2 and ignores armor, excepting those with an environmental seal. For more distant or armored targets, the EM round does 2D10+2 (type 2) damage AP4. Using this round, the weapon has a ROF of 2, Range 50/100/200. Its weight is 35 and it can only be used by Deep Ones or Hybrids due to its unique psychic interface. Any human attempting to use it must take a Sanity check and suffers 1D10 damage.

Fnords

Fnords are a group of entities that feed upon and destroy information. Because of this, very little data about them exists. It can be assumed that research has been done about them and even counter-measures devised that have been discovered and then lost many times over. It's possible that this information isn't completely lost and still exists in scattered pockets or even in the mind of an individual. If an agent comes across such information, they should use their own best judgment on how to proceed.

Ghouls

Occasionally mistaken for Zombies (a comparison that they find offensive), Ghouls are in fact a mutation of humanity brought about through natural as opposed to magical means. Unlike Zombies, only living humans can become ghouls. Ghouls also have their own culture and society that dates back millennia.

Ghouls are created when individuals occupy an area rife with death, such as a war zone or an area struck by famine, disease or natural disaster – indeed, the transformation may be an attempt by the body to adapt to these circumstances. While cannibalism can act as an accelerant to the transformation process, it is not necessary and usually only occurs when an individual is already well along into it.

The first signs that a metamorphosis is taking place include feelings of comfort, satisfaction, a sense of religious awe and/or safety in places where the miasma of death is present. The affected person will not want to leave such places, even when offered a chance to escape to a place of relative safety. The individual will then begin to lose interest in human endeavors and society, eventually wandering off to a hiding place where they will wait until their transformation is complete.

What happens next largely relies on the person in question. Many become bestial in nature, losing all human reason and seeking only to feed and revel in their charnel home. Others hold on to some or all of their reason and choose to continue their past pursuits in the service of the Ghoul community. They will rarely continue their association with humans, since this would not only mean separating themselves from their preferred environment, but also having to take significant steps to hide their true nature from those around them.

Ghouls range from a pale white coloration to mottled gray. They are hairless, with elongated hands equipped with sharp talons. Their jaws are large, unhingable and very strong, capable of snapping the strongest bones in order to get to the marrow. They reek of carcasses and decay, although this can be masked with perfume if they are attempting to pass for humans. They eventually go blind, with their eyes turning milky white. This is compensated by strongly enhanced senses of smell and hearing, as well as the ability to see astrally. Some Ghouls get their vision restored via cybernetic means, but this is extremely expensive as the entire visual cortex must be reconstructed. In addition, they heal very quickly and are immune to disease.

Ghouls can use all types of equipment if they have kept their reason, often wearing armor to protect themselves from both their hazardous environment and marauding humans who usually consider them little more than vermin. Their ability to use ranged weapons and devices with a visual interface is compromised, but this can be worked around by using a VR connection. Ghouls have even been known to use Ginserts or similar devices to communicate with the outside world and obtain needed information – they can also be fitted with cortical stacks.

Currently, a rogue colony of Ghouls called Abattoir exists openly in what was formally the south eastern portion of the United States. While its status is recognized by few other nations, the facts on the ground speak for themselves, with even some of the major cities having to be evacuated by the human population who risk undergoing metamorphosis if they remain. While the United States is diverting considerable resources to fight this, the influence of the Ghouls is spreading, with many fearing that it will eventually engulf the entire nation. The resources used to combat this spread are often military in nature, a 'solution' that often does more harm than good since Ghouls are immune to poisons and other pathogens while their warrens make for natural fortifications. Meanwhile, corporate and government leaders seem conceptually unable to embrace the idea that better healthcare and other infrastructure improvements would at least contain the problem. Instead, the focus is on how to best profit from the situation, which many of these organizations have done with some success. The corporate response treats both Ghouls and the citizens who oppose them as differing marketing demographics, while local governments see Ghouls as a convenient way to dispose of corpses of the indigent while simultaneously advocating for their eradication.

On becoming a Ghoul, a person usually loses their national citizenship, being considered dead by their former homeland. A rare few with highly marketable skill sets can be given corporate citizenship, but even this won't be recognized in places outside of the corporation's direct control. While this rejection adds to the trauma of transformation, those who are willing to move on will find Ghouls have a very ancient civilization with its own artwork, literature, architecture, religion and magic. Their history is, in fact, far more integrated and complete than anything currently available to humans.

The Ghouls attempting to colonize the surface in the United States are a rogue faction that embraces violence as a means of extending their influence, an idea that is strongly at odds with the more conservative majority who views their relationship with humanity as a sort of distant symbiosis. This rebellion is currently being tolerated, but those participating are considered beyond the pale of Ghoul culture and receive none of the ancient benefits available to the majority.

These resources are considerable, and include carefully concealed, closely guarded warrens beneath every major city. Some of the deeper tunnels have an integral gate that connects to the Dreamlands, a place where Ghouls can walk about openly, under no more threat than any other creature that exists there. If a Ghoul wants to visit a distant warren, they will often use the Dreamlands as a means of transit, traveling across its landscapes until they find a tunnel connecting to the place they wish to go.

Being generally peaceful in nature, they are careful to maintain cordial relations with any who wish to reciprocate, having pacts of understanding with the Tcho-Tcho, Nosferatu and even some tentative contacts with the CU. Their religion focuses on worship of past Ghouls of note, noting their accomplishments and setting them up as examples to emulate. To be included in this pantheon is the highest honor a Ghoul can receive. The only Outsider worship that is tolerated is that of Shub, as a symbol of the cycle of life on which Ghouls depend. That the surface colonizers are violating even this stricture by forming cults that seek the favor of Nyarlathotep, Yog-Sothoth and other powerful beings almost guarantees conflict with the conservative sect unless some accommodation can be reached.

Attributes: (These are meant as an example for a common Ghoul – individual stats vary widely)
Agl. D8, Smts. D6, Spt. D8, Str. D10, Spt. D8, Vig. D10
Pace: 8, Parry: 6, Toughness: 7

Skills: Fighting: D8, Stealth: D10, Notice: D10, Athletics: D12

Special Abilities:
Astral Perception
Natural Attack: Claws (D6+Str type 1)
Immunity to Disease, Pathogens and Aging
Regeneration
Fear

Hindrance:
Blindness

Hounds of Tindalos

As one of the few creatures known to inhabit the angles of time, the Hounds have acquired a fearsome reputation among those who walk the corridors of that dimension. Only the Yithians and Yog Sothoth have assured ways of avoiding them, and while they may occasionally assist travelers with this ability, their means of doing so remains a secret.

The entities in question are called hounds for their habit of pursuing interlopers they detect in their realm as opposed to any resemblance to canines. Their bodies are best described as a combination of ichor and mist with a five-lobed 'head' that contains its primary sensory organs and a barbed proboscis that it uses to lash out at its prey to drain mana. They have an unending howl that can only be detected by their potential prey when they are sleeping or in a hypnagogic state, which can lead to terrifying dreams and night terrors. As the Hound draws near, this is enhanced by a static like scratching sound that is louder in corners and other sharp angles as the hound parts the final veils between itself and its prey. When it finally emerges, it will be without warning from a cloud of vapor that issues from one of these angles.

Hounds are not intelligent, although they will sometimes cooperate with each other to bring down especially challenging prey. They seem to have no motivation other than feeding – while their usual sustenance comes from creatures who exist naturally in their plane of existence, they take special interest in those not native to their strange habitat.

Attributes: Agl. D10, Smts. D8, Spt. D8, Str. D12, Vig. D10
Pace: 12, Parry: 6, Toughness: 7 (9)
Skills: Fighting D12, Stealth D10, Tracking D12+2, Notice D12+2

Special Abilities
Phase Shifting: Armor 2 (type 1), -2 to hit
Outsider: Called shots do no extra damage, cannot be Shaken.
Regeneration: Can recover one wound per action with a successful Vigor roll.
Ichor: Creature can spew a sticky, acidic substance using a cone template once per encounter. Unless a turn is taken to wipe off exposed areas of the body, the character will become Shaken unless they can pass a Vigor check.
Proboscis: Str+D6 AP 6 type 1– with a successful hit, the victim will be temporarily drained of one point of Vigor (reduce die type by one). If all Vigor is drained, the character will suffer a cardiac arrest and take three wounds. Vigor will return at a rate of one die type per hour.
Teleportation: Hounds can teleport instantly anywhere within one kilometer, but need to appear

through an angled surface in order to manifest.
Fear: -3

Hunting Horror

Hunting Horrors are the servants of Nyarlathotep. He uses them to fulfill his whims, even granting supplicants temporary authority over one or more, although in the end they are answerable only to him.

Like their master, they excel at deception, being able to duplicate an individual in every respect after a few minutes of physical contact with them. The person being imitated must still be alive while this transformation occurs and once it has been completed, the Horror has access to their memories and knowledge as well as their appearance.

Horrors are known for their unwavering determination, and will follow any quest given to them to the bitter end, utilizing any and all means to fulfill their objective and often expressing a great amount of creativity and cunning in doing so.

In their true form, they have a four-lobed mouth that opens to a circular collection of teeth, with three photosensitive eye spots on each side of their long neck. Their bodies consist of multiple folds of flesh that are in constant motion, elongating and being reabsorbed, sampling the environment around them with receptors that can detect the faintest sound or scent. They are also capable of astral perception and projection, often using the latter to find the location of their target .. and what they see Nyarlathotep sees.

In combat, they prefer to use their innate offensive spells, but are capable of rending targets with their jaws or with claws formed from their tough, malleable flesh.

Attributes: Agl. D12, Smts. D10, Spt. D12+3, Str. D10+2, Vig. D10
Pace: 10, Parry: 5, Toughness: 5 (13)
Skills: Fighting D10, Notice D12, Stealth D10, Spellcasting D6

Special Abilities:
Armor 4 (type 1)
Bite/Claw: Str+D8+2 (type 1)
Flight: (Pace 48, Climb 12)
Inherent Spells: Up to four that can be cast at no penalty.
Hardy: If Shaken, further Shaken results have no effect.
Low Light Vision: No penalties for darkness
Large: +2 to hit
Mimic: Can create a nearly perfect imitation of a person. It will only take a few seconds of contact for an unmodified human being, but to several minutes for anyone with extensive artificial implants such as a Morph. As long as there are some organic elements remaining, the transformation can take place. Even though all of the person's knowledge and memories are copied as well, sensitive individuals or creatures will feel uneasy around them, and any astral examination will reveal an Outsider presence.
Outsider: Called shots do no extra damage, cannot be Shaken.
Fear: -2 (while in natural form)

Illoigor

Illoigor are more ancient than even the Deep Ones and wide spread across the cosmos, drawn to the Earth when the first sapient life appeared eons ago. Unlike the Deep Ones and other races, they have no civilization to speak of, being highly individualistic and territorial. They are attracted to systems of sapient organization, however, and use their abilities to insinuate themselves with the rulers, military commanders or other people of influence and have many times co-opted religions and cults. Once they have the confidence of one or more of these groups, they offer their power to help attain whatever ends these leaders find appropriate. Such immense power comes at cost, of course, and must be sustained.

The energy the Illoigor feeds on is the kind produced by conscious minds when in heightened states of agitation. Using their psychic abilities, Illoigor can both create these circumstances and feed off of the results within the radius of a dozen or more miles. Those experiencing this attack will suffer nightmares, anxiety, migraines and a heightened fear response. As a result of the Illoigor feeding off of these responses, the victims will also feel exhausted. The violence, suicide and sickness that come from this only add to the Illoigor's banquet.

These creatures have no compunction about draining an area until everyone within it is dead, dying or insane, but their hosts will usually ask them to move on before too much damage is done, with exceptions being made for areas with troublesome populations.

Illoigor are never seen unless they wish to be, but their presence in a general area can be detected by an individual who is familiar with them. There is a hazy shimmer to the air and sounds tend to be louder but less distinct. Focusing is difficult and it is an effort of will to do even moderately difficult tasks.

They will occasionally make themselves visible, and they will do this sometimes when conversing in order to intimidate their listeners, or briefly do so in order to heighten the tension and fear in the area they are feeding in. Like many Outsider entities, its appearance is beyond human comprehension – in such cases, the mind will superimpose the closest approximation in its memory in order to process what is being seen. For those unlucky enough to see an Illoigor, they will usually describe it as a dragon.

Attributes: Agl: D8, Smts: D10, Spt: D12, Str: D12+10, Vig: D10
Tough: 10 (6) type 2, Spd: 8, Parry: 7, Fear -2
Skills: Fighting: D10, Notice D8, Intimidation D8, Stealth D10, Spellcasting D10

Special Abilities
Natural Attacks: Bite (1D8 type 2, AP4), Claw (1D4 type 2, AP3)
Two or more inherent spells that can be cast with no chance of negative effects.
Armor: 6 (type 2) due to natural armor plates and a non-centralized nervous system.
Ethereal: The Illoigor is immune from physical attacks while it is non-corporeal, but is affected by magic normally. It can manifest physically, and must do so to use its fighting skill.
Fear: The Illoigor exudes a miasma of fear even when invisible. When it's feeding, this can extend to miles in all directions. Anyone failing their check suffers the effects listed in the Illoigor's description.
Essence Drain: Any person failing their fear check suffers the 'Fear/Nausea' effect of the fear power

and gains a level of Fatigue. On a critical failure, they roll on the Fright table. Illoigor generally only feed once per day, more if they have been injured.
Thermal Vision: The Iloigor suffers no penalties for darkness if the target is giving off heat.
Hardy: Two Shaken results do not wound
Huge: +4 to hit,
Level Headed: Acts on best of two initiative cards.
Outsider: Called shots do no extra damage, cannot be Shaken.

Who Will Be Your Gateway There?

The King in Yellow

The King in Yellow remains a cypher. He causes no direct harm – he doesn't even speak. Usually his only action is to appear, and then fleetingly at a distance. But as a person draws closer to Carcosa, the King appears nearer and may favor them with a glance. When the person in question is at the threshold of the city, the King may appear in their home, longingly looking over certain possessions as if with nostalgia. It's then that the person's home will begin to change, with items that hold no actual importance to them replaced with artifacts that reflect their own perceived sense of entitlement, status and persecution. If they are artists of particularly vivid obsessions, these will be on display as well or instead.

The King will continue to appear to the affected individual, both near and far away, at any time or place, staring out the window of a passing train or behind the person as they look up into a mirror, giving them a sign of benediction. Such encounters will become less and less a cause of anxiety and instead instill a feeling of gratitude and relief, as the time of pretending is almost over.

The King in Yellow is a manifestation of a particular form of insanity where the individual craves a sense of significance far outside what could be considered necessary or deserved. If this significance can't be experienced in a real sense, then it will be invented. Thus one's individual struggles take on national or even cosmic relevance via religion, nationalism, racism, conspiracy theories or various narratives of persecution that have no basis in reality. Artists whose ideas and creations seem more real to them than the world that surrounds them are also vulnerable. *Please keep in mind that many persecution narratives are quite real if they are based on disenfranchised people struggling for equality.*

The King in Yellow is an ancient man in appearance, wearing bits of tattered yellow cloth that are draped over his body to form a trailing robe or gown. This cloth is often dirty or stained, and the manifestation itself is stooped and weary as it shuffles slowly about. He always wears a makeshift crown of some sort, usually made of yellow paper or cardboard crudely painted in gold. His face is at least partially obscured by a mask of paper or porcelain.

Carcosa was a city inhabited by people from an unknown time and place. Pre Human writings mention it (including those of the Yithians), and that one could reach the city using gates or via a treacherous route through the Dreamlands that crosses over into that world much as the Plateau of Leng crosses into ours. It is possible that these paths still work.

Any route that goes to the world where Carcosa once existed will find nothing of that metropolis, not even a memory, as the city has vanished from that place, becoming a dream of itself. The incident that caused this to happen was a play that was written either in eons past or future. The playwright was consumed by a vision of melancholy, ruin and the tales people told of reality that were in fact lies. The play was called 'The King in Yellow', and there was only one known performance. The artist was able to convey their vision so effectively that their reality became that of the audience, transporting them and all that they had perceived to a timeless dimension where all were free to explore the ramifications of the revelations put forth. It is unknown if the King in Yellow also appeared during the play or is a manifestation of the artist themselves. Other cities have since joined Carcosa, merging their architecture with its own and disappearing from memory except in certain books written by those with eyes to see.

Existence in the city is nearly a seamless transition for most, with many not even realizing that they are there. Whether it is heaven or hell depends a great deal on what brought a person to Carcosa – though it is far more often the latter, some artists create beautiful visions that they forever become a part of (although even in this case, endless corrections need to be made, as everything is never quite perfect). The reality of most, however, is an ever increasing anxiety as manifestations of their delusions continue to haunt them, but without the possibility of resolution. Circumstantial evidence mounts as to the accuracy of their claims, but no proof. Technique improves, but never to satisfaction. Knowledge is acquired, but every new piece of information points to several more. Correspondence is exchanged, liaisons planned, but the person dreamed of never actually arrives and is, at best, seen only from a distance.

Everything is provided. The individual is as impoverished or as lavishly wealthy as they require, any substance or materials available for as much struggle that will suffice – but never, ever, the thing itself. It is always the next phone call, message or conversation away.

Note: Characters must be careful when investigating the activities of Carcosians, and take care even when moving about places that they inhabit, lest they fall prey to the visions that have consumed the souls of those who dreamed them. Each time a person comes into contact with a Carcosian artifact, they must make a knowledge roll at -10, with each point of Corruption they possess adding +1 to the roll. Any further encounters with other related artifacts calls for another roll, with a cumulative +1 for every such encounter. If they succeed, they are drawn into the vision of that particular Carcosian – it becomes an increasing obsession that preys upon their minds until they themselves are drawn into that eternal city.

Being in an area that several Carcosians inhabit has a similar effect – for each hour spent in such a place, the character must make a roll like the one described above. If they succeed, they are drawn into an obsession of their own creation. It is up to the GM to decide if there is any escape for them, and if so, what must be done to obtain it.

Seeing the King in Yellow does not trigger a Fear check.

Migo

Migo are a race of intelligent fungi that have small, scattered outposts throughout this galaxy and others. Their origin is unknown, but it has been speculated they are a nomadic species with groups settling in a particular location until it no longer has use for them and then moving on.

The species is well adapted to this life, being able to exist without protection in environments ranging from the upper atmospheres of gas giants to a total vacuum. They are even capable of navigating through space by utilizing adaptable cells in their bodies to convert charged particles like those found in solar wind and radiation into propulsive energy.

They prefer the relative safety and higher speeds of their spacecraft, however, which carry highly destructive weapons as well as the sensors, lab equipment and computers necessary for their research. These ships are capable of interstellar travel, utilizing a series of permanent gate spells that are linked together throughout the cosmos. The location of these gates are a closely guarded secret, the ones in this solar system having not yet been discovered by humans.

Migo physiology is a network of highly adaptable cells whose make up and configuration can change depending on the task it's undertaking. Migo can even combine to increase their abilities, share information or aid one of their number in repairing damage that has been done to it. They are extremely resilient and can regenerate rapidly when injured, often regrowing entirely from mere fragments.

Their language consists of changing body coloration and the rapid flashing of multi-spectrum photocells combined with various configurations of the body itself. They have a written language as well, whose letters and glyphs can in themselves constitute hyper-geometric principles, drawing certain concepts and ideas in their original form from other dimensions in order to better illustrate certain ideas. Humans can try to comprehend the language, and while some have done so, it is not conducive to sanity. Those who have managed it can create spell glyphs of great subtlety that are in high demand among collectors and practicing magicians. The majority of these capable linguists have very comfortable lives behind a wall of intense security, with those few at large having to remain in hiding.

Migo are a highly technological species, able to incorporate magic in everything from personal weapons to battle mechs and spacecraft. This has several advantages, ranging from improved performance against conventional targets to enhanced capabilities against Outsiders. While human weaponry might have little or no effect against entities that cross over from other dimensions, the Migo have the ability to combat such incursions, at least against some the less capable species. Other equipment that utilizes magic is not constrained by many of the physical limitations that affect its human counterparts. Migo spacecraft, for instance, have few limits on their rates of acceleration and deceleration, effortlessly performing maneuvers that conventional craft would find impossible.

Migo worship many Outsider entities, but do so for practical reasons. They are more than willing to aid an agenda by one of these beings in exchange for knowledge and other considerations, but their own interests always come first and foremost.

The Migo view humanity as a threat since they combine the qualities of creativity and individuality with all of the narcissistic short sightedness the latter quality implies. Humanity's creation of artificial intelligence is viewed with particular alarm, as a singularity event could rapidly transform the entire solar system. Given this, the Migo seek to destroy AI and AI research whenever possible.

Attributes: Agl: D6, Smt: D8 Spt: D6, Str: D6, Vig.:D8
Speed: 8, Tough: 6, Parry: 4
Skills: Fighting: D4, Shooting: D6, Knowledge (Sciences) D8, Notice D8

Special Abilities
Robust: +2 to recover from being Shaken
Adaptable Cells: Can move up to two dice from up to two different attributes to reinforce a third (ex: moving a die from Agl and Str to reinforce Smt would change a Migo's stats to Agl D4, Str D4 and Smt D12)
Immune to poison or disease
Fungal Mass: Non-area effect weapons do half damage. Can regenerate one wound per turn.

Merge: If merged, give the Migo +2 attribute dice, +2 skill dice and +2 Toughness. Number of wounds that can regenerate increases to two. Merging happens instantaneously, but the two Migo must be adjacent.
Fear: -1

Nosferatu

Nosferatu are not Outsiders, having existed on Earth alongside humanity since time immemorial, even preying upon our semi-sapient forebears. While they superficially resemble humans, they can be recognized as monstrous even from a distance. They are hairless, with elongated skulls, small, pointed ears, needle sharp teeth, lidless eyes and hands that resemble talons. They are extremely thin and average two meters in height, although they often move around with a stooped posture.

Due to these attributes, they often go about with a Glamour spell cast upon themselves to better blend in, although some will use this to affect their appearance as little as possible, delighting in the unease they cause. All of them have the Arcane edge – given their longevity and nearly endless time to learn and acquire knowledge, they are formidable practitioners of magic. As if this didn't make them dangerous enough, they also have innate abilities that vary between individuals, making dealing with a Nosferatu unpredictable.

Although they are very rare (their current population is approximately one Nosferatu for every 5 million humans), there are enough of them to need a global governing body to handle hunting grounds and to make sure the majority of humanity remains ignorant of their existence.
Despite being personally unaffected by the increasing Outsider incursions (the differing structure of their minds make them immune to possession), the Nosferatu operate against cultists or others who seek to bring about the return of the Great Old Ones, knowing their population would suffer collateral damage from such a catastrophic event. They have nothing against working with Outsiders, however, if it suits their interests, and they regularly deal with Nyarlathotep and others that haunt the Dreamlands or Carcosa.

Nosferatu are blood drinkers, and are indeed incapable of ingesting anything else. They must feed at least once a week to keep their reason intact. This degeneration happens rapidly, hunger turning them into ravenous beasts if they are unable to consume blood for fourteen days. Death comes swiftly after, with their lives ending in excruciating convulsions at the end of the twenty-first day. Such ends rarely happen, of course, with most Nosferatu using their longevity to amass fortunes, protecting their lives and hiding their true identities behind layers of wealth.
If they are able to ingest a large quantity of blood over a short period of time, their power and abilities also increase (albeit temporarily), even to the point where they can draw life energy from an ever widening circle around themselves. This in turn can lead to a frenzy that can depopulate an entire area in a very short period of time. This behavior is strongly discouraged by the council, as it draws unwanted attention to the existence of their species. Even so, use of this ability can go unnoticed in an area where plague or other catastrophes are known to occur.

Attributes: Agl. D8, Smts. D10, Spt. D10, Str. D8, Vig. D8
Pace: 6, **Parry:** 5, **Toughness:** 6
Skills: Fighting D10, Stealth D8, Athletics D8, Notice D10, Spellcasting D8 (the GM should feel free to add other skills as appropriate – the Nosferatu have no hindrance or disinclination from using Human technology).

Special Abilities (all vampires have these)
Inherent Spells (up to 3 – can be cast with no penalty)
Fearless: Immune to Intimidation and Fear checks.
Natural Attack: Claws (Str+D6 type1)
Low Light Vision: No darkness penalty)
Undead: +2 to Toughness, +2 to recover from being Shaken, no additional damage from called shots, immune from disease and poison, does not suffer wound penalties.
Regeneration: Can instantly heal damage if able to drink at least a pint of fresh blood.
Charm: Can use puppet power on one victim.
Drain Life: This powerful ability can only be used if the vampire has consumed several pints of blood. It will cause one level of fatigue to anyone within a large burst template unless the person can pass a Vigor check. If able to drain at least one person in this way, the vampire is invulnerable to normal damage.

Optional Powers (Up to the GM)
Reanimation: If the vampire is slain, it can be brought back to life by submerging the remains in blood.
Shadow/Mist Form: The vampire can change into a shadow or mist, making it immune to normal weapons and able to move into any unsealed environment. +2 to Stealth rolls.
Change Form: The vampire can change into one type of creature of the GM's choice.
Change Form (Swarm): The vampire can change into a swarm of insects or small animals of the GM's choice
Animal Control: Can control one type of insect or creature of the GM's choice
Wall Walker: The vampire can move at its normal pace across any surface
Astral Projection: The vampire can astrally project and manifest.

Nyarlathotep

Since the Outer Gods cannot fully manifest in our universe (yet), Nyarlathotep was created to carry out their will on this planet and possibly others. He freely moves about this world as well those created by its inhabitants, including the Dreamlands and Carcosa. It is supposed that he has carried out this role as long as intelligent life has existed on Earth, with references to him in the writings of the Elder Things, Deep Ones, Yithians and ancient Hyperborean, African, Chinese and Australian Aboriginal cultures. He has left the largest impact on human civilization of any Outsider, and is represented by dozens of different legendary figures that appear across different cultures, including the Wandering Stranger, Pale Rider, Man in Black and even made an appearance in a song titled 'Red Right Hand'.

He rarely acts directly, going through intermediaries whenever possible, providing them with whatever they need to accomplish their tasks. He will even slowly change an individual's personality over time to better suit his ends and purpose, delighting in spreading corruption this way, always listening, always sympathetic and understanding. He never seems to be in any particular hurry, seeing time as his canvas and eternity the plain he wanders. With each passing millennia, he gets closer to his goal of allowing his masters free rein, and like them he is timeless and endlessly patient.

Nyarlathotep will usually manifest in a corporeal body and appear as an ordinary man of a particular time and place. This is entirely arbitrary, however, and he has been rumored to have a thousand different forms. In fact, he has far more and can appear in whatever shape he feels will aid in accomplishing his goals. Many times this is a reflection of whatever image a summoner or supplicant expects in order to command their obedience. The bodies he forms around himself can be damaged, but even if this should happen, his essence would remain unharmed and he would be able to form a new body out of the remnants of the old one, a process that has made many turn the corner into madness.

Shaggoth

The Shaggoths were created by an extraterrestrial race called The Elder Things, a species that existed on Earth for millions of years before being encountered in small numbers by the earliest examples of humanity. While fragments of evidence of their existence remain in ancient books, there is no visual record of them and only the barest remnant of one city remains in Antarctica, closely guarded by the CU. It's not entirely clear why they vanished, although the books hint at some catastrophe that overtook them. Whether they are now extinct or exist elsewhere is unknown.

The legacy they left behind shows they were masters of magic and genetics, making changes in several terrestrial species to better suit their ends, with humanity perhaps being an accidental byproduct of these modifications. They were known to experiment with protomatter, a matrix of proteins and other organic compounds that can either be introduced into an already existing life form to make mutations or to create an entirely new species.

It was by using this latter method that Shaggoths were created. Designed to be the ultimate organic tool, Shaggoths can create whatever limbs or sensory organs are needed to complete any task, ranging from micro manipulation to the construction of entire cities. They have martial applications as well, being able to project deadly bolts of electricity strong enough to shatter steel or stone. If necessary, they can produce thinking organs capable of abstract thought to solve problems they find insurmountable, even forming the necessary speech organs should communication be required. The one thing they can't do is reproduce, an element perhaps introduced as a fail safe by the alien race that created them.

While the Elder Things are gone, they left their organic machines behind. Their current purpose is a mystery – are they simply reenacting their last orders, or do they have an agenda of their own? While it is rumored some humans know the secret of commanding them, many more have died trying.

Attributes: Agility D6, Smarts d6, Spirit d10, Strength d12+2, Vigor d12
Skills: Fighting d12, Notice D8
Pace: 8; Parry: 8; Toughness: 8 (16)

Special Abilities
Alien Physiology: +2 to recover from Shaken. Called shots do no extra damage. 8 Armor (type 2)
Fast Regeneration: Shoggoths make a Vigor roll each round to heal wounds - a success heals one wound or removes incapacitated status while a raise will heal an additional wound. +2 to recover from Shaken.
Huge: Attackers add +4 to their Fighting and Shooting rolls when targeting a Shoggoth due to its great size.

Improved Sweep: Shoggoths may ooze over all adjacent enemies as a form of attack. A successful attack will do Str damage every turn without need for a successful attack roll.
Hardened, Sharp Tentacles: Str. + D8 AP6 (type 2)
Fear: -3

Shan

The Shan are a decadent insect species from the planet Shaggai, arriving on Earth centuries ago after the destruction of their home world in a cataclysmic event involving their worship of the god Azathoth. Only those involved in the ritual and a few others were able to make their escape before the disaster incinerated billions of their kind.

With no coordinated escape plan, their few spacecraft fled to different corners of the Universe, with some finding themselves in Outsider dimensions due to hurried navigational calculations that left them forever lost in some of the most hostile environments imaginable.

One ship managed to escape such a fate, its engines detonating due to a cascading series of failed hyper-geometric calculations as it reemerged into the realm we call reality. Space fractalized around its entry point just outside the orbit of Jupiter, the ship burning as it tumbled toward the Sun. Utilizing what little control they had left, the Shan managed to redirect their trajectory to the third planet where it impacted into the Sea of Japan, within a few hundred meters of Sado Island. Their ship plunged into relatively shallow water which managed to slow their speed considerably, but enough velocity remained to partially bury their vessel into the sandy seabed.

Being a robust species able to partially phase into alternate dimensions (allowing them to pass through most objects), none of the Shan were harmed in the crash, although many had succumbed when their engines detonated on entering our solar system. Able to survive in water but unable to float, a party of Shan made their way across the sea floor to the nearby island. Finding the conditions on the island well within their limits of tolerance, the Shan explored the lush plant life and encountered many species of insects and other fauna that interested them not in the slightest. Then the first humans sent to investigate the impact arrived.

The Shan are 20 centimeter long intelligent insects with tremendous psychic ability. Being able to gain sustenance passively from the dimension they can phase into, they spend most of their time searching out strong emotional impulses from other species then voyeuristically enjoy them via their telepathic abilities. If the subject in question isn't in a mental state that is of interest to the Shan, they can evoke it using the abilities they have at their disposal, often sharing traumatic images they themselves have witnessed in their worship of Azathoth or any a number of experiences gleaned from humans or other alien races they have encountered. Included in these images are desires read from the mind of the victim, ones they cherish but would never acknowledge. The Shan also use these images to control behavior, inflicting combinations of mental pictures on the target to wear down their will until they're willing to commit any act to make them stop.

The first humans to encounter the Shan were monks from the nearby Saihoji temple who came to investigate the impact site of the fiery streak that had disturbed their evening meditation. The Shan, desperate to keep their ship from being discovered (parts of it would break through the surface at low tide), bombarded the monks with images that sent them fleeing back into the forest.

Following the monks back to their refuge, the Shan continued to inflict visual atrocities that would break down even the most disciplined mind. Fearing his temple was under demonic attack, the temple's master sent a messenger to the island's daimyo to tell him what had transpired.

Having witnessed the falling star himself, the daimyo agreed to send several armed retainers back with the monk to investigate. By the time they returned, they witnessed many of the monks visiting terrible atrocities on a nearby fishing village and others who had not yet succumbed to the Shan's torture begging to be killed before they did so. The samurai massacred the monks and the villagers, but the Shan began to influence them as well once the monks were dead, with the majority of the Samurai turning their swords on themselves once they felt the first stirrings of Shan imagery in their minds. Those who didn't end their lives made their way to the mainland accompanied by their Shan masters, where they would write their own gruesome stories, many of which would live on in legend. The year was 1575, and the Shan were to exploit the chaos of the Warring States period to the utmost. Some remained in Japan, while others eventually made their way to Portuguese trading ships in the company of the sadistic and capable, seeking places of the greatest unrest and using their abilities to stoke the fires of misery and ruin. They always found a way home, however, sometimes after decades of travel to share their experiences with their brethren.

They remain as a plague to humanity to this day. Their ship still rests off the coast of Sado Island, the immediate area around it abandoned and avoided by locals. Modern Japan, which has declared itself allied with and an autonomous region of the CU, is aware of their presence but has yet to locate them. They are convinced that it is only a matter of time, and when the Shan are discovered they don't plan to leave any alive, the species considered too dangerous even for the Zoo.

The Shan are aware of this, and there is a faction among them that advocates using the considerable fortune they have amassed to purchase the exotic items needed to repair their ship. Earth, while extremely desirable for the titillating nature of its inhabitants' emotions, was also becoming increasingly dangerous. Dozens of Shan had met their ends already, with the number of dead steadily increasing over the years as humanity's awareness and means of dealing with them grew.

Earth's atmosphere also isn't conducive to their reproduction. Unless something is done, it is only a matter of time before they are no more. Another faction of the Shan advocates creating artificial environments for breeding, with even the possibility of utilizing humans as hosts for egg sacs, something they insist is possible with proper experimentation. Others point out that this will only raise the possibility of their discovery even more. Given the individualistic nature of Shan society, this debate will probably not end soon.

The consequences of Shan possession are severe - only the truly amoral or sociopathic would walk away from the experience unaffected. While the Shan do seek out such individuals, they also enjoy victimizing those who are utterly horrified by the actions they are forced to do. In the past, suicide, institutionalization, or elimination by law enforcement, self-defense or vigilantism were almost universal ends for all cases of Shan possession. While these outcomes are still common, those with digitized memories can have the experiences redacted and still live the semblance of a functional life, even though the subconscious stain has proven to be harder to eradicate, with victims often experiencing night terrors and other symptoms of PTSD when exposed to something that might stir a memory of their past experience. They may also encounter people they dealt with while possessed who either expect certain behaviors from them or wish vengeance for the acts they committed but can no longer recall. In these cases, their shattered lives may end up being short as well.

Attributes: Agl. D10, Smts. D12, Spt. D12, Str. D4, Vig. D6
Pace: 4, Parry: 4, Toughness: 5
Skills: Fighting D4, Outsider Knowledge: D10, Stealth D12, Notice D10

Special Abilities:
Out of Phase: Can pass through solid objects, -2 to Notice, -2 to hit.
Telepathy: Each hour a person is exposed to Shan telepathy, they must make a Spirit roll at -2. Failure inflicts the loss of one point of sanity. If the character goes insane, they become the willing accomplice of the Shan. While under the influence of the psychic assault, all actions taken by the victim are at -2.
Small: -2 to hit
Neural Disruptor: This psychic attack that causes mental agony. The target must make a Spirit roll at -1 or be Shaken.
Fear

Shub

Shub is a fertility god whose cult is perhaps the largest of any of the Great Old Ones, spanning countless worlds. Anywhere there is a symbiosis between people and the land, Shub will seek to make itself part of it, tempting numberless races with its aid and protection.

It does this chiefly through various avatars, which include its Dark Young as well as priests to teach hunting and gathering techniques, agriculture, animal husbandry and methods of worship. The priests are contacted directly by the entity, and taught first how to summon a fragment of its persona. Once present, the persona immediately engulfs the priest, altering their minds and physiology to make them suitable for the priesthood. For humans, this process is extremely traumatic and can result in total loss of sanity. The priest's new responsibilities are hard coded into their consciousness, however, so they are able to perform all of the required rituals of their new station for which sanity would only be an impediment. In addition, internal changes to their physiology makes harming them very difficult.

Once this is done, the priest will summon Dark Young and gather followers, their next move being to usurp any other religious or secular authority in the community, replacing it with their manifestation of Shub's will. If necessary, the authorities in question or others can be altered to become priests as well, with the original convert only having to summon another instance of the God to do so.

Once the transformation of the community is complete, Shub will be summoned during a once yearly fertility festival, where it will watch over the ritual of the reawakening of the Dark Young (see Dark Young entry). It can also be summoned if the community is facing dire circumstances, but doing so requires a sacrifice that includes the high priest. Once the crisis has been dealt with, the God will choose a new one.

Shub Priest (use these additions to modify another character template)

+1D to all attributes, reduce sanity to 0, add +5 to corruption
Add following skills: Outsider Knowledge (Shub) D10, Aklo D8, Summon Dark Young (automatic – creature will arrive in 1D4 turns).
Add following abilities: Immunity to disease, poison and aging, Armor 4 (type 1), called shots have no effect

Star Spawn

Star Spawn are Cthulhu's brethren, having followed him to this world from their own remote dimension. They live only to assist their high priest in his quest to Godhood, their individual wills completely subsumed to Cthulhu's psychic domination. Even though Cthulhu is now sleeping due to being unable to access the energies and parts of himself that exist in other realities, his followers are under no such restrictions and continue to attempt to speed the awakening of their God and pave the path for his ascension once he returns.

While being contemptuous of humanity, viewing our primitive species merely as biomass with the souls their master requires, they realize that human assistance can occasionally be useful. To this end, they will aid their cult if it suits their purpose, assigning them tasks they would find difficult or dangerous, or if they require stealth or assets that are both deniable and expendable.

In appearance, Star Spawn are similar to Cthulhu himself, but with their outline and form less complex due to only existing in a few parallel dimensions simultaneously. The human mind usually interprets the resulting visual input as them being 'smaller' than their master. Although descriptions vary, the consensus points to an octopoid head with a dozen or more tentacles, attached to a body able to generate limbs of the required shape and size as needed.

The Star Spawn do not have technology as we understand it. Being accomplished magicians, they alter reality in minor ways to suit their purpose, having access to several spells of Heroic level or even Legendary in a few talented individuals. They will often make use of artifacts, mostly of their own creation that they style in a terrifying aspect, but which also hint at an elusive beauty that draws people to them when seen.

Although extremely robust, they can be killed by either physical or magical means. Because of this, they will try to avoid direct confrontation and will instead try to attack targets with ritual magic or more commonly, use cultists to solve the problem. If it comes to close quarters combat, they are extremely dangerous, and will use a combination of deadly magic and physical attacks that, due to their extradimensional nature, ignore most armor.

Due to their sole remaining city of R'lyeh being sunk beneath the waves, Star Spawn live an underwater existence. They tend to stick close to their city, located in the vast reaches of the South Pacific Ocean, leaving it only in pressing need. Although the Deep Ones know of their existence, they give the city a wide berth, having no interest in a conflict with Cthulhu or his deadly minions.

Attributes: Agl. D6, Smts. D12+4, Str. D8+2, Spt. D12+4, Vig. D8+1
Pace:12, Parry: 6, Toughness: 20 (6)
Skills: Fighting D12, Notice D10, Athletics D8, Spellcasting D12 (Star Spawn are very intelligent, resourceful and creative – the GM should feel free to give them any skills they feel are appropriate)

Special Abilities

Armor 6 (type 2)
Natural Attacks: Tentacles (4): Str.+1D4 (type 2), Claws: Str.+D8 (type 2)
Jack-of-All-Trades: No -2 for unskilled tests if Smarts based
Hardy: If Shaken, further Shaken results have no effect.
Fearless: Immune to Intimidation and Fear checks.
Huge: +4 to hit
Inherent Spells: 6+ (GM choice)
Astral Possession: Star Spawn have this and access to all other astral abilities – see the New Edges section of this book.
Fear: -3

Swarm

Swarms are manifestations of ambulatory biomass that spills over from a dimension that consists entirely of living matter. It is unknown if this migration is deliberate, but given a Swarm's ravenous properties (it can ingest any organic matter), it seems likely. Researchers are divided as to whether there is a gestalt conscientiousness controlling them, either singularly or as a whole.

The use of gates both to travel to our dimension and to withdraw once satiated suggests an intelligence since such sophisticated constructs can only be sustained by a complex neural net – however, a creature developing this power naturally cannot be discounted.

A related ability is the Swarm's tendency to 'fade' when threatened with a peer or superior opponent. 'Fading' takes anywhere from one to 10 seconds depending on distance, and involves the Swarm teleporting en masse to a different location. A one second Fade will transport the creatures a few dozen meters away, while ten seconds could transport them several thousand kilometers, with an equal amount of time needed to fully manifest in their new location. Individual components of a Swarm are almost always left behind in the old location after a transfer takes place and these almost always act as separate elements instead of in concert. They will scatter and hide, emerging when they feel it's safe in order to commit acts of mayhem ranging from sabotage to attacking vulnerable humans or other creatures.

The individual components of a swarm are anywhere from 1 to 5 centimeters long and will number in the thousands, although groups of a million or more have also been reported. Such concentrations are extremely difficult to destroy, with the 'Black Tide' incident in Mumbai requiring a total commitment of the city's militia units, with other regions mobilized to deal with any teleportation.

The creatures are generally black and insectoid in appearance, although many other colors and forms have been observed as well. They can alter their shape to fit into almost any space or opening, no matter how small. An environmental seal will keep them out, but they are adept at getting past such hindrances by employing a molecular acid that will rapidly dissolve any terrestrial metal. They will also utilize this acid to attack, using it to enhance their bites.

Attributes: (Average sized Swarm covers a medium burst template – change attributes as needed for larger or smaller examples.
Agility d10, Smarts d6, Spirit d12, Strength d8, Vigor d10
Skills: Notice d6

Pace: 10; **Parry:** 4; **Toughness:** 7

Special Abilities:
Bite or Sting: Swarms inflict hundreds of tiny bites every round to their victims, hitting automatically and causing 2d8+2 (4 AP due to acid) type 1 damage to everyone in the template. Damage is applied to the least armored location (victims in completely sealed suits are immune).
Split: Some swarms are clever enough to split into two smaller swarms (Small Burst Templates) should their foes split up. The Toughness of these smaller swarms is lowered by –2.
Swarm: Parry +2; Because the swarm is composed of so many creatures, cutting and piercing weapons do no real damage. Area-effect weapons work normally.
Fade: See creature description.
Molecular Acid: Can be made once per round in addition to its other attacks against a single target with a range of one meter. Exposure causes any material to lose 1 AP per turn. Once it burns through, it will continue to dissolve anything it comes in contact with until it is removed. Exposed flesh will take 1D8+2 damage.
Outsider: Called shots do no extra damage, cannot be Shaken.
Fear: -2

Tcho-Tcho

The Tcho-Tcho are a semi-nomadic ethnic group whose range extends from Nepal and Bhutan to the highlands of Bangladesh, Myanmar, Laos and Vietnam. They may well be the world's oldest culture, perhaps even surpassing Australia's aboriginal population in this regard.

They have records in the form of sutras that outline their rituals and mythology that could shed light on their past, but these are closely guarded and they will not allow outsiders to see them. The Tcho-Tcho claim that there is no reason to restore or copy the texts, as they are indestructible and if lost, will find their way back to their clans with dire consequences to those who stole them. Whether this is true or not, to this date no one has been able to do a detailed ethnographic study of them. What little information is available is from the histories of neighboring peoples, where they have been known to show up in frescoes as well as mentioned and portrayed in illuminated texts. In these, they are portrayed as harbingers of corruption and decay as well as calamity from the sky and referred to as 'The Dream People'.

This last reference is probably due to their production of Soma, a drug that first acts as an opiate and then slowly transforms the user so they are in a permanently blissful state, capable of uttering only a single unique syllable and capable of no other acts of volition. Once they have reached this state, no amount of persuasion or violence can stir them out of it. Indeed, all a person needs for continued life after this is an infusion of Soma once every new moon. If this is done, they are immune to disease and will not age, nor will they need to eat or drink anything else. They can be killed, but only fire or acid will accomplish this, with other injuries rapidly healing. That there is a large underground demand for people so afflicted should go without saying. The people to whom this drug is offered are always from the lowest strata of society – every culture has its 'untouchables', and it's to the least of these that this future is offered. Occasionally Tcho-Tcho descend from their remote villages to gently lead one or more of these people off to an unknown destination – and while there are always witnesses, nobody thinks to stop them or interfere in any way.

There is a temple somewhere in the wooded, misty forests of the Laotian highlands where the Tcho-Tcho practice their ceremonies to Azathoth. It is said the afflicted (although the Tcho-Tcho name for them translates to 'blessed') people they lead away end up here, joining a chorus of their brethren to offer eternal praise to that which whispers, sighs and laughs at the center of creation.

Several criminal syndicates and corporations have tried to synthesize Soma, without success. Teams sent to recover samples more often than not simply vanish after walking into the jungle or the labyrinthine alleys of slums and shanty towns. Others return empty handed, having found nothing, or with tales of ambushes by heavily armed Tcho-Tcho or flayed skins hanging from trees coming to life and tearing their team to shreds in a horrifying whirlwind.

'The Dream People' could also refer to their presence in Carcosa and the Dreamlands. In the former place, they are not trapped as the other inhabitants are, but are usually there on an errand or using it as a conduit to some other reality.

William Burroughs was inspired by Tcho-Tcho culture, writing about a rumored empire these eldritch people control that exists simultaneously in the distant past and future, the infamous 'Cities of the Red Night'. While a few brave archaeologists seek out these cities, it is a practice the Tcho-Tcho actively discourages.

Their contact with the outside world is limited, and they purposefully settle in regions of little interest to corporations or major SMMs. They have shown no interest in the initiatives of either Temple or the CU, with both organizations quickly withdrawing after tentative attempts to contact them, the consensus seeming to be the culture could not be assimilated into either.

While potentially dangerous, the Tcho-Tcho want to stand separate from the outside world and only bring their power to bear if threatened. This summation is borne out by their interactions with the various criminal syndicates and corporations that have attempted to make inroads into their society – while the fates of these interlopers were subtle and malignant, they hinted at a far greater power that is perhaps best left undisturbed.

Attributes

The Tcho-Tcho are human and share most human attributes, skills and have the same access to Edges and Flaws. The main difference is they do not have a sanity attribute, being able to witness the manifestation of entities that would leave most other terrestrial intelligences in a vegetative state with a simple glance. They can similarly read any text or use any artifact without penalty and are fluent in both Enochian and Aklo.

Despite their insularity, they are not intimidated by other cultures or by traveling. They usually speak at least two terrestrial languages in addition to their native tongue and will study the customs of foreign places they wish to visit in order not to stand out.

Toxic Elemental

Elementals represent forces of nature made manifest in a pure and often intelligent form. As such, they are neutral in regards to humanity, but will follow the instructions of a magician who summons and controls them. Elementals usually make their home in their dimension of origin, places embodying their nature that are quite dangerous to humans - this is due not only to the indifference of these environments to human life, but to the myriad creatures who thrive and make their homes there.

Elementals existing on Earth end up there in any number of ways, either summoned by magicians or finding their way through weak spots joining the two realities. In the first case, especially intelligent Elementals may choose to remain in our dimension after the spell caster has dismissed them, or the summoner may have been killed before dismissing the creature or lost control of it during summoning. In all cases, once free, the Elemental will make its way toward a place it feels best embodies its nature and remain there, sometimes for centuries or millennia.

Toxicity can enter the picture either through human or Outsider intervention. Any poisons introduced into its environment will affect the Elemental as well, changing its nature to reflect the means of contamination. This sort of mutation is intensely painful, and it will first and foremost seek out a means to eliminate the source of its distress and will be hostile to any terrestrial life intruding in its domain.

Attributes and Abilities:
As per the rule book with the addition of the following.
Since Elementals represent primordial forces, the level of damage they can inflict is potentially extreme. Because of this, the power of their attacks should reflect their size and strength.
Cannot be Shaken, +2 to Toughness, Fear -1, Berserk, Frenzy
Toxic elementals receive +2 modifier to damage due to their taint. In addition, characters will receive one level of fatigue if they fail a vigor roll after being hit due to exposure to toxic elements. Characters protected by an environmental seal are immune from this additional damage.

Wendigo

Even though they are best known for populating Arctic climates, Wendigo are very adaptable and can be found in nearly any environment, with specimens found from Greenland to Australia, with suspected cults as widespread as the orbital ring and Lagrange colonies.

In their usual state they are large simians, covered in white fur and with sharp, enlarged canines. They are also capable of appearing human for extended periods of time. This mask can slip if they are hungry or agitated, however, slowly revealing their true form if the condition continues.

Wendigo are a specific type of carnivore, deriving energy from both feasting on the flesh of sapient species and by encouraging others to do so. For the latter and other assistance, a Wendigo will have an associated circle or cult. Over time, the members of this circle will no longer have the volition to refuse the Wendigo any request and will eventually lose their sanity and the ability to get sustenance from any source other than the flesh of their own species. The source of these recruits can be anyone from jaded corporate drones to the desperate and hungry that populate the numberless shanty towns around the globe. The Wendigo will usually trick the prospective supplicants in some way, and those receiving the tainted meal will find it unusually difficult to refuse, with the meat seeming to radiate a desirability bordering on the carnal. Once they feed on the flesh, they will crave it more and more with each passing day. This diet will slowly change them into predators with increased strength and speed, though externally they will still appear fully human. It should be noted that this sustenance, both for the Wendigo and its Circle, can only be from flesh from a corpse less than an hour old. Flesh older than this is the province of Ghouls, whom Wendigo despise as scavengers. While some Wendigo have infiltrated modern societies, others refuse to do so, preferring a more 'traditional' lifestyle.

Wendigo have a number of abilities that can only be sustained through a regular diet of their unspeakable repast, with each gram of flesh providing them with power points both for spells and abilities. If a Wendigo or Circle member goes for more than three days without at least a taste of flesh, they will suffer a point of fatigue, with another point suffered for each day they are unable to feed until they die.

Wendigo

Attributes
Agl: D10, Smt: D8, Spt: D10, Str: D12+2, Vig. D12
Pace: 8, Parry: 8, Toughness: 10 (type 1), Fear 0 (only if in monstrous form)
Skills: Athletics D10, Fighting D12, Intimidation D10, Notice D10, Stealth D12, Tracking D12, Spellcasting D8 (Note that these skills are only those that the Windigo inherently possesses – in human form, they can and do use more high tech skills such as Hacking or Firearms if they've taken the time to learn them.)

Special Abilities
Bite/Claw Attack (monstrous form only): Str+2D6 type 1
Immune to Weather: No natural terrestrial weather will harm or fatigue them.
Fearless: Immune to Fear and Intimidation.
Low Light Vision: No penalties unless in total darkness.
Size +2 (monstrous form only)
The Wendigo also will have the following inherent abilities if they have fed within the last 24 hours: **Regeneration, Puppet, Armor** (level matches that of Wendigo – see spell listing)
Fear (when in natural form)

Wendigo Cultist

This represents a person who has been completely corrupted by a Wendigo. Those in earlier stages will have only some of these abilities, or have them to a lesser extent.

Attributes: Agl: D8, Smt: D6, Spt: D6, Str. D8+2, Vig. D10
Pace: 6, Parry: 6, Toughness: 7 type 1
Skills: Fighting D8, Notice D6, Stealth D8

Special Abilities
Bite: Str.+D4
Combat Reflexes: +2 to recover from being shaken
The Hunger: Each bite attack that inflicts a wound gives the cultist +1 die to vigor and strength to a max of +2 for 5 minutes.
Improved Frenzy: 2 attacks per round.

Xenomorph

Xenomorphs are artificially constructed lifeforms, created using a neutral protein base sculpted by nanobots. An AI oversees every part of the creation, from the first cell to the finished product, giving the designer complete control of the creature's appearance, instincts and other motivations. Xenomorphs come in many sizes and have a variety of applications, ranging from combat and security (Xenomorphs are used by the United States to combat Ghouls in their complex cave systems and by various corporations to find and remove squatters on their territory), explorers of hazardous environments, bodyguards or even pets.

The advantages of a Xenomorph are manifold, having all of the advantages of an organism (self-repair, reproduction, adaption) with only as many of the limitations as the designer wishes - fear, attachment, empathy or other traits can be included in the creation's psychological matrix, or not.

The compulsion to explicitly obey the instructions of their owners are deeply implanted in the creature's psyche as a key aspect in every design. It is important to note, however, that no fail safe can be one hundred percent effective. Xenomorphs score highly in this regard, though, with less than one percent acting in a manner outside of their orders on an individual level. Mass failure of a single genotype is even more unusual, coming in at less than .01 percent. Production is immediately halted in such circumstances until such a time the problem can be isolated and excised. While the news feeds tend to sensationalize such events, it should be noted that any casualties resulting are well within the norm for many other cutting edge technologies.

Xenomorph Warrior Model
Attributes: Agl. D12, Smts. D10, Spt. D8, Str. D12+2, Vig. D10
Pace: 10, Parry: 8, Toughness: 8 (2)
Skills: Fighting D10, Athletics D12, Notice D8, Stealth D12

Special Abilities:
Armor 2 (type 1)
Natural Attack: Bite/Claw (D8+Str AP 2 type 1)
Hardy: If Shaken, further shaken results have no additional effect.
Immune to Fear and Intimidation
Fear

Yithians

It is difficult to say when this time traveling species first appeared. The incarnation that time travels to interact with humanity existed about 1 billion years ago, remaining in that form for 200 million years before moving on to their next incarnation. Throughout our existence, they have been studying our cultures and technology, making special note of sorcery techniques and Outsider contact. It is unknown if they have interacted with other intelligent species like the Deep Ones or Elder Things, but it certainly seems possible, even probable, that they have. They are the undoubted masters of our planetary history, with an extensive catalog of all life, civilizations and catastrophic events ranging from different extinction level disasters to the end of the planet itself. They explore dimensions in addition to that of time, so it seems unlikely that the end of this world will mean the end of the Yithians. With their extensive knowledge, however, they probably know what will ultimately bring about their own demise as well.

The Yithian method of time travel involves projecting their consciousness to the desired era, where they find a creature capable of hosting their intelligence and take over their central nervous system. The host intelligence can then either be put in a dormant state or destroyed, although the Yithians will only do the latter if they are planning to take up permanent residence.

The Yithians store any knowledge they gain from these expeditions in extensive libraries that exist in particular moments and places in time, always in geologically stable regions when the Earth is devoid of intelligent life. This makes finding the libraries extremely difficult, as the time traveler must not only know the location, but the narrow window of time when it actually exists, which can be as small as a few seconds. Given the Hounds of Tindalos and other hazards of time travel, no one known to humanity has ever visited one and survived – and yet some books taken from the libraries exist in our time, in the hands of SMMs or individuals.

The books are folio sized, constructed of thin, lightweight indestructible metal. In order to decipher them, one must know the complex Yithian language. Even without this knowledge, the painstakingly rendered glyphs and mandalas make them priceless, even though they require full spectrum vision enhancements to fully appreciate.

The Yithian's physical appearance can vary, depending on the temporal frame of reference. The form humanity is most used to seeing them in is a species they inhabited eons past, a robust life form naturally shielded against the intense radiation present at the time. Its small head has three eyes, placed to give it all around vision. The head is attached to the body by a long, flexible neck, while the body itself is knobby and chitinous with an appearance similar to that of porous volcanic rock. Coming out of its back is a long tentacle that can vary in length depending on the creature's needs – attached to it are four fleshy cones that contain enhanced senses that it uses to investigate objects it is curious about. It also uses them for speech and respiration.

Two arms emerge from either side of the body, each covered in knobby deposits that act as armor. They end in pincers that are strong and sharp – these are excellent for close-in defense, but what's truly remarkable about them is that inside they contain a collection of microscopically thin tendrils, each one of which is capable of fine manipulation. These can be used to absorb nutrients from a variety of sources, but the Yithians also utilize them to craft technology and artwork of remarkable utility and subtlety. The body is supported and moved about by a dozen or more sharp bony limbs that extend out from the bottom of the torso, providing locomotion with a silent, elegant grace.

Yithians have no religion and worship no Gods. While they are certainly aware of Cthulhu, Nyarlathotep, Azathoth and others, they do their best to have as little to do with them as possible, considering the cost of dealing with such entities far greater than any benefit gained.

Their civilization is a highly organized caste system, but without the variations in status so common to human institutions of this type. Each individual is assigned an occupation suitable to their abilities, and they tend to remain in their field for their entire existence. They have no ego as we would understand it, with every member of the society working tirelessly toward the greater good of their species and wishing to do nothing else outside of their assigned tasks. The majority of their resources are utilized in understanding the details of upcoming catastrophes so they can be avoided, and in learning all there is to learn from other times and places for the purpose of using this knowledge for their benefit. They have little in the way of empathy, no nostalgia or anything that humans would recognize as emotion. Despite this, they are not needlessly cruel and tend to be excellent caretakers of whatever biosphere they find themselves in, even reversing any damage previously done to the environment.

Yithian technology is equal to or surpasses that of humanity, with a few notable exceptions. They do not create machines that think independently and have little industry, with most of their tools and machines hand crafted. The low output from the latter is balanced by the low demand their society has for such things, with an individual acquiring a device only if it is required for their profession. The resulting machines are beautifully, even artistically designed and can last in a functioning state for centuries or longer. The few examples available in our time are closely guarded in state controlled vaults, or in private collections of privileged individuals.

Attributes (This is for the incarnation listed above. For other manifestations, it will use the physical stats of the creature it is inhabiting and retain its own mental attributes).

Agl. D6, Smts D12+2, Spt. D8, Str. D10, Vig. D12
Pace: 8, Parry: 5, Toughness: 8 (12)
Skills: Fighting D6, Shooting D6, (Profession) D12, Notice D8

Special Abilities
Immune to Radiation
Bony nodules: (Armor 4 type 1),
Natural Attack: Claw (1D6+Str type 1)
Astral Possession: In addition to the normal benefits this Edge provides, Yithians can also use it to move through time and other dimensions without penalty.
Telepathy
If they are present in an unfamiliar era, they gain the **Clueless** hindrance.
Fear

Yog Sothoth

Yog Sothoth is an Outsider of near God-like ability, and as such cannot be directly harmed by humans. It can be summoned, but will only appear if it feels that it's in its interests to do so.
As the 'Key and Guardian of the Gate', Yog Sothoth can exist in several times, places and dimensions simultaneously and will often do so in order to carry out its unfathomable agendas. It does have limitations – it is not omniscient or omnipresent and can only alter reality on a local level when it is directly present - thus it will often rely on cultists and avatars to act on its behalf in many situations. Many who seek its patronage or wish to be transported somewhere and/or somewhen outside of their ability to reach will find themselves in this role. Contacting this entity is extremely dangerous, with many rituals encoded in books incomplete or otherwise inaccurate.

Yog Sothoth doesn't have morality as we understand it, only agendas. Humanity and other lesser species are tools to be used in accomplishing these, but their existence in part or whole does not concern it, and it will not hesitate to bring about immense destruction and death if it would help to achieve some minor end.

Moses Mountain Convergence

THE WORLD OF ADVENT OF CARCOSA

Azrael has divided up the world into different regions, labeled The Corporate Unity, Temple, Corporate, Nationalist, Toxic (Sacrifice), Preserve and 'Other'.

Any inhabited region, with the exception of the Preservation and Sacrifice Zones, can change its affiliation by plebiscite. Plebiscites are announced by Azarael two weeks in advance and all sapients living there aged sixteen or over have a vote.

Those living in Corporate Zones have their votes controlled by the business that employs them, while the CU and Temple run sophisticated memetic and other marketing campaigns in combination with strong psychological controls to ensure the continued loyalty of their citizens. Nationalist Zones will also use these tools to a greater or lesser degree, and in addition can depend upon the strong sense of identity their citizens derive from living under their rule.

Toxic, or Sacrifice Zones, are areas that have been rendered unlivable by human or Outsider agency. While Azarael identifies and marks these zones, they take no action to enforce these boundaries (although nearby municipalities may do so).

Preservation Zones are areas that contain plant and animal life that are vital to the ecosphere's continued viability. Humans are allowed to live in these places, but only at the lowest levels of technology and societal organization. Unlike the Toxic Zones, Azrael enforces strict compliance in the way these areas are affected and utilized. Such enforcement is swift, without warning, fatal, and done in such a way as to minimize environmental impact and other collateral damage.

'Other' is a catch-all category for any other viable means humans have to organize themselves. Azarael seems to have deliberately left the definition for this category vague in order to encourage experimentation with alternative SMMs. Any sized group can petition Azrael, who will then give a yes or no answer to the petition. The AI will then choose what they consider to be an appropriate area or installation for the group to inhabit.

The Seattle Metro Post Human Autonomous Zone (SAZ)

While the CU has a functioning Post-Human (PH) society, the benign authoritarianism it embraces is not attractive to many adherents of the idea, leading to many PH city-states around the globe. Most of these areas are anarchist-libertarian or anarchist-socialist in nature, with some notable exceptions - Seattle, with its progressive history, has embraced the anarchist-socialist model. While anyone is allowed to live there, immigration by those possessing physical bodies is at present strictly controlled due to overcrowding. Any non-corporeal intelligences are welcomed (many fleeing oppressive SMMs and seeking asylum), as are those who can offer a valuable service to the community. While there are some who are not PH living in the Zone's borders, most would find it challenging to their physical existence and sanity to do so.

The current most fashionable mode of existence is a nano-fog that incorporates Maker technology. The fog can take any shape the user wishes and can produce any number of objects, dependent only on the sorts of templates the individual has available.

Those who are unable to use their abilities and technology without the well-being of the community in mind will find themselves opposed by a militia that handles all aspects of public safety. The individuals who make up this unit are very capable, their rapid reaction time and constant adaptation challenging even the CU's attempts at infiltration. If things get too out of hand, the Zone also has a Platinum Contract with Occulus Solutions to intervene with any assets necessary to contain the problem.

The laws of this regional SMM basically boil down to the individual is responsible for their actions and for anything that they create. Also, sapient entities cannot be owned.

While these rules are simple, the Militia never finds itself at a loss for things to do. When responding to an emergency, their prerogative is always community safety first and foremost. If the individual responsible for the incident survives the deployed counter-measures, their status is determined afterward. If they still pose a threat, they will not long survive the situation they created. If they do not, they will most probably be exiled – even if this course isn't determined to be necessary, the responsible party's deeds will be widely known and they will suffer a significant loss of reputation. As chaotic as all of this sounds, day to day life in the Zone is for the most part peaceful, and the region has a strong economy based on the creation of templates and other software. Other production is on the artisan/craftsman level, with heavy industry and spacecraft launching facilities regulated to the nearby Moses Lake Sacrifice Zone.

SAZ points of interest include the Membranous Undersea Habitat, an underwater archology that is fully alive, living in symbiosis with those who call it their home. The habitat consumes anything it can find to sustain its growth, including animals, plants, garbage, heavy metals and other pollutants. It has currently spread to the shallows of Bainbridge Island and shows no signs of slowing down. It generates food, water, oxygen and comfortable living accommodations for its inhabitants should they require them, knows several languages and can play games like Chess and Go fairly competently. To the chagrin of its creators, it has applied for full citizenship, and with it, the right to decide who can live within its spaces and who cannot.

The Needle Drone Hive is another local landmark, occupying the same area as the former Seattle Center with its famous Space Needle, the latter still being faintly recognizable amidst the blooming tendrils that encircle its base and support struts, said tendrils feeding materials to trees that produce base block materials as fruit. The Hive is a collective of digitized consciousnesses that produces drones for a number of different uses, including mobile art installations. Occasionally, an intelligence will leave the Hive and inhabit one of the drones – other times, the drones are self-aware in their own right, but in either case, most make their way back to the collective to reintegrate. The Hive is a valued citizen of the SAZ and can produce swarms of state of the art drones to combat any local emergency.

The Boeing Skunk Works is also worth a look as long as those doing the observing keep their distance. This facility produces unique, artistically designed aircraft for the stratospherically wealthy. The customer has input on the basic type of aircraft desired, with options running the gamut from small propeller driven aircraft or helicopters to semi-ballistic spacecraft. The engineers at the Skunk Works will then design a machine, with every component fashioned to provide optimal performance, comfort and a strong aesthetic impact based on the psychological properties of the client.

Perimeter security on the facility is tight, composed of aerostats with cyber security provided by a digitized consciousness named Kevin whose favorite pastime is optimizing his neural net for his job, even going so far as to incorporate bits of code taken from defeated but worthy opponents into his own synaptic map.

There is also a magical element to security – a shimmering ward that blocks astral movement and is strong enough to prevent entry by a minor Outsider incursion. It also impairs visual inspection of the facility, having the aspect of a silvery heat mirage that organic visual receptors have a tendency to skip over. Focusing on it is not recommended, as this can cause severe migraines, nausea and the occasional brief flash of images detrimental to one's sanity. Approaching within 50 meters will cause a Fear check to anyone without a ward. This aspect of security, as well as certain design elements of the aircraft constructed (some utilize hyper-geometric principles or exotic metals), has sent tremors of alarm out to the various agencies created to contain Outsider activity, ETM included.

Other Outsider activity in SAZ is suspected, the region rife with technology created, in the words of the ETM, 'with very little regulation and no oversight whatsoever'. SAZ insists to all of their concerned neighbors that they have a handle on it, and with their ability to defend themselves and, if necessary, retaliate, no one is stepping forward to insist that they do otherwise.

The Cascadia/Okanagan/Olympic Preservation Zone

The Preservation Zones are Azrael's most controversial edict and the deadliest in terms of enforcement. Decades ago, the AI made an announcement declaring certain parts of the world off limits to humanity unless those present were willing to accede to an extremely environmentally low impact standard of living. Those who wished to leave would be compensated and provided with transportation, with arrangements made for them wherever they might wish to relocate and host SMMs provided with rewards in exchange for accepting refugees. Alternatively, those who wished to stay would be provided with instruction, aid and protection if they wished to live within the guidelines Azrael provided. The consequences for not complying were described as 'dire' – 100 days were provided for those inhabiting these regions to make up their minds.

The reaction was varied. The CU, understanding what it was up against, immediately arranged for the evacuation of all of its citizens, accepting aid from Azrael when necessary and resettling them in existing ocean, orbital or Lagrange settlements. Few from other SMMs indicated a willingness to try living within the guidelines provided while a disconcertingly larger number said they would organize and fight against the edict with any means at their disposal.

With all attempts at negotiation ignored, the days leading up to the ultimatum passed quickly. The people who had organized to resist were ready, many equipped with weapons supplied to them covertly from nationalist and corporate SMMs. The first hint of what was happening involved all of the affected regions reporting a haze that was affecting visibility. Then all communication ceased.

Satellite imagery showed all infrastructure had vanished, as had all the people who had decided to remain in violation of Azrael's directive. In the pandemonium that followed, it took several weeks to work out exactly what had happened. Azrael had created clouds of nano-fog of unprecedented size, positioned them above the Preservation Zones and had them settle to the ground at the appointed hour. All of the machines, weapons and all of the people who had chosen to resist had been disassembled into their component elements and returned to the ecosphere. It all happened in a matter of seconds. Untold millions were dead. Power and computer resources in surrounding areas were affected as fusion plants, power transformers and server farms vanished. Hundreds of thousands more died as a consequence.

The reaction was swift, sustained and utterly ineffectual. Hackers from around the world tried to bring down the AI, but all failed with the loss of their lives or with permanent neurological damage. Those attempting to cross into the Zone with banned technology only lasted a few seconds before they and everything they carried vanished as well. Attempts to isolate and study the nano lead to several catastrophic lab accidents.

At present, low tech civilizations inhabiting the zones can be observed via satellite, although the view is indistinct through the permanent haze. If a person's SMM doesn't prohibit it, they can visit or relocate to the Zones. To do so, one simply has to petition Azrael, who will provide a short answer that cannot be appealed. Sometimes the AI will even issue invitations to certain individuals, which can be heeded or ignored at the receiver's option. The inhabitants are free to leave, but may not be allowed to return (and are not treated kindly by the outside world if their origin is known). Permanent residency is also not guaranteed. If a person is exiled (which can happen for any of a variety of offenses against the environment), they are given a certain period to depart, after which they will suffer the fate of trespassers.

Meanwhile, the fog has decompiled all of the toxic elements in the environment and the land is as pristine as it was before the arrival of civilization.

Outsider worship is not unknown here, usually focusing on entities like Shub or Windigo. Such pacts are generally seen as toxic, however, and warfare has been known to erupt in response to a particular settlement using them to enhance their powers of production and productivity.

Settlements tend to cluster along the coasts, or rivers, lakes and valleys. Populations are usually no more than a few hundred, although trading centers have sprung up in former metropolitan areas that number a thousand inhabitants or more. Village production varies depending on region, with each settlement having specialists that hunt, fish, farm or perform artisanal duties such as blacksmithing, baking or beer or wine production. Some have a warrior class, but this role is generally taken on as a secondary profession by all of the able bodied adults.

Amidst all of the simple technology and natural splendor, Azrael's drones stand in stark contrast. Constantly patrolling overhead, they tend to not interfere in any way with the human activity taking place below them, although they can be utilized by the inhabitants to speak with the AI if they wish.

Seattle tends to view this area as its own private security moat and is careful to never allow any of its activity to affect the environmental sanctity of the surrounding region.

Places of note in the region include the rain forests to the west of the Olympic Mountain Range that have merged in an unprecedented period of growth, spreading to the shores of the Pacific Ocean and as far south as the Chehalis River. The terrain has become dense even by rainforest standards, with reports of green light in the interior of such unusual hue that it brought explorers up short or caused them to flee wildly and become lost. The people who make their home in the forest seem unaffected by these changes, and indeed seem to be able to move with unnatural speed through terrain that would halt or at least seriously delay the progress of others.

The volcanoes of the Cascade Range are another area of interest, having become active far in excess of what should be occurring naturally. Deep One Hybrids have said this is due to their brethren tapping geothermal power along fault lines with the goal of producing an energy surplus, which will be utilized to speed the colonization of coastal regions once humanity has been wiped out by the Outsider incursion.

The constant eruptions have led to extensive loss of life and have rendered large areas of the Cascade area uninhabitable as well as spewing ash into the air that has affected the global climate. The magic being used in the project has had other impacts as well, causing gates to spontaneously open on the sides of the mountains, as well as infusing the ash that spreads over the globe. Those in the path of the fallout are encouraged to take shelter, as contact with it can have bizarre physiological consequences. Other animals and vegetation can be similarly affected. Strange plants have been known to sprout in the aftermath of exposure to the ash, along with other Fortean events. All of this hasn't stopped intrepid explorers who brave the slopes to find the unusual ores that result from the eruptions, or investigate the gates for artifacts or other treasures.

While Azrael has observed the activities of the Deep Ones and disapproves, they know better than to engage in a conflict with the ancient aquatic race.

The Okanogan Preservation Zone is another area off limits to SMMs, and contains a phenomenon called the Moses Mountain Convergence, which is similar to the Plateau of Leng in that different realities and times can co-exist in the same space. While the Leng event is stable and much larger, its sister in North America is much less predictable in its intensity, boundaries and destinations. Oddly enough, the region still has a population, although it's open to question whether the identities of the individuals change or if they remain constant over time. There are occasional noticeable differences in geography and weather shifts can be rapid and unpredictable. At night, alien cries echo through the empty spaces under the shifting constellations above. Mountainous shadows can be seen moving through the mist while strange insects and other small creatures make their way along the ground and through plant life that is often at close inspection thoroughly unfamiliar.

The event horizon of the phenomenon is constantly shifting, and is usually only known through a subtle shift in light, strange weather or spotting one of the more unusual inhabitants. Visitors from other realities cannot leave the borders of the Zone, and their stay is usually brief. At the same time, those from this reality that vanish usually return after a period of time, but are sometimes older, younger or in a different state of mind.

The CU and other SMMs know of these circumstances, but given the nature of the Zone, exploration has proven to be problematic.

Moses Lake Sacrifice Zone

This region maintains its stark beauty despite its Sacrifice designation, which was given due to its position in the shadow of the Cascade volcanic fallout and the bizarre radioactive pollution from the Hanford area that refuses to be contained, spreading at a rate of dozens of meters per year with no signs of stopping. Life in the area has adapted, often in ways that suggest more than simple mutation from exposure to radioactive elements – it is postulated that the effects of ash from the Cascade range is the cause of both events (see below), although cult activity has not been ruled out.

Those who live in the Sacrifice Zone generally do so unwillingly, and either can't leave for economic reasons or because their SMMs have dumped them there for any of a variety of offenses. In the latter case, enforcement of the sentence is usually accomplished by an injection of Cutter Nano that activates the moment the condemned leaves the area of the Zone. This also gives those who tire of their exile a way out if they desire it - this is such a popular option that the borders of the Zone are nicknamed 'The Rust Belt'.

Of course, there are many who thrive here and there are even some who come to the Zone voluntarily, attracted to the lawlessness and unchecked violence that is not only tolerated but celebrated in marked contrast to the tightly controlled societies of the CU or Temple. Others come for the economic opportunities, criminal or otherwise - there's a surprising variety of merchandise that can be found for sale on the black market. The lack of any sort of regulation allows programmers to make templates or software limited only by their fevered imaginations, all of which they find a ready demand for in the desperate society that surrounds them. More traditional professions and crafts thrive as well for those who can't afford the perfection of something from a Maker.

Makers themselves tend to be few and far between – those that exist are well guarded or a closely kept secret. While the CU did once attempt to distribute Makers here like they do elsewhere, the crime syndicates and gangs destroyed any they could find and dealt harshly with any in possession of them, seeing the devices as a threat to their businesses. Major players in the Zone also run strong memetic campaigns against the CU, the most common portraying them as organ harvesters or a hive mind looking for raw material. This, along with ambushes set up for the CU baited with false distress calls has made incursions into the Zone a rarity for the SMM.

Those with the proper credentials can get employment at one of the SAZ facilities, although to get a job, one has to be at least at a savant level of expertise to compete with the AI work force. Lateral thinkers will also find themselves welcome, as are those capable of envisioning and working with hyper-geometry, something AI have been unable to do without being corrupted by the very forces they are trying to control. Many exiled Deep One hybrids find employment in the latter category (exile or death being quite common for these beings in SMMs that value physiological conformity – in other words, pretty much all of them outside of the CU).

In terms of cult activity, Carcosa has the largest following here, the combination of altered states of consciousness and despair causing many to dream of that distant shore. Little is done to contain such outbreaks, leading to large sections of inhabited areas having a baroque air about them that is tinged with a furtive longing and desperation.

Worship of other Outsiders is also present, mostly in remote areas like the Hanford Reach or Channeled Scablands. The CU and other SMMs monitor these where they are known and will intervene if it appears the ceremonies are reaching some sort of climax.

Places of note include the town of Pasco, located on the southern border of the Zone, adjacent to the Columbia River that marks its boundary. To the south lie the eastern reaches of the anarcho-socialist Cascadia SSM, a successful but rather dour collective that focuses on sustainable ranching, farming and energy production.

Pasco serves as something of a steam valve for Cascadia, an exciting if sometimes dangerous place for locals to go for a more diverse set of experiences. For the people of the Sacrifice Zone, it's a gathering place for those who wish to escape. To this end, shops claiming the ability to deactivate Cutter Nano exist in profusion, with some of them actually capable of doing so. Those who survive crossing the border will more often than not find a fresh start available, with automation and AI being at a minimum in Cascadia. Those unable to abide by the simple but harsh laws, however (usually dealing with violence or environmental destruction) will find themselves with a lifetime sentence to the Cascadian penal colony on Vesta.

The rest of the Pasco economy deals with vices that are illegal or discouraged in Cascadia – while many of these transgressions can be practiced safely and legally using virtual means, for a certain segment of the population this simply isn't enough. Cascadia officially turns a blind eye to these activities, allowing unrestricted crossing for any of their citizens who wish to do so.

The Moses Lake Spaceport is another locale of interest, serving a launch facility for SAZ payloads as well as anyone else who needs to send something up the gravity well. While Earth does have a space elevator in Central Africa, this is under control of the CU, who guards its use jealously.

In addition to providing cheap orbital insertions to all comers, the Spaceport also provides lifestyle packages to those in the Zone who have the skills they require. Knowledge is the only criteria for employment, with the details of one's past being of little or no consideration. Those who perform to expectations will find protection and a standard of living comparable to many mid-level corporations. With the exception of restrictions on movement (recruits from the Zone are not allowed to leave the compound), there is little of the oversight and 'community building exercises' that has become the standard with other employers. All that matters is the successful completion of projects within the specified time – anything less and the recruit will find themselves back at the mercy of the Sacrifice Zone.

The Port covers hundreds of kilometers and is made to be self-sufficient, with the crown jewel being the circular, stepped monolith that is the Columbia Basin Launch Facility. With its workshops located in the middle of the massive structure, rockets and payloads are assembled and launched from the pad in the center of the archology. When it has been completed, electromagnetic coils eject the rocket skyward, where its engines ignite once it's a safe distance away. The Spaceport's most valued personnel are housed here, where they can work on their employer's most valuable projects in comfort, safety and secrecy. Other launch sites are scattered around the Port, with their attendant housing, workshops, hydroponic gardens clustered around the launch pad that will send their project to orbit or beyond once finished.

Security is provided by an aerostat fence that surrounds the port, which can be reinforced by armed aerial drones if necessary. There is also a small human security element provided, equipped with advanced battle armor and weapons. Seldom called upon to act in a military role, they also act as the Port's police force and all-around emergency first responders.

Corporate Unity Pacific Coastal Region 6

Bordered to the north by the Chehalis River, by the Cascade foothills to the East and the Columbia River to the South, PCR6 occupies an area of lush natural beauty that the CU preserves by blending its infrastructure into the surrounding environment whenever possible. As tranquil as the interior seems, fierce memetic wars are being fought with the SAZ and the Cascadians, which on rare occasions spills over into actual violence.

Portland is the lively border town in the region, currently under the control of Cascadia, but heavily infiltrated and influenced by CU elements. Tourism and trade in both directions is common with both parties taking pains to ensure that their citizens are safe and closely watched. Trade with the CU usually involves technological products being exchanged for clean surplus energy from Cascadia's ample supply of renewables.

The eastern border is mostly quiet since it abuts the Cascade Preservation Zone. However, several designated immigration corridors exist that allow travel on foot or with zero emission vehicles. Following old state and interstate highways, these corridors are a constant scene of low intensity warfare between the security forces of PCR6 and various organized crime elements from the Sacrifice Zone. PCR6 wants to use the corridors as a funnel for aid and refugees from the Zone, while gangs wish to seal them and resent the CU's attempted interference in their economies of scarcity. Border outposts, aid stations and refugee processing centers are all targets for various attacks, mostly of an asymmetric nature.

To the North is the dense forested wall of the Olympic Peninsula. The rainforest has been slowly but steadily making its way south, growing at an alarming rate until border outposts a kilometer within CU territory began to become engulfed. After the commitment of a reconnaissance unit to investigate, the CU evacuated the entire northern border region and committed main force infantry units to the region along with the 21st Mech Brigade from the CU central reserve. ETM has also mobilized teams to be sent in an investigative and advisory capacity. An Annihilator Mech battalion has been put on alert but not yet sent.

CU Regions are notable for their lack of specialization, with each area producing everything it needs in terms of food, durable goods and defense. Since all industrial and agricultural production is accomplished via Makers, most imports involve matter feeds and base blocks from areas capable of producing these along with energy – lots and lots of energy. Software design tends to be shared across regions to maximize creative input.

Each region expresses cultural differences through the production of music, sculpture, architecture and clothing. Templates found in Minifabs in Region 6 will be very different from those in Tokyo or Mumbai.

In terms of defense, each Region has an array of forces specialized for its own particular type of terrain and size. A combined arms unit in excess of local needs is kept in reserve to be sent to any region that might require it. These forces are seldom at home, however, as they are usually abroad training together in terrain and weather conditions that fall outside of those that they normally operate in.

While the CU does its best to make corruption and other crime literally unthinkable to its citizens through stable communities, therapeutic regimens for anti-social behavior and memetic campaigns, these things exist in PCR6 as well as the rest of the CU, although not at the same levels as the world at large. Along with the usual illegal items like weapons, hacking software and consciousness altering drugs and media, there is also demand for Outsider art, artifacts and books. Illegal Morph mods are also popular, ranging from increasing a body's maximum stats (especially intelligence) to making the mind more of a personal space, immune from surveillance by the Law or one's Ginsert. The CU finds these latter devices particularly obnoxious, as they not only block scans but also send a false image of a mind untroubled by deviance.

These rare dark undercurrents aside, PCR6 presents a picture of perfect domestic symbiosis and contentment, with the clear majority of residents going about their quiet and peaceful lives.
Places of interest include the city of Olympia, a popular destination for visitors and citizens alike for its ergonomic beauty and large bartering culture. People from all over the region will bring their crafts to trade, and most will gladly exchange something of their own creation for an authentic artifact from a different SMM.

The first thing a visitor will notice is the air of languid ease with which the people carry themselves – no one seems at all hurried or in a rush to accomplish anything in particular. Many are put off both by this and their boldness - it's not unusual to be followed by one or several curious citizens, none of whom will be shy about asking all sorts of questions, with the concept of personal space also being something of a mystery to them (although all are very conscientious about asking for consent before approaching or initiating any form of physical contact). While this is the way they naturally interact with the world, they understand others are different and travelers will be left alone if they adjust the settings on their AR profile to indicate that they wish this. Even then, a traveler might find they are being followed at a distance – if this is a problem, a brief conversation with a Law Drone (all of whom take an active interest in visitors) will result in the perpetrators being told in no uncertain terms that they are making a nuisance of themselves.

People from profit/status motivated SMMs find the experience alien, many of them to the point of being offended and leaving after only a few hours. Those who mistake what they witness for weakness, however, are in for an unpleasant surprise – the Law takes its mandate of protection very seriously. In this SMM, people aren't traumatized into being afraid to ask for help – if a citizen is in any sort of distress, they will summon aid and it will arrive quickly.

Those with a taste for natural beauty won't want to miss the Columbia River Gorge, whose habitat was entirely restored by a cooperative venture between Cascadia and the CU. Both sides of the river are considered an International Park, with citizens from both SMMs free to come and go as they please. Both SMMs are responsible for patrolling the region, although these are more concerned with safety, rescue and preservation issues than anything else. A close eye is kept on the north eastern most regions, however. Since this borders on the Sacrifice Zone, the public is not allowed to enter and a close watch is kept for any sign intrusion or trouble.

Temple: Salt Lake City Diocese

This Temple region occupies a vast amount of territory, encompassing a region that consists of much of the former American states of Utah and Idaho, as well as sections of Eastern Oregon and Nevada. Despite the large land area, the population is small and widely scattered, following mostly agricultural pursuits. They have a wary but overall friendly relationship with Cascadia, with lightly controlled borders and a wide variety of trade taking place. In contrast, the border with the Moses Lake Toxic Zone is strongly garrisoned with heavily fortified agricultural settlements whose young farmers do double duty as militia. Anyone attempting to emigrate from this direction is treated with a great deal of suspicion and will most likely be sent back.

To the east lies the long border with the United States Nationalist Zone. While relations between the governments of the two zones are cordial, there are elements of the Nationalist population that take exception to the presence of large non-Christian communities within the borders of the Temple Diocese. Because of this, travel between the two regions is infrequent with strong surveillance and a considerable paramilitary presence along the border. Tourism is allowed but usually with armed escort, both to protect visitors and keep an eye on them.

The Diocese has very strict business and banking regulation, with exacting environmental standards, no extraterritoriality for corporations and no interest allowed on loans or credit for any reason. Wealth above a certain level is also heavily taxed – the idea behind all of these laws being that labor is essential for an ethical life and wealth brings corruption. Because of this unfriendly business environment, most corporations won't locate in Temple areas, with many refusing to do business with them at all. Temple doesn't see this as a problem, with all vital industries and banks being state owned. People are employed in agriculture, by the state, their local religious communities or in small businesses. Energy is the chief export, with solar farms producing energy far in excess of the needs of the Diocese. The CU is their main customer, and a great deal of anxiety and contingency planning concerns what would happen if the CU's Helio Array were ever fully brought online.

Few heavy military assets are present, most of which are drones used to patrol the airspace of the Diocese and defend against the occasional raid from the Sacrifice Zone. While there are distant concerns of an attempt by the USNZ for forceful reunification, the Diocese could depend on aid from more heavily armed Temple locations for support.

The Diocese, like other Temple locations, has a Glyph of Piety that subconsciously compels the citizens to adhere strongly to the tenets of their faith. Located on Fremont Island in a church that combines elements of all the faiths represented in Temple, the Glyph is ensconced in a seemingly impossible assemblage of floating, warded stones that constantly shift to contain its different manifestations. During its more dynamic changes, it's possible to glimpse it through its protective wall of stone, and many have despite warnings not to. Those who have witnessed the Glyph describe it as a waxy sun surrounded by a melting sky. If one focuses on it, they get the sensation of falling, but if they maintain their concentration they can see the sophisticated hyper dimensional workings of the glyph within the hazy orb. Doing so will increase their belief in their religion, but also decrease their sanity and increase their corruption

Every citizen of Temple is required to be linked to a Glyph, the necessary ritual usually being incorporated into a given tradition's baptism or naming ceremony. Given that their influence reaches out to thousands of kilometers, citizens can travel almost anywhere on the globe and feel its comforting presence. Being outside the range of a Glyph can result in severe anxiety and panic attacks, leading those who travel to distant orbital or Lagrange habitats to do so in stasis. All Temple off-Earth facilities will have a Glyph, but the limitations of it's range makes visiting the habitats of other SMMs problematic.

A ritual exists that will destroy a Glyph's influence over an individual. This is extremely traumatic, and the person in question will need weeks to recover. Temple does not look kindly on those who practice this ritual, and will send the Inquisition anywhere it's being practiced with or without the permission of the SMM it's occurring in.

Due to the Glyph's presence and the stable nature of Temple society, crime of all kinds is extremely low, exceeding even the CU in domestic tranquility. The combination of reinforced faith, meaningful work and multiple social safety nets provides each Temple municipality with strong social cohesion and unity of purpose.

While the Glyphs are effective for the most part, their protection is imperfect in the sense that some people sincerely believe the correct interpretation of their faith lies in the worship of Outsider entities. Indeed, there is a long history, dating back to before existing records of civilization, of sects of every current major religion and others doing exactly this. Although Temple encourages sincere faith, such interpretations and their resulting consequences can't be tolerated – hence, the Inquisition.

Given the dark history of this institution, one of the first suggestions made by an Elder about the concept was 'While I recognize the necessity, perhaps we should call it something else." Her point of view was duly acknowledged, but the majority felt that the title carried the necessary gravity and authority required to fulfill its mission and instill its officers with a sense of purpose.

While the Inquisition is eager to publicize the fact that it doesn't use torture like its namesake, its presence in an area still evokes feelings of fear since its mission is the literal elimination of heretical sects. It also means that these sects are at least suspected as being present nearby, which can lead to a wave of paranoia and other symptoms of anxiety. Because of this, Inquisition Agents tend to work through the local constabulary whenever possible and try to keep their investigations low-key. Despite these precautions, word seems to get out more often than not, leading to complications that inevitably end up impeding their work.

Areas of interest include Salt Lake City, the capital of the Diocese and the spiritual center of the Mormon religion. The city and its environs are best described as well ordered and immaculate, with all the work of keeping it so done by human hands. In the interest of full, meaningful employment, automation is kept at a minimum, with all jobs contributing to social well-being given nearly equal status. Crime in the city is so low that there is very little police presence, and those are mostly employed with crimes committed by foreigners, either purposefully or by mistake. Ignorance of religious stricture is considered a mitigating circumstance and will receive leniency, but could get a person deported so its best to read up on local interpretations of correct behavior.

Visitors tend to be impressed by the uniformity of purpose, friendliness and the almost complete lack of social friction. There is also no visible poverty or pollution, the latter due to the city's zero emissions status. Mormons take pride in the fact their city makes such a positive impression that many who only intended to see the sights end up staying and converting.

Zion National Park is another place worth a visit. It's an area of immense natural beauty, as well as potential danger. Its reputation for the latter began a few years ago when a group of a dozen students from a girls school vanished, along with their teachers. As night approached, a small team of Rangers, long familiar with the terrain and possessing excellent survival skills, also disappeared after checking in three hours into their search. Drones equipped with ground penetrating radar were employed. They did find something, but their results ended up posing more questions than they answered. The remains of a modern adult male skeleton were found 20 kilometers away from the search area, but far underground and well over a million years old. Damage and age rendered dental records useless. Had this been a member of the search party?

The incident was treated as an isolated anomaly until recently, when a group of campers vanished under similar circumstances. In this instance, satellite imagery clearly showed their campsite, while another pass a few hours later didn't show a single trace, like they hadn't been there at all. Conventional investigation revealing nothing, the Inquisition has been called in to look into the matter further.

ARIA LAPINE

Cascadian Landscape

Cascadia

Cascadia arose from a movement of old-school environmental activists and anarchists who wanted to form an SMM away from what they considered to be the corporate, theocratic, oligarchic and fascist policies of the United States. During the chaos of the global war triggered by the CU's declaration of autonomy, the Cascadian movement saw its chance to not only spare their land from the ravages of war, but to carve out their own place in the sun where they could be free from the ravages of Capitalism forever.

Their uprising was perfectly timed, coming as it did when Azrael shut down all manner of infrastructure to spare the world from a fatal self-inflicted cataclysm. With the armed forces of the US stranded elsewhere, they easily took control and after the AI's announcement of the new world order, declared themselves the Cascadian SMM. While their application gained immediate approval, they were disappointed that they were granted only part of the area under their control, with much of it doled out to other SMMs that Azrael deemed worthy. Seeing the writing on the wall, they withdrew from the contested regions and focused on preserving their freehold in an environment of increasingly sophisticated memetic campaigns, low intensity warfare and destabilization efforts launched by other SMMs in an attempt to coax their population into a different way of living by one means or another.

Lacking the strong societal controls possessed by the CU and Temple, Cascadia nonetheless maintains its place with its preservationist/humanist philosophy that attracts immigrants from around the globe. If they seem dour, it's due to the hard work and watchfulness that characterizes so much of their lives and their attempts to preserve everything they've built in a world that appears increasingly alien and strange.

Cascadia's main exports are surplus energy (for the US and CU) and organically grown produce and livestock, the latter having a strong market for those with allergies to insecticides, growth hormones and other additives regularly found in food products. While these demand a high price in most markets, Cascadia always donates a large portion of its output at low or zero cost for those in need. Cascadia manufactures its own armaments and software, but does not allow these to be sold abroad.

The territory controlled by Cascadia is vast, extending through the former state of Oregon and continuing south to the outskirts of the US controlled Los Angeles Corporate Zone. Its diplomatic stance is one of armed neutrality, a policy it practices deftly with a large but defense oriented military and participation in global initiatives that include disaster relief and peace keeping operations. Because of this, conflicts along its borders are infrequent and mostly concern infiltration and terrorist attacks by far right US organizations.

Cascadia's defense policy is best described by the first line of its military instruction manual, which states 'Civil Defense is every citizen's responsibility'. As part of their education, each person is trained in military science and tactics, disaster response and de-escalation techniques. Every able citizen is given a suitable weapon and a suit of light body armor they keep in their home, along with survival and first aid gear, with heavier equipment available in the local arsenal. Citizens drill once a month and are assigned to a unit in the local militia, with training covering a variety of contingencies. These are backed up by a professional force that is highly mobile and can assist in any civil emergency as needed. To patrol its airspace, long borders and coasts, a variety of drones are employed. These are always on autonomous control unless something suspicious or out of the ordinary occurs, in which case a human operator virtually jumps in to have a look and respond to the situation.

Areas of interest include the capital of San Francisco. While it appears a little run down, its neighborhoods are colorful and cheerful, filled with the smells of sidewalk restaurants and the flowers grown in rooftop gardens. Like all Cascadian cities, it takes pride in its zero toxic emissions status and the air is always fresh and clear, with no motorized vehicles allowed at all in the city center. However, with no consensual crimes on the books, outsiders may find some scenes they come across as shocking.

The High Sierras are a Cascadian success story, with the habitat entirely restored and left in its natural state. The public are allowed to visit, but only using non-motorized means, and even then, mounted and armed park rangers keep a close watch, especially on foreign visitors who may be unfamiliar with Cascadia's strict environmental laws. Outsider and other paranormal presence is minor, limited to cryptids and other anomalies – these are dealt with by the rangers on an as-needed basis and they will only reluctantly request aid from the outside.

Visitors are advised to stay away from the area that borders the Los Angeles Corporate Zone, as this area is a scene of constant conflict between corporate security forces and elements of the Cascadian militia over toxic emissions and dumping. Cascadia charges that the US is trying to turn the border region into an uninhabitable Sacrifice Zone where they can practice their operations with no oversight of any kind, much as they have in the area between LA and San Diego. The CU has been known to intervene against the US as well in particularly heinous infractions, usually using deniable methods like cyber attacks or armed drones that are in use by many different organizations.

Being a society that has strong, organic community ties that strongly renounces materialism, there is little of the alienation or ambition in Cascadia that leads to Outsider worship. Not to say it doesn't happen, just much less frequently than one tends to find elsewhere. There is an instance of an entire artists' commune located in Kings Canyon whose members found themselves pulled toward Carcosa over the course of a year, each of them vanishing into the city singly or in pairs before anyone realized what was going on. Patrols sent to investigate either ended up following them there or lost much or all of their sanity among the artwork and other relics left behind.

Informed by their intelligence network of this alarming development, the CU offered to send advisors and other aid through diplomatic back channels to assist Cascadia in this and other Outsider matters. Unaware of the extent of the Outsider threat, Cascadia accepted, but gave the ETM teams very little latitude in pursuing operations. In most cases, the affected community must approve of ETM involvement, and even then have the right to oversee and accompany the CU operatives on any mission with their own people.

Thus far, these joint teams have been active in investigating current and potential outbreaks of Outsider influence, in one instance wiping out a Windigo cult operating in the area of Mt. Shasta. Meanwhile, an outbreak of tremors, night terrors and horrifying waking hallucinations has led to the evacuation of Death Valley. The ETM advisors suspect Cthonoian activity and have recommended the intervention of CU heavy units, a request that has been flatly denied by Cascadia.

Low Tier Worker/Resuscitated Asset Housing LAP CZ

Greater Los Angeles and Phoenix Corporate Zones (LAP CZ)

While nominally separate, these two extraterritorial corporate areas have effectively merged, with their suburbs, shanty towns and fields of detritus joining under a toxic cloud of perpetual twilight. If someone has the right lifestyle package they might never notice, living as they do in luxury archologies or domed habitats well furnished with hydroponic gardens, full spectrum lighting and high resolution screens that show more ideal scenery. Even the less well off can usually afford a good AR or VR rig - when combined with a suitably equipped urban survival jumpsuit, this can also deliver a full sensory experience of any environment the user wishes. Those of lesser financial means must make do with what they can, with goggles and a filter mask being the absolute minimum if one wants to survive longer than a few months.

The Corporate Zones (CZ) are a creation of the United States Nationalist SMM and feature areas that are free of any of the environmental or labor regulations that are present in other places. Others include Chicago, Detroit, New York and the Florida Reclamation Area. Corporate citizens are officially the sole occupants of these areas, but squatters, rogue machines, cryptids and the occasional Outsider also call these places home. Corporate citizens come in all stripes, running the range from CEOs all the way down to prisoners purchased from the US penal system. All citizens have a lifestyle package to meet their needs, but of course the quality of these vary widely depending on the perceived value of the person in question. The packages cover everything from food, shelter, medical care, entertainment, transportation options, clothing and even the method of one's recycling after death. The corporate overlords also understand that not everyone is born with equal amounts of motivation, so this can be provided using various implant and psychotropic techniques, all included as part of the lifestyle package.

The LAP CZ's military and police assets are considerable, with each corporation having either its own paramilitary and police force or subcontracting this out to an organization who specializes in this kind of work. While suitable for black ops and policing, these forces lack the numbers of heavy weapons, military vehicles and logistics capability required for a sustained conflict. If this kind of conventional military force is needed, the Zone's corporate parliament can request assistance from the US SMM, and these requests are nearly always granted.

The corporate parliament oversees the day-to-day governance of the CZ, with each business having representation equal to its net worth and physical presence in the zone. This parliament exists only to oversee commons and to smooth out day to day communications and problems between the different businesses that might otherwise result in open warfare that would only serve to damage valuable personnel and infrastructure. It also serves as the point of contact between the Zone and the US SMM, allowing a forum behind closed doors for both entities to make their needs known.

Tourism is popular, with most major corporations having dedicated campuses for hosting visitors, with amusements provided for little or no charge. Heavily discounted examples of their products are also available, along with displays of other merchandise and a museum dedicated to the corporation's history and benefits to humanity. These museums provide many AR and VR entertainments, with Deep Green featuring a 'You're a Member of the Board!' corporate decision making interactive game. Families are the usual visitors, appreciating the safety and predictability of the vacation packages on offer that make planning easy and less stressful than other destinations. Virtual tours and getaways are also available for those who can't make the trip, again at very affordable prices and can feature time dilation for those with a busy schedule.

Outsider activity in the LAP CZ is not uncommon, but is usually ignored unless it's impacting operations. Suppressing these outbreaks is the second most common reason for infiltration of the CZ by the CU (the first being the destruction or sabotage of especially toxic facilities), with ETM teams using any means at their disposal to root out the problem, be it in a board room or in the endless miles of landfill and shanty towns. These teams have more than once found themselves working at cross purposes with corporate forces, whose mission is usually to wipe out the problem in the quickest and most economical way possible with a secondary objective of recovering anything potentially useful.

The nature of the incursions vary, running from Carcosian communities taking up several square miles in the wastelands to executives having research groups summon Shoggoths to work on asteroid colonies in order to save on life support and other labor costs. While the US SMM has its own resources it uses to combat or co-opt Outsiders, it takes the extraterritorial nature of the LAP CZ seriously and won't intervene unless asked. Lines of communication between the CU and US are tenuous at best, leading to occasional fire fights between teams or ambushes if intelligence has informed one side or the other of the presence of rival forces.

The economy of the LAP CZ mostly consists of the production of items whose process of creation is toxic and/or has toxic by-products. The industries that produce these items are ideally exo-global in order to avoid the consequences to the environment, but given the extraterritorial nature of the CZ, this is not a concern. Because of this, the attendant costs of exo-global production, along with the prohibition of the CU for use of their orbital beanstalk for certain items, can be avoided entirely.

Notable product lines include fusion reactor cores, psychotropic biological weapons, primordial protein matrix (an exotic form of base block - when combined with a suitable template and Maker, this material can be used to create made to order lifeforms), and xenomorphs. The latter two items are especially hazardous, as they have been known to be hijacked by Outsider entities capable of possession. Several other, more innocuous product lines are produced here as well, ranging from robotics to cosmetics, all made at the low cost only possible in a terrestrial based CZ.

The Virtual States

The Virtual States number in the hundreds. The only quality they share in common is they exist digitally, running on a battery of servers requiring massive amounts of power for their processors and cooling. Those not owned by SMMs or corporations are usually supported by trust funds meant to keep them operating in perpetuity, with better resourced examples having their own fusion power plants and AI controlled maintenance bots. The latter examples have contracts with security organizations to intervene if there is an unauthorized approach to their facility or if any other if their physical interests are threatened.

The interior reality of these worlds are varied, ranging from utopian pastoral settings to soulless office environments where no one ever needs to take a break or go home. They cover a variety of time periods and realities, with all, some or none of the inhabitants realizing that they exist within a simulation.

Some of the more affluent Virtual States own entire corporations or their own exo-global habitat. These will often make use of real world agents to do their bidding, or even have Mophs standing by for more adventuresome members of their community to inhabit and take care of business on their own.

The following is an adventure I'm including to help introduce players to AOC – I hope you enjoy it and the game!

TIME IS THE FIRE IN WHICH WE BURN

Philip Stokes is a project manager for Czarny Dom Mining (CDM), a specialist in locating rare earth asteroids and setting up extraction procedures. His operations are notorious for being high risk/high reward – the attrition rate for the contracted miners he hires averages 15% due to the speed with which the extractions are carried out (to avoid pirate and claim jumper interference). Despite this, there are always individuals and crews willing to bid on the jobs he offers since he offers large bonuses for a full depletion of recoverable assets on a given site. Because of this, his contracted laborers will often fight encroachers instead of abandoning an operation and fleeing.

When not overseeing mining operations, he has proven invaluable as a troubleshooter in Czarny Dom's Trans-D efforts, figuring out ways to store and utilize elements that would not otherwise be able to exist in our reality. His ability to do these things is not looked into too closely by his superiors at CDM, who accept his explanation that he has a knack for conceptualizing these elements and their properties due to his arcane abilities – a rare if not unique ability.

The truth of the matter is that Stokes is not fully human at all, but hosting the essence of a Yithian named Shubrir who has been exiled from his own time hundreds of millions of years in the past and forced to live with the alien primitives of the modern era. The ability to visualize the properties of higher dimensional elements without going mad is natural to his species, while his personal knowledge of geology and advanced mining techniques has ensured that he's rapidly risen through the ranks of CDM.

After years of work, Philip has finally maneuvered various elements into position that should make his wish to return to his own time a reality. That this will come at a severe cost to the sapient and other species currently inhabiting the planet is not his concern.

PHILIP'S PLAN

The Yithians have a very ordered society with strict laws meant to ensure the continued survival of their ancient species. Of these laws, among the most paramount is that no Yithian may attempt contact or commerce with a trans-d entity. Shubrir, who had studied trans-d species at length in order to gain insight on the origins of the Flying Polyps, thought he had found a way to banish these entities for good – doing so, however, would have meant dealing with Yog Sothoth, who could move the Polyps to some distant location in time and space. Yog Sothoth, however, usually only provides favors in exchange for its preferred currency – energy released through sapient deaths that it can then use to enable its own agendas.

To Shubrir, the math seemed to more than balance out in favor of the Yithians- say, a city's worth of his brethren in exchange for the effective eradication of his species' ancestral enemies. Shubrir put a proposal together and presented it to high ranking members of the military caste. After recovering from the shock of a Yithian violating one of their most sacred taboos, the military caste were sympathetic to Shubrir's motives, but nonetheless considered him tainted by his studies and therefore had his consciousness exiled. They were also aware from studies of other times that arrangements made with entities like Yog Sothoth seldom went as planned and were best avoided.

The lesson that Shubrir learned from his experience was that the next time he had such an opportunity, he would not make the mistake of asking for permission. Indeed, the very instrument of his return would serve as a field test for the method he would use to rid the planet of the Polyps.

To make his plan to return a reality, Shubrir must engineer a mass casualty event. To ensure success, he has two plans in place – the first will gather the energy he needs slowly, hopefully escaping notice and allowing him to slip back with no one the wiser. The second plan is an emergency fallback that can be rapidly implemented, to be used in case he's discovered. This will incur a great deal of collateral damage, but this can't be helped if he is to bring his great work to fruition.

The first plan involves erecting an obelisk outside of a major urban area that already experiences a high mortality rate. The glyphs on the obelisk will slowly drain the needed energy from the nearby population, causing thousands of extra deaths over several months, with most of the inhabitants also experiencing sleeplessness and excess levels of anxiety and aggression.

The second plan is much more difficult to implement, but Shubrir is convinced it is necessary due to his previous experience – except this time, it wouldn't just be exile – if he were lucky, failure would simply mean death. To be captured in his current time and place would be horrible beyond imagining.

This plan involves steering a near Earth asteroid into a lower orbit, the reason being to more economically extract the valuable rare earths contained within it. In reality, the asteroid would be directed at a heavily populated area, the resultant energy then being collected by Shubrir's orbital command post, ostensibly being used to direct local mining operations. He could then summon Yog Sothoth right there and then. The resulting manifestation would undoubtedly destroy the station, but by the time that happened, Shubrir would be back in the correct time and place.

The city Shubrir has selected is Dili on the island of East Timor. Formerly a free trade zone operated by Czarny Dom, East Timor has recently been incorporated into Temple after a long struggle by the island's Catholic population. CDM hasn't given up yet, however, and has responded to the small nation's change of status by slashing wages and benefits for its workers, citing higher operating costs due to Temple's stringent environmental protection laws. In addition, it has brought Dili's organized crime organizations into the fray by funneling them weapons and mercenaries. The bosses of these gangs are more than willing to fight, knowing that their days would be numbered under a Temple administration once it found its feet. While none of them really enjoy the nearly one sided 'profit sharing plan' in place with CDM, it's infinitely better than extinction.

Shubrir plans to utilize one of these gangs in an operation his superiors consider to be inspired. He will accompany a small group of Triad members to an isolated location near Dili for the purpose of erecting his obelisk. As far as CDM knows, all this will do is increase the background count of misery, weakening the determination of its citizens and making it easier to bring them back into line. They don't know about its ability to store the energy it has stolen or of Stokes' ambition to travel to the distant past.

Shubrir's plan will be successful, but with complications. He and his group of mercenaries will stumble on a group of villagers hunting an Alsban that had been stalking their village. After a brief firefight, the villagers are killed, but during the raising of the obelisk, the Alsban is able to lure one of the mercenaries away by imitating one of the villagers and devouring him. Not wanting to risk an extended engagement with the dangerous creature that might get them discovered or killed, the team withdraws, believing that the Alsban has devoured any evidence.. which it (mostly) has, but it also still possesses the mercenary's memories.

Shubrir's terrible engine of extraction ends up working a little too well, however. Rapid increases in death and incidental violence are red flags for ETM, both being indicators of Outsider activity such as an Illoigor, Fnords or even Nyarlathotep.

With this information in hand, ETM has to proceed carefully. In addition to CDM being the CU's only source of rare transuranic elements, the political situation in Dili is precarious due to East Timor's attempt to join Temple, abandoning its role as CDM's corporate vassal.

All of this will be outlined by the team's briefing officer. ETM plans to infiltrate the team into Dili using whatever means the team deems best. The agents will have any needed field gear (weapons, medical gear, skill/enhancement modules, armor, vehicles) prepositioned – they will need to make their request for these items after the briefing to FO (Fieldwork Outfitting). Alternatively, if this is being used as an introductory scenario, the FO personnel can have gear already prepared for the agents - this will also give the GM a chance to explain various types of common ETM gear to the players (wards, hexaphones, etc). Resleeving support will be provided by an offshore submarine that will deliver the characters back to Dili once they have been integrated into new bodies.

On arrival in Dili, any means used to detect malignant magical energies will reveal that something is very very wrong. Following where it leads will take the characters first to the village of Nelio in the shadow of Mt. Kakusa – here they will learn that an armed party of men set out to hunt a person or creature that has been stalking the village over a matter of weeks, killing several people. The creature responsible is an Alsban, who has found the chaotic situation around Dili to be very conducive to hunting.

When a drone sent by the Temple authorities was unable to locate the parties responsible, the villagers decided to take matters into their own hands. Led by the village constable and his deputies, they walked into the jungle weeks ago and never returned. To make matters worse, the Alsban has returned, luring villagers to their deaths with its uncanny psychic lure. Villagers have also been getting sick and feeling lethargic due to the proximity of the obelisk – any that the team talks to will be distracted, tired and irritable. If the team needs a guide, Bethari, the wife of one of the missing men, will accompany them. A veteran of years of fighting against CDM, she is proficient in field craft and with firearms.

Bethari (Wildcard)

Bethari is a devout Catholic who considers Mophs and genetically modified humans anathema, but will try to keep these opinions to herself since the characters seem to be the only means of finding her husband. Since she was a little girl, she discovered she could turn invisible when exposed to extreme stress. While this terrifies her, it has saved her life more than once.

Like most of the villagers of Nelio, she constantly wears her Urban Survival Bodysuit to protect against the toxic emanations of Dili and nearby CDM facilities.

Str. D6, Agl. D8, Smt. D6, Vig. D6, Spt. D8

Toughness: 5 (9)
Parry: 5
Sanity: 6
Power Points: 8

Spells: Infiltration (Veteran Level)

Skills: Firearms D6, Fighting D6, Notice D8, Athletics D4, Stealth D6, Survival D6, Spellcasting D6

Edges: Dodge (-1 to hit), Quick (Discard draw of 5 or less on initiative - draw again), Arcane Background (limited - one spell only that will only activate with a Fear check).

Hindrances: Narrow Minded (Strict Catholic) - 1 Charisma outside of Catholic community.

Gear: Machete (Str + D6), Glock 9mm 12/24/48 2D6 AP1 type 1 16 rounds, spare magazine, Urban Survival Bodysuit

The way up Mt. Kakusa is difficult – it is overgrown with jungle with all of the usual hazards (ants, mosquitoes, snakes, crocodiles, rain, heat, humidity [roll athletics - failure means fatigue]). With Bethari's help, the team will be able to track the villager's posse to the place where it was ambushed by the Triad mercenaries – the growing putrid smell of corpses will make finding them easier once the team gets within a hundred meters. As they get closer, warded characters will feel their skin tingle as if it were being subjected to a weak electric current. Those who are unwarded will have to take a fear check at -1 - any who fail must turn around and run until at least 200 meters away. Afterward, they will be unable to speak of the experience or describe where they had been.

Any team members who remain will discover the fate of the villagers who went searching for the Alsban. The corpses are in an advanced state of decomposition and partially devoured, but despite this it will be obvious that the team was shot – some of them obviously executed and many have had their heads removed. Bethari is beside herself and thinks she recognizes her husband's body, but can't be sure. Towering above the horrible scene is an obelisk, carved with glyphs that seem to shift in the uneven light, its surface a dull silver interspersed with milky white veins.

A closer investigation of the clearing will indicate an aircraft had landed there, a helicopter or tilt-rotor from the evidence of downwash in the surrounding flora and the fact that several medium and small branches have been sheared off in nearby trees.

Any readings done with a Thaumometer will confirm the Outsider nature of the artifact – a character who has a magic or Outsider related skill can find out more with a raise on a skill test. Its abilities closely resemble those of an Illoigor in that it slowly drains life from creatures in the surrounding area, but unlike that creature, it only affects sapient beings. It also appears to be storing the energy it collects.

A simple ceremony will release the energy slowly (a simple success with a magic or Outsider related skill will suffice to work it out) – when the ceremony completes, the obelisk will dissolve into sand. Simply destroying the Obelisk (a weapon or explosive capable of type two damage or higher will be required) will release it in a violent explosion (large burst template, 3d6 type one damage).

During the investigation into the Obelisk, the Alsban will be stalking the team. Recognizing Bethari from her husband's memories, it will call out to her in his voice, trying to lure her off into dense jungle where it will have the advantage of being able to use its considerable close combat abilities. If the rest of the team follows her, so much the better (it's rather easy kills in this locale so far has made it overconfident).

Asalban

Attributes: Agl. D8, Smt. D8 (A), Spt. D10, Str. D12+4, Vig. D12
Pace: 8, Parry: 6, Toughness 12 (4)
Skills: Fighting D8, Stealth D12, Notice D10, Athletics D8

Special Abilities
Size +2
 Armor 4 (type 1)
360 degree Awareness (cannot be surprised)
Sonar: No low light penalties, most camouflage ineffectual
Puppet: Power can be used against a target if the Alsbans digested the brain of someone close to them.
Tentacle blades: Reach 2", 1D8+Str. Type 1
Fear

After the Asalban has been dealt with (or the characters resleeved and returned to Dili), the characters can begin their investigation into who created the obelisk and their purpose for putting it there. They know some kind of STOL (short take-off and landing) aircraft was used - now it's just a matter of tracking it down and finding its owners.

There are a few ways of doing this - one is accessing CU ReconSat data over the area at the time. Accessing this information, the characters will be able to trace the route of the aircraft from CDM's corporate airfield at Dili International Airport. They can zoom in to try and identify the individuals involved, but all are masked. Finding more details would mean hacking CDM's flight logs.

GM Note: It might be good to use a Quick Hack if the players choose this route in order to keep the story moving - see Hacking rules pg. 122 AoC Rulebook

The second method involves finding one of the Triad mercenaries who had been partially devoured by the Asalban. His head is gone, but sampling his DNA could lead to an identification if the characters are able to access police records in Dili (their options for doing this being highly related to their chosen method of entry into Timor). These will point to his Triad gang and association with CDM (Stokes has used his influence more than once to get him out of custody).

Another route to discovering Shubrir's involvement is by finding a video that was posted online by an aircraft enthusiast who witnessed the mission aircraft catching fire and recorded a video of the heavily armed team switching to another aircraft, taking a huge, heavy crate (the obelisk) with them. For more info about this, see below.

The final method is grisly, but may end up providing the most information. If the Alsban has been killed, consuming a gland in its brain will provide access to its accumulated memories. The character who does this must be organic (Morphs fit this category if not synthetic). If they pass a Spirit check at -2, they can isolate the memories they require, while a failure causes them to be overwhelmed with the memories of the Asalban's terrified victims - in this case, no information is gained and the character must roll on the Fear table.

On finding Phillip Stokes is responsible for the incident at Dili, ETM will order the agents to apprehend him by any means necessary and return with him to the CU so he can be interrogated. Shubrir will be alarmed at the destruction of his obelisk and will immediately put his back-up plan into operation. He'll also try to find the parties responsible in order to slow down or eliminate them. His attempts to find out what happened via recon satellite feed over the site are frustrated by the jungle canopy. He will put out feelers to try to acquire any information he can get about individuals inquiring about himself or the events surrounding the placement of the obelisk.

These inquiries will turn up a video placed online that records their first mission aircraft suffering an engine fire. A passerby witnessed it and recorded a video on their phone of the event, including a heavily armed party evacuating the aircraft, switching to a different plane, then taking off into the night. Shubrir's agents will take down the video and ensure the person taking it suffers the fate of being killed while having their apartment robbed. If the team can get their hands on the video, they'll be able to identify Shubrir's alter ego Phillip Stokes by comparing his body language and movements to recorded footage of other CDM executives (Computer Use -1).

If the team tips their hand in any way (makes underworld, local police or online inquiries about Stokes or has their location traced while hacking), Stokes has a hit team waiting that will be sent in the quickest but most innocuous way possible (the team will all be Triad members to make it look like an organized crime hit).

Triad Hit Team

While the Triad working for Stokes values their partnership, they are unwilling to use any of their scarce magical assets in a confrontation with powerful outsiders. The team they send is of relatively new, untried members who are not widely known to be affiliated with the Sun Yee On

Triad. While not highly skilled. the team will be eager to prove themselves.

They will try to fight hand to hand at the start of combat to keep from drawing police attention, switching to weapons only if the PCs do.

Soldiers (equal to number of players)
Str. D6, Agl. D6, Smt. D4, Spt. D6, Vig. D6

Tough: 5 (9)
Parry: 5
Sanity: 5

Skills: Fighting D6, Shooting D6, Stealth D6, Notice D6

Edges: Martial Artist (+D4 unarmed damage, never unarmed), Fanaticism (+1 to Shaken tests)

Gear: Tactical Vests, MP5 SMGs 12/24/48 2D6 type 1, ROF 3, Shots 30

With his pursuers hopefully taken care of, Shubrir will requisition a space plane to take him to his orbital HQ (CDM Orbital 29) which he is using to oversee resource extraction on a near Earth asteroid.

Hacking Shubrir: While extremely intelligent, Shubrir is not exactly up to speed on the latest security software, and he's too paranoid about being discovered to entrust it to an expert. Because of this, he uses high grade security software to defend his files, but has no hacker on duty for more active defense. He also needs to be able to access them anywhere at any time, which of course means an enterprising hacker could as well. A Quick Hack would be appropriate to access this info, with failure escalating rapidly from a -2 to Hacking rolls to Attack (Wound) software that will cause three wounds unless warded off by a successful Hacking roll. Shubrir's Firewall is -3.

If Shubrir makes it to his orbital HQ, getting to him will be difficult. The station itself has minimal defenses, but is guarded by a picket ship that also enforces CDM's claim on Apophis. There are many ways they could gain access, the most prudent being to hack their way in, find out what Shubrir is up to (if they haven't already) and put a stop to it (see supplemental section for cyber defenses).

The Yithian has a section of his orbital base set aside for a basalt pillar with Aklo runes painted on its surface. The station is in geosynchronous orbit over Dili - once the asteroid hits the city, the pillar will store the energy that's released from the hundreds of thousands of deaths and act as a conduit for the summoning of Yog Sothoth. When the entity appears, time will be locally frozen while Shubrir makes his exchange. When the ritual is completed, the station will explode from Yog Sothoth's presence - whether or not Shubrir succeeded will not be known.

The obelisk is similar to the one that was outside of Dili and can be destroyed using the same process.

Regardless of Shubrir's fate, the runes on the surface of Apophis have been activated. A science roll will reveal that the complete destruction of one of the runes will change the asteroid's course, driving it into deep space. The surface is not unguarded, however, with several resuscitated assets deployed on the surface to prevent any tampering.

SUPPLEMENTAL SECTION

Shubrir (Stokes) and his entourage

Needing utterly loyal and reliable people around him, as part of his contract Shubrir requested his personal assistant and bodyguards be murdered and resuscitated as zombies. Although not the most monstrous thing requested in a contract, it was certainly one of the more expensive - it cost CDM a great deal of capital to outsource the procedure, and Shubrir now has his utterly devoted undead entourage that can be expected to follow orders and keep secrets. CDM has had no reason to regret its decision, as Stokes has more than made up for his considerable expense with his mining operations and his expertise in Trans-D operations. Shubrir and Brad are a formidable challenge by themselves, but if the GM feels their players need more of a challenge, they should feel free to include a few more high quality undead bodyguards.

While Shubrir is highly skilled magically, he won't risk the delicate brain of his host (if it goes, he goes) by casting spells using that method unless he feels his life is at risk, limiting himself to the options given by his Hexaphone.

Like many corporate citizens, Shubrir and Brad had their last names changed to that of their corporation on signing their contracts.

Phillip Stokes CDM (Shubrir - Wildcard)

Str. D6, Agl. D8, Vig. D8, Smt. D12+2, Spt. D10
Pace: 6, Tough: 6 (8), Parry: 6 Sanity: N/A Power Points: 12

Skills: Fighting D8, Shooting D6, Notice D10, Computer Use D10, Hacking D8, Earth Science D12, Geology D12+2, Outsider Knowledge D10, Trans-D Physics D12, Aklo D6, Enochian D8, Spellcasting D10

Edges: Bureaucratic Fu (+2 to hinder or help a bureaucratic process), Eidetic Memory (+1 to all Knowledge skill rolls), Social Chameleon (+1 to Persuade or Networking tests), Attractive (+1 Charisma), Dodge (-1 to hit), Arcane Background

Gear: Armor Clothing, 9mm SDW (12/24/48, 2D6+2 type 1, AP 2, Shots 12, +2 Stealth to conceal), Maker, Hexaphone capable of assisting with spells up to Seasoned level.

Know Spells: As an entity thousands of years old, Shubrir knows the entire spell catalog, but is limited by the technology available to him.

Brad Chad CDM (Undead Personal Assistant - Wildcard)

Brad is such a loyal company man that he actually considers his own murder and resuscitation into an undead servant to be a good power move on the part of Stokes.

Str. D8, Agl. D10+2, Vig. D10, Smt. D8, Spt. D8
Pace: 8, Tough: 9 (13), Parry: 7, Sanity: NA

Mods: Adrenal Booster (+1 to Agl. and Agl. linked tasks for 2D6 rounds if activated), Wired Reflexes (act on best of two cards drawn - if face card or Joker, get second action after everyone else has gotten one), Military Smart Gun Link (+1 to Shooting rolls - this +1 is included in determining if the shot 'Aces')

Skills: Fighting D10+2, Shooting D8+2, Notice D10+2, Stealth D8, Intimidation D8, Throwing D6, Driving D6, Piloting D6, Athletics D6

Hindrances: Overconfident

Edges: Counter Attack (additional attack at -2 if opponent misses a Fighting attack), Martial Artist (+D4 unarmed), Alertness (+2 to Notice rolls), Bodyguard (-1 Agl. to take damage in place of target if within 1"), Undead (+2 to Toughness, +2 Shaken recover, called shots do no extra damage with the exception of the head. Undead Wildcards take no modifiers from wounds).

Gear: Tactical Armor Vest, Memory Blade, Shock Gloves, SPR-12 CAW Flechettes: 5/10/20 1 – 3 D10 (depending on range), halves type 1 armor, area effect (cone), Shots: 6

Alpha Loyalty (Pioneer Class Science/Recon Vessel)

If the PCs don't have a spacecraft yet, this one will be assigned to them for the mission. The Pioneer Class of ships are designed for short to medium duration reconnaissance and science missions- their lack of amenities makes them unpopular with crews, with many commenting that some offensive capability could be traded off for a lounge or garden module. Despite these shortcomings, the ship is ideal for intel ops due to its ubiquity - the CU exports many of these to various clients, with many ending up on the black market.

While its multiple avionics bays make it vulnerable to damage, its designers felt that the extra capability more than made up for this weakness. This ship's components are of superior quality, receiving a +1 modifier to their operations.

Toughness: 11 (2) type 3
Acc: 20, TS: 700, Climb 0
CU Ship: Rerolls critical failures, can ignore Disaster results in chase rules.
Stealthy Hull: -1 for other ships to Notice and to hit
Carbon Composite Hull (+2 Toughness)
Extra Armor (+1 Armor)
SOTA Sensors (+2 Notice, +1 to hit)

Modules: Bridge, Armor, Avionics (includes Auto Pilot, ECM [-2 to hit] and ECCM [negates enemy ECM]), Avionics (includes SOTA Sensors, Science Module (+1), Quantum Targeting), EMAG (+1 hit/dam - turret), Onager Missile (+1 hit/dam - turret), Crew Module, Med Bay, Lab, Escape Pods, Propulsion

Wolverine (Protector Class Base Defense Ship)

Literally built around a 12 MJ laser spinal mount, the Wolverine is designed solely for area defense of potentially vulnerable installations, the Protector Class is all about strike power and very little else.

Toughness: 7 (1)
Acc: 50, TS: 500, Climb 2
SOTA Sensors (+2 Notice, +1 to hit)

Modules: Bridge, Avionics (ECM, Auto-Pilot, SOTA Sensors), Fighter Drone (Tough 8(2) type 3, Acc. 75, TS 1000, Climb 3, Turreted EMAG Gun 1D6 type 3, AP2, ROF 3), Sparrow Agile Missile System, (6 shots, each has 50% chance to destroy incoming missile, ROF 6, takes full turn to reload), 12 MJ Laser (Spinal Mount, needs card draw of 10 or higher to use - 3D6 type 3, AP4, ROF 2

CDM Orbital 29

Designed as a research platform, this space station has well appointed facilities meant to ease the rigors of long term habitation by high value personnel. As such, it is heavy on amenities but somewhat lacking in defenses, relying on its guard ship to handle any security problems.

Toughness: 14 (4)
High Quality Sensors (+1 to Notice and Science rolls)
Improved Armor +2

Modules: Bridge, Armor, Cargo (3) (used for provisions, expedition gear, etc), Crew Modules - luxury (3), Probe Drones (2), Escape Pods, Garden, Labs (4), Lounge, Medical Bay, Science, Turreted Hornet Missile Pack (Damage 1D6+1 type 3 AP2, Shots 8, ROF 8 - once all shots are fired, module is spent), Turreted Sparrow Agile Missile System (Stats: Type 3 Damage 1D4, Shots 6, ROF 6 - each missile has a 50% chance of shooting down an incoming enemy missile)

The space station has a security squad of six guards - these personnel have been demoralized by the bizarre goings on and the imperious behavior of Stokes and Chad. Like everyone else on board, they're just looking for a plausible reason to head for the escape pods - an attack by the team will be just the encouragement they need. The guards will stage a fighting withdrawal to make it look like they made an effort (engaging for one turn, then running for a turn until they reach the escape pods). If any take a Shaken result, they will either flee, making straight for the pods, or surrender and ask to be allowed to go if that seems to be the best route to survival. In the latter case, they will gladly give the players the location of Stokes and Chad.

Nervous Guards (6)

Str. D6, Agl. D6, Smts. D4, Vig. D6, Spt. D4

Toughness: 5 (9)
Sanity: 4
Parry: 5
Pace: 6

Skills: Shooting D6, Fighting D4

CDM Orbital 29 Cyber Defenses

Firewall -2

Each time the team's Hacker fails a Hacking rolling, apply the following in order

5. All Hacking rolls at -1
6. All Hacking rolls at -2
7. Trace program. Character must succeed in a Hacking roll to defeat it. On successful completion, if the players are on a ship nearby, the station will alert the Wolverine to investigate. If not, CDM security will be alerted to their location.
8. Counter-Attack! A new trace attempt as above, but unless the Hacker succeeds in their roll, their Hacking device will be damaged (-4 on all future Hacking rolls until repaired). The character must pass a Spirit check or get Shaken and dumped from the system. If they pass, they are able to log off before the trace is completed. If the character is dumped, the target system's trace attempt automatically succeeds.
9. Security Hacker alerted! Hacker stats: Hacking D8, Firewall -2, running Notice D8, Attack (Stun) D8. If the Hacker is able to incapacitate the PC, they will proceed to destroy their hacking device. If the Security Hacker suffers a single Wound, any Fatigue or is Shaken, they will log out.
10. Deadly Force Authorized! The character must succeed in a Hacking roll or have all content on their device uploaded to the system they're attacking. The device is then destroyed as above, and the character is Shaken and takes three wounds that can be resisted normally. If the character is dumped, the target system's trace attempt automatically succeeds.
11. Trace program (lock on) - on successful completion, the computer will have enough information on the player's location to generate a firing solution. If they're onboard a ship, the station will alert the Wolverine and open fire with its own rockets. Due to knowing the exact location of the player's ship, all fire directed at it will be at +1 to hit. If not on a ship, the info will be fed to a satellite, which will fire a 12 MJ laser at the Hacker's location unless they're in an affluent area. In the latter case, the local authorities will be informed of a terrorist incident originating in their locale.
12. The system shuts down. The system under attack will attempt one final attack as above before shutting down. Every subsystem the computer controls will immediately cease functioning. The character has two more turns before they are dumped – if this happens they have to pass a Vigor check or be Shaken.

Apophis

Given Shubrir's sinister plans for Apophis, he's made sure that its operations center is manned only by resuscitated assets that will follow his instructions to the letter. There are also human and robotic miners scattered around its surface, but these are focused entirely on their work and know nothing about the unfolding disaster. Anyone not broadcasting a CDM id code will be assumed to be a claim jumper or pirate - contract miners might engage such trespassers with whatever weaponry they have at their disposal, but will not act foolishly if they're obviously overmatched. CDM corporate employees and robots will conceal themselves as best they can and report any incidents to the operations center.

Shubrir installed a failsafe in the event that he needed to postpone or cancel his plan. Explosives have been placed around the runes - they can be destroyed singly to modify the asteroid's course or entirely to keep the asteroid from getting underway at all. If Apophis has already been set on its course, the former is the only option as its inertia will cause it to hit Earth unless its trajectory is drastically modified.

To defend this vital aspect of his plan, Shubrir has installed some sinister psychotropic software. The first failed Hacking roll will get a warning that deadly force will be authorized with any further tampering - following Hacking rolls will be at -2. The next failed roll will have the Hacker take a Spirit roll at -1. Failure means that they will attack their teammates with the most dangerous means at their disposal while their hacking device burns itself up. A simple success will cause the Hacker to become Shaken, while a success with a raise will have no effect. Any further failure will trigger a self destruct program that will destroy the entire operations center.

Op Center Personnel

Technicians (2)

Raised by a Necromancer of exceptional ability, these Heroic level zombies are fully capable of doing any of the numerous technical tasks required of them without the need for breaks, sleep or compensation. Meant only to oversee operations at the mining base, they have no weapons but will fight using their natural attack or flee if up against heavily armored opponents.

Str. D8, Agl. D8, Smt. D10, Vig. D8, Spt. D4
Tough: 7
Pace: 8
Parry: 7

Natural Attack (Claw, Bite) Str.+ D6 type 1

Skills: Fighting D10, Mining Operations D8, Sorcery (Knowledge) D8

Guards (6)

The guards in the Ops Center will get a couple of chances to detect the PCs. If the players make a stealthy approach in their ship, let the pilot make a Stealth roll. Then have a guard make a Notice roll to see if the players' ship is detected. If the guard's roll is higher than the pilot's, the ship is detected and four guards will be deployed outside the base in cover with their heavy weapons with the other two providing security inside.

If the ship lands undetected, the guards will get another chance to notice the players when they approach. Make another opposed test like the one above. If the players' succeed, they will be able to get the drop on the guards, getting a surprise round when they enter. If they fail, they will find the door sealed (Toughness 10, type 2) and the guards ready for them when they enter, weapons drawn in positions of cover. While four try to hold the players off, the other two will run back to the armory to acquire better weapons.

Str. D8, Agl. D8, Smt. D4, Vig. D8, Spt. D4
Tough: 7 (15)
Pace: 6

Natural Attack (Claw/Bite) Str. + D6 type 1

Skills: Fighting D8, Shooting D8, Notice D6

Gear: Assault Armor, Peacemaker .44 (12/24/48, 2D8+2 dam, weight 2 Shots: 15, AP4 Min. Str. 6, Full auto recoil -3)

If the guards are alerted, those deployed outside will have access to the following weapons from the armory: AM24 LAW (24/48/96 2D6 type 2, Snapfire, weight 5, Shots: 1, ROF 1, 1 Action to reload, Burst MBT) with four reloads, 1 MJ88 MSW (30/60/120, 2d8+4 dam, AP6, weight 15 Shots: 50, ROF 4, Min. Str. D8), 1 M24 HB Sniper Rifle 50/100/200, 2D8+4 dam, AP8, Snapfire, Shots: 10, ROF 2 Has integrated scope that will eliminate range penalties with an aim action.), 6 PK-49 TAW Battle Rifles (25/50/100, 2D8+2 dam, weight 5, AP6, Shots: 45). Has an integrated grenade launcher (50/100/200 3D6 dam area effect with adjustable blast radius – use small or large template) that can also fire shotgun rounds (damage/range per SPR-12). A HEAT round is also available that does 1D6 type 2 damage (no area effect).

The guards remaining behind will equip themselves with any remaining PK-49s.

ABOUT THE AUTHOR

Aria Lapine

"We were built, trained conditioned to disappear - we shall stay in the shadows, in the meadows afire.
We shall remain invisible - we travel light. We do not rush toward the light and we dance when we can - with our eyes closed all along the border."
~ Rome

Aria Lapine lives in Seattle, Washington

Made in the USA
Columbia, SC
20 April 2023